German J

Steve

Granger

ISBN: 978-0-244-54401-0

PUBLISHNATION

www.publishnation.co.uk

For Anastasia, thank you for believing in me.

CHAPTER 1

31.08.1988

'Bloody hell.'

'What have we got?'

'Oh shit, what a stench.'

'Move out the way and let me have a look'

Erster Kriminalhauptkommissar Sven Gerling moved around his long-time friend and colleague, Kriminalhauptkommissar Gottfried Fischer, known to all as Freddy, and let out a deep sigh. 'Poor cow, how can anybody do this to another person?'

'I don`t know boss, but it ain`t right.' said Freddy.

They had been called out to visit a murder scene outside the Sankt Maria zur Wiese Kirche, shortened and known locally as the Wiesenkirche, which is located in the northern part of Soest. Built in the 14th century, the church is a formidable building with its two towers reaching over 81 meters high can be seen from all over the town. Over the main doors, several figurines attached to the architecture look down onto the church forecourt. Pope Saint Gregory 1st, commonly known as Saint Gregory the Great and the Madonna holding her child, were witness to an awful tragedy.

The young victim lay on her back outside the main entrance. The ground was soaked in blood, obvious even to a blind man that the majority of it came from the cut throat, which was spattered against the closed doors and the walls. The rest of the blood came from the deep, open wound of her lower abdomen where the intestines glistened under the street lamp on Wiesenstrasse. The blood had formed a small pond under and around where the victim lay. She was found wearing tight jeans, a white blouse and comfortable flat shoes.

'OK,' said Sven, 'let`s back off and wait for the forensics to turn up. Who found the body?' he asked a policeman standing as far back as was appropriate.

'I was first on the scene, sir. We got a call from a lady living in one of the apartments behind us. She was on her balcony, said she couldn`t sleep and came out for some fresh air and saw someone running away from the church.'

'And you are?' asked Sven.

'Polizeimeister Grünewald, sir.'

'Go on, what else do you have?'

'Not too much at the moment. We got the call at the station around 02:30 this morning, said she saw a person legging it and thought they may have broken into the church and nicked something. Happened a couple of times apparently. I was sent here to have a look and did not expect to find a dead woman lying here. I called the station over the radio and I was told to stay here and secure the area.'

'OK, son,' Sven said, 'you look pretty shaken up. First body?'

'Yes sir, only out of training since 4 months. I joined the Schutzpolizei as my dad is also a copper and I wanted to follow in his footsteps, but he never told me I would see anything like this.'

'Did you touch anything?'

'No sir, as soon as I saw the blood and guts, I ran over to the bushes and puked. Not proud of it. I thought I was big and tough, obviously not.'

'Don`t beat yourself up about it,' said Freddy, 'None of us feel good at the sight of a murder, no matter how many you get to see. What else did the lady say?'

'Well, she heard me puking and asked me if I was alright. I asked for a glass of water and she came down. I asked her if she saw anything and she told me that she didn`t hear or see anything apart from seeing the person running off.'

'What`s her name and where is she now?' asked Freddy.

'Er, I have it all down in my notebook. Here it is, a Frau Sabine Richter, lives in house 26a, first floor.'

'We`ll need to give her a formal interview later on down at your station. Where is it, by the way?'

'If you go up the street here, sir, turn left on Krummel, then turn right on the main road and the station is about 300 meters on the left.'

'Right,' said Sven, 'You stay here, make sure that nobody gets near the church or body and give us a call when forensics turn up.'

'Where will you be, sir?'

'At your station having a brew. Not nice being woken up at 3 in the morning and having to drive the 50 kilometres from Dortmund. And before it gets much lighter, try and clean your shoes and trousers. Got slices of carrot and God knows what pebble dashed all over them. Don`t need the public to see the contents of your last meal displayed all over your uniform.'

'Yes sir, sorry sir.'

With that, Sven and Freddy walked off towards their car.

'Well, first impressions?' asked Freddy

'Hard to say until the local bobbies get the scene lit up properly and the body is examined. Mind you, did you see how deep the cuts were?'

'Not really, had my eyes closed for most of it. You`re the hard man, thought I would leave it to you.' replied Freddy.

Sven had joined the police force after leaving school at the age of 17, firstly stationed in his home town of Iserlohn as a normal policeman. After 5 years on the job, he applied to be a detective and after a successful assessment and interview, was transferred to Dortmund Eving to serve as a Polizeikommissar in the detective unit. Being keen and not shy, he swiftly proved himself and was then asked if he would like to join the Mordkommission, the murder squad. He jumped at the chance and was transferred from Dortmund Eving to Dortmund Mitte, the main police station called Polizeipräsidium and after being in this department for the last 8 years, he was seen by his colleagues as being a good boss, friend and confidant. Now at the age of 36, he was content with his life. Married for the last 12 years to Johanna, a beautiful woman two years his younger, they had two children together, both girls aged 7 and 9. What made his job even more satisfying was that he worked alongside his best friend, Freddy, whom he had known since basic training when they had both joined the police force back in 1969. Although he was Freddy`s direct boss, he treated him the same at work as like he did at home.

Sven was 172 centimetres tall, weighed a trim 72 kg and kept fit by training in his local boxing club. He had been crowned twice as the West German Police boxing champion as a welterweight whilst in his 20s with a record of 43 fights, winning 36, but with his ever increasing workload and getting on in years, he had decided not to compete in the ring anymore but still trained regularly on the bags and was often used as a sparring partner for the up and coming, which suited him well, as this was a good way of releasing all the pressures his job provided.

Never one to use his rank to boss anyone around, he was known as being fair, firm and friendly. His sense of humour and quick wit made him likeable amongst both men and women and was not shy in meeting people for the first time.

Freddy was from a small town called Werl, around 36 kms to the east of Dortmund and about 15 kms to the west of Soest. Freddy was 180 centimetres in height and carried a weight of 90+ kilos on his feet. Big built but not all muscle, he was not as fit as Sven, but his presence made any trouble maker think twice about giving back lip.

Although being one year older, Freddy had not had the opportunity of moving out of uniform until several years after Sven had made the transition. However, as soon as hc was able to hang up his "greens", Sven was able to pull a few strings and have him transferred and be assigned to his team and they had stayed together ever since.

Freddy got married when he was just 20 to a girl he had known since kindergarten, but after 5 years, they both realised their mistake and amicably separated and divorced. He then met his present wife, Heike, whilst at a crime scene in Dortmund. She had been a victim of an attempted rape when she was 23, which had gone badly wrong for the perpetrator. A good looking woman with a nice body, she was into keep fit and had no troubles in kneeing the spotty faced bastard in the nuts and putting him in a choke hold until the police arrived. Freddy interviewed her at the scene and was smitten from the first moment he saw her. Obviously he knew a lot about her from the interview, some of these questions were not needed for the report, but she answered them anyway stating that she was single, had no current boyfriend and yes, she lived on her own. He broke every rule in the book and asked her out for a drink. They married two years later and were still very much in love even after being married for 6 years. They had no children but this suited them both, as they were both egoistic in that they did not want to give up their lavish lifestyles.

Now, walking alongside his best friend, they got back into their silver Volkswagen Golf II and headed in the direction given them by Polizeimeister Grünewald and swiftly arrived at the Kreispolizeibehörde Soest. Sven parked the car in one of the visitor's parking places and both entered the building on Walburger-Osthofen-Wallstrasse.

'Can I help you two gents?' asked a voice behind a sheet of plexiglas.

'You most certainly can,' said Sven, showing his badge and ID to the duty desk officer. 'We are from the Mordkommission in Dortmund and been sent here to assist in the murder by the church. First and foremost, do you have a canteen where we can get some breakfast and secondly, who is in charge here?'

'Well sir, we do not have a canteen but you can find a vending machine when you go through the glass doors, up the stairs, turn left and the break room is the third on the left. As for who is in charge, normally it would be Erster Polizeihauptkommissar Schneider, but he is off on holidays at the moment, won`t be back for another week, so you will need to speak to Polizeihauptkommissar Backhaus. He is also upstairs, this time instead of left, take a right and his office is the second along on the right, just after the toilets.'

'Well, thank you for your precise A-Z of the station, sure to come back to you if we need any further directions. Now buzz us through so we can get something to eat and get on with it and hopefully get home today.'

'Good luck with getting something to eat sir, I don`t put much hope that you will find much. The machine hasn`t been filled in days.'

'Bloody typical. Called out in the black of night and no sodding grub. Ok, thanks anyway.'

The door was buzzed open and both men walked through the first door, this being the barrier from letting the public getting any further into the building uninvited. They walked through a small waiting area with out-of-date magazines and the usual stand of police pamphlets about how to report a crime, what to do if your house is broken into etc. and the notice board with various pages taped to it, one advertising a local boot sale, another of a missing cat called Cindy and the normal boring stuff nobody actually read. 26 stairs later, they came to the first floor, followed the directions and walked over to the vending machine in the corner of the break room. Well, a normal room with several hard plastic chairs dotted around two Formica tables and a waste basket filled with empty coffee cups.

'What do you want?' Sven asked Freddy. 'You want the cheese sandwich with the curly ends or do you want to share the last Mars bar?'

'Told you yesterday, can`t eat chocolate, on a diet.' Freddy said.

'Oh yeah, so you won`t want a hot chocolate out of the machine then?'

'Well, we can make exceptions. Although we have the back end of summer, still a nip to the air this morning. Yeah, I`ll have a cup of hot chocolate if you`re buying.'

'Cheeky sod. I`m always buying. At home you might live and spend like a king, but at work you`re a fucking scrooge.'

'Bollocks,' Freddy replied with a smile on his face. 'I had to pay for the kebab yesterday when you suddenly up and left the café. Remember?'

'Some bugger was peeing in the doorway and I went out and politely asked him to piss off. And if I remember correctly, you scoffed half of mine yourself. Diet my arse.'

Sven took some change out of his pocket and slotted 30 Pfennig into the machine, pressed the button and waited for the plastic beaker to fill up. It filled up, but the substance was not brown as expected. The beaker was filled with a yellowish coloured liquid and when taken out, green bits could be seen floating on the top.

'What the fuck is this?' Sven asked nobody in particular. 'I've never seen chocolate this colour before.'

'Oh, sorry about that, you won`t know about the twat who mixed up the powders when filling up the machine. You are now the proud owner of a cup of chicken soup. Hot chocolate is the second button down, the one labelled tea. Oh, and glad to meet you. Downstairs called me and said you were on your way up. Polizeihauptkommissar Backhaus at your service.'

'I`m the proud owner of diddly squat. How the hell can a police station not have a canteen, nothing to eat in the vender and some dyslexic put in charge of filling up the coffee machine? Pulled out of bed in the early hours of the morning to attend a murder scene, and so far I am not that impressed with Soest. I`m Erster Kriminalhauptkommissar Gerling and this is my colleague, Kriminalhauptkommissar Fischer.'

'Well, come into my office and I will rustle up a cup of coffee and I`ll see if I can find some biscuits.' Backhaus replied, indicating that they should follow.

'If you need to find the biscuits, go downstairs and ask the plod on the front desk. Wouldn`t be surprised if he is able to tell you which shelf and in which cupboard you`ll find them.' Sven answered back without a smirk, but Backhaus could see the glint of a smile in the hazel coloured eyes.

'Ah yes, that would be Günther, nice chap, been here for donkeys. Rumour has it that he was sitting on a chair at the side of the road and they built the police station around him. He's part of the furniture. Talented in sniffing out time wasters at the desk though, happy not to have to go out and do any real police work. Mind you, need any typing done, he`s your man. Able to type around 60 words a minute without any mistakes. Took a typing course with his misses about 10 years back. Can`t remember the last time I saw a bottle of *Tipp-Ex* on his desk. So, follow me and let`s see if we can wet your whistle.'

They followed Backhaus to his office which consisted of working space for two. On each desk was a type writer, a telephone, a selection of pens, pencils and note blocks and several plants that were trying to remember what water tasted like and two overfilled ashtrays. The walls themselves were coated in a two tone green, the lower half darker than the top. The ceiling was a dark cream colour, but had started life out white until the years of nicotine had taken over and won the battle. On a side table was a radio set connected to all units in Soest, several dog eared files that looked like they hadn't been read or moved in decades and a facsimile.

'Sit down, please,' Backhaus said, pointing to two uncomfortable chairs next to the wall. 'Bring the chairs here and let's see about the coffee. I hope you like it black as we don't have any milk. Ran out and no bugger thought to buy some yesterday evening. Got some sugar though.'

'It's ok,' said Sven, 'Freddy here is on a diet, he doesn't need sugar. As for me, can't stand it black, so I'll go without.'

'I'll take a miss as well if there's no cow juice.' stated Freddy adamantly.

'Please yourselves.' replied Backhaus. 'Cigarette anyone?' he asked, lighting one up as soon as he had finished asking the question.

'No thanks, we both do not smoke. So, let's get down to business. What have you got in the way of movement in regards to the stiff by the church?' asked Sven.

'So, let's see, the call came in at 02:36 from a Frau Richter living in Wiesenstrasse 26a, which overlooks the church. Said she thought there was another break in at the church. Wouldn't be the first time. Sent young Grünewald over there on foot and he called back saying he had found a dead woman by the church doors. So our suspected break-in has turned into a murder. The duty sergeant sent out two car patrols and then called me at home. We don't have many murders here in Soest, fights, theft and aggravated assault, but not murder. So we play by the book and as we have no murder squad here, we contacted the Kriminelhauptstelle in Dortmund and were told to expect a team soon. We are still waiting for the arrival of the forensics team from Dortmund, so until then we have cordoned off the area and will be carrying out door to door interviews when it gets light and more people come on duty. So you now know as much as I do.'

'We're a bit stretched at the moment,' said Freddy, 'normally we'd come with a whole team of 5, but with the school holidays and a couple off sick, we're slightly undermanned. Not to worry, we're known as the Dynamic Duo, so you're getting the best. Saying that, the forensics team and the meat wagon should be here soon. There's nothing we can do until they get here. Is there any place we can get some breakfast? Want to get some soon before I lose my appetite when I have to look at the dead body again.'

'Well, you can either drive around and look to see if there are any bakery's open or you can follow me over to the Marienkrankenhaus where I know one of the cooks. Sure she can magic up an omelette or something.' replied Backhaus with a smile across his face. 'Used to bed her when her old man was in the nick, now we have to settle for sharing a meal together in the hospital canteen.'

'Sounds like a plan,' said Sven. 'Come on then, let's go'.

CHAPTER 2

'Well, Gaby, that was delicious. Nothing beats scrambled eggs on toast. Thank you so much for banging that together at such short notice.' Backhaus praised, looking across the condiments and sauce bottles at his once upon a time bed partner. 'Remember, if you want your old man locking up again, all you have to do is ask.' he said.

'Now, now Bernhard, don't be going and putting any ideas in my head. And lose them dirty thoughts you might be having at the same time.' she replied, chuckling as she did. Well, it was more like a bull elephant clearing phlegm from its throat than a chuckle, but that is what smoking 40 fags a day and being about 20 kilos overweight did to you.

'Yes, fine breakfast that was Frau Müller, thank you.' said Sven, wiping some tomato ketchup from the corner of his mouth with a napkin.

'Yep, I'll second that. Best bit of bacon and eggs that I have eaten in a while. Simply delicious. Pity that the normal hospital breakfasts are not this tasty.' Freddy replied.

'If they were,' Gaby replied, 'the patients would not want to leave and we'd be chock a block before you knew it. And if you are working with my Bernie, then please, call me Gaby. Frau Müller makes me sound old.'

'Right you are.' said Sven. 'Best be off now, see what the daylight has thrown up. Come on guys, move your butts.'

'I'll, er, meet you outside in two minutes,' Backhaus said, 'Just need a quick chat in private, if you don't mind.'

'No problems, just don't take too long. Me and Freddy here want to get home sometime today.'

'Ok my loves, remember, if you need some sustenance, you know where I am. Normally have a 12 hour shift over the summer holiday period, so come back this afternoon if you can and I'll have a cake ready and waiting.' Gaby replied, shifting her excess weight up out of the chair and wobbled towards the kitchen where her staff was busy preparing breakfast for the whole hospital, Bernie Backhaus in tow.

Outside, Freddy said to Sven 'Nice woman, but a bit on the large size.'

'Well, people come in all shapes and sizes. Give it a couple of years, you may look like that:' Sven said smiling.

'Fuck off, no way. If you ever see me getting that size, shoot me.'

'Will need to use a harpoon gun then.' Sven said, opening the entrance door and letting an old man carrying a urine bag out. 'But would never believe old Backhaus would happily bed her. Imagine her being on top, he'd be crushed.'

'And his pecker would need to be the size of a horses prick in order to get any penetration.' Freddy stated. 'Oh well, big woman, big heart, that's what they say.'

'Funny, only fat people say that. Quiet now, Backhaus is coming.'

Backhaus joined the two murder detectives from Dortmund and had a slight blush on his cheeks.

'I know that you are laughing and talking about Gaby and myself behind our backs, but we have history.' he said. 'I helped put her old man away after he clunked her a few times too many. He went down for 5 years, we got to be friends and we both got the benefits. Plus it also means I don't have to do much cooking at home on my own. She makes a mean beef roulade with red cabbage.'

'We were just discussing fishing, that's all.' Sven said straight faced. 'As far as I am concerned, every man to his own, that's what I say. Isn't that right Freddy?'

'None of my concern what and who you do,' Freddy said, 'as long as it ain't my misses.'

'I would never do anything to a colleague's wife, that goes against my principles.' retorted Backhaus.

'Principles you might have,' replied Sven, 'scruples you don't. Who in their right mind would get together with the wife of a wife batterer? I don't mean any disrespect or nothing, but she does lean more towards the large size, so if she let her old man whack her around, how big is he? Dancing with fire I'd say.'

'Well, believe it or not, she is so gentle, wouldn't hurt a fly. And her husband is about your size and took advantage of her forgiving personality and bashed her a bit too hard when she was beating him at Monopoly. Something to do with him owing her rent when he landed on one of her hotels and couldn't pay.' Backhaus lengthened his stride and it was plain to see that he was slightly hurt from the discussion they had just had. He wasn't used to the frankness in the way both Sven and Freddy spoke, and would never have dreamed to speak to someone of his rank with such openness.

'You play with fire and dance on ice, not dance with fire like you said.' Backhaus murmured over his shoulder towards Sven.

'No mate, you are definitely dancing with fire. One day when you are doing the Samba horizontally, Herr Müller will turn up and set your testicles on fire, you mark my words. Then you will be looking for some ice to play with, even if it is to cool down your balls.' Sven replied, clapping Backhaus on the shoulder in a manner to diffuse the rising tension. 'Only pulling your plonker, nothing meant by it, honest. Ain't that right, Freddy?'

'Course it is guv. Only banter. Without it, wouldn't get through the day, would we?' Freddy reached out his hand and offered it to Backhaus, who hesitantly took it in his own and shook hands. 'No hard feelings.'

With the gesture complete, Backhaus immediately changed tune and led the way on foot back to the murder scene. They crossed the hospital car park and entered immediately the road that led to the church and arrived within one minute of leaving hospital.

'Bloody hell, that didn't take long to get here,' said Freddy, 'no time for my breakfast to have digested. Hope I don't taste it a second time.'

'Stop your whining. You've been fed and watered, now back to work.' said Sven.

The road was blocked off by police tape and a local constable was standing guard, keeping any early risers away.

'Good morning sir.' the constable said, raising the tape so that Backhaus, Sven and Freddy could pass under.

'Good morning Obermeister Horst. Have the team arrived yet?'

'Yes sir, about 30 minutes ago. We tried to raise you on the radio but couldn't get through.'

'What? Oh bugger, got the volume turned right down. Give me a squawk will you'

The constable pushed the pressel switch on his own radio and a sound of static was heard from Backhaus's set, proving that he was back in touch with the rest of the force. 'Was having a meeting with the murder squad so needed it on silence.'

With that, they left the constable guarding an empty road and moved towards the church. When they got near to the junction to get to the front of the church, they heard a generator running and saw that there were portable spotlights on, shining towards where several people were busy doing what they were trained to do, all clad in white paper over suits complete with surgeons gloves, face masks, head cap and blue over boots.

Sven called from behind the area that had been cordoned off with more police tape to the paper suits. 'Can anyone give me an update?'

A muffled voice answered 'Give me a sec, just need to finish what I'm doing and I'll be over.'

'Right Bernie, I want a door to door sweep underway before anyone leaves to go to work. Maybe someone else saw something that Frau Richter didn't. Call up the next town if you need more bodies, give them my name and they will cooperate. Then I want a sweep of the area, say a radius of 5 streets either way and look for any knives, axes, swords or other large, sharp weapons. Don't think a firearm was involved, not with all those knife wounds. I want drains, bins, garage roofs, gardens, any shallow streams, under all vehicles checked. I noticed when we walked across the hospital car park a sign pointing in the direction of some nurses living quarters. The victim looked to be in her late teens to early twenties, maybe a nurse or trainee nurse. Get a list of all those who live there, track them down and maybe we will come up lucky quickly. Any questions?'

'No sir,' answered Backhaus. 'I'll get on to it right away. Will you be needing anything else?'

'Yes, I would like you to set me up with some office space as we will be working out of your station until we have everything and anything anyone can think of. Then and only then will we get out your hair and bugger off back to Dortmund'.

With that, Polizeihauptkommissar Bernie Backhaus walked back the way they had come and disappeared around the corner.

'Decent sort of fellow, I think.' Freddy said. 'Just a bit weird that he is shagging Gaby the Giant.'

'Maybe he has a fetish for all things that wobble.' Sven replied back. 'Bet he gets turned on eating a trifle. Remember that woman last year down in Unna? You know, the woman who was stabbed 3 times in the stomach and the fat folds basically sealed up the wounds and she hardly bled at all. If it wasn't for the keen eye of that young rooky, the bitch could have walked around for days thinking she was just punched a few times in the belly and not stabbed like she was. So for her it was a blessing she was not skinny.'

'Yeah, how could I forget? I was the one who had to help the ambulance crew cut her clothes off. Couldn't sleep for weeks without dreaming of humpback whales wearing Motorhead t-shirts.'

One of the figures kneeling over the dead body by the church door slowly stood up, straightened, stretched and started walking across to where the two men stood waiting.

'Hi boys,' she said. 'Not seen you two for a while. I just wish it was somewhere where there were no dead bodies.'

'Hi Steffi,' Sven replied, 'You're looking as gorgeous as ever. New outfit or something?' he said jokingly.

'Yes, the department has gone all Vogue and purchased the latest overalls from the Paris mode show. When the photographer has finished taking my photos and also those of the corpse, you can come over and take another look. You can get suited and booted over by our van.'

'Hi Steffi.' Freddy answered, blushing slightly as she looked into his eyes.

'Hi Freddy, how's Heike?' she asked.

'Keeping well thanks.'

'Ok,' she said, 'come and join me once you're ready. Looks like "Flash" is finishing up.'

With that, Steffi pulled the mask back over her nose and mouth, turned and walked back to where she had been working.

Sven and Freddy walked over to the forensics van and started rummaging in the box marked 'Protective Clothing'.

'What is it with you two?' Sven asked. 'Every time you are in close proximity to Steffi, you go all red and get tongue tied.'

'Remember that Christmas party, 1985 I think, I had a few too many sherbets and I was dancing with Steffi and a couple of others when the DJ played 'Cherish' by Kool and the Gang. Well, she latched onto my neck like a limpet mine and wouldn't let go for dear life. We landed up snogging in one of the cubicles in the ladies loo. Bad thing is, her and Heike are good friends. I love Heike to bits, but I get all rubbery knees when I see Steffi just thinking how close I came to shagging her.'

'Wow, you never told me that.' Sven said with a big grin plastered all across his face.

'Have to have some secrets for myself.'

'Your secret is safe with me. You and Heike are made for each other and I am glad you thought with your head and not your penis. Mind you, Steffi is quite beautiful with a good figure to boot. Something must be wrong with her to be still single.'

'Yeah, well, maybe she is waiting for Mr Right to come along.' Freddy mumbled.

'Come here guys, I need to show you something.' Steffi shouted.

'Coming my dear.' Sven shouted back, nudging Freddy in the side of the ribs.

'Good job these paper suits are baggy,' Sven said to Freddy, 'will hide your hard on when you get close to Steffi.'

'Fuck you.' Freddy replied.

With that, Sven stepped down from the van and with a little snigger, walked over to the cordon, ducked underneath and joined Steffi at the inert body on the ground.

'So, fill me in.' Sven said.

'OK, this is what I can ascertain here at the scene. Obviously you will get a full report when I have the body back at the lab.

'Victim is a female aged between 18 and 25, her throat has been severed by two deep cuts which would have been the killing factor as you can see by the blood spurts on the church door. Her lower abdomen has been ripped open and she also received several stab wounds to her abdomen. She would have been dead by the time the perpetrator decided to slice her open like a pig in a slaughterhouse.

'I would estimate the time of death to be between 01:00 and 04:00 this morning. Rigor mortis has started to set in at the eyelids, neck and jaw, which is a good indicator that she wasn't killed any earlier, as it takes around another four to six hours for it to affect the other muscles and internal organs. Her intestines are just starting to harden up now, so the time window fits.'

'Yes, our witness saw someone running away from here at just after 02:30 this morning. See anything else that could be useful?' Sven asked.

'Nope,' she replied, 'I want to get her back to the lab now where I can then tell you what weapon you are looking for.'

'Any sort of identification on her? Maybe a handbag with her Personalausweis in it?' he asked.

'No, sorry. We checked her pockets and moved her over to see if she was lying on a handbag, but nothing found. Strange that she wasn't carrying her ID like she should have. She has some money in her jeans pocket, so not a robbery.' she replied. 'The coroners are waiting to take her back to my lab. If there is nothing else, I'd like to get moving.'

'No, go on. Keep in touch and please let me know the soonest you have the report ready. I'll be available through the Soest station.'

'Right on,' she said. 'Speak to you later.'

And with that, Sven walked over to where Freddy was shirking.

'It's alright, Samantha Fox is going now and little Freddy can come back out to play.' Sven said teasingly.

'Wish I hadn't told you now.' Freddy replied. 'Always taking the piss, you are.'

'Leave it out, you love it. Come on, let's get out of these overalls and get back to the station and see how the door to door is going and see if Mr jelly lover has bought some milk.'

CHAPTER 3

'What time did you stroll in last night?' Lance Corporal Tony White asked.

'Must have got in around just after four. Picked up a bird in *Big Ben* and went back to her place afterwards.'

Big Ben was a pub/disco which played the latest popular English (and on occasions) German chart music. The club boasted two bars, one on the right hand side when one entered, the other consisted of a large square in the middle of the floor so that many could sit around the bar on all four sides whilst the drinks were served from the inside. Over to the far right corner was a small dance floor, speakers and flashing lights. The back wall was of a painting of the houses of parliament, the prominent feature being Big Ben, hence the name. This was located in a street named Thomästrasse and was a well known hunting ground for the British soldiers stationed around Soest. The majority of the clientele were British soldiers and this is where the local German girls would come, knowing they would have a good night. A few local German men would also be present, but they were few and far between. Sometimes the pub would be visited by a group of Belgian soldiers, but they were normally not there long, as they would be outnumbered and told to leave. All in all, it was known to be a club for the Brits.

'So you're no longer a virgin then?' chimed in Ian Goodwin, the oldest in the four man room.

'I've had more women than you've had hot dinners.' replied Billy Jennings. 'You're just jealous that you can't pull.'

'Listen to him,' Tony said jokingly, 'first bit of fluff he's had since he's been here and he thinks he's John Travolta. What's her name then?'

'Mind your fucking business.' Billy retorted.

'See, all porkies. Full of shit and fantasies you are mate.' Tony replied, winking at Ian when Billy could not see.

'No I ain't, seeing her again tonight if you must know.'

'Where?' asked Ian.

'Bogs free. May want to give it a few minutes though' said Paul Meyers as he entered the room, carrying a towel over one shoulder and his wash kit in his hand.

'If you must know, her name is Anja.' Billy said. 'And I'm meeting her in *Old Germany.* She's a trainee nurse.'

Another club in the centre of town, this one situated on Walburgerstrasse, *Old Germany* was in a better condition than *Big Ben* and here the clientele also differed slightly. Although also visited by many British soldiers, these would be the ones who would prefer a quiet drink and have a dance with a good possibility of not getting involved in a fight. Several, regular, older German men would prop themselves along the bar and watch the mating rituals between the squaddies and local lasses and wonder what would have happened if the 1945 home match would have turned out differently.

'Alright lads, looks like we're all going out tonight, don't it. Got any friends has she?' Tony asked.

'Why can't you just leave me alone? Always trying to ruin whatever I plan.'

'What have I missed?' Paul asked.

'Nothing' Billy said.

'Billy's got a bird, apparently meeting up with her tonight. Some girl wearing a nurse's uniform. He doesn't want us to go with him.' said Ian.

'Come on boys, leave him alone. Stop bullying him or I'll knock you one.' Paul said. 'And that goes for you as well, L/Cpl or not.'

'Only having some fun,' Tony said, 'not our fault if he can't take a joke.'

'Alright then. So Billy, what's she like?' Paul asked.

'21 years old, blonde, pretty, trainee nurse.'

'Good on you mate. Just be careful. These wankers will probably turn up and try and steal her from you. If they do, just let me know.' With that said, Paul finished dressing and went for breakfast.

'Typical of Paul, that is. Always sticking his nose in and ruining the fun. Mind you, I wouldn't want him to punch me. Arms like Schwarzenegger.' Ian said.

'I'm off for some scoff. Anyone care to join me?' Tony asked.

'Yeah, c'mon, let's go before it's all gone.' said Ian. 'You coming, Billy?'

'No, I'm not hungry. Gonna have a shower when you're all gone.'

With that, both Tony and Ian left the block and crossed the road to the cookhouse, leaving Billy alone in the room.

After about five minutes, Billy walked quickly to the washroom which was located in the middle of the block. The washroom itself consisted of sixteen sinks, eight on each side of the room. Behind a dividing wall were four showers and over the other side of the corridor were the toilets and a single bath.

Billy went to one of the urinals and closed his eyes as he peed. The barracks block was now quiet as the majority of soldiers were enjoying the pleasure of eating an army breakfast. After shaking the last drops, Billy flushed the urinal and headed towards the boxed off room where the bath was situated. He found the plug on the floor by the door, cursed at the state the last person had left the bath in, left the bathroom, went to the blocks cleaning cupboard, took out some Vim and a scouring pad and went back to the bath and got rid of the dirt ring that had been left. Job done, Billy put the plug in and started filling the tub up with warm water. From out of his wash bag he took out some bubble bath and put a generous squirt into the flowing water from the tap.

Once the bath was full, Billy removed the towel from around his waist, placed the wash bag on the ledge behind the tap and slowly and tentatively stepped into the bath and lowered himself down. He reached behind him, groped in the bag and came out with a nail brush. He then started scrubbing his body rigorously from head to toe with the brush and Vim, leaving his skin a bright pink.

Once this task was complete, he let the water out, dried himself sparingly and cleaned the bath again. Still no voices were heard, so he quickly moved over to the showers and finished cleaning himself, this time using shower gel to clean his body. He turned off the shower, dried himself and walked around the wall to one of the cleanest sinks, splashed some water on his face, took out his shaving kit and started to get rid of the bum fluff he called a beard.

Now that he had finished with his ablutions, he walked back along the corridor to the end room where he lived and closed the door behind him. He took his clothes that he would be wearing to work out of his locker and started dressing.

He had just finished tucking his shirt into his khaki trousers when he heard voices approaching. Tony was the first through the door, followed by Paul and Ian.

'What's that smell?' Tony asked.

'Smells like a brothel if you ask me' replied Ian.

'That's my aftershave I got for my birthday.' Billy said, not looking at anyone.

'Don't wear that when you meet up with your bird then. It stinks to high heaven.'

Each soldier then checked themselves in the mirror, adjusting either a shirt collar, pulling the cuffs of the jumper down, made sure the beret was on correctly and that there were no scuff marks on their boots. Once this morning ritual was complete, all four left the room and went outside to join the rest of the troop who were all sauntering towards the parade square, which was situated behind the gymnasium. Start of another day, the same like many.

Billy Jennings was born in Brighton in 1969 and was the younger of two children, his sister being born two years before him. His father was a butcher in the local supermarket. His father hardly spoke to him as he was always busy pruning his roses in the small garden they had at the back of their terraced house or watching taped videos of the dog racing he missed whilst outside. His mother was a cleaner at the local comprehensive school. When she was not working, she kept herself occupied with the church group, planning activities for the local youth club or, when at home, busy with her knitting needles or crocheting until the late evening. His sister was out most nights and normally came home when all were in bed. Billy suspected this was a plan so that his parents would not smell the cigarettes or booze on her, as both frowned upon this as a waste of money and such things led to worse habits.

Feeling suffocated and not knowing what to do after finishing his A levels, Billy went along to the local Army careers office and told the Sergeant that he wanted to join. After watching two short films of what units there were and being shown several pamphlets, Billy confirmed he would like to join as soon as was humanly possible.

Some three weeks later, a letter arrived for him with a train warrant, informing him to travel to Sutton Coldfield for a selection weekend. He had not told his parents or sister about his plans and packed a small sports bag with a change of clothes, a sports kit, wash bag and a book.

On arriving at the Sutton Coldfield train station, he was met by a likeable Corporal who told all those waiting on the platform to follow him, and they all walked apprehensively behind, like ducklings following their mother. They were all told to get into the back of a Bedford four tonner, to keep their noise down and enjoy the journey. The short drive took them through the town and out into the countryside, where they soon came to the army camp.

After debussing, they were all led into the barracks where they were told to line up and confirm they were present once their name was called. Once everyone was accounted for, they were led to the place they would be sleeping for the night, which turned out to be a very large room with 64 beds.

After they put their bags into their allocated locker, they were all marched to a room which consisted of row upon row of chairs, a film projector, a table and several mean looking men dressed in army uniforms.

They were shown several short films about the different services and units, different trades one could choose and were all handed many pamphlets showing the same as they had seen on the screen.

They were then taken into another room and instructed to sit down and complete several written tests and puzzles and were then interviewed by a Staff Sergeant and a Captain.

Then they were told to go and wait outside the room opposite and were called in one by one by an army doctor. After an examination where they had to strip bollock naked, had their testicles held whilst told to cough, they were then measured, weighed and told to dress again.

After the interviews, assessments and medical were completed, they were all led to a cookhouse where they were given some watery beef stew with dumplings, a bowl of rice pudding and a cup of tea.

They were then informed that they should go back to the dormitory and get some sleep, as they will need to get up early to complete several physical tests and were advised not to masturbate as this would sap their energy, which they would need in the morning.

At 06:00 hours, they were all woken up by a Corporal shouting 'Hands off cocks, on with socks.' They all dressed quickly into their sports kit, a variation of tracksuits or shorts, trainers or plimsolls, sweatshirts or t-shirts. They were all herded outside and were taken on a 1.5 mile warm up, alternating between running and walking before they were instructed they had to run around the field twice, another 1.5 miles and that everyone had to get to the finish line in less than eleven minutes or they would fail. Although not the best runner, Billy managed to get around in just over nine minutes and was nearer the front than the back.

They were then taken to the gymnasium where they took part in what is known as an APFT, an Army Physical Fitness Test. After finishing the shuttle runs, pull-ups, sit-ups, jump test and step test, they were again marched outside and told to get themselves cleaned up for breakfast and to be ready for the final interviews at 10:00 hours.

When it was Billy's turn for his final interview, the troop Captain informed him he had scored well in the aptitude test, that his fitness was good and that he would be able to apply for any trade that was on offer. Billy had been impressed by the first film he had seen and said he would like to join the Royal Signals as a Radio Operator. The soldier in the film had been seen walking through the jungles of Borneo with a radio pack on his back and a rifle in his hands and then of another soldier relaxing on a beach with crystal blue sea in the background. Billy signed on the dotted line and was told he was now enlisted in the Royal Signals as a Radio Operator with the belief that he would be sent to places like Belize, Cyprus, Malta or Hong Kong.

Back to the cookhouse for a late dinner and then herded onto the Bedford and driven back to the train station and sent on their way with the words that they would receive by mail their recruitment papers with when and where they were to report to for basic training.

Billy arrived home on the Sunday evening to find his dad had had an accident with his pruning shears and sat nursing a bandaged index finger on his left hand and his mother on the telephone to Mavis, their next door neighbour, telling her all about the long wait they had in the casualty department of their nearest hospital and how lucky it was that it was only his index finger and not his whole hand. It was as if his parents had not noticed he had been away at all.

When his letter finally arrived, he told his mum that he was joining the army and would be reporting for training in October of 1987 in Catterick Garrison in north Yorkshire. After wiping away a stray tear, his mother said she would miss him and that he should write regularly. His dad just grunted and said it was about time he done something with his life and become a man. His sister was more than likely in the back of a Ford Escort with her knickers discarded and getting a good rogering from her latest boyfriend and would not know he had left the family house until she needed something from him, which was not often.

After completing the ten weeks of basic training where he learned how to iron his kit properly, how to make his bed, bull his boots, clean the barrack room, march and salute, fire a rifle, get over the assault course and many other tasks, he had his Passing Out parade in the middle of December. He was provided with another set of rail warrants to travel back home and needed to report back for trade training at the barracks down the road from where he had spent probably the best ten weeks of his life so far.

When returning from a dreadful Christmas back at the family house, he was only too eager to get back to military life where he had a sense of belonging and purpose. 8 Signals Regiment was his new home for the next fourteen weeks, where he polished up on his drill, was able to shoot more weapons and learned all about being a Radio Operator. He also learnt to drive, this being done in an army Land Rover.

He was told to fill out his ‘wish list’ for his first posting and was hoping that it would be somewhere overseas, someplace exotic like Hong Kong, Cyprus, Borneo or Belize. These were the places where he had seen the soldiers in the recruitment films, so he entered these on the list.

After finishing his trade training, he moved out of the training block and into the transit block, where he waited for his posting papers. He was still ordered to drill, keep fit and keep his kit and room in tip top condition, but he had more time on his hands.

One morning whilst on parade, the squadron Sergeant Major handed out the papers to the soldiers and Billy eagerly opened his, only to find that instead of sea, sand and sun, he had been given Echtrop, West Germany. Germany had not been on his list, not a place he would have chosen willingly and was disappointed to say the least. He was told by a couple of seasoned soldiers attending an upgrade course that Echtrop was a village near Soest and added that 'Soest' consisted of two British camps, one called San Sebastian, otherwise known as 'Top Camp' as this was on top of a hill overlooking the Möhnesee, a large stretch of water with a dam at one end. The other camp was called Salamanca and was known as 'Bottom Camp', if only for the fact one had to travel downhill to get there. These camps were about 15 kilometers or 10 miles apart from each other but worked closely together. The upgrade soldiers also informed Billy that both top and bottom camp were shit holes, the dormitories were old Nissen huts left over after the war and that there was bugger all to do when one knocked off for the evening.

Soest has had a military presence since several years after the Second World War. From approximately 1953 to 1971, there was a garrison of Canadian soldiers and their families stationed near Soest as well as in Werl, Hemer-Iserlohn and Deilinghofen. There were also several Belgian camps located in Soest itself. From 1971, the British military took over the former Canadian camps and also the married quarters along Hiddingser Weg, just south of the B1, known to all soldiers as "The Patch".

A week later, after boxing up his belongings and having his MFO box shipped off for him to meet in Germany, he was sent home again and told to wait for his travel documents and be at the airport on time, or else he would be jailed for being AWOL.

He spent two weeks at home with his mum fussing over him as if she would never see him again. His dad actually proved that he was able to put more than five words together and form a coherent sentence and told him all about his time when he was in the army during his two years national service and what the army would do for Billy. He only saw his sister when she came home to change her underwear and was back out being the local bike, letting anyone ride her if they had some spare cigarettes or a can of lager.

After the New Year, Billy's papers arrived and he made sure he was not late at the airport as he did not want to miss his flight and be reported for being absent without leave and was soon in the air, bags stowed in the belly of the Boeing 737 and not knowing what to expect on landing in Düsseldorf.

The flight took just over 90 minutes and he disembarked without any hassle and picked up his suitcase and holdall from the carousel. After passing through customs, he was met in the hall and told to join the other soldiers who were either arriving back off leave or, like him, joining their new regiment for the first time. All were herded onto a military bus and were whisked away into the night. The journey was broken up as the bus stopped in several places along the way, dropping off soldiers at their relative barracks. With the number of bodies depleting, there were only himself and two others left.

They arrived at San Sebastian barracks, home of the 3rd Armoured Division, Headquarters and Signals Regiment on the evening of 10th January 1988. He was met at the gates by the duty Sergeant and told to go to block 29 with his bags and report to the block Corporal. He was given directions and informed that a meal was waiting for him in the cookhouse if he was quick. The other two had stayed on the bus and were driven further, most likely Salamanca.

Block 29 looked the same as block 28 and even the same as blocks 27 down to 25. These were the living quarters of the single soldiers. The buildings were single storey made of concrete and did not resemble anything like the Nissen huts like he was led to believe. Although it was dark, security lights shone outside each building, illuminating the way.

Block 29 was the second to last along the road on the right. He hesitantly opened the door and saw the sign for the blocks junior

NCO on the first door after entering the building. He knocked on it hesitantly and heard someone mumble something under their breath, waited and was then confronted with a small man wearing shorts and a bath robe.

'Signalman Jennings reporting Corporal.' Billy said, standing to attention.

'Steady on, anyone would think you were just out of training.' the Corporal replied.

'I am Corporal' Billy said.

'I can see that you wally. Come on, I'll show you to your room. I'm Cpl Andy McIntosh, you can call me Andy but Corp when senior ranks are around, clear?'

'Yes Corp.' Billy replied.

'Andy. You're in room two, you'll be joining L/Cpl Tony White and Signalers Ian Goodwin and Paul Meyers. Watch Tony, he can be a bit of a cunt at times. Got his stripe straight out of training, Technician and full of himself. Ian is alright and easy to get along with. Paul will look after you as he takes shit from no one, not even me. Keep close to him and he'll show you the ropes.'

Andy opened the door without knocking and Billy followed him into the room. There were four beds, one in each corner of the room, and each bed space had its own locker. Each occupant was lying either in or on their bed. Tony was watching TV with a set of headphones on, Ian was listening to a tape playing on his stereo unit and Paul was reading a book whilst eating a packet of crisps.

'Guys, this is Signalman Billy Jennings, he will be your new roommate for the foreseeable future. Please make him feel welcome and at home or I'll jail the fucking lot of you. Understand?' Andy stood there looking at the three soldiers.

'What?' This was from Tony.

'Shh,' said Ian, 'I'm listening to the new album from *Wet Wet Wet.*'

'Hi Billy, guess what bed is yours.' Paul said without looking up from his page.

'Well, that's the introductions done, doss down there, be ready for parade at 08:10 in the morning. Good night and sweet dreams.' And with that, Andy walked back out the room, closed the door and went back to his bunk.

Billy emptied his suitcase and holdall and hung up all his clothes and stored his belongings in his locker.

'Bogs are down the corridor, same as the washrooms. Cookhouse is straight down the corridor and out the other end, directly opposite. I'll let you use my iron tomorrow after me. Not a bad posting if you behave yourself. The Möhnesee is not far from here, you know, the lake where the Dam Busters blew up the dam in 1943, just like in the film. Keep your noise down and I'll see you in the morning.' With that, Paul put the crisp packet in the bin, picked up his toothpaste and brush and headed down the corridor.

Tony and Ian ignored him, but as he was used to eighteen years of loneliness, this was rather normal for Billy. He left the room, followed the corridor as explained and walked over to get some food. After trying both sets of doors, he understood that the kitchen was closed and the duty cook had probably gone home or to his room for the night. With nothing else to do and nothing to eat, Billy himself went back to his room, got a towel and wash kit and went back to the washroom before getting into bed.

Over the next few months, Billy slowly came out of his shell and was gradually accepted as a roommate, although he was always reminded he was the sprog, a new recruit and would always be until someone new joined the room, where he would then rise up the pecking order. As the others had no plans and were not scheduled to be posted anywhere soon, he took the jibes easily enough and just rolled with the punches. This was the beginning of the making of Signalman Billy Jennings, 18 years old, a loner all his life and now in a foreign country for the first time.

CHAPTER 4

At the time when Billy was being inspected on parade by his troop Staff Sergeant, Rudolph Mertens was washing his pride and joy after working the night shift. The taxi he drove was a Mercedes 190 D, cream in colour with light brown seats and he looked after it as if it was the love of his life. A day would not go by without him polishing the bodywork, wiping down the dashboard, checking the tire pressures or just cleaning the windows and lights. Yes, Rudolph was happy.

He had just finished drying the car off with a chamois leather and he opened the rear doors and took out the foot mats to give them first a bashing and then a hoovering, when he noticed that an identity card on the floor under the passenger seat. He leant in and retrieved it and held it up to the light to get a better look. He saw the picture of a young woman with a pretty face and a cute smile. She had blonde hair pulled back in a pony tail and the ID showed her name as being Anja Schmedding, date of birth 25th April 1967 and her address showed she came from a town called Herzfeld.

He looked around him and after checking that no one was watching, he was took out his own wallet and slipped the ID card in between his driving license and his own ID. His wallet went back into the rear, right hand pocket of his baggy jeans. With a smile on his face, he finished cleaning the floor mats, put away the pressure washer and dried his hands.

Born in Berlin in June 1943, his mother fled west with her newly born when she received news that her husband had been brutally killed whilst serving in the 2nd SS Panzer Division at the battle of Kursk in the first week of August of the same year. She believed that as the Russians had been able to so easily defeat the German tanks in such short time, it would not be long before they travelled west and took Berlin. None of her friends listened to what she said and so she made her way slowly out of Berlin, first stopping in Helmstedt for several months, but deciding that as it was not far enough away from her husband's killers, she travelled further west and settled in a town named Salzkotten.

Rudolph was bullied at school for the simple fact that he was different. He was shunned by all of the boys and laughed at by all of the girls. His mother told him that he had nothing to worry about because they were all stupid and did not know that he was special.

As Rudolph got older, he started growing, much faster than other children. Although the war had ended only 10 years before and poverty was still the norm, by the time he celebrated his twelfth birthday, he had started to get obese. The children in the town would call him names and throw sticks and stones at him when he walked past and he would run home crying, where his mother would smother him with affection and from the folds of her shawl, she would always produce some sweet item for him, which she had required from some source or other. So he learned the rule that the more he cried, the more treats he would be given, meaning he would put on more and more weight as the years went on.

When he was nineteen, he was instructed to enlist in the newly founded German national service, the Bundeswehr. Because of his size, the commanding officer of the newly formed unit made the decision to have young Rudolph made his driver, as it was plain to see that he was not the most athletic of the conscripts. Rudolph underwent an intense driving course and found that ferrying around the CO had its advantages. For one, he did not need to do any guard duties and secondly, he was always told to wait in the kitchen or hallway when the CO was invited to the officer's mess or other functions.

On returning home after 24 months to his mother after his conscription time was finished, Rudolph found the opportunity in helping a local farmer drive his tractor and plough the vast acres of fields. This suited the young Rudolph, sitting high up, able to look down on those who walked or cycled by. Here he was king, ruler of the fields, the engine drowning out all insults thrown at him from the local youths about his size.

One sunny morning in September of 1973, Rudolph's life was shattered. He woke up in the bed he still shared with his mother in the one room flat to find that she had died peacefully in her sleep. Not knowing what to do and with nobody to ask for help, he left her lying in bed and went to work, as he had promised the farmer that he would have the south field ploughed and ready for seeding by the afternoon. His mother had told him that a promise made is a promise kept, and he lived by this rule.

Once the field was completed, he parked the tractor back at the farmers' house and waddled home to find that his mother was still in the same position as when he had left her. Never having learned to cook, Rudolph started eating raw vegetables and apples that he had collected the weekend just gone.

His mother stayed sharing the bed with Rudolph for another two weeks until one day he could stand the stench that was wafting off of her decomposing body no longer, nor watch the flies feasting on her lips and the maggots wiggling out of her mouth and nose. He wrapped her up in the bed sheet and went and collected the tractor. As he was a big man, he was able to pick up his slight mother with ease, lift her into the tractors cabin and drove off towards the trees at the bottom of the road that led to the farmers' field. Here he dug a hole large enough to lay his mother inside. Once finished, he collected her body from the warm cabin and carried her to the freshly dug grave, where he tenderly put her on the ground and gradually rolled her in. After saying a silent prayer, he filled in the earth on top of his mother, wiped the tears and sweat from his face and got back into the tractor.

He knew that he would not be able to stay in Salzkotten without the one and only person who had ever loved him, so he drove back to the farm, abandoned the tractor and walked back to the room they had shared, collected the meager belongings he had along with a picture of his mother and left town.

Rudolph was able to catch a bus travelling to Lippstadt, some 20km or so to the west. He had no job, no food, no money to speak of, nowhere to live and no thought as to what he was going to do.

After sleeping in the Stadt Park for two nights, he was reading the newspaper he had found and used during the night as a blanket, when he came across an advertisement about a new taxi firm opening up and was looking for good drivers. He decided that if he stayed one night longer in the park, he would surely die from lack of food and hypothermia as the nights were turning cold. With this, he walked down to the Lippe, a river that runs through Lippstadt, originating in Bad Lippspringe and ending some 220 km further down the line where it joins another river called the Weser, and stripped off his clothes and washed himself for the first time in days.

On the way out of the park, he rummaged around in the rubbish bins looking for some food, anything edible that a passerby may have discarded. With an apple core and a not so yellow banana skin, breakfast was quickly eaten on his way to the local train station where he knew he would find a taxi waiting to pick up passengers after they disembarked from the trains. Rudolph showed one driver the advert and was told that yes, he worked for this particular company and would take him to see the boss, told Rudolph to jump in and off they went.

Herr Springer, the owner of the new taxi company, was not overly impressed with the state and appearance of Rudolph, but as he had a good heart and could see he was in trouble, decided to give him a chance after learning all about Rudolph's driving experience whilst in the army. That said, Herr Springer told his wife to find a set of clothes that would fit him from her late father's wardrobe and to show him the bathroom was so he could have a descent wash and a shave. Rudolph had to sit a test in able to gain his taxi license, but after studying for this for a week and also learning the streets from a book of maps, Rudolph was handed his taxi license and a set of keys to go and pick up his first customer.

Things were looking up for Rudolph at this time, as now he was earning regular money he was able to rent out a small room in the attic of an old couple in the middle of town. He provided the authorities his new address and occupation and settled down to live a solitary life driving passengers to and fro and for an extra cost, he was allowed to share the evening meal with his landlord.

Some 4 years later at 04:00 hours on the 2nd of February 1977, the doorbell was pressed and not released until the house owner let the police in and Rudolph was rudely awakened in his attic room, this being filled with a bed, a set of drawers, a long mirror, a sink in the corner and now four burly policemen. Rudolph was taken to the police station where he was charged with failing to inform the authorities of the passing away of his mother and for illegally disposing of her corpse.

Two randy teenagers had gone into the trees to have some uninterrupted sex. The girl had been lying on the ground with her boyfriend, who was pounding away on top as if sex was going out of fashion, when she started to climax. She reached out with her hands and grabbed hold of a tree stump. Or at least that is what it was until it came away in her hand and she saw herself holding a human thigh bone. When she let out a loud shriek, the boy thought he was doing good and pounded harder until she hit him on the head with the bone. When she managed to disentangle herself from Don Juan, they both saw that a skeletal body was partially uncovered, this being the work of ground frost pushing the body higher as it froze and then the carcass being dug up by foxes and other scavengers wanting to get in on the action. The teenagers went straight to the police, admitting only that they were only walking through the trees when they spotted the body. The autopsy provided a set of dentures and it was only a matter of time before the police would track down the identity of the body, which they did from asking several dentists if they had any records of providing the false teeth. Then it was easy to find the next of kin and learned that her son had just upped and left and moved away from Salzkotten.

Other charges were threatened but the interrogating officer could see the truth told him by a broken man who seemed a bit simple.

Rudolph appeared in court and was jailed for a year after admitting the charge of concealing a body and preventing a lawful burial.

After his release from prison, he decided he did not want to go back to Lippstadt as he did not want to be confronted with people who knew him as the 'Mother Smotherer', a title given him by the local press, not for the fact that he killed his mother by smothering her, but because she smothered him with more affection than was normal all his life, and as we all know how the press works, any headline that rhymes sells papers. He knew the area well so decided to find somewhere to live in Soest and find employment.

Looking more presentable than he did at his first job interview, Rudolph found another job driving a taxi and was still working for the same company some 10 years later.

Now at the age of 45, still overweight, swiftly balding, he had bad eyesight, bad health and bad breath. The lenses of his glasses were so thick, people used to say they were made from the bottom of Coke bottles. He had no friends, other colleagues shunned his presence, he was never invited out for a drink with the boys and he never went out looking for a drinking buddy himself. All in all, others would have said he was a fat, lonely man. But others did not know what thoughts went on inside his head.

CHAPTER 5

'Guten Morgen allerseits,' Klaus Lodde said, greeting everyone in the staff room. 'All ready for another crazy day?'

'Not really,' replied Sandra, 'Julia kept me up most of the night with her coughing. If it gets any worse, I'll need to take her to the doctors. Have kept her home from school today and my mum is looking after her. Would like to curl up on the sofa and have a kip for a couple of hours.'

'Well, there's no chance of that happening today. Gregor's pulled a sicky and Mechtild is helping out downstairs on 15/1.' answered Klaus. 'So it looks like it is just the four of us today looking after that lot out there.'

"Out there" was the ward of 15/2, where 6 nurses per shift took care of 30 patients.

The patients housed in Eickelborn were here because they were in no fit state to understand right from wrong due to either their psychological state of mind or because they were under the influence of alcohol or drugs at the time they committed their crime. The aim of the institution is to provide the patients with care and therapy with the goal of being able to one day release them back into the general public.

The clinic first started in Benninghausen in the early 1800s to take care of the mentally ill and was called the Westfälische Landeskrankenhaus Lippstadt. In 1883, the Eickelborn clinic opened its doors to the ever expanding science of psychiatry and was aptly named the Westfälischen Landeskrankenhaus Eickelborn. In 1984, both clinics merged and were renamed the Landschaftsverbands Westfalen-Lippe (LWL).

Depending on the seriousness of the offense committed and the nature of the patient, the stations dotted around the grounds vary with the care they receive and also the security. It is not that uncommon to see patients shopping in the local Cooperative or queuing up to by bratwurst and chips at the local snack shop down the road. However, these were the patients classified as being "safe" which meant they were not classed as being violent or a danger to the general population. The patients who were marked as being a high risk were put in the wards or stations which were situated behind high walls and fences, barbed wire included. And it was behind one of these walls that the stations 15/1 and 15/2 found themselves, at the back end of the grounds out of view from all eyes unless you happened to take a walk in that direction. Each patient was locked up in their single room from 22:00 each night and the doors were reopened again the next morning at 06:00.

'Who's turn to make the coffee?' Petra asked.

'I'll do them. All want one?' asked Klaus.

Both Petra and Sandra nodded, but Detlef appeared not to have heard and was standing staring out the window at nothing in particular, lost in thought.

'Detlef, do you want a coffee?' Klaus asked again.

'What? Oh, no thanks. Just finished one'.

'How long we got before we have to start?' Sandra asked, resting her head on the table.

'Another 10 minutes before official handover.' Klaus stated.

Coffees made, all three sat at the table waiting for their 8 hour shift to start.

'Detlef, all OK?' asked Sandra, 'looks like you haven't slept much either.'

'Yeah,' he replied, 'didn't get home until late. Went out for something to eat in Soest. May have had a couple of bevies too many, heads killing me.'

'Want a pain killer?' she asked.

'No, as soon as I start moving it'll go away.'

At that moment, they were joined by the nurses who were going off duty after their night shift had ended.

'Any trouble last night?' Klaus asked.

'Nope, quiet as a cemetery.' came the reply from the station lead. 'I now officially hand our patients over to your care.' he said grinning. 'Off now to do a bit of fishing. See you all tomorrow.' And without waiting for a reply, he was out of the room, off the ward and out of the building before the others had a chance to finish their coffee. The others who were on the night shift all said their goodbyes and clocked out at the same time.

'Come on then, let's get a move on. They'll all be wanting their breakfast soon. Better unlock the bastards.' Klaus said quietly so that his voice would not carry itself into the corridor in case it was heard by one of the patients.

Working as a Krankenpflege, a male nurse, was not the first choice Detlef Krome had chosen as a profession. When he left school at the age of 17, he completed a 3 ½ year apprenticeship and became a builder. The money was good, there was always some work to do on the side and obviously he did not inform the local tax authorities of this extra work. Then at the age of only 25 he started having back pains and after exhaustive examinations by the doctors and hospitals, he was advised to retrain into another profession. As he had lived in Eickelborn all his life, he knew all about psychiatric nursing, and that it was an "easy number", so he filled out an application at the job centre and was accepted to join the next intake of trainee nurses.

Although he had to learn basic nursing and work in normal hospitals, he wanted to get a job in either Eickelborn or Benninghausen so that he was close to home and could carry on living with his parents and not have to pay any rent.

He passed his exams and was given the opportunity in starting in Eickelborn, as the director was friends with his father and it all made good sense.

Now at the ripe old age of 34, Detlef was bored with his job, hated the "inmates" and wanted nothing better to do than get out of the "prison" where he worked. Most evenings he would be in one bar or another and come to work the next day with a hangover. He knew he was drinking too much, but what the heck.

He walked out of the staff room, put his hand into his trouser pocket and took out the "key". This opened all the doors to the patient's rooms on this particular floor, a second key was used for getting off the station and out of the building and a third to unlock the outside gate. He unlocked the door to room 3 and was greeted with the words 'Took your fucking time. What have you all been doing?' This came from the English patient, Gary Stiles.

'Sorry Gary, had to do the handover first as you know.' Detlef replied.

'Why am I always the last to be let out? Why can't you start unlocking the doors from this end?'

'Old habits die hard.' Detlef retorted and moved along to open the final door.

'Are you going to play chess with me today like you keep promising?'

'Yeah, but it'll have to wait until later. Got things to do first.'

'Well don't forget.' And with that, Gary moved off down the corridor to the day room and joined the other patients.

Gary was a bit of a novelty on the station. Being the only foreigner, he was treated differently than the rest. When he had first come to Eickelborn back in 1982, he could only put a few German words together and did not understand much what was said to him. Now he was able to speak and understand the majority as long as it wasn't medical terms.

He had served in the British army as a medic and had been stationed in the British Military Hospital in Iserlohn and then transferred to BMH Berlin where he became a staff nurse. During his time in Berlin, Gary came in contact with probably the most infamous patient BMH Berlin had ever treated. This was Rudolf Hess, the deputy leader to Adolf Hitler and the Nazi party. Hess was sentenced to life imprisonment at the Nuremberg Trials and was imprisoned at the nearby Spandau Prison. During periods of ill health, Hess would be admitted to BMH Berlin where an entire floor would be shut off and secured for his treatment and his treatment only.

Gary read all the books he could find on Hess and admired the courage Hess had shown when he flew solo to Scotland in an attempt to negotiate peace with the United Kingdom during the Second World War.

One night whilst out on the town, Gary had been drinking heavily and was on his way home when he got into an altercation with some German punks. They were spraying something unreadable on the Berlin wall which separated the East and West when Gary decided to poke his nose in and claimed in a rather loud, drunken voice that

Hess would not have tolerated their behaviour if he had still been in power. Not knowing that the punks were students at the nearby university and could speak English, one decided to tell him that he should fuck off back to England from where he came.

Gary, never one to back down, decided to take the law into his own hands. He also decided that the bottle he was drinking from was as good a weapon as any and smashed it over the head of the youth who had spoken. Gary then proceeded to use the broken end and stabbed the punk several times in the side of the neck, severing his artery. Not only seeing red but covered in at as well, Gary moved towards the remaining two but was too pissed to follow at the pace they were running.

He was found that night by the Berlin police along the side of the Olympic stadium unconscious on the ground. He was rushed to hospital as it appeared to the police that he had been attacked and had suffered some extremely, violent injuries due to being covered in blood, but when the doctors stripped off his clothing they found no wound marks on his body at all. What they did find was someone who had taken rather a bit too much to drink, so a blood test was taken and the results showed an alcohol level of 0.32%. Most people would be near death with this level, but years of training put Gary in good stead for a recovery.

Whilst under observation by the nurses and under guard be the police, the body of the punk rocker was being transferred to the morgue and his friends told the police how their friend had been killed and gave a good description of the attacker, one that was pretty accurate and matched Gary.

Although a serving soldier in the British army, Gary was arrested, tried and sentenced in a German court and ordered to serve 15 years in a psychiatric facility to receive help for the ruthless crime he had committed, one he could not remember doing.

Now in Eickelborn, he used his own uniqueness to his advantage. If he did not want to do something, he would claim he did not understand. If he was refused something, he would shout loudly that he was being racially discriminated. So in order to keep the peace, the nurses generally went out of their way and provided him with items that were not purchasable from the clinics tuck shop i.e.

English newspapers. These were purchased specially for him and he would receive six copies of last week's *The Sun* newspaper the following week. So although he was reading "old news", it was still news from home and after he had read them back to back, he would do the crosswords and then he would leave them in the common room for anyone to read or at least to look at the pictures.

Detlef was able to get through the morning and made it to lunch time. He went into the staff room and devoured two cheese and ham rolls his mother had made him and finished the liter bottle of Coke he had started earlier. Headache now gone, he felt like a human being again. He sat at the table on his own and was lost in thought when Sandra entered the room.

'Hey, Detlef, want to come and baby sit at mine tonight?' she asked. 'Mums looking after her all day so won't want to stay there tonight and I need to get out for a drink.'

'I can't tonight, sorry,' he replied, 'have already made plans myself. What about Petra, have you asked her?'

'She was the first I asked. Her boyfriend is coming home tomorrow and she needs to tidy up the flat. Oh well, looks like I'll be staying in again.'

'What if I swing by when I am finished what I'm doing. I'll bring a bottle or three and we can have a good time.'

'I've told you before I'm not interested in you that way. Only friends. We both know what you get like when you've had a few. It's ok I'll survive until the weekend.'

'Have you been able to trace Julia's dad?' he asked.

'Nope, looks like the arsehole may have left the country or changed his name or something. Whatever it is, the authorities cannot find him under his name in Germany. Better off without him but I could use the alimony that he owes me.'

'If I ever meet him, I'd give him such a beating, he'd wished he'd stayed for the wedding and not buggered off when he found out you were pregnant.'

'You and me both. Whatever. So what plans have you got tonight?' she asked, changing the subject away from herself.

'I think I lost something in the restaurant last night. Need to go back and check if they found it or if it was handed in. Must have fallen out when I was paying the waiter.'

'Restaurant hey, who did you go with?'

'Girl I met the other day. Met her in the hospital when I took my mum in to get her ingrown toenail looked at. She a bit younger than me, but we really hit it off.'

'Good for you.' she said before turning and leaving the room.

Detlef stayed sitting and stared out of the window trying to remember where he could have lost it. Could he have dropped it in the restaurant? What about when he paid the taxi driver when he was outside his house? He definitely needed to be more careful in future and maybe even cut down on the drinking and have a clear head for once.

With that last thought, Detlef put away his lunch box and went back onto the station to see what the commotion was all about in the corridor.

CHAPTER 6

Soest has early origins dating back some 1000 years and is situated in the middle of North Rhine-Westphalia, West Germany.

Around 1180, Archbishop Philipp von Heinsberg of Cologne expanded the area of Soest to around 102 hectares and had a defensive wall built around the town which included towers and 10 entry gates. The wall had a total length of 3,8 km, around 2,6 miles. With this defence in place, Soest was one of the strongest and richest towns in Westfalia and was considered to be one of the most important trading towns in its day.

Today, the population of Soest is around 30,000 in the main town and another 15,000 in the outlying areas.

'OK, the scene of crime is completely sealed off and the surrounding streets are being searched for any clues or weapons. Door to door inquiries are underway to see if anyone else witnessed anything out of the ordinary last night, anybody seen hanging around, any noises etc.

'We have also established that three trainee nurses from the Marienkrankenhaus have not shown up for work this morning. And before anyone asks, yes, we have checked their rooms in their accommodation and they have not been there all night. We are interviewing their friends, work colleagues, anybody who would have known them in the dorms. Officers have been sent to each of their parent's houses in case they went home and still not returned. Nobody else has been reported missing by the general public, so it looks as if our mystery lady could be one of these.

'The Staatsanwaltschaft (the prosecutor's office) in Arnsberg have been informed and are waiting for the autopsy results, just like we are. They are in contact with our own press office here and an early press release is scheduled for this lunch time. Then the local press will get the story and this should hit the local news by this evening and by tomorrow morning will also be in the local papers. And that is where we are at the moment. Erster Kriminalhauptkommissar Gerling, anything you would like to add?'

'Thank you for the update, Polizeihauptkommissar Backhaus. All I would like to add is that we need to catch this vicious bastard soon. The tech team are going all out trying to find any evidence of the attacker at the church. So far they have turned a blank. Due to the location, we have been unable to find any footprints, so we have no idea of the size or weight of the culprit. That said, we need to get the witness woman and press her for more details. I don't care if we have to take her away from her work place, this has priority. Other than that, we just have to wait for the autopsy results like you said. Any questions?'

'Yes sir, would you like to be present when I hold the press conference at 12?' asked Polizeihauptkommissar Ahrens, the press officer for Soest.

'No, I'd like to leave that honour to Polizeihauptkommissar Backhaus as this is his territory.' replied Sven. 'Anyone else?'

'Yes, have you seen any other murders like this one, sir?'

'Good question, but no. I have witnessed several throat cuttings and one or two disembowelments but not both together. And in the ones I have seen, these were mainly related to gang fights.' Sven said, looking the constable in the eye. 'Ok, keep doing what we are doing and let's hope for an early break.'

With that, the meeting was over.

'Bernie,' Sven said when most had left the room, 'who was the constable dishing out the coffee?'

'Ah, that was Polizeimeister Trilling. Very keen and not shy in sticking his chin out. He started at the same time as Grünewald but you can already see the difference. Where Grünewald is still a bit green behind the ears, Trilling is proving to be an asset to us. Boxes for Soest so has his face in the local rag quite often.'

'Would like to keep him on this if you don't mind. Asked a decent question back there. Most newbie's would have kept their mouths shut and been scared to speak. I like him.'

'Ok, I'll pull him off his current task and get him on boarded.'

With that, both officers left the room and went to their appropriate offices.

'Good afternoon ladies and gentlemen of the press. For those of you who do not know me, my name is Polizeihauptkommissar Ahrens and I'm the press officer for Soest.

'I would like to inform you that on 31.08.1988 at 02:36 hours this morning, a body was found outside the main doors to the Wiesenkirche here in Soest. The victim is of a young, unidentified female believed to be in her late teens or early twenties. She was found with her throat cut and her stomach sliced open. All details will be released of cause of death etc. once we receive the autopsy report, in which case another press conference will be scheduled.

'We have so far no clues as to the perpetrator and have one witness seeing a figure running away from the scene at the time we believe the victim was murdered.

'Apart from that, there is nothing more I can add at this present moment.'

'Is it true that she was a trainee nurse?' asked Thomas Loch of the local newspaper, the *Soester Anzeiger*.

'As I mentioned, we are unable to confirm her identity, but as the nursing quarters are only located some 150 meters away from the murder scene, it is a possibility that she was from there, but please let's not jump to conclusions, we don't want to scare every parent who has a daughter studying here to be worried.'

'Is it true that her heart was ripped out and taken?' This question was asked by Michael König from one of the national newspapers, the *Bild.* This tabloid is keenly read by many tradesmen as some say it contains more tits and scandal than facts and that it can be read from cover to cover within a day's coffee break time.

'No, this is not a fact that has been substantiated. Again, we are waiting for the autopsy report and until then, no details apart from the cuttings are known. Very nice to have some sensationalism, but let's keep any stories of missing organs and vampires away from this one.

'As soon as we hear anything new, you will be invited when we hold the next conference.' With that, Ahrens stood up and walked out of the room amongst shouts from other reporters.

'Here, where did you get the angle of her being a nurse?' König asked Loch.

‘I was in the hospital canteen interviewing a hit and run victim when the police came in asking all the staff if they had anyone missing from their shift. As I’m over there quite often, I get recognised. One of the biddies behind the till told me what the police were asking, so watch this space.’

‘Let me buy you some lunch,’ König said, ‘then we can put our heads together and come up with a headline.’

‘Sorry mate, I’m not interested. We report facts in our paper, not fiction. And besides, why should I share my story and contacts?’ he said.

‘Surely it makes sense to combine our thoughts’ König stated, ‘if only to be one step ahead of the rest.’

‘No thanks, I’m the local and this is my patch. You want to report something, go out and find the story yourself.’ Loch stood up and made his way swiftly through the room, trying to put some distance between him and König.

Stefanie Becker, the pathologist, had just finished examining the body with her colleague when the phone rang in her office. She quickly walked over to her desk and picked up.

‘Dr. Becker speaking, how may I help?’ she asked the caller.

‘Steffi, Sven here. Any updates? We are now at a crossroads and cannot proceed any further without your report. The Techies have called and stated that they have not been able to find any conclusive clues as to the murderer. With so many people going in and out of the church all these years, all fingerprints on the walls and doors are non recognisable. The blood splattered on the walls and floor shows that whoever killed her was standing behind her for the initial attack and was careful not to step in any blood. Please tell me you have so good news for me.’

‘Yes and no. I think it would be better if you could come back to Dortmund and I will show you what I have found out. Then at least you will have a clearer picture about what I am saying. I’ll send a fax to Soest with my findings and you can read what I have written on your way here.’

‘Ok, I’ll leave as soon as you send the fax.’

Steffi put the phone down and started to play the tape she had made during the autopsy and started typing up her report.

'Boss, fax has come through. I'll get the car to the front, that will give you time to read it whilst I am driving.'

'Cheers Freddy, yeah, meet you outside in five. I'll just let Bernie know where we are going.'

Freddy left the office and Sven walked towards where Bernie was situated.

'Bernie, here's a copy of the fax from the pathologist. Freddy and me are off there now. She wants to talk me through her findings. If it is something big, then we'll be back later. If not, then we'll leave it in your capable hands and see you in the morning.'

'Alright,' said Bernie, 'see you later. Hopefully we'll have an update about the missing nurses soon.'

Sven went back to the office he and Freddy had taken over, grabbed his jacket and left the room, skipped down the stairs two at a time and walked out through the security door and out through the main door. Freddy was there waiting in the Golf, engine running, eating a chocolate bar.

'Give us half,' Sven said, 'getting a bit peckish.'

Freddy bit into the bar and offered the remaining piece to Sven, who took it and placed it in his mouth. As Freddy slotted into the traffic, Sven started reading the report out loud for Freddy's sake.

They travelled out of Soest and joined the Autobahn 44, the motorway leading to Dortmund and arrived at the "Institute für Rechtsmedizin" within 50 minutes and on entering, walked towards the office and workplace of Steffi.

CHAPTER 7

Stefanie Becker grew up in a family of five in Bochum, some 20 km west of Dortmund. Her father worked at the Opel car factory as a designer, her mother was a school teacher in the local elementary school. Her eldest sister married a musician and moved to Paris when Steffi was thirteen and her twin brother was last known to be exploring the Amazon rain forest as part of a television production company.

Steffi became intrigued with medicine as a child when she was taken to a hospital after cutting open her calf muscle on a barbed wire fence. She decided from an early age that doctors were the best people in the world and she wanted to help others who were in pain.

Then, when she turned fifteen, a friend's brother had been killed under dubious circumstances and had needed a post mortem to determine the actual cause of death. Steffi was intrigued to what they were able to find out and decided that the living was for others, she needed to help the dead.

After finishing her A levels at the age of 18, she went to medical school where she studied medicine for 6 years and a further 5 years of hard work and studying to get the title of being a Forensic Scientist. She was then able to find immediate employment at the Institute für Rechtsmedicine which is the Institute for Forensic Medicine in Dortmund. Here she started as the "junior" doctor but soon impressed her then boss, Dr. Kalkhofen, who kept his eye on his protégé and assisted and taught her everything he knew. Although younger than the other doctors, upon Dr. Kalkhofen's retirement, Steffi was asked if she would like to become the head of the Institute. So, at the young age of 35, she was now in charge of four other doctors, two preparation assistants and two secretaries.

Steffi opened the door when she heard the buzzer. Freddy jogged up the stairs to the second floor followed closely by Sven.

'Hi gorgeous,' Sven said when entering, 'not an ideal location for a date. But if this is what rocks your socks, who am I to complain.'

'You wish,' she replied, 'all it would take is for me to lock you in the cold room with all the stiffs, then we'll see how romantic you feel.' she said smiling. 'Freddy could stay here and keep me warm, though.' she added, looking directly at Freddy. 'Why, if I didn't know better, I'd say you're blushing.'

'Er, no, just jogged up the stairs a bit too fast. Besides, I'm married to Heike, remember?'

'Of course, excuse me. I thought your panting breath was because of your close proximity to me.' she said teasingly.

'Ok, I think we've had enough of the "glad to see you" routine. What have you got for us that we could not read in the report?' Sven asked.

'No time for play time?' Steffi asked. 'Ok, follow me to my domain and I'll show you what I want to show you.'

Steffi led both men back down the stairs to the first floor and into the lab which was kept constantly cool. There was a single, metal table in the centre of the room, accessible from all sides, a set of large operating lights hanging down from the ceiling and a body lying on her back.

'Ok, as you can see, the killer really went to town on her. She has a bruise on her jaw on the right side of the face most probably caused by a blow from a fist or pressure from a thumb. On the left side of her neck, she has an incision 2 cm below her jaw and 10 cm in length and runs from a point immediately below the ear. On the same side, but about 3 cm below the first, she was sliced again. This incision is 20 cm in length and ends at a point 7 cm below the right jaw. This second incision completely severed all the tissues down to the vertebrae, severing the carotid artery, the trachea and the jugular vein. She also received a 7 cm wound to the left, lower part of the abdomen. This wound is some 6 cm deep and has cut into her intestines. All the injuries have been caused by a very sharp, long-bladed instrument.

'So, to put it simply in layman's terms, she died from exsanguinations or to put it even more bluntly, she bled to death. The artery and vein cuts would have stopped the flow of blood to and from the brain. Simultaneously, the cutting of her trachea, the wind pipe, would have had her gargling and coughing for air. She would have lost consciousness within 10 seconds. As like all arterial cuts, her heart would have continued pumping whilst unconscious, squirting blood in all directions until there was not enough in her body to pump. She would have been dead within about 40 seconds due to excessive blood loss and her body shutting down in shock.'

'Have you found any clues on her from her attacker' Freddy asked.

'We have taken scrapings from underneath her fingernails to see if there is any skin or clothing fibres from her attacker, but we came up blank.'

'So, we know how she was killed, where she was killed and when she was killed, all we have to find out now is who she is and who killed her. Not going to be easy.' Sven stated. 'Ok Steffi, if you find out anything more, please call us immediately. Come on Freddy, let's go home and get some rest. I think tomorrow will be a very long day for us. I'm sure the others can do without us for now.'

When the two policemen left, Steffi told one of her prep. assistants he could close up the body and put her back in the body bag and wheel her into the fridge which was able to hold nine bodies at any one time.

CHAPTER 8

'Good afternoon ma'am, sorry to bother you. Are you Frau Wenderling?'

'No, Frau Wenderling is still on holiday, expected back on Friday. Can I help?' she asked.

'And you are?'

'I'm Frau Schmidt, live next door. Come in to water the plants and take the letters out of the box whilst they are away.'

'We need to ask you a rather delicate question. Would you mind if we come in, don't like to talk about these things on the street.'

'What is it about?' Frau Schmidt asked.

'Not here, hallway will be fine.' Polizeihauptmeister Grote and Polizeiobermeister Cord stood on the steps of the terraced house, cars driving by on the Werler Landstrasse in Ostönnen. 'Best if we do.'

Frau Schmidt moved her body backwards, allowing the two policemen into the house.

'How long have you known the Wenderlings'?' Grote asked.

'I'd say coming on ten years or so. Why?'

'We are trying to track down their daughter and would like to know if you are aware of her whereabouts? Would not normally ask anyone who is not a family member, but we really need to move fast and cannot wait for two days before her parents come home.'

'Has something happened to Agnes? Has she had an accident?'

'Sorry, we cannot divulge that information, we just need to check where Agnes is at this moment.'

'She should be at work. She's training to be a nurse in Soest, ever so caring. She has a room there in the nurse's home. Have you tried there? She replied.

'Yes, but she has not been seen there last night. Would you know where else she could be?' he asked.

'Well, she has a boyfriend, bit of a loser if you ask me. Beat his own mum up when she caught him stealing money for drugs. Dad kicked him out of the family home. Living in some sort of shared accommodation I heard.'

'And his name is?'

'Daniel something or other. Don't know his last name, I'm afraid. Or where he lives. But last I heard is that he is started a plumbing apprenticeship in Bad Sassendorf. Don't know what company'

'Ok, that is something we can follow up with. If you do happen to see Agnes, could you please tell her to contact us in Soest. It is important.'

'Of course I will. Anything else you would like to ask or tell me?'
'That's all. Thanks for your help.'

And with that, the two policemen left the house and got back into the car.

'How many plumbing firms are there in Bad Sassendorf?' Grote asked his colleague.

'Two or three I think. Shouldn't be that many Daniel's, so should be able to track him down quick.' Cord replied back.

The police turned the car around and headed back the way they had come, followed the B1 sign posted for Paderborn and turned off towards Bad Sassendorf.

'Excuse me miss, can I have a word?'

'Has my brother been arrested again? What for this time?'

'Is your name Tina Peters' asked Polizeiobermeister Pister.

'No, that's my sister, I'm Astrid.'

'Do you know where your sister is?'

'Last time I heard, she was upstairs taking a shower.'

'And when was that exactly?'

'About five minutes ago when I came out to hang up the washing.'

'We would still need to confirm that we have seen her. Could you ask her to pop some clothes on and come down?' Pister had the patience of a priest.

'Come on in yourself.'

Pister followed Astrid into the side of the house and into the hallway.

'Sis, police are here to see you. Are you decent?' she shouted up the stairs.

'Hold on, be down in a jiffy.' came the reply.

A jiffy turned out to be exactly three minutes and eighteen seconds long when a girl with legs up to her armpits descended the stairs in a way only good looking women can.

'Hi, I'm Tina. Have I done something wrong?' she asked nervously.

'No, nothing wrong. Just trying to ascertain your whereabouts. You did not show up for work this morning and your colleagues are concerned.'

'Seriously?' she asked. 'I was given the day off as I worked a couple of hours extra yesterday and they send out a search party. I'm not due back until tomorrow.'

'It's alright, just that we have to trace down three girls who did not show up for work today. Your name was on the list, but as I can see you are safe and well, then I'll be on my way.'

'Did the hospital send you because 3 nurses didn't turn up for work? That's a bit much isn't it?'

'No, there's been a murder and we think one of them might be the victim. So we are trying to trace the three not accounted for, that's all.'

'Oh shit. Who are the other two? Maybe I know where they are.'

'Sorry, we have to speak with the next of kin first. But I'm glad you're ok. Best be off now. Glad to have met you. Bye.'

Pister left by the front door and as he was getting into his car, he saw Tina standing at the side door and heard her telling her sister that a nurse had been murdered and she thinks it is one of her friends and the police would not tell her the names of the missing girls and she's really scared because if a murderer was walking around killing nurses, she was bound to be next because she was far more prettier than the rest, apart from Natalia, but she doesn't count because she isn't German and…

He closed the door and drove away and as he did, he turned his head and had another, long look at her. He was glad he was given this girl to check up on. With a stirring in his trousers, he drove further.

*

'Hello, we would like to speak with Herr Schmedding, please.' Polizeihauptmeister Sander stated.

'I'm sorry but he's in with a patient and won't be out until about five o'clock.' came the curt reply.

'I'm afraid we cannot wait until then. Could you please ask him to come out or we will need to go in, and we don't want that do we. So, we'll be over there in the waiting area and you show him to us, there's a good girl.'

The girl was a twenty eight year old dental receptionist at a surgery in Herzfeld, a small town some 12 km north of Soest. Like most who sat behind these desks, she had perfect white teeth and fingernails that would make Freddy Krüger jealous.

'Unfortunately I cannot interrupt him. He is doing a root canal and this takes time.' she stated.

'Either you go and ask Herr Schmedding to come out or we will open every door until we find him, cause more unrest than is necessary and then arrest you for obstructing the law. Your choice.' And with that, Sander stood to his full height and gave her his best stare.

The receptionist wilted, walked around her desk and knocked on a door numbered 3. She walked in without waiting for a reply and was followed out some thirty seconds later by a man dressed in white trousers, a green smock over a white t-shirt and a mask over his face, which he politely removed on his approach.

'Yes officers, my receptionist told me you need to see me immediately. Can't be too long, patients tooth is wide open, need to remove the dead pulp tissue. What can I do for you?'

'We'll be as quick as we can. Do you have an office where we can go, somewhere in private?'

'Of course, follow me.' They followed and were led into a room numbered 1. 'So, what is it?' he asked.

'Sir, would you be able to tell us the last time you saw your daughter Anja?'

‘Yes, I saw her last night. She came home for dinner, her mother made her favourite dish, Spaghetti Carbonara and she left again by taxi. May I ask why you are asking?’

‘Would you know the destination she was going when she left your house sir?’

‘She said she was going back to Soest to meet up with someone, she didn’t say who, expect it was a boy. Then she would have gone back to the nurses’ home. Why?’

‘Because sir, she never returned to the nurses’ home. We are at this minute trying to ascertain her whereabouts. Would you know of any other place she could have gone to? Friends or family’

‘No, she would not have stayed away all night. She’s not that sort of girl. She may change her boyfriends more often than most, but she is young, pretty and does not want to settle down.’

‘41/01 to 41/35, 41/01 to 41/35, come in over’.

The radio attached to Sanders’ belt squawked out the message from headquarters and Sander excused himself and left the room.

‘41/35 receiving, over’

‘41/01, we have had confirmation from 41/26 that Agnes Wenderling is accounted for. After they visited the boyfriend’s place of work, they were given the location which building site he was actually at that day and once they tracked him down, he told them where she could be found. She was sitting in the park painting a picture. So, that is two out of the three accounted for. Looks like you have got some bad news to break, over.’

‘41/35, that’s what I thought. Ok, wish me luck, out.’

He was back inside room 1 within two minutes.

‘Sir, I am sorry to inform you that we have reason to believe that your daughter was murdered early this morning. We would like you to accompany us to the station and ask you to identify a photo we will show you. If you identify the photo of being your daughter, we will then need you to make a formal identification at the morgue, where we will of course drive you to. But we will need to wait for confirmation that the autopsy has finished. We have not been able to locate your wife, so if you would like to contact her so she can join you, then please do.’ Sander had learnt long ago to provide the facts in a professional manner, direct and to the point, leaving no room for misinterpretation or questions.

'Are you sure that it is my daughter?' Schmedding asked quietly.

'No sir, that is why we need you to confirm. Three nurses did not turn up for work this morning nor were seen to sleep in their accommodation. I just received a message when I left the room that two of the girls have been accounted for, only your daughter not. If you would contact your wife?'

'No, she is away for the day in the spa with one of her friends. Leave her there, I'll do this myself. Just give me five minutes to close up next door, cannot leave my patient laying there with an open tooth and an open mouth all day.'

With that, Schmedding left the room and closed the door to number 3. In next to no time, he was out again and followed the police out of his surgery and into the waiting car and was taken to Soest.

'And sir, is it Anja?' asked Sander, showing Schmedding some pictures of the face of the dead girl, cleaned up and made presentable after the autopsy.

Schmedding just sat there, not answering, not moving and apparently not even breathing. He held on to the faxed photograph of his beloved daughter.

'Sir?'

'Sorry, yes, that's Anja. Can I ask what happened? Was she raped? Did she suffer?'

'I cannot answer that I'm afraid. Not until we have all the results from the lab. Until then, it is not worth conjuring up scenarios that are not facts.'

'When will I be able to see my princess?' he asked.

'Shouldn't be too long, sir. As soon as we get the go ahead, we'll drive you down to Dortmund so you can formally identify her for the records. Then we can leave you alone to say your goodbyes.'

'Thank you,' Schmedding said. 'I just feel so numb. It is as if it hasn't really happened. Not yet. This could all still be a mistake and Anja will come bounding through the doors saying sorry for causing all the trouble, her beautiful smile across her face. She's a good girl, always good to her mother. God, don't let it be her.'

Schmedding slowly crumpled up the paper in both hands as he started a slow, low moan, rising in pitch until it reached a full blown cry. Then the tears started falling and he completely lost control. Huge sobs were interspersed with gulps of air and snot ran unabated from his nose and dribbled over his lips and onto his trousers. Seeing this, Sander handed him a packet of tissues but Schmedding just held onto these along with the crumpled photo. With face contorted and still dripping, Sander decided to allow Schmedding some privacy and silently left the room, informing the female officer outside to keep an eye on him. God, Sander hated this part of the job.

CHAPTER 9

01.09.1988

'Ladies and gentlemen, thank you for joining us at such short notice. As before, if you are new here, I am the press officer Polizeihauptkommissar Ahrens. With me today is Erster Kriminalhauptkommissar Gerling who has just returned from the Institute für Rechtsmedizin. Please refrain from asking any questions until the end.

What we can tell you now is the following. The murder victim has been positively identified as being Anja Schmedding, aged 21 from Herzfeld. She was a trainee nurse at the Marienkrankenhaus, just 150 meteres from where she was murdered.

Currently we have no witnesses who can identify the murderer and we also have no suspects.

Frau Schmedding was found by the main entrance of the Wiesenkirche on 31.08.1988 with her throat cut twice and her abdomen sliced open. She would have lost consciousness almost instantly after her throat was cut and died within the minute from losing too much blood.

We are following up on several leads as to the last known movements of Frau Schmedding leading up to her demise.

If anyone has any details, please come forward so that we can catch the murderer before they can strike again.

Thank you for your attention. Any questions?'

'Yes, Michael König, *Bild*. Is it true that the murderer is preying on young nurses, as only 5 weeks ago, a nurse from the Stadtkrankenhaus here in Soest was sexually assaulted.'

'No, we can categorically rule out any comparison. There is no evidence that a weapon was used in that event.'

'Siegfried Kotten, *Die Glocke*. What are the police doing to make sure that this does not happen again?'

'Well, as you can imagine, it is very difficult to say it will never happen again. All we can do is make sure that we follow up with all inquiries that are open and also on new leads that come to light. Only then, with methodical process, will we be able to catch the offender.'

'Thomas Loch, *Soester Anzeiger*. Could you say why Erster Kriminalhauptkommissar Gerling has been brought into the investigation?'

'Well, now that you have brought me into the discussion, let me fill you in on a couple of points. I have been sent from the murder squad in Dortmund in order to assist in the brutal murder of Frau Schmedding. Why me? No reason other than the fact that I was available. Why from Dortmund? No other reason than the fact that we cover all major criminal activities for all serious crime and murder for this region.'

'Ulrike Klever, *Die Welt*. When will the body be released and when is the funeral planned?'

'The prosecutor's office has not yet released the body, so no burial or cremation can be planned at present. But I have spoken to the deceased's family and they want the funeral to be private.' Sven replied adamantly.

'If there are no further questions, then I can announce this conference has ended. As per normal, if we find out any meaningful information that may be in the public's interest, then we will contact you all accordingly. Thank you.'

Ahrens stepped away from the row of microphones, tidied his papers together and left the podium with Sven in tow.

Several hours later, Sven walked into the break room and spoke to the officers sitting drinking something out of the machine.

'Right you lot, we've got a confirmed pickup by taxi from the Schmedding house on the evening of the murder. We need to find out the taxi company involved and speak with the driver. Where was she dropped off and at what time? Did the driver see anyone meeting her? Do any of her friends know of any current boyfriends? At her age, which bars and clubs would she have visited? Too many open questions left unanswered. I want you to find them for me.' Sven looked around the police conference room at each and every face present. 'Only by answering every question can we piece together

Anja's last movements which may lead up to identifying her killer. Any questions?'

'Just one question sir, if she was out clubbing, and Soest does have quite a few, the majority are normally filled with the British soldiers stationed here and about Soest. What if it was one of them she was dancing with? What if one of them saw her leave the club on her own? What if it was one of them that killed her?'

'Thank you Trilling, that was three questions, not one. But yes, good points. This makes our lives even harder. Not only do we need to track down the taxi driver which should be pretty easy, we will also have to contact the Royal Military Police and speak to their liaison officer before we can question anybody. That itself can cause a few upsets. All we need is for one of them to come under suspicion from us and the British Army will more than likely close ranks and ship the bleeder back to Blighty. Seen it happen before in Dortmund. Young soldier raped a girl and all fingers pointed at him. When we went knocking at their door again, turned out he had been posted out of Germany for reasons not provided and that no, they were not obliged to say where he went as this was against security protocol. So, we were left with a raped girl and the only suspect was allowed to walk scot free.

'Well, we'll have to tread extra careful if fingers start pointing in their direction this time. We'll keep the information close until we can prove something. Until then, let's get out there and start policing.'

CHAPTER 10

'A bit over the top ain't it?' Ian said to Billy as they were both getting dressed.

'Why? Can a man not dress when he is going out? Why is it that we expect our women to always look nice, why can't we dress up for them?'

'Only saying, that's all. Just not too many guys wear ties and a suit when going downtown.'

'If you're on the pull, you've gotta look cool,' Billy replied, 'that is probably where you are going wrong. You're always dressed in scruffy jeans and shitty trainers. No girl will look at you, especially if you're around me. Fanny magnet I am.'

'Listen to Casanova talking. Got himself laid by a nurse and thinks he's God's gift to dating. What happened to her by the way?'

'Met up with her last night, she wanted to start a serious relationship with me so I broke it off. All good for a poke, but too many girls out there.' he said as he was lacing up his shoes.

What Ian and the rest of the roommates didn't know was that when Billy went out last night as planned, he didn't meet up with the nurse, Anja like he said. He did not want to lose face in front of his mates so he told an elaborate lie to get himself out of being cross examined. With her now out of the way, Billy could carry on as if nothing had happened.

'So, where are we off to then?' Ian asked.

'Thought we'd skip Soest tonight and head off to *Klabautermann* in Schmerlecke. Nice young girls there for you to take a pick. But do me a favour first and change that fucking shirt. It's got stains all down the front. Haven't you got any pride at all with your appearance?' Billy asked.

'Alright, alright, I'll just need to iron another one. Take two minutes. Anyone else going?'

'Nope, just the two of us. I'm "Maverick" and you're my wingman "Iceman".

Once they were ready, the two soldiers walked out of the block and moved towards the guardroom to sign out.

'Where are you two off to then?' asked the guard commander.

'Off to Schmerlecke tonight, Corp'

'Behave yourselves. Heard there was trouble there a few nights ago. Don't want the RMPs bringing you back if you get involved in any fighting.'

'No Corp, I'm a lover, not a fighter.' Billy replied, grinning.

'Lover, my left testicle.' the guard commander retorted.

After both had signed out in the leaving book, they left the guardroom and were let out of the gates by the sentry on guard. Across the road were several taxis lined up, as Thursday evenings was the start of the clubbing weekend for most soldiers. Billy and Ian crossed the road and opened the door to the first taxi in line. Billy jumped into the front and left Ian to take a seat in the back.

'Schmerlecke, bitte. *Klabautermann.*' Billy said, informing the taxi driver in his best German where they wanted to go.

The alarm clock on the side table by his bed showed it to be 16:25 when Rudolph was awoken by the noise of the dustbins being emptied. He tried to get back to sleep, but the sun shone through a gap in the window blinds directly into his eyes. He rolled and wriggled his way out of bed and padded off to the toilet to relieve himself. Once he had finished, he went to the small kitchenette and took his wallet off of the table and took out the ID card he had found. With this in hand, he walked the few short steps back to his bedroom and lay back down on his bed. After meticulously placing a tissue on his vast stomach, he held the ID card in his left hand and vigorously masturbated, fantasizing that he was being wanked off by the pretty girl in the picture.

After ejaculating in the open tissue, he wiped his rather small manhood of excess cum and got back off of the bed and went again into the bathroom, where he washed his privates with the flannel first and then his face. He then proceeded to shave.

After getting dressed, he drove to the nearest Schnellimbiß where he ordered a king size hamburger with double chips topped with Rot-

Weiß, this being tomato ketchup with mayonnaise, and a large coke without ice.

Once devoured, he went to the kiosk on the corner and bought that days copy of the *Bild*. He climbed back into his taxi and at 18:00 he was back on the clock. He drove around looking for fares and by early evening, he parked opposite the camp gates of San Sebastian and waited for soldiers to come out for the evening. His first customers were Billy and Ian.

'You go dancing?' Rudolph asked his passengers in English.

'Yep, got my dancing shoes on tonight,' Billy replied, 'no girl will be safe with me on the dance floor.'

'Are you meeting up with your girlfriends?'

'Nope, out looking for some new ones, aren't we Ian?'

'Yeah, that's the plan'

Rudolph drove away from Top Camp and headed off towards the B475 which would take them to the B1, which would eventually get them to their destination.

Whilst driving along, Ian picked up the German newspaper that Billy had taken off of the front seat when he had sat down and thrown it in the back. On the front page were the headlines that 92 American Pershing missiles were being decommissioned as per the INF agreement between the United States and Russia. Also on the front was a picture of a 21 year old, clad only in a school tie claiming she was studying to be a veterinary surgeon and had perfect measurements of 90-60-90 cm.

Page two was boring and his German was not that good, so he looked at the pictures.

On page 3 was a picture of a pretty girl who had been brutally murdered in the early hours of 31.08.1988. What Ian did not understand was that the police were asking for any witnesses who had may have seen Anja Schmedding, aged 21 from Soest on the night in question to come forward so that they could piece her last steps together. It was also mentioned that there were currently no suspects.

Ian turned over to page 4 when the taxi started slowing down as it approached the town of Schmerlecke.

'Here we are, Ian. Let's get ready to party.'

Ian put the paper down and was forced to pay the taxi driver as Billy had already gotten out.

'Have a great time.' Rudolph said.

'Thanks.' Ian replied, 'keep the change.'

'Thank you.'

Ian climbed out and closed the door to the taxi and walked over to where Billy was standing, talking to the doorman.

Rudolph watched two young girls walk from the car park and stood behind the two soldiers. One was wearing black tights with a white blouse and a wide belt over the top, the other tight jeans and an extra small t-shirt to show off her cleavage. It appeared like both sexes were out hunting tonight.

Rudolph put his car in gear, radioed into central and informed them of the drop off and that he was heading back to San Sebastian camp.

'You're not going out again are you?'

'Yes mum, off to Lippstadt with a couple of people from work.' Detlef called back. He was upstairs in the bathroom brushing his teeth. 'Don't know what time I'll be back, so don't wait up. I'll cut the grass tomorrow when I'm back from work.' he said.

'You said that yesterday and the day before.' she shouted back.

'Couldn't do it yesterday, had to sort something out, remember?' And with that, he closed the door on his mother's voice.

Detlef looked at his face in the mirror and saw that he had black bags appearing under his eyes. It had been another late night again last night.

Yesterday after he had finished work, he had gone home to eat. Then he quickly changed and left the house before his mum had time to come up from doing the washing in the cellar and start to nag him. He had walked to the local Co-op, bought himself a can of beer and then went to the telephone box on the corner and called a taxi.

Whilst waiting for the taxi to arrive, Detlef had reflected on the nurse he had taken to the restaurant the night before. If only things had turned out different.

When the taxi arrived, Detlef informed the driver where he wanted to go and sat at the back with his eyes closed. As the taxi drove under the railway lines near the Bahnhof, Detlef asked to be let out and paid the driver what was owed. He crossed the road at the lights and headed left towards the Marienkrankenhaus, the hospital where he had met Anja.

As he approached the hospital, he saw that there was a lot of police activity around the area and the streets "Am Wiesenkirchhof" and "Wiesenstrasse" were cordoned off and guarded by police officers.

'What happened?' Detlef asked a young looking constable.

'Don't you listen to the news?' replied the policeman.

'Didn't have time, been working all day.'

'Young nurse had her throat slit and her belly ripped open.'

'Caught anyone?'

'Not yet, but it will only be a matter of time. There's blood all over the place. Crime technicians are still collecting clues. There's talk that that new DNA stuff will be used so they can catch the murderer.'

'I didn't know that it was being used in Germany,' Detlef said, 'thought it was only in England and America.'

'Well, I'd use a crystal ball or Tarot cards if it would help catch the bugger.' replied the policeman. 'Were you around here anytime on Tuesday evening or early hours Wednesday morning?'

'Me, no. Just going into the hospital now to pay my nan a visit. It's about time I visited her, she's been here a week. You never know what she'll leave me in her will.' he replied and walked off towards the hospital entrance.

Once out of sight of the policeman, instead of going in through the entrance, he turned right on Lentzestrasse, right again on Kleine Osthofe and right again on Severinstrasse. This brought him out further down on Wiesenstrasse near the Hallenbad, the public indoor swimming pool. From here, Detlef walked to the town square where the restaurant "*Im Wilden Mann*" was located and had been in the same spot since opening its doors in 1618.

He went inside and asked the waiter if anyone had handed in an ID card, as he had lost one the evening before. The waiter asked the girl behind the bar and after a swift look stated no, nothing had been handed in or found.

Detlef immediately left the restaurant and walked around some of the old streets in deep thought, worrying about the ID card he had lost and wondering where it could be. On seeing a taxi parked outside the main Sparkasse bank, he got in and asked to be driven home.

CHAPTER 11

02.09.1988

'Sir, we've got a hit. The taxi company Velberts confirm that they had a call to Herzfeld and picked up a young girl and took her to Soest. Drop off point was the main train station.' said constable Trilling. 'I've also got a name of the driver and the taxi central has informed him to report here soonest.'

'Well done son, good news.' Sven was studying a street map of Soest that was pinned to the office wall he had taken over with Freddy. 'As soon as he arrives, let me know please. I want to sit in on the questioning.'

'Right o sir.' Trilling replied and ducked back out of the room.

'Freddy, the ball has started to roll.' Sven stated.

'Fucking hell Sven, you said the ball has started to roll. Look at the size of him. Push him off his legs and he'd roll as well.'

'You're right there Freddy. Did you see him getting out of his taxi? It took all of five minutes before he was able to get both legs out from under the steering wheel. I can't wait to see him get back in. Might even charge ring side seats for people to watch the event.'

'Hey, imagine him and Gaby getting it on together. Be like two samurai warriors having a fight.' Freddy smiled at the thought.

'Alright, I'll lead, nice and gentle. Got to coax anything he may know out of him.' Sven said to Freddy.

'Thanks for coming in Herr Mertens. My name is Erster Kriminalhauptkommissar Gerling and this is my colleague Kriminalhauptkommissar Fischer. You may have read or seen the news about the nurse who was murdered two days ago. We would like to ask you some questions as we think you may be able to help us with our inquiries.'

Rudolph looked at both policemen and cold sweat ran down his spine. Freddy laid a photograph of Anja Schmedding on the table and turned it so that Rudolph could see the smiling face, the picture given them by her father, this one taken when she had finished school.

'Do you recognize her?' Sven asked. 'Take a good look and try to remember.'

The picture on the table and the one in his wallet was nearly identical.

'Yes, I remember picking her up in Herzfeld and dropped her off at the train station.' he said.

'Can you confirm the times, please?'

'Yes, pickup was around 7 o'clock yesterday evening and it would only have taken about twenty minutes to reach the station.'

'Did she say anything during the drive? Where she might be going, who she was meeting?'

'No, I tried to get her in a conversation but she just sat at the back and ignored me.' Rudolph explained.

'When she got out of your taxi, did you see her meet anyone? Was there anyone waiting for her?' Sven asked.

'No, she just got out and stood there by the main doors as if she was waiting for someone. As soon as she had paid me, someone else got in the taxi and I left. Didn't see her after that, I'm afraid.'

'Can you confirm to us what she was wearing?' This came from Freddy.

'Er, blue jeans and a white blouse.'

'Did she seem happy, disturbed or apprehensive?'

'Couldn't say. Bloody rude is all I'd say. Young people today. In my day, if someone spoke to you or asked you a question, you'd answer them back politely. She just ignored me totally. The only words she said to me was where she wanted to go. Didn't even say thank you or goodbye when she got out.'

'Ok Herr Mertens, thank you for taking up your time. If you do think of anything else, please inform us immediately.' Sven held the door open and Rudolph squeezed past and went out through the glass doors.

'So, we didn't learn anything new there. Still, good to dot the i's.'

'Talking of t's,' said Freddy, 'let's get a brew and see what else they have found upstairs.'

"Upstairs" was getting frantic. It was now early evening and they appeared to be going nowhere until they hit a breakthrough. Anja's father had told the police she had eaten a meal at home, but Bernie Backhaus had an idea and had made many copies of the photo Herr Schmedding had provided. With these, he made sure that they were left in every restaurant and pub in Soest and see if she had been seen the night of her murder. Bernie was leaning over the radio in his office with Sven and Freddy both waiting for the constable on the other end to finally finish talking.

'Will you get to the point?' Bernie said into the microphone.

'Yes sir, sorry sir. Well, when I went into the restaurant *Im Wilden Mann*, a waitress can clearly remember the girl there with an older man. She said that what made her surer is that the man came back the next day looking for his ID. All they did was drink something and they got into an argument. The waitress does not know what they were arguing about but heard the man say loudly that he would fix her for good. After rowing a bit more, she stood up and left him sitting there.'

'Now that is good news. Get her down here immediately so we can get a photo fit of the man.' Bernie replied.

'What time did she leave the restaurant?' Sven ask loudly, hoping that the mike would transfer his question. Bernie had to relay the message to the constable.

'Waitress says around 10 o'clock. Didn't see what direction she went when she left.'

'Ok, bring her in and I'll get the artist ready.'

Bernie was beaming as he put the mike down. 'We could be on to something,' he said to no one in particular. 'Two witnesses in one day.'

The time was now 8 o'clock in the evening of the 2nd September and Sven was in full stride, standing in front of the squad.

'I want this photo fit circulated as far and wide as is humanly possible. Restaurants, taxis, bus drivers, pubs, clubs, the lot. He might not be our murderer but he was seen with the victim. And they were arguing. We need to find him and find him fast. With no other evidence, all we can do is hope and pray.

Get on to the forces in Lippstadt, Werl, Arnsberg and Beckum and have them distribute also. Our man may not live in Soest, but you can bet your bollocks to a barn dance he will come from an outside area not too far from here. Hopefully someone will recognize him and then we can start the fun part.'

'Fun part?' asked Trilling.

'Yes, interrogating the swine.' replied Freddy.

'Right, piss off and don't come back until you find me something.' Sven said to all.

The majority stood up and filtered out the room as ordered. Bernie stayed behind with Sven and Freddy.

'Tell me,' Bernie asked, 'what do you think the chances are of finding him and him being the killer.'

'Only the ancient Gods know the answer to that. All we can do is saturate the area and hope for him to be recognized or picked up in a random check.' Sven answered.

Several days passed by without any new leads. Nobody recognized the photo fit and no new clues appeared. All that the police could do was go over the material again and again and hope for a breakthrough.

CHAPTER 12

03.09.1988

'All right you lot, fall in,' the troop Corporal shouted so that he could be heard over the babble, 'C'mon, we ain't got all day.'

P troop all fell in, meaning that they lined up in three ranks or rows, each an arms width apart from the next man.

'Troop, troop shun.' the corporal bellowed and all lifted up their left knee and slammed their left foot solidly onto the tarmac so that both feet were next to each other, arms straight at their sides in the attention position. 'All present and correct sir.'

'Thank you Corporal McIntosh, troop, stand at ease,' the troop Captain said, allowing the soldiers to stand in a relaxed stance. 'OK, now listen in. I have just come back from the Training Wing and Staff Sergeant Bones has confirmed he is holding a survival course and that he is keeping the places open for P troop, in other words you. There are only ten spots available so I'm looking for volunteers to go. The course is for four days and nights and you will need to take your webbing and accessories, backpack with spare clothes and sleeping bag, obviously your first aid kit and you'll need to wear full combats. Transport leaves from the drill square at 10:00 hours. So, who wants to learn how to be Rambo?' he asked.

Everybody kept their hands to their sides apart from Signalman Jones.

'No other volunteers?' the troop Captain asked. Not a movement. 'Ok Corporal McIntosh, I'll leave it in your capable hands. 10:00 hours I want to see ten soldiers on the back of the truck in full combat uniform. Any questions?'

'No sir. Troop, troop shun.' he shouted again and the troop all came back to attention. The Corporal and Captain saluted each other and the Captain walked away briskly back to the comfort of his office.

'I want you all in one line in front of me.' Within seconds there was a long line of twenty eight soldiers standing next to each other.

'Numbers from the right.' he commanded and the first soldier on the end right shouted one, the next two, three and so on until all soldiers had a number.

'On my command, odd numbers take one step forward, even numbers take one step back. Move!'

Now there were two rows of soldiers, one in front of the other. 'Front row, numbers.' he commanded again and the soldiers in the front called out as before. 'On my command, numbers one to ten take one step forward. Move!' and ten soldiers all moved forward together as one. 'So, you ten are the lucky volunteers. Double back to your bunks, change into combats, pack your kit and see you on the truck. Anyone late and they'll have my boot up their arse. Now, fall out.' All the soldiers turned ninety degrees to the left, marched three paces and then split to go about their tasks.

'For fucks sake, why do I always get the fucking shitty end of the stick?' complained L/Cpl Tony White.

'You can fucking talk, got a date planned for tomorrow, that's out the fucking window. If I don't show, she'll think I've stood her up.' Billy told his comrades.

More moans and groans were heard amongst them all. All ten were now doubling back to the barracks room where they slept to get packed as instructed. One thing the army could do, get fully grown men to run from point A to point B as a single unit.

At 10 o'clock, ten not so willing soldiers were waiting to mount the truck when SSgt Bones walked up and instructed them to empty the contents of their packs, webbing and to turn out all their pockets, and yes, they will be getting patted down. Reluctantly, a variety of kit and supplies were spread out on the floor around the soldier's feet for the SSgt to inspect.

'Who's kit is this?' he asked.

'Mine Staff.' came the reply.

'And what the fuck do you think you are doing with half the fucking NAAFIs supply of meat pies in your bag?' he shouted. 'We are going on a survival course to learn how to survive off the land, not going on an army fucking wives picnic. Pick them up and put them in the sack.' SSgt Bones said, pointing to where a blue bin liner was waiting to be filled.

'Who's got the sweet tooth?' he asked. 'More chocolate here than a Mars Bar factory. You got shares in Cadbury's or something? Bin them.' These also went into the bag.

'And what the fuck is this?' he asked bewildered. All eyes turned to see what he was staring at and all started to snigger. 'Who the fuck in their right mind would pack a flask of some beverage and a collapsible bed? Are you taking the piss?'

'No staff. Just thought that if we are in the field, sleeping on the floor isn't good for my bad back.' said a young soldier, not too long out of training.

'I'll show you bad back. Mag to grid, get fucking rid. And remind me to jail you when we get back for being a stupid twat.'

After about thirty minutes had been wasted and all soldiers relieved of any comforts, they were told to quickly pack their kit and get on the back of the truck so they could get moving. Ten minutes later they were on their way. They left camp and drove for around two hours when the driver stopped the four ton truck and the SSgt informed them all to debus.

'Welcome to the field, gents,' he said. 'Over the next four days and nights, I am going to show you how to survive with only the bare minimum. I want you all to place any knives and lighters you may have on the floor in front of you. Then I want you to step away over to the right.'

All the soldiers rummaged in their webbing and packs and took out what was required and moved to the side.

'You,' he said, pointing to Billy, 'throw all the packs and webbing onto the back of the truck.' Billy done as told. 'Now, I want you all to pick up your knives and lighters and line up again. You will not need your sleeping bag as I will show you how to make a bed from the things around us. You will learn how to build a shelter to protect you from the elements, how to find water so that you can drink, teach you how to survive off the land. I will show you what you can and can't eat. I will show you how to collect insects so that you eat lots of protein. I will show you how to stalk and kill animals and I will show you how to dissect and skin them so that you can cook a proper meal. Now, follow me.' And with that, SSgt Bones walked briskly into the forest without glancing back.

'Why the fuck did we need to pack our kit if we weren't gonna use it in the first place?' Tony said out loud, but not loud enough for it to reach the front.

'All psychological. If we all came empty handed, we'd be in a foul mood before we got here. This way we were led to believe all was good until it is too late to do anything about it.' one of the lads replied.

'Could be fun, this.' Billy thought to himself.

Detlef sat at the back of the counselling room that was to the side of the station and was near sleep as the group of patients talked openly about why they were locked up and which crimes they had committed.

'She had a nice pair of tight shorts on, tits sticking out and she was gagging for it.' Jonas was saying.

'Did she actually voice out loud that she wanted intercourse?' asked the counsellor.

'Didn't have to, sitting on the swing, lollypop in her mouth acting all innocent like.'

'And did she give you any indication that she wanted you to approach her?' he asked further.

'She kept opening and closing her legs. That was a sign she wanted fucking.'

'But she never spoke to you at all at this point in time?'

'Well, not really. But why would she do that if she didn't want it?' Jonas asked frantically.

'You must understand that just because you want something, doesn't mean that you can have it or take it. You do understand don't you?' asked the counsellor.

'Of course I understand. I'm not stupid.'

'No, you're just a kiddy fiddler who likes to rape little girls.' This came from Benjamin, who lived in the next room to Jonas.

'I didn't rape anyone. I told you, she was dying for it, you could see it the way she moved.'

'Dying for it? You killed her after you raped her you sick fuck and she isn't moving any more is she?' Benjamin retorted.

'Ok Benjamin, this is not for you to interrupt. We are trying to get you all to understand the terrible accidents you have committed and that you realize what is right from wrong.' the counsellor butted in before the session got out of hand. 'Carry on Jonas.' he said.

'I don't want to talk no more, not if Benny keeps interrupting and calling me a rapist.'

'Benjamin won't interrupt no more, will you?' he asked, prompting Jonas to continue.

'Then the second time I saw this lady out playing in her garden. She had lots of babies around her and was playing in the sand. I asked if I could hold one of her babies and she said yes. She had a plaster on her knee and when I asked her what she had done she asked if I wanted to see. I watched her peel back the plaster and saw she had grazed her knee. My mum used to kiss my knee better when I fell over, so I kissed her knee the same way my mum did mine. I remember she had white knickers on and she was flashing these at me as I was kissing her. I could smell the smell of pee on them and when I touched her there, she started crying, so I cuddled her and told her it was alright to cry if her knee hurt. So I kissed her again but on the lips this time. I knew she wanted to have sex because she didn't say no. I put the babies we were holding on the floor beside us so they could see her mummy and me. Then her mother came out screaming at me to leave her baby alone. But the babies were on the floor watching us. Her mother did not believe me when I said I was only stopping her knee from hurting. She then started to hit me and said she would call the police, so I got up and ran away.'

'And that is when the police found you and arrested you?' asked the counsellor.

'Yes.' replied Jonas.

'We all know that the "lady" was a little girl and that her "babies" were dolls. So you tried fucking another toddler.' Benny said loudly with a laugh in his voice. 'Let's face it Jonas, you couldn't get it up with an adult, so you preyed on little girls. You sick fucker.'

'Stop him saying that.' Jonas commanded the counsellor.

'Ok Benjamin, that's enough, I won't tell you again. Right, thank you Jonas for opening up, let's move on to someone else for today. Felix, would you like to tell the group why you are here?'

‘Are you sure this is the right place?’ he asked. ‘Don’t want to scare these wimps so they piss their beds tonight.’

‘I’m sure it will be alright,’ said the counsellor, ‘please go ahead.’

‘Well, it all started when I was a teenager, about fifteen years old. My granddad was a farmer and he kept a lot of livestock, sheep and pigs mostly. Also had some fields at the back where he grew grain and stuff, but the real business was livestock.

‘One day, he decided that I was old enough to watch him kill a pig, as this was going to be our Sunday dinner. We went into the shed where he sharpened a knife on the grinder so that it was razor sharp. He also took his .22 rifle with him.

‘He asked me to select the pig we should kill and I pointed to one with a black blotch on its shoulder. My granddad put on his boots and apron and told me to do the same. He then aimed at a point on the forehead of the pig and shot, stunning the pig only, not killing it. Then he jumped forward and before the pig had a chance to move, he sliced the throat, making sure to go through the jugular vein. He would cut all the way to the spine to make sure he done the job properly. It was then my job to tie its legs up so that we could hoist it up so the pig would bleed out. He would then cut open the belly and chest, making sure not to cut the intestines. Then he would pull the entrails into a bucket. Once this was done, he would take a saw and…’

‘Boring,’ Benny said, ‘What the fuck has that to do with why you are in here?’

‘Because you dumb shit, one day I decided to practice this with my sister when my granddad was at church.’

‘And? What is so bad about that?’ Benny asked.

‘Because I didn’t kill a pig to practice on, I used my sister.’ ‘Am I right in understanding you shot and bled your sister and then proceeded to eviscerate her?’ asked the counsellor, feeling the session wasn’t going in the direction he wanted.

‘I never liked her anyway. Right stuck up cow. Mind you, should have seen her piss her pants when I aimed the rifle at her. Did you know that they say a pig is very similar to a human in anatomy terms?’

'Well, isn't that interesting.' intervened Benny again. 'Another cunt killing girls'

'Fuck off, she was older than me.'

'Alright, times up for this week. We'll continue same time next week.' the counsellor said. 'If you'll all put your chairs to the side so that we can get the table tennis table back in the centre of the room.'

Detlef was wide awake and had been listening to Felix's story intently.

Rudolph was excited in more ways than one. Not only had he kept his cool whilst being questioned by the police the day before, but he had actually had the ID card of the murdered girl in his wallet. If that was not exhilarating enough, he was then let out without any accusations of any kind.

Now at home, he put in one of his favourite VHS videos from his collection and pressed play. The screen took a few seconds to light up but then the video started playing. It was a cheap made movie, not a movie such as those made in Hollywood, nor were any of the cast known as they all wore masks. But all of this was irrelevant. The story and the scenes were why the watcher paid a lot of money to purchase these films.

On the TV screen in his bedroom, Rudolph watched how a young woman of around twenty or so was chatted up in a bar somewhere in South America. She was light brown in colour and was pretty to look at, even if she had small breasts. The scene started out with her getting chatted up by two local men, one aged between twenty five to thirty years of age, the other was in his late forties or early fifties.

After the young woman was given several drinks, it was plain to see that she was either drunk or her drink had been spiked. The two men carried her outside to a pickup truck and put her in the back.

Rudolph stopped the film at this point and went to empty his bladder and on the way back to his bed, bypassed the kitchen where he collected a bag of crisps and a bottle of beer. He pressed play when he was once again settled and opened up his refreshments.

The next scene showed the girl already tied to a bed and all of her clothes had been removed. She was still unconscious and the men stood around waiting for her to wake up. The film then jumped forward as the men suddenly appeared on film to be in different parts of the room than where they were first seen, so obviously the editor had just cut out a portion of the film and spliced it together in an amateur way.

When the young woman started to move, both men decided it was time. First, she was raped in the missionary position by both men, one after the other, tag team style. She was then turned over, her legs were again spread apart and tied to the posts as were her arms and she was taken from behind, sometimes in her vagina, other times in her anus. Then for the finale, both men simultaneously spurted their cum onto her upturned face and was then left to lie alone for a while.

This is the point where Rudolph really concentrated on the screen. The men turned her back over so that she was laying face upwards and each man took a knife out of its holder and the woman, who by now was fully conscious and aware of her surroundings, started to struggle against her bindings, screaming in Spanish to be set free. The eldest man grabbed her hair and with his knife, sliced off her right breast. The woman writhed and thrashed around and her eyes were open so wide, it seemed they would pop out of their sockets. Blood was spilling onto the bed and soaking into the sheets when the younger man sliced off her other breast. Still holding her hair, the eldest put the tip of his knife to her vagina opening and slowly moved his hand upwards until he reached the point between where her breasts had been not so long ago. She was sliced fully open and her inners spilled out onto the floor, steaming as they fell. At this point, the woman's brain finally flicked the self defence fuse and she fainted, but this did not stop what happened next. The younger man then took his knife and sliced her throat from ear to ear with such force, her head was nearly severed. More blood gushed out as the heart pumped its final beats, splashing both men with her life's vital liquid.

At this point, both men rubbed each other's body with the dead woman's blood and proceeded to masturbate each other until the point of ejaculation, where they then proceeded in having a blow job with the dead woman's head.

Rudolph wiped the cum off his hands and belly as the final scene died and the men moved out of view of the camera. Rudolph pressed rewind on the remote, got out of bed and retrieved the ejected cassette and put this back in its secret place at the back of his wardrobe. This was his favourite film as it showed more than just killing. He had watched this particular film about fifty times so far and he was always aroused and never got bored watching it. Still, it was time he needed new wanking material. He would have to go at night into the old part of town and see what he could find.

CHAPTER 13

07.09.1988

On the second night in the forest, SSgt Bones was showing them the benefits of eating most insects, this being demonstrated by each soldier being told to collect what they could fine. Several caterpillars, spiders, moths and a large amount of ants later, SSgt Bones had instructed them to eat the insects and creepy crawlies alive, making sure to chew first before swallowing, after all, one wouldn't want a spider to climb up out of his stomach and back into his mouth now, would they?

At this point, every soldier heard a crashing and a high-pitched, piercing cry in the trees and realised that something big was moving very fast towards them. Suddenly, a wild boar came charging out of the undergrowth and stopped in the middle of the clearing. It was a huge, massively built animal which was made up of a short body with short thin legs, a short thick neck with a hump rising behind the shoulder blades and sported an oversized head. Its eyes were small and deep set and had long, broad ears. And then there were the teeth. The upper canines were growing sideways out of the mouth and curved upwards like tusks whilst the lower canines were much sharper and longer, measuring about 10–12 cm in length. Its coat consisted of long, coarse bristles and the bristles along its back were standing erect due to the animal being agitated. The beast must have weighed in the region of 80 kg and stood at a height of around 75 cm from floor to shoulder. Although its eyesight is very poor, it not being able to see anyone standing about ten meters away, it made up for it with its keen sense of smell and acute hearing. The animal can run at a maximum speed of around 40 km/h.

If everybody had stayed still all would have been good. But no, as soon as one soldier ran for cover, this started them all running, including the boar. With its head down, it charged at the nearest moving shape and without a care in the world, bowled it over before turning its attention onto the next figure running away from it. The screams of fright from the soldier's only made the matters worse by agitating the pig even more. With red eyes glowing, long teeth protruding and head down in the charge position like a huge plough, it charged another soldier who had the misfortune of tripping over his own feet and them of his comrade and landed heavily on the forest floor. Just as the boar was reading itself to ram the downed soldier, Billy jumped close and was able to stab the pig in its neck. Pure luck was on Billy's and the downed soldier's side that day. The sudden attack from Billy meant that the boar changed its run so that the grounded soldier could roll away and Billy had actually cut the jugular. The boar went down pretty quick and this gave the SSgt enough time to move himself from behind a tree and slice its throat.

The animal lay on the forest leaves, its breath coming in loud grunts, blood still pumping out of the gash in its neck, but slowly the spurts became less as the animal's heart stopped pumping.

The rest of the soldiers started to appear from where they had tried to make themselves invisible and no one had suffered any major injuries. SSgt Bones stood with a huge grin splitting his handsome face from ear to ear.

'Brilliant reflexes Jennings, stood your ground and didn't buckle. I'm sure you'll make a fine soldier. Well, thanks to a lot of luck and for Jennings's braveness, I will now show you how to slice, eviscerate, cut and cook a wild pig. Anybody bring any potatoes with them?' he asked jokingly, motioning all to gather round.

Now, back in the barracks, a nice hot shower and a change of clothes was what he needed. Ablutions complete, he headed back to his room where jeers of "Billy the Butcher" rang out on his entering.

'Oi, Billy, have you got any pork scratchings?' asked Ian, good humoured as ever.

'So, that's another pig you fucked, hey Billy? This time a male pig.' roared Tony.

'Laugh all you want, if it wasn't for me, everybody would still be looking for worms to eat.'

'Alright, keep your hair on Billy. You know these wankers like to be a couple of wind up merchants. They're just pulling your pud.

Tony pissed himself when the wild pig came charging out. As for the rest of those whoosies on the exercise, you are a fucking saviour. Relish in the thought that you are the bee's knees.' Paul stated matter of factly.

'Well, I'm off down town, see what's been happening whilst I've been away.' Billy said. 'And before any of you ask, no, you cannot come. You all cramp my style.'

'I'm strapped for cash as it is and it's only the beginning of the month.' Ian said.

'I'm off to the gym, important session tonight.' Paul said.

'Then fuck off on your own then.' Tony finished. 'Gonna do my washing anyway.'

So, once Billy was dressed and ready, he left the room without saying goodbye to his roommates. He signed himself out of camp in the guardroom and caught a taxi into town, getting dropped off near the town square. Since the survival course, he was far more aware of his surroundings than ever before. Every movement and noise was registered in his brain and his sense of smell had improved drastically.

Walking from one street to another, he registered the houses and alleyways as if he had never seen them before. As had been taught him over the last few days by SSgt Bones, he was looking for places of concealment, places he would not normally have thought of before. Thinking back, he was glad that he was number seven and was chosen for the survival course.

During the evening, he successfully tracked several people who had passed him by without them seeing him hidden in the shadows and he was pleased with himself that only one person had turned to see Billy walking about three paces behind. The man had crossed the road and Billy had sought out a new target.

It was so much fun being a trained hunter and killer.

Detlef had spent the afternoon chatting with Felix in a casual manner asking certain questions so that Felix again divulged his crime in more detail than he had in the therapy group. Felix decided he wanted to have a game of draughts with another patient and left the table, so Detlef sauntered over to Gary and asked if he would like to play chess, which Gary did. Pieces set up on the board, Gary asked matter of factly if Detlef was finished with the newspaper he had lent him the other week.

'Sorry Gary, had an accident at home. I was reading through it and reached to pick up my English – German dictionary when I accidently knocked over a glass of juice onto the paper, which I had to throw away. Was there anything in particular about that paper?'

'Yeah, there was a double page spread about something that happened a hundred years ago. It made interesting reading.'

And Gary told the story about what he had read in the newspaper and what he knew from history lessons from when he was at school.

Now, evening time had arrived and after finishing work, Detlef was washed, dressed and ready for another few beers in town. He went down through the cellar and left the house so that his mother would not spot him. Although the grass was now cut, she would surely find something else for him to do.

The taxi dropped him off in Soest and he moved from bar to bar, drinking one beer in each location. As he moved around, he pretended he was somewhere else a century ago and tried to visualise what it would have been like. As he walked down one of the old streets between the half timbered houses, he was suddenly aware he was being followed. He looked around suddenly to see that a young man had emerged from nowhere and was following him only a couple of paces behind. To be on the safe side, Detlef crossed the road and looked to see if the young man followed, which he didn't. So Detlef went into the next bar and had another glass.

Throughout the night, Detlef had visited nine bars and had drunk as many glasses of beer and had walked all around the old town, taking in the small streets with the dapper houses and the alleyways and parks. He decided he had seen enough for the evening and after peeing against someone's garage, he walked back to the train station where he got into a taxi and told the driver to take him home.

Rudolph sat in his cab and slowly drove through the streets, looking for a particular location. The night was dark and this suited him for the task he had planned. He parked his taxi in a car park across from the old slaughterhouse and informed the taxi central he was having his lunch, this being at 22:30. He got out of his vehicle and proceeded to walk along the outside of the town wall, following the path that led through the park. He walked for around fifteen minutes when he saw an old acquaintance of his, waiting near an opening in the wall that led to the inner city. After money and package were exchanged, the acquaintance moved away and told Rudolph not to follow. Rudolph did not know the man's name or where he lived. All he had was a phone number that he called when he wanted to buy certain items that were not for the general public. And he did not want anyone to know of the secrets he kept.

Rudolph put the brown paper bag into his jacket pocket when he noticed how secluded an area he was in. The acquaintance had certainly chosen a good spot for the trade off point, secluded but accessible from two sides of the wall. He walked back the way he had come and got back into his taxi where he put his latest video into the glove compartment and locked it with his key.

Dinner time over, Rudolph logged back in with central and was told he was late back and that he should go to the station and wait for fares as it was a slow night. He sat in his seat thinking about his night and was pleased with what he had seen.

CHAPTER 14

08.09.1988

Nicole Kühn liked to look after herself. She believed she was loved and liked by all who knew her and would have put her hand in fire that nobody would say a bad thing about her. The fact was everyone she knew sniggered behind her back and made ridicule of her appearance.

At the ripe old age of thirty four, Nicole still dressed as if she was a teenager. At first glance, her body was full and shapely, still looking young and vivacious, but on closer inspection she was mutton dressed as lamb. Her fake tan was acquired after hours of lying on a sun bed in her bedroom and her frizzy hair was blond, this coming out of a bottle. Her finger nails were false as was the appearance of her cleavage. Her small breasts were held in place by a push up bra, turning her from a B cup to a C cup. Her waist was squashed together under a corset whilst her face was hidden from the sun by layer upon layer of makeup, false eye lashes and red lipstick. If she was to undress in front of anybody (which she never did), they would be amazed at the sudden appearance of lumps and bumps around her body that had not been there previously. But from a distance she was stunning.

What also went against her was she was thick as pig shit. Her so called friends accepted her only for the reason they had something to giggle over once she left.

When she was a baby, she had natural blond curly hair and a chubby face and legs. Well loved and protected, she was an only child and spoilt rotten. Her parents had tried many years to have a baby but all efforts went unanswered. When her mother turned forty two, all thoughts of getting pregnant were no longer considered and they had accepted the fact that they would grow old childless. But modern day miracles still occurred and her mother became pregnant, where she was forced to go through the morning sickness and putting on weight but was delighted when their daughter was born healthy, if not a few years too late.

Nicole was from an early age never shy. Always trying to be the centre of attention, she would not see resentment in the other children's eyes when she would always get her way. At school she did not do too well. More interested in boys and preening herself, she failed at language, mathematics, physics and literature but excelled in art and sports.

On leaving school, her final report informed any future employer that Nicole needed constant guidance, was a dreamer and would never excel at anything other than simple labour.

Her mother was able to persuade a friend to give Nicole a chance of an apprenticeship in a local hairdresser, as Nicole was always helping to colour her mother's hair. With apprehension, she was taken on and surprised everyone, including herself, how she mastered the different cuts, curls and colours with ease.

Nicole grew up in a fantasy world where Prince Charming would one day be around the corner and would sweep her up in his arms and cart her off to his castle. This never happened. Now nearing her mid thirties, she was destined to grabbing one night stands wherever she could find one, making sure that all lights were turned off first before she disrobed. She wasn't that stupid after all.

So after finishing work for the day, Nicole had gone home and sat in front of the television watching a favourite soap whilst eating a jar of pickled cucumbers with some slices of ham. At around eight o'clock in the evening, she decided that she was bored and was in the urge for some company. She threw away the empty glass jar, put the remaining ham back in the fridge and went in search of an outfit for the night. After a quick shower, making sure not to get her face and hair wet, she dried herself, got dressed and fixed up her appearance. By 9 o'clock she was out the door and headed towards the *Bäärenkeller*, a pub at the corner of Freiligrathwall and Jakobitor.

Several glasses of wine and no man showing interest later, she decided she needed to look for somewhere else where the lighting would be better and the men would admire her beauty.

She left the pub and clumsily walked along the Jakobistrasse heading into the centre of town. Halfway down the street, she saw a man walking towards her. He was casually dressed and looked like fun.

'Fancy having a drink with me?' she asked as he neared.

'Sorry love, just on my way home.' he replied.

'And where is that then?' she asked.

'Just around the corner,' he replied, 'my wife is waiting for me.'

'Well, if you change your mind, I'll be in the *Pesel*, and if you play your cards right, I might be willing to give you a hand job after.' she said.

'I'll keep that in mind. Maybe I'll see you later.' he said, stepping around her and heading home.

"Yep, he'll be coming after me soon," she thought. She continued walking and finally arrived at the *Pesel*. She opened the door and went inside. Music was playing and as the beer was two for the price of one, she ordered two beers at the bar and looked around for somewhere to sit. She spotted a table in the corner away from the loud speakers and walked towards it.

'Is this seat taken?' she asked.

'No, you can have it.' replied the girl sitting on the other stool.

'Thanks. Nicole,' she said, introducing herself, 'would you like a beer? Bought two but you can have one if you want.'

'Ulli,' came the reply. 'And no thanks, I have to drive home so I'm on soft drinks.'

'What would you like,' Nicole asked her new friend, 'I'm buying.'

'Oh, I'll have an orange juice with lemonade, please.'

Nicole walked back to the bar and ordered the soft drink.

'Ein D-Mark bitte.' said the barman, asking Nicole for the money.

She opened her purse and noticed she had run out of money. 'Shit,' she said, 'run out of cash. I'll just pop around the corner and get some out of the wall.' she informed the barman. 'Don't tip it away, it's for my friend Ulli over there.'

She quickly opened the door and walked outside. Ulli did not notice her leave.

Slightly disorientated, she turned left to go towards the Sparkasse bank on the main square, not realizing that if she had turned right, the nearest Sparkasse would have been around the next corner. As it was, she took the next left down the side of the pub and walked down a dark, narrow alley, this being called the Corduanergasse. As she walked past the two garages on the left where the Corduanergasse joined Mariengasse, an unseen figure came out of the recessed door as she passed and struck silently. The first she knew was a hand grabbing her head from behind and the last she knew was that she was going to die.

Nicole's body was found some ten minutes later when a young couple left the *Pesel* to head home. They had taken the same alleyway and noticed something on the floor. On getting nearer, they recognized the body of a woman lying sprawled on her back, her clothes either ripped open or discarded on the ground next to the body. Her face was badly swollen and her left arm was lying across her left breast whilst her right arm was at her side. Her throat had been cut deeply right around her neck and all her life's blood had spurted and leaked out on to the walls and ground. Her abdomen had been cut open and they saw the woman's intestines were above her right shoulder and two flaps of skin from the lower abdomen lay above the left shoulder. If the young couple had looked closer amongst all the blood and gore, they would have seen that her womb, the upper part of her vagina and her bladder had been removed and taken. The woman screamed, the man hysterically shouted at her to stop screaming and both backed out of the alleyway and went back inside the *Pesel* and shouted what they had just found.

'For fucks sake, are you telling me the bastard has struck again?' Bernie shouted down the phone.

'Yes sir. Where the Corduanergasse and Mariengasse join. This time the killer has stepped it up a bit.' the duty sergeant said. 'I've notified Dortmund and they're on their way as we speak. This time they're bringing a few more men with them.'

'Alright, give me a few minutes to get out of bed and find my socks. I'll drive straight there.'

'Right you are sir' the sergeant said and waited for his boss to put the phone down first.

'Bit of a déjà-vu don't you think? Two murders in one week. Streets are getting more violent as time passes.' Freddy reflected.

'According to the phone call I took, looks like the killer decided to go the whole nine yards with this one. Organs ripped out and everything.' Sven answered as he drove along the autobahn at a speed of 160 km/h.

'Well, let's hope someone saw something this time. We're still chasing our tails trying to find the suspect in the photo fit picture.' Freddy said.

'Well, with us two back from holiday, pound to a pinch of shit we'll have this wrapped up in no time,' Kriminaloberkommissar Peter Schwarz stated to his colleague, Kriminaloberkommissar Dennis Schmidt, both sitting in the back of the car.

'Well, seeing that we'll have more plods on the ground for this one, only stands to reason that we'll catch the wanker sooner rather than later.' Dennis replied.

'Just hope you both haven't forgotten what freshly ripped open body's smells and looks like.' Freddy said to his two colleagues in the back.

They exited the autobahn and drove towards the town centre. Freddy had the A-Z of Soest map out on his legs that showed all the street names.

'Take the next right at the lights and go to the end.' Freddy directed. 'Then turn left.'

As they got to the junction, they could see the blue flashing lights of the emergency services. A constable stopped their car and on recognizing the front two occupants, instructed where they should park. All four policemen got out, went around to the car boot and each took out a torch, a pair of surgeons gloves and a notebook.'

'Come on, let's go and take a look at the delights that are awaiting us.' Sven said.

They all moved towards the area where the most activity seemed to be. The technicians were already on the scene and the alley was lit up like daylight. A crowd had gathered on the pavement at the beginning of Petristrasse, but nothing of the crime scene could be seen from there. Sven flashed his badge to the constable behind the police tape, stated that the other three were with him and were all let through. As they walked past the *Pesel*, they looked inside and saw several civilians being questioned by detectives. They walked on past the pub and stopped at the beginning of the alleyway.

'Sorry boys, you can't come down here just yet, still looking for clues and prints.' one of crime scene technicians shouted from a distance.

'Ok, we'll be in the pub, give us a shout when you're ready.' Sven shouted back. They all turned and entered the *Pesel.*

'Who's in charge here?' Sven asked.

'Until Polizeihauptkommissar Backhaus gets back, I am. Hauptmeister Zimmermann, sir.'

'And where is Polizeihauptkommissar Backhaus?'

'He went back to the station to rally up more troops.'

'Ok, so what have we got here?'

'Couple over there with the female officer. They found the body as they were going home. Went through the alley and saw her lying there, ripped open like a pig's carcass. Both really shook up. They saw no one else in the alley. They recognized the victim as she was in here drinking earlier and the barman confirmed she had only just left to go to the bank to get some more money. Nobody followed her out of the door at the time and the next people out were the young couple who found her.'

'Was it an opportune victim or was she targeted? Do we know anything about her yet?' Freddy asked.

'Techies won't let anyone in and they haven't come out yet. But if she was going to the bank, she'll have ID on her. All we know is a first name given as Nicole' Zimmermann replied.

'Was she with anyone when she came in or did she meet someone whilst she was in here?' Freddy asked.

'We've spoken to all the clientele who were still here when we arrived and have confirmation from several independent witnesses that she came in on her own and sat talking to a girl named Ulrike Berghausen, Ulli for short. She also confirms that they had only just met and that Nicole went to the bar to buy her new friend a drink. Frau Berghausen saw her go to the bar but did not see her leave the establishment. The next she knew was when the young couple came back in blabbering to the barman to call the police because something dreadful had happened. Everyone piled out to see but some bright spark told everybody not to enter into the alleyway as they would destroy any clues. Obviously watches cop shows on the TV but could have done us a favour in the long run.'

'Ok, I want a full catalogue of who saw what at what time in regards to Nicole coming in and going out and what she spoke about with Frau Berghausen.'

'Yes sir.' Zimmermann replied and walked back amongst the throng.

'I've got a feeling that this could be the work of the same killer,' Sven confided in Freddy, 'just that he is only one step ahead of us. Right, what I want is to step up the search for our missing date with Anja, get the picture out on local TV and splash it all over the local papers. Someone must recognize him and will come forward and he may even come forward if he is innocent and maybe tell us something more. Can I leave that with you to deal with?'

'Yeah, no probs. What will you be doing?' asked Freddy.

'I'll get cracking with this new murder so we'll have two fronts to contend with. You take Peter with you, I'll keep Dennis. Need any extra manpower, just shout. Use whoever you want but find me that face. Here, take my car'

'Ok, I'll get back to the station and will meet up with you later.'

Both teams walked away from each other, one back to where the car was parked and the other back towards the carnage in the alleyway.

Mariengasse and Corduanergasse joined each other and formed a "T" shape, the top upper left being the Corduanergasse which was about 30 meters in length and the top right and lower part of the "T" being the Mariengasse, also being around 30 meters each in length. There was no street lamp located anywhere along the alleyways as the buildings along each were either the back ends of half timbered houses, three individual garages to house cars or the back of a shop. The location for a murder was ideal. Dark and gloomy and not much foot traffic, it was overlooked but not viewable from the houses that had the garages, which blocked the view of even the nosiest neighbour. The streets themselves were cobbled and sloped away from Corduanergasse.

Six sets of Arc-lights had been set up by the technicians and lit up the night sky as if it was day. Several bodies clad in paper suits, protective hats and shoes danced around each other like a well rehearsed ballet school. Each technician had their own job to do, always being mindful of the others, as it was not good to be a prima donna and hinder the important work of someone else, as all were professionals and wanted to gather as much evidence as was humanly possible to assist in the capture of the killer. With the body still in situ, there was a lot of swearing and cursing heard amongst anyone who glimpsed the victim and the mutilation taken upon her.

'Yo, Sven.'

'Talk to me,' Sven replied, 'tell me you've wrapped this one up and know the name of the killer.'

'Can't help you there, but I can honestly say this is one of the most gruesome murders I have seen in a long time. And I've been around the block a few times.' Dr. Egbert Freckmann was one of the colleagues who worked under Steffi and was known to Sven as being a very thorough, easy going individual and went out of his way to assist anyone who needed his help. 'What I can say is this, when I assisted Steffi with the autopsy from your victim last week, she had been cut up pretty bad. This latest victim has the hallmarks of being killed the same way as the last but the killer decided to have a bit more fun with this one. I can't let you down to see because we'll be here a while yet gathering evidence etc. but I can tell you that she has been ripped open and had certain body parts removed. I won't know for sure if anything is missing and what weapon was used until we get her back to the lab. We've got someone studying the blood patterns which will ascertain what and where she was cut first and in which order, each cobble stone is being scrutinized along each street for clues and of course the place is being sprinkle with enough powder for fingerprinting for it to look like it has been snowing.'

'Ok, Dr. Freckmann, thanks for the preliminaries. We'll let you get on and ask you to keep me informed if and when you find anything here useful.'

'Will do.' replied Dr. Freckmann and turned and moved back down to the body between small markers that made a corridor for people entering and leaving the scene.

'Come on Dennis, let's go and start coordinating the early morning wakeup call of all the houses backing onto these streets. If no one in the pub saw anything, maybe someone did from their house and has not yet been asked.'

Dennis followed Sven as they both walked around the corner looking for where the houses would have their front entrances. By keeping the Arc-lights always on their right, they turned down a couple of streets until they found what they were looking for.

'Hey, boss, look at this one. Looks like to be about four storeys high at the back. Shall we start here?'

The building in question was situated on the corner of Marktstrasse and Kungelmarkt and also sported the half timber design as like most of the buildings in the old part of town. Sven took the honours and rang the doorbells of all tenants simultaneously. It took three successive rings for anyone to buzz open the door and allow the policemen in.

'Erster Kriminalhauptkommissar Gerling, this is my colleague Kriminaloberkommissar Schmidt. We would like your permission to come into your house and look at what we can see through your back windows at the alleyway behind your house.'

'Certainly, please come in but would you be so kind as to remove your shoes? I only scrubbed the carpets the day before yesterday and what with my arthritis, can't kneel down for too long.'

The old lady who had opened the door appeared to be as old as the house, which would have made her to be around two hundred years old. Although small in height, she was shortened even more by the chronic crouch she possessed making her upper body lean forward at an angle of around 80° from the waist. She had pure white hair cut short, had more wrinkles than a well folded map, wore thick lensed glasses and had a hearing aid in her right ear. She wore a pair of long, woolen tights under a grey cardigan and a night robe and she also wore a pair of slippers that looked similar to a pair of Eskimo moccasins.

‘Yes, of course, only too willing to oblige.’ Sven replied, nudging his colleague in the side as the old woman turned away to lead them in. They took off their shoes as requested and carried these with them. The room they entered was obviously the living room as it contained a two seated couch and two individual matching armchairs. A coffee table made of ceramic tiles was in the centre of the three piece suite and a sideboard held various photos of many people, most probably those of her children and grand children. In the corner was a cat tree with various ledges, a ladder, some toys hanging off and the obligatory box for the cat to sleep in. Obviously there was no litter tray for the cat as not only did the room stink of cats piss, on closer inspection the small items under the sideboard and coffee table were dried up cat faeces. Either the old lady’s eyesight was a lot worse than what the glasses should have corrected or her sense of smell was non-existent and she was oblivious to the odour and cat poo solidifying under the furniture.

‘So, what is happening out there?’ she asked. ‘I was soundly asleep when all of a sudden I heard a loud shout and sometime later the heavens have been lit up as if we were expecting another air raid.’

‘When you say you heard a shout, what time would this have been?’ Sven asked.

‘I don’t rightly know,’ she answered. ‘I went to bed straight after the 10 o’clock news and fell asleep pretty quickly. My eyesight isn’t what it used to be so I can’t see the clock anymore, even with my glasses.’

‘Did it sound like a female?’

‘No, most definitely a man. Never heard so much foul language in all my life. Not even from the children I used to teach at the local comprehensive school. Something you would not want to hear at my age.’

‘Can you remember what was said?’

‘Just a string of profanity shouted in a random order not making any coherent sentence at all.’

'Would you be able to identify the voice again?' Sven asked hopefully.

'Don't be so daft, of course I wouldn't. All I do know is that it scared the living daylights out of me. And talking of daylight, what is it with all the lights?'

'Well, to put it blankly, some poor girl was murdered at the back of your property and the lights are those from the technicians so they can carry out their duty in gathering all the evidence they can find. I see you have a patio. Mind if we pop out and take a look?' Sven said, opening the glass door and putting on his shoes.

'Don't let my Molly out, she's an indoor cat. I don't let her out so please go outside and close the door behind you.' And with that she pushed the policemen outside and closed the door on them before the cat was able to make any attempt of escaping captivity.

'Ok Dennis, I'll ask you to arrange to have the living dead visit the local nick for an interview. We need to find out about what she heard. Did our attacker get injured himself? Hopefully our victim was able to get a few blows in herself and made him bleed or scratched him somehow and has his blood under her fingernails.'

'Yes will do.'

Both finished lacing up their shoes and headed to the end of the patio, which was situated on top of one of the garages. Both Sven and Dennis leant over the railing and had a bird's eye view of the crime scene.

'Hey, found a great spot for taking more photos,' Sven shouted down to the crowd of technicians going about their business. 'Ring the doorbell and the old biddy will let you in. Bring a clothes peg for your nose if you don't like cat's pee.'

'Nice one, Sven. I'll come around when I have finished up here. What's the house number?' asked Bjorn, the murder squad photographer.

'Didn't pay too much attention, just rang randomly. Sure you'll figure it out though, just follow the scent of cat piss and you'll be right on the mark.'

From the view that both Sven and Dennis now had, they could see the length of the first part of Mariengasse in front of them, showing the entrance onto the small church square and then by turning their heads slightly to the right they could see the body being placed carefully into a body bag by the end garage. The buildings along the Corduanergasse had several windows overlooking the alleyway but there were no doors.

‘I would go so far as to say this was not an opportune killing but a well planned one. Look, three entrances and all only a short distance from one end to the other. Hardly any lighting would get down this end and nothing that really overlooks the location. The killer would then be able to slip away without being noticed. What do you think?’ Sven asked Dennis.

‘I’m not one to argue with that, boss. Have you noticed that the only garage out of the three that doesn’t have a door flush with the brickwork is where he attacked? Was probably in shadow the whole time when she passed him. And going by the amount of blood we can see, he ripped her throat open like the last victim.’

‘I’d bet my police pension on it that the killer has the same M.O as with the last victim, meaning that our killer has struck again. Looks like we may have a serial killer on the loose. Come on, let’s get out of here and have the local bobbies do a door to door immediately like planned and we’ll just hang around and see if anything comes out of down there. And that won’t be the only murder being committed tonight.’

‘What do you mean, boss?’

‘Let’s go and do some more questioning in the pub and you’ll witness me murdering a pint. As you’ll be driving me back to Dortmund later, I’ll let you have a coke.’ Sven smiled and led the way to the house once again.

‘And, did you find anything?’ the old lady asked, holding a fat feline close to her bosom.

‘We’ll need you to come to the station later for a formal interview, we’ll arrange for transport for you when it is a more sociable hour. In between time, if you can try to think of what you heard, that could really help us in our enquiries in catching the killer.’ Sven said, heading towards the front door.

‘I don’t think I’ll be able to help you that much you see. Whilst you were both outside, I’ve been trying to piece together what I heard and as I have already said, all I heard was a lot of swearing and cussing going on.'

'Exactly, so that may be because our victim fought back somehow.' Sven interjected. 'We'll be on our way now, so please make yourself available for later. Much appreciated and we'll see you down at the station.' And with that, both Sven and Dennis left the building and gasped in a lungful of fresh air when they hit the street.

'Come on, last one to the pub buys the drinks'. Sven said, walking off at a fast pace back the way they had come.

CHAPTER 15

09.09.1988

'Ok Steffi, this is our latest victim from Soest, so prepare yourself as she is not a pretty sight.' Dr. Egbert Freckmann said.

Egbert unzipped the body bag that had been placed on the metal table and with the help of a lab assistant, they slowly removed the bag from under the body.

'Oh my God,' Steffi said when she could see the complete body lying in front of her, 'What animal could do this?'

'Beats me,' Egbert replied, 'all I know is that I would not like to meet the killer on my own if he is capable of doing something like this.'

'Oh, I would love to meet whoever is responsible. I'd slice the skin off their body and tip them in a saline bath. That would get them screaming.' Steffi smiled inwardly as if she was able to see the scene playing out in her mind.

'Didn't put you down for a revengeful vigilante.' Egbert grinned.

'Well, one can fantasize I suppose' she said. 'Ok, let's get to work.'

And with that, both doctors and the lab assistant turned their attention to the body and the job at hand.

The lab assistant wrapped the body with a plastic sheet, both doctors helping by lifting the victim up so that the sheet could go underneath first. Once wrapped, all took hold of a part of the body and slowly turned it so that it was lying face down on the table. Then the lab assistant carefully cut the plastic sheeting so that the back of the corpse was free, leaving the front still lying on the sheeting. With the lights turned on and the air conditioning running at a comfortable speed, both doctors stood on opposite sides of the corpse. Steffi took a scalpel in her right hand and slowly inserted the tip of the blade into the skin and flesh just under the shoulder blade and carried on this incision until the blade met the spine. She then done the same to the other side and when both points met, she sliced the skin down along the spine until it reached the coccyx, then continued slicing both sides from the middle to the hip bone. Once these cuts were complete, both doctors took hold of the skin and slowly peeled each segment away from the muscles so that the skin flaps lay on either side of the body. Then they meticulously cut through the muscles and fat tissues to see if and what injuries had occurred from the front. They stopped often to speak into the microphone that was hanging near the lights, making a recording of the steps they were undertaking and of what they could see and had found so to provide an accurate post mortem report later. Once the back had been examined, the flaps of skin were pulled back together and swiftly sewn up. Maybe not the neatest one would expect from a medical professional but it would suffice for what they further had in store. Cleanly closed back up, each present slowly turned the body onto its back and removed the plastic sheeting that was still in place.

Steffi spoke clearly into the microphone as she and her colleague worked.

'I can see that there are several bruises to her head, these consisting of a large contusion on her right temple, probably made from a blunt instrument or a fist and also some bruising over the right eyelid. This is consistent with being grabbed from behind and the head held in place by someone using their left hand. The throat has been severed from left to right, the point of the blade scraping across the neck bone, nearly severing the head from the body. This is the cut that would have killed her.

The stomach contains no traces of food, so I suppose she either had not eaten or she had eaten more than two hours before she was killed, as this is the time it takes for food to be digested and passed along to the intestines. However, there is a large amount of fluid inside her stomach which we will examine later. The abdomen has been cut open and the large intestines have been removed and placed on the shoulder of the victim. What for is a mystery. Two flaps of skin have been cut away from the abdomen and this had been placed over the left shoulder which I am reading from the notes taken by my colleague who was present at the crime scene.

Also removed from the body is the uterus and its appendages along with the upper portion of the vagina and the bladder. There are no traces of these body parts as these are not present, meaning that maybe the killer has taken these as a trophy. All of the incisions are cleanly cut, suggesting that maybe this is the work of someone who has a certain anatomical knowledge. Again, all we can ascertain is that a very sharp knife has been used to slice and cut the victim before and after death but are unable at this point to confirm the length of blade.'

Even though the room was cool, Steffi wiped sweat off her brow with the back of her sleeve.

'Well, what do you think?' she asked her colleague.

'As you have said, looks like whoever did this knew what they were doing. Could be someone from the medical profession, a vet, maybe a butcher.' replied Egbert.

'That may narrow the field down somewhat than just looking for a random person, I suppose.'

'Wouldn't want to be the ones looking for the culprit, so many unanswered questions and no clues as such to go with.' he answered.

'Oh well, they get paid for doing their job just like we get paid for doing ours. Ok Marc, if you could run the blood tests for substances and also check out what is in the stomach, as soon as that is done along with the needlework, please would you inform us of your findings so that we can write up our report.' With that, Steffi and Egbert left the lab technician to follow Steffi's instructions and moved away from the table and walked through the plastic doors and proceeded upwards to their offices.

'I'll put the kettle on, you start writing up?' Egbert asked.

'See you volunteer for the easy job. See if you can find a packet of biscuits from somewhere to go with the tea. Brigitte always has one or two packets stashed in her desk draws for when she doesn't go out for lunch.' Steffi was referring to one of the two secretaries who worked alongside the doctors and assistants. 'And remember to put the milk in after you have removed the teabag.'

'You're worse than my misses,' Egbert said jokingly, 'never happy unless you are moaning.' And with that he moved towards the small kitchen and was heard clinking the cups together on the work surface.

Steffi turned on her computer and monitor and placed the recorded post mortem tape into the cassette player and started typing up her report and findings.

'Polizeihauptkommissar Ahrens, can you confirm that the latest killing is from the same hand as the first victim?'

'Herr Loch, you know that it is too early to make conclusions and as I have just said, as soon as we have more information, we will hold a further press conference and keep you all up to speed.'

'But surely if the same modus operandi is present, then it must be the same killer or not?'

'Again, no. Let's not jump to conclusions and scare the public. We are still working on the first victim and looking for witnesses who may have seen something to come forward and help us with our enquiries. Don't forget it has only been just over one week and these types of crime take a bit longer to solve than your local thief.' Ahrens stood his ground in front of the bank of microphones and looked for any other reporters to ask a question.

'Michael König, *Bild*. Is it true that some body parts have been taken from the last victim and are we looking for a cannibal?'

'No, we are not even suggesting that a cannibal is on the loose. Wherever do you think up such stories?'

'Well, some of your coppers are talking about it, so something must be true. Does Soest boast its very own Hannibal Lecter?' König asked.

'I will be very disappointed if I see anything in print suggesting that we have a cannibal called Hannibal roaming around our streets taking body parts from his victims. Is that understood?'

'Only saying what I heard is all.' König replied, hiding the smirk on his face behind the head of a female reporter sitting in front of him. König had learnt to just throw shit at a fan and see what stuck to the wall. Just by adding some utter nonsense, Ahrens was now on the verge of losing his cool and may let something slip that was being held back.

'And I'm saying if you print any of the shit that comes out of your mouth, you will get to see the inside of a police cell first hand. Understood?'

'Alright, keep your hair on. Only fishing is all.'

'Is it a coincidence that both victims have been killed within the walls and in the old part of town?' asked the blonde in front of König. 'Has the killer found the spots before he kills or are the victims just at the wrong place at the wrong time?

'It may be a coincidence, but until we know the identity of the murderer it is hard to be certain.'

'Ron Wilhelm, *Patriot.* Can we confirm that the killer has some anatomical knowledge in that the victim was sliced and diced pretty professionally?'

'Again, I do not want to jump to any conclusion at this point. Yes, it does appear that the killer may have some knowledge, but to what degree we cannot ascertain. He could be from any number of professions. Someone with a medical background, a doctor or vet maybe.'

'Someone who works in the slaughterhouse, maybe someone who has watched a lot of gory films, maybe even a soldier who has seen battle?' This last remark came from Thomas Loch of the *Soester Anzeiger.*

'As you can see, Herr Loch, you are not even able to comprehend the vast array of professions our killer may come from. If we now have to take into consideration that the killer maybe a soldier, then our job of finding him has been made even more difficult. Let's not forget, we have two British army camps around here, we also have a large camp of Belgium soldiers directly in Soest as well as a small American camp just outside and of course the German army in and around the area. Getting access to interview all of these potential "suspects" will be impossible. No, we will have to rely on our police work and capture the killer using what we do best, policing.'

'Where is Erster KriminalHauptkommissar Gerling? Why is he not present at this press conference?' asked König.

'Because he is leading up the investigation of this latest killing and will not be available for some time.' Ahrens replied. 'So, that will be the end of this conference, be prepared for an update as soon as we have one.' Ahrens then turned to his right and exited through the door in the corner of the room, ignoring the shouts of more questions and remarks.

'Well, that got him a bit red in the face, don't you think?' König asked the blond in front of his chair.

'I like your style,' she said. 'I reckon behind that façade of indifference and sensationalism, there is a real reporter in there somewhere.'

'Why, that is mighty nice of you to say so,' he replied. 'How about I take you out for a late breakfast and we can go over what I know and see if you have any fresh ideas.'

'Don't listen to him, he talks crap at the best of times. Thomas Loch, local rag.' he said introducing himself to the only reporter he did not recognise.

'Bettina Feldmaus, but please call me Betty.'

'And which paper do you work for, Betty?' König asked, not wanting to lose his place in the queue crowding around this beauty.

'That is my secret and for you to find out' she said smiling. 'Let's see how good you are at digging up the truth the good old honest way.'

'Don't let this local yobbo fool you just because he comes from around here. He knows as much about this case as the rest of us. But I bet my purse strings are not as tight as his. Who can turn down a free meal with someone who can help you out?' König asked.

'Well, seeing that I have my own story to cover and I do not want to be biased in any way, I would prefer to work on my own, thank you very much. As for the free meal, I do not consider a baguette with a warm tea of being taken out for dinner. If you want to impress me, then you will need to smarten yourself up, have a shave and book a very expensive restaurant with the best wine on the menu if you want to a) work with me and b) have any chance of getting into my knickers. Have I said that clearly enough?'

'I know this great restaurant that brews it's own beer not too far from here,' he stammered, 'maybe we can go there for lunch?'

'You just won't give up will you?' she answered. 'I have some work to do and I would appreciate it if you would let me get on with it.'

Betty turned and started to walk away, her buttocks swaying seductively in the black pencil skirt she wore. She knew that all the men and probably most of the women reporters in the room were watching her leave, but heck, she was quite beautiful and she knew it. As her dad used to say, "If you've got it, then flaunt it."

Freddy was sitting at the desk he had commandeered and was going through the reports he had received regarding the person they were still looking for. Peter Schwarz was reading through all the files to get up to speed. Being a power reader, he was able to dissect many a page as if he was just scanning the contents, but in reality he was reading nearly every word written.

'How far are these circulated?' Peter asked Freddy. 'Looking on the map, Soest is in the middle of quite a few towns and many villages are dotted around. We are looking for someone who took a girl out for a drink and had a row, this being overheard by a waitress, the girl then got up and left him sitting there. That is the last information we have of anyone seeing her. But where did she go after that? Was she with anyone else? Did our mystery man know where she was going and followed her some time later? Is he the killer or did he see her with someone else?'

'Wow, slow down cowboy, you're full of beans today.' Freddy answered. 'On the case for five minutes and you set off like a hurricane. Good questions, we have a lot of ground to cover so all of your input is welcome.'

'Ok, what I can do is get this picture circulated, I'll drive around the areas making sure that this gets a wider circulation and is seen by more eyes.'

'Yep, I like that idea. Grab one of the plods from here and get him to drive you wherever you need to go. Keep me posted as to where you are and what you can find out.'

'Will do, who should I speak to in getting a car with a driver?' he asked.

'Polizeihauptkommissar Backhaus, office near the bog.' Freddy replied.

Peter grabbed his jacket and radio and left Freddy scanning another document and headed in the direction of getting the transport organized.

CHAPTER 16

'And what is this place?' Peter asked the driver, Polizei Obermeister Suzanne Baumgarten.

'This is a psychiatric clinic for the mentally ill. Some are just old and suffer from dementia, others are just born with a brain defect and others are criminally insane and spend their time here rather than in prison. This is our local nut house.' she replied. 'Place has many stations or wards dotted all over the place, I have no idea how many patients are actually housed here but I can't understand how normal people can live here in this town when the building across the road is full of nut jobs.'

'I'm sure it's safe or they wouldn't allow such facilities to be so close to the general population,' Peter answered, 'but at a guess, how many stations are there here?' he asked.

'Again, no idea. We could stop at the main office and ask if you want.'

'I have an itch and I just think that I can get it scratched if someone can answer one or two questions I have. Yes please, drop me outside the office and wait for me in the car.'

Suzanne drove the police car up to a barrier that was blocking a side road that led into the hospital grounds and waited for the security guard to raise the bar from his booth. She drove on and stopped outside the main building, large and white and parked where it said "visitors".

'Wish me luck,' he said and did not wait for a reply. He headed towards the main doors and walked up to the reception desk.

'Can I help you?' asked a woman of middle age. 'This isn't a place where you can just walk in without an appointment.'

'Well, I did and I can,' he replied, not liking the way that he was addressed, 'I am Kriminaloberkommissar Schwarz and I need to speak to someone with authority.'

'You are speaking to someone with authority. There is not much that goes on here that I do not know about and I am the first line of defence. If you want to know something, then ask, but be quick about it as I am rather busy.'

'And you are?'

'Frau Hellweg, I am the senior front desk executive.'

'Then, Frau Hellweg, if you know about most things, then you can tell me who I can talk to who is not someone who appears to be sucking on lemons and does not have a broom shoved up ones backside. I am here on a matter of police business and have never in my fifteen years on the service been spoken to in such a rude manner before I have even addressed the reason why I am here. Now I suggest you direct me to someone with a bit more authority than a simple desk clerk and be quick about it yourself, otherwise I might just be in the mood to arrest you for obstruction of justice. Now, have I made that clear enough or would you like me to write it on a memo pad for you?' It wasn't often that Peter got riled, but certain personalities did, and one of them was sitting behind the large desk.

'Well, I never. I am a well-respected person in this facility and all I am doing is trying to ascertain what your business may be so that I may help you so we do not need to bother anyone else. But if you want to go over my head, then you will need to wait over there in the waiting area and I will page Dr. Heimeier. He is currently in a conference but I am sure he will be able to find some of his valuable time for someone who has no appointment.'

And with that, Frau Hellweg turned her chair away from Peter, stood up and disappeared through a door. Peter sauntered over to the waiting area, a place in the corner with several hard backed chairs and a low table with old magazines scattered on top, a water dispensing machine that gurgled every two minutes and a potted fern that was urgently in need of water.

Fifteen minutes had passed since the battle axe had left her sanctuary from behind her desk and had still to return. Had she gone to personally speak to the doctor? Had she actually just left him sitting there out of spite and had contacted nobody? Would she dare to do something like that? Peter was getting slightly anxious and was just about to walk over to the door she had disappeared through when another door opened and a man walked over, hand outstretched.

'Dr. Heimeier at you service, how may I be of assistance?' he asked politely.

'I am Kriminaloberkommissar Schwarz and I would just like to ask you a few simple questions if I may. I appear to have been shown both barrels by the receptionist and may not have got off on the right foot. I just need to speak to someone with some authority, not necessarily someone as highly qualified as yourself.'

'No, no, all is fine. Glad to get out of there. Hate these "important" conferences where all people want to do is hear their own voice and go round in circles without anything ever getting done. And I would like to apologize for the rudeness you may have received from my sister-in-law. Has never been the same since she caught her husband of twenty two years in bed with the next door neighbour. Wouldn't have been too bad but the neighbour was a widower as his wife had died two years before. So she now thinks that all men are bastards, myself included, and will do anything to upset the status quo. Mind you, my wife's brother was always a bit feminine, so it wasn't much of a surprise for us to see him shacked up with another man.'

'Maybe she should be employed in another office where she has no contact with the outside world?' Peter replied.

'No, she does a fine job, even if she thinks she is better than what she really is. Come, follow me and I'll see if I can find a cup of coffee for us both.'

Peter followed the doctor through the door and up one flight of stairs, down a long carpeted corridor until they came to the last door on the end.

'Please, take a seat,' the doctor invited, 'I'll see about the coffee. Won't take two ticks, sit tight.'

Several minutes passed when Peter heard some scuffling at the office door. He went over and opened it and was just able to catch the doctor from falling over, as he had two cups with saucers balanced in both hands and carrying a packet of biscuits under his left armpit. He had been trying to open the door with his elbow when the door opened suddenly and all the coffee in one cup landed up either in the saucer or dripping on to the office carpet.

'Bugger, looks like one of us will have to go without I'm afraid, as this was the last of it that was left over from the conference.'

'No worries, I am sure you need it more than me.' Peter said politely. 'I really don't want to take up much of your time and I really do only have some simple questions.'

'Then take a seat and fire away.' the doctor answered, putting both cups on to the desk and wiping his hand on the arm of the chair.

'Well, I am investigating the murders that have recently happened in Soest and it appears that our killer may have some medical background. As I was being driven through this town, I was made aware of the vast facility the place houses and was wondering what training would a psychiatric nurse undergo and how many nurses and doctors do you have working here?'

'Well, every nurse is fully qualified and has to work on every station there is in any normal hospital just like other nurses. That means that every nurse would have spent time on the wards for the geriatrics, paediatrics, accident and emergency, the natal clinic and also the psychiatric wards. That is where they then decide in which field they would like to work in. Here in the forensic clinic, we have around 250 trained medical staff working in eight buildings which are divided into eighteen wards. But surely you cannot be thinking that someone of our profession would stoop so low as to murder someone?'

'And why not? It wouldn't be the first time that a nurse or doctor committed heinous crimes. Surely you can remember the story of Dr. Josef Mengele, one of the main doctors at Auschwitz extermination camp. And how many nurses carry out so called "mercy killings" when they state that the patient would be better off dead? Who are they to be judge and jury?'

'Point taken.'

'If there are so many medical personnel here, would it be possible to hang some pictures up in all the canteens, locker rooms etc. on the off chance that someone recognizes the person we are looking for? The man in question is not a suspect to the murders, just that he may be a vital witness to some information we require.'

'Yes,' replied the doctor, 'Leave a pile for me and I'll make sure they get distributed today. I give you my word.'

'That's awfully kind of you to make sure these get full coverage, let's hope we can get something positive out of this visit.' Peter remarked. 'So, thank you for your time and the nearly cup of coffee.' he said grinning.

'The pleasure is all mine. And maybe you can do me a huge favour yourself.'

'Yes, what is it?' Peter asked.

'If you see old grumpy draws downstairs, upset her a bit more would you. Can't stand the woman.' And with that, the doctor winked at the policeman and led him out of the office.

Outside, Suzanne was sitting in the car with the door open for some air. On seeing Peter approach, she closed the door and started the engine and waited until he was sitting before she pulled off.

'And, how did it go, sir?' she asked.

'Rather well I think. Doc will distribute the photo to all canteens and locker rooms etc. Maybe someone will recognize him and come forward.'

'Where to now?' she asked.

'I would like to visit every taxi and bus company in Lippstadt to see if they can recognize our man. If he works here, only stands to reason he may live either between Soest and Eickelborn or Eickelborn and Lippstadt, meaning he would call for a taxi if he hasn't got his own wheels.'

Suzanne drove the police car out onto the main road and turned right and headed towards Lippstadt. They passed through the villages of Benninghausen, Herringhausen, Overhagen and entered Lippstadt some ten minutes after leaving the hospital.

'So, I only know of four taxi companies, we'll start on the furthest on the right and make our way to the left of the town.' Suzanne said.

'We can also stop off for a bite to eat as well. Bloody starving. I'll put it on the accounts. What do you fancy?' he asked.

'Oh, thank you sir. Something quick in the hand or a proper sit down dinner?'

'I was thinking on the lines of a Bratwurst in a roll or a burger in the hand. We've got a lot of ground to cover and haven't got the time for a romantic dinner with candles.' he responded.

Suzanne blushed and turned her head as if she was looking out of the side window. She thought how would he put the price of two Bratwursts on the accounts? Definitely not a womanizer or a big spender.

After another two hours, all taxi companies had been visited and most of the taxi drivers on duty had been personally spoken to by Peter himself. Each driver was handed a small copy of the photo of their mysterious man and told to call either the local police or the Soest police directly if they were lucky enough to pick him up. They then drove to both of the hospitals in Lippstadt and asked again for the picture to be distributed to all the staff rooms on each ward. After saturating the town, they moved on and done the same with Beckum, a town to the north of Soest, and finally finished in Werl, a town some 15 km to the west of Soest.

'Right, nearly my bed time. Let's get back to the station and see what else has been happening since we departed.' he said.

'If you don't mind sir, when we get back I wouldn't mind knocking off. Been on duty since eight this morning and it's nearly seven now.'

'You lucky so and so. I was called out of bed when we first got the call last night. Been working ever since. Yeah, get us back and you can bog off. I'll just close my eyes now for a few minutes to have a cat nap. Wake me up when we get there.' And with that, Peter closed his eyes and was soon snoozing in the front seat, head resting against the side window.

Some twenty five minutes later, they arrived at the station.

'Sir, we're back.' Suzanne said, softly shaking his arm.

'All right, thanks for the ride. Didn't mean to upset you over our dinner arrangements,' he said. 'I'd like to make it up to you some other time, take you out for a proper meal and all.'

'Will have to check my diary,' she answered, blushing again when he looked at her, 'but I am sure that there is nothing in there that cannot be either cancelled or moved. Not that you think I'm desperate. I'm not, I mean just that I have nothing important, if you know what I mean.'

'Don't sweat it, I have no idea how long I will be in Soest, but yes, I would really like to take you out and get to know you a bit more. Have a nice evening and I hope to see you tomorrow. Any more chauffeur duties, I'll ask for you.' he said, winking at her.

Suzanne went into the building first and went straight to the locker room where she quickly got changed into her civvies, stamped out and handed the keys in to the duty officer, hoping to see Peter before she actually left the station.

Peter was at this time sitting down and telling Freddy of what he had done the whole day, where he had distributed the photo fit pictures and that tomorrow he would walk around Soest doing exactly the same.

Sven radioed in and informed Freddy that it was time to knock it on the head for the day and that they should all meet for something to eat in a restaurant in the old town and maybe have a couple of beers to loosen up the limbs.

CHAPTER 17

10.09.1988

Rudolph was feeling good with himself for two reasons. The first reason was he had been able to add another video to his ever growing collection, this latest purchase was by far the best he had collected, and the second reason was that the daily newspaper was reporting another woman being killed in Soest and was being linked to the first murder just over one week before. He read the complete story from beginning to end three times and noticed he had goose bumps on his lower arms from excitement. If only all his days could start like this.

After eating a large breakfast consisting of four fresh bread rolls filled with crispy bacon, hamburgers and all covered in tomato ketchup, two large glasses of cola and some crisps, he put on his jacket and made sure his wallet was in the pocket. He took his car keys from the hook by the door and went outside to where his pride and joy stood in the sunshine. The weather was turning and the days were starting to get colder, as were the nights. But at least it was dry and not raining. He opened up the car boot, took out his cleaning basket and started cleaning the windows and lights like he did every day.

Once this task was finished, he put the cleaning material back in the boot and squeezed in behind the steering wheel. He then logged onto the taxi radio and informed central that he was ready for any pickup needed and that he would wait at the train station if there was nothing outstanding. As there were no clients waiting, he drove to the station and parked up, waiting for the next train to spill out its passengers in the hope that he would be able to pick up a fare. Whilst he was sitting there waiting, a police car drove on to the taxi rank and someone in civilian clothes got out and started talking to the driver in the taxi at the head of the line. After a few minutes, the man then proceeded to move down the line, stopping at each car as he went along. Finally, it was Rudolph's turn. He unwound his window just as the man stopped by his door.

'Can I help you?' Rudolph asked.

'Hopefully, yes.' replied the man dressed in a dark suit, white shirt and black shoes. 'I am looking for some information to see if any taxi driver recognizes this individual.' He held a small copy of the photo fit that he had shown to all the taxi drivers and the hospitals the day before. 'We are looking for information if anyone knows or recognizes him as he may hold vital information with regards to the murder that happened on the night of 31st August. Maybe you have picked up this gentleman yourself?'

'I'm sorry, but I get so many fares per day, it is impossible to remember them all.' Rudolph stated.

'Quite, but maybe you can recollect the particular night in question and recollect if you had taken this man either to or from Soest?'

'Again, sorry, but I really do not recognize the man in the picture. If I did, I would be only too pleased to help.'

'Ok, thank you for your time. I would like to leave this photo with you so that if you do happen to pick him up, then please call the number on the back as soon as you have delivered him to where he wants to go. He may be a suspect and could be dangerous, so please do not attempt anything heroic on your part. Understood?'

'Yes, I certainly will. And you are?'

'Kriminaloberkommissar Schwarz from the murder squad from Dortmund. On attachment to Soest'

'I'll keep my eye out like you asked, but he just looks like a regular male to me. Nothing that distinguishes him from the next guy.'

With that, Peter left Rudolph and walked to the last taxi that was parked behind and went through the same procedure. Rudolph looked at the picture again and tried to remember if he had taken this man somewhere or if he had seen him at all. After giving the thought about ten seconds, his mind started to drift and he was remembering what he had read in the newspaper over breakfast. He should have brought it to work with him for when it got dark.

*

‘Good morning Detlef, I’ve made your sandwiches and left them next to the kettle. Coffee is out here by your door. Don’t spill it when you come out, don’t want any stains on the carpet.’ Detlef’s mother knocked one final time on her son’s bedroom door and disappeared into her own room to get ready for the trip to the fruit and vegetable market in Soest, it being a Saturday. Once fully dressed, she went back out onto the landing and saw that the coffee was still outside his room. ‘Detlef, you’ll be late for work. Get up now. I’m off so will see you tonight. I’ll cook us a nice meal for when you finish your shift.’ And with that she was down the stairs, shoes and coat on and out the door.

Detlef heard the front door close and heard his mum talking to one of the neighbours about the weather forecast and what her day entailed. He didn’t want to get up as he was very tired after the last couple of late nights he had had in a row and wanted to sleep some more. But he really had to get up and ready himself for work.

After a quick wash and a shave, he dressed in a pair of jeans and grey sweatshirt and went down the stairs to the kitchen, carefully carrying the full cup of cold coffee. He dispensed of this in the sink, swilled the cup under cold water and left it on the draining board to dry. He put on his coat and shoes and remembered to take his lunch box with him as he left the house to walk to his place of work. It was a clear sky and sunny with the temperature warmer than expected for the time of year, but welcomed by everyone all the same.

‘Oi, Detlef, not seen you in a while. Where have you been hiding?’

‘Oh, hi Paul, no, been busy and all that. How’s the new car?’ he asked.

‘Not bad, mate. Getting the windows tinted this afternoon so it will be a real fanny magnet. You wanna go for a spin tonight and see who we can pick up?’

‘Yes, I finish work at seven today, how about we meet at around eight tonight?’

‘Yep, sounds like a plan. See you later.’ And with that, Detlef’s next door neighbour but one got into his new Audi 80 and drove slowly down the street, hoping that all would see his new set of wheels.

Detlef walked slowly up the road to the main road of the village and crossed the street and walked along until he came to the main gate of the clinic. He walked past the porter and into the clinic grounds. The grounds themselves were carefully cultivated, having many flower beds with the seasonal flowers planted, bushes and trees and vast areas of grass where visitors could sit down or on the benches dotted around the area. He past several buildings and eventually saw his place of work through the trees. Just as he approached the gate that led into the security area of 15/1 and 15/2, he heard a voice behind him and he turned to look.

'I don't suppose you could take these for me, please? Top pile is for 15/1 and bottom pile for 15/2.' The person who spoke was sitting on a bicycle with pannier bags on both sides. His name was Johannes and was the internal postman for the clinic. 'Saves me having to get off etc. Want to knock off as early as possible as I want to go and watch Eickelborn play Rüthen. If we win today, we'll be top of the table.' he said.

'Yeah, alright. Anything special in the post today?' Detlef asked.

'Not really, usual amount of letters for the patients, a couple of flyers for you lot and Gary's newspapers.'

'Ok, give them here so you can swan off and watch football whilst I'm stuck here slaving away all day.'

'Cheers.' Johannes said and handed the bundle to Detlef.

'Is everything alright?' Detlef asked.

'Er, yes, why?'

'Because you are looking at me in a weird way. What is it, have I got a bogey hanging out of my nose or something?'

'No, nothing, sorry.' And with that, Johannes turned his bike around and started to cycle the way he had come, but not before he took another look at Detlef just to confirm his thoughts.

Detlef put the post under his arm and unlocked the gate, walked through and relocked it from the inside. He then unlocked the door to the station and again relocked it after getting inside. He walked up the stairs and unlocked the door that led onto his ward and heard the daily noises from the men who had been locked up all night conversing with each other.

'Morning all,' he shouted, 'hope you're all gonna behave today. Weather is good outside so maybe we can have a game of basket ball. Who's up for a game?'

Several patients confirmed and started arguing who would be on which side and who was better at shooting etc. Detlef walked into the staff room and greeted his colleagues with a smile and put the bundle under his arm on the table.

'Morning handsome,' Sandra said, 'you're in a good mood today. Get your leg over or something?'

'Nope, still waiting for you,' he replied smiling. 'You know you want me, so why deny yourself all this time?'

'I honestly don't know how I can resist from pulling your clothes off you right now in front of everyone and shagging you on the table, but somehow I manage it.' she replied with a smirk across her face.

'Alright you two, let's have less of that kind of talk in here, don't want to give the patients any ideas now, do we?'

'Sorry Klaus,' Sandra said, 'I know that you have forgotten what a good old shag is at your age, but don't deny me the pleasure of winding Detlef up when he starts his daily mating ritual. I mean, the day he comes in here and doesn't make a pass at me will be marked on the calendar on the wall'

'Very funny,' Detlef said, 'I'm off downstairs for a game. Anyone want to join?'

'Not me, too old for running after a ball.' Klaus said.

'I'll come and watch.' Sandra said.

'I'll stay here with Klaus and mind the others here,' Petra stated. 'On your way down, take the post to 15/1.'

'Come on you lot, get your trainers on, let's get outside before downstairs decide to do the same.' And with that, Detlef led several patients down the stairs and outside into the outside area, encircled by a six meter high wall with barbed wire on top.

It being a Saturday, breakfast in the barracks was changed to brunch, enabling the single soldiers to have a lie in. Only those on essential duties needed to get up for work, so the majority of the soldiers only worked Monday until Friday. At 09:15, the cookhouse was not that busy and the duty chefs were frying the eggs on demand but keeping the bacon and sausage trays full. The soldiers who had been on guard the night before had all eaten before the change over and the new guards needed feeding, so it was arranged that four soldiers could get their breakfast and swap over so that the remaining soldiers on guard duty could have theirs.

'My misses told me last night that there was another murder in Soest a couple of nights ago,' the guard commander told the soldiers sitting at his table. 'She works in one of the travel agencies in town. It is all over the local news and in all the papers.'

'Is your wife German then?' asked a soldier through a mouthful of beans on toast.

'Yep, I met her when I was posted to Herford.'

'What was said in the papers?' Billy asked.

'She said that the latest victim had her throat cut like the first, but this time half of her organs were ripped out. Police are chasing up a couple of leads but nobody has been arrested yet.'

'Must be a sick mother fucker to rip out all her organs.' This voice came from another table behind the one where all of those on guard were sitting. 'If I ever saw the wanker in the act, I'd cut his fucking Jacobs off.'

'His what?' asked the guard commander.

'His Jacobs. Jacobs cream crackers, knackers.' came the reply.

'Oh, never heard that one before.'

'Whoever is doing this definitely needs some serious help. It's one thing to kill someone, done enough of that myself in Northern Ireland, but to do it to an innocent woman, no, something is mentally wrong with him.' the guard commander stated.

'Hope this doesn't scare all the girls down town,' Billy commented, 'some of us need regular nookie. If they are all too scared to go out at night, where can I get my next lay?'

'Glad you have the heart of a valiant knight and are only thinking of their welfare,' replied another soldier at the table. 'I mean, what with all the upset and everything, all you are thinking about is who you can stick your prick into next.'

'Too right, remember what we were all taught in basic training. Rule one: Look after number one. And guess what, I'm number one.

If some sad fuck goes on a killing spree, then that affects the playing field so all the women stay at home.' Billy said adamantly.

'And if all the women stay at home, then there will be nobody else for him to kill.' came the reply.

'Whatever. Listen Corp, just going back to my block to take my washing out of the washing machine. Should be finished now and I'll quickly hang it up to dry. I'll be back at the guardroom in about ten minutes.' Billy informed the guard commander.

'Alright, I'm going to have another brew before we all go back, so no worries. See you back there.'

And with that, Billy left the table and the cookhouse and walked the few steps it took to get to his block and went inside and walked to the laundry room to carry out what he had said he would be doing.

'41/01 to 41/22, 41/01 to 41/22, come in, over'

'That's us,' Suzanne Baumgarten told her passenger, Peter Schwarz, 'I wonder what base wants' she said. She took the handset from the dashboard and spoke into the microphone '41/22 receiving, over'

'41/01, we've just had a call from some bloke in Eickelborn. Apparently he's the clinics postman and may have recognized the guy we are looking for in the photo fit. I've sent 41/28 over there as first response, don't know if you would like to team up and go there yourselves, over.'

'Tell him we'll meet 28 by the porters building along with the postman and they are not to go in without us.' Peter told her.

'41/22, we're happy to respond and will meet 28 outside the porters building. Please have the postman available and tell 28 not to go in without us, over.'

'41/01, will do. Let's hope this is our man. Out.'

'ETA?' Peter asked his driver.

'Estimated time of arrival will be 11:30. Earlier if you want me to use the sirens.'

'No, this is not an emergency as such. Just shift it a bit please.'

They had been visiting the many rehabilitation clinics in Bad Sassendorf, distributing even more photos when the call had come through. They left immediately and drove through Bettinghausen, Ostinghausen and entered Eickelborn, the drive only taking ten minutes. ‘Looks like we’re here before the others,’ Suzanne stated.

‘Ok, park up here, I’ll go into the porters place and speak with the postman. You wait here for the others and we all go in together.’ Peter left the car and walked the few steps to the small building.

‘He’s in the back using the toilet.’ The porter informed Peter when he was shown the ID card.

‘Thanks, anywhere I can talk with him in private?’ Peter asked.

‘Either you talk to him in the toilet or you go outside. I’m not allowed to leave this building unattended.’

‘Ok, send him outside when he comes back, please.’ Peter turned and walked back outside the small building.

After about two minutes of waiting and as if everything was choreographed, both the postman and the second police car appeared at the same time.

‘Good morning sir, I am Kriminaloberkommissar Schwarz. I understand that you have called the police station in Soest with information about recognizing the face in a wanted photo. Is that correct?’

‘Yes, I deliver all the internal post to all buildings and stations and when I was collecting all the post from the main office, I saw a piece of A4 hanging on the notice board with a photo of a man. Although the poster didn’t say anything to me at the time, when I delivered some post to 15/1 and 2, I recognized him immediately. I can take you to where he works if you like.’

‘That’s good of you to be so observant. Just for the records, your name is?’

‘Johannes Werner. I’ve been the postman here for the last four years.’

‘Ok, Herr Werner, and who exactly is it that you suspect looks like the man in the photo?’

‘I don’t know his name, all I know is he’s a nurse who works with the dangerous ones at the back.’

‘Ok, jump in the back and we’ll drive there. Porter, open up and let both cars through.’ he shouted and the barrier was electronically lifted, allowing both police cars into the clinic grounds.

‘Drive to the rhododendrons and follow the road to the left. Now drive to the end and take a right and first left through the trees. See the building through the trees? That’s where he works. Ok, we can park here and walk the last twenty meters.’ Not only did Johannes rate himself of having excellent recognition skills, he also had balls the size of coconuts to tell the police when and where they should park.

‘Do you have any keys to get us inside?’ Suzanne asked.

‘No, can’t have any keys. Just in case and all that. Have to ring the bell. Someone is here 24/7 so never an issue.’

Johannes rang the bell and waited for the intercom to speak. ‘It’s me, Hannes the postie, I have a special delivery for you.’ he replied.

‘Be down in a sec.’ replied a metallic female voice.

Petra came out and opened the gate and had the look of shock on her face when she saw three people in police uniforms and another man standing beside Johannes.

‘Sorry, but we need to come inside and ask some questions.’ Peter stated, taking advantage of the woman being rendered speechless.

‘Um, wait, er, what’s happened?’ she finally stammered.

‘We’ll need to come in and all will be explained.’

‘Ok, but I don’t know if I can let you in carrying your guns.’

The German police all carried the 9mm SIG Sauer P225, otherwise known as the P6 which carried a magazine of eight rounds. They also sported a small baton, a pair of handcuffs and a can of CS gas each.

‘Well, as it is part of our uniform and that we are required to wear it at all times when on duty, I am afraid that we cannot leave them outside. But don’t worry, we won’t draw them if we do not get attacked.’

With that, Peter walked past Petra and motioned for the others to follow, Johannes included. Petra then unlocked the first door, walked them up to the station and unlocked the next door. Klaus was waiting for the visitors as he had been able to catch a glimpse of the police wearing their moss green and beige uniforms.

‘Hello, I am Klaus Lodde, the station manager. May I ask what has brought the police to my ward?’

'Certainly, I'm Kriminaloberkommissar Schwarz and these are my colleagues. Is there a room we can all go into?'

'Yes, follow me. Petra, can you keep an eye on them in the day room. I'll let you know later what is happening.'

Petra moved to the day room to look after the patients whilst the others followed Klaus into the staff room.

'Right, we have reason to believe that a male nurse works here and looks similar to someone we are looking for. Here, do you recognize the person in this photo?' Peter asked, holding out a sheet of paper. Klaus took it and after several seconds replied 'It does have a vague resemblance to Detlef Krome, yes. He is currently outside in the yard playing basketball with some patients. Shall I go and ask him to come in?'

'Not just yet. Tell me, what is he like? Has he been acting strange the last few weeks? Is he focused at work or does he appear to be somewhere else?'

'Well,' Klaus answered, 'everyone appears to be somewhere else when you work in a place as long as we have. It's only natural. He has been coming into work looking more tired of late, but he says he has been out on the town with some mates. Maybe his way of switching off. Not as easy as one thinks working alongside some of our patients. Some of their stories would make your hair stand on end. Why are you looking for him? What is he supposed to have done?'

'All in good time sir. If you could ask him to come up, but please do not inform him that we are here, there's a good chap.'

'Ok, I'll go down and relieve him. I'll tell him he has a phone call.'

And with that, Klaus left the room, the station and the building whilst the visitors all waited in the staff room. Several minutes passed when they heard the key turning to the station door and heard footsteps walking towards them. No sooner had he walked into the room, one of the policemen who was standing behind the open door closed it, blocking any chance of escape.

'A very good morning to you, Herr Krome, my name is Kriminaloberkommissar Schwarz and I would like to ask you some questions.' Peter looked into Detlef's eyes and only saw a rabbit trapped in headlights. 'We are here to investigate the last sightings and killing of a young woman and you have been recognized as the man fitting the description.'

'Sorry, but I don't know what you are on about. Who am I supposed to have killed?' Detlef asked, finally getting some sense back into him.

'Yes, I can see the resemblance. Herr Krome, we would like you to accompany us down to the police station in Soest, where we would like to ask you a few questions.'

'Am I under arrest?'

'At this moment in time no, you are not.'

'Then I can refuse to come with you. Is that not correct?'

'Yes and no. You can refuse to assist us with our enquiries but we would then be forced to arrest you as we believe you may be holding some vital information. So, don't be a prick, grab your coat and follow us downstairs.' Peter left no room for argument. The only room that was left was the staff room, all following Peter as he headed to the exit.

As Detlef unlocked the door, Petra poked her head out of the day room and asked 'Detlef, all ok?'

'Yes, just off helping them with something or other. Be back soon.' And with that, they all headed down the stairs and out into the open and carried on to the cars. Johannes held back but was able to see Peter give him the thumbs up as he was getting into the car.

'Fuck it,' Klaus said when he went back upstairs with the patients. 'I will have to call someone in from their day off to cover. Stupid bugger, knew he was up to something.'

CHAPTER 18

'What room can we use?' Peter asked the desk Sergeant.

'Interview room two is free.' came the reply.

Peter and Suzanne escorted Detlef into the allocated room and told him to sit down on one of the four hard backed chairs available around the table that was bolted to the floor. Detlef sat down as requested and looked around the place. The walls were of a two-tone colour, the bottom half of the walls being a light brown, the upper half was some sort of dark yellow. The lighting came from a single neon tube attached to the ceiling and a tape recorder was fastened to the desk.

'Do I need a lawyer?' Detlef asked as both Peter and Suzanne sat down.

'No, as I stated earlier, you are voluntarily assisting us with some open enquiries we have. If, however, you feel the need to have a lawyer present, then just say so and we will stop the interview so that you can get some legal guidance. Is that ok?' Peter replied.

'Yes, alright.'

Suzanne turned on the tape recorder and Peter spoke clearly.

'The time is 14:05 on Saturday the 10th of September, 1988. Present in the room is myself, Kriminaloberkommissar Schwarz, my colleague Polizeiobermeister Baumgarten and Herr Detlef Krome. So Herr Krome, what can you tell us about the evening of 31.08.1988?'

'What day was that?' Detlef asked.

'That would have been a Wednesday.'

'I was probably at home watching TV with my mum. Other than that, maybe I was having a couple of drinks with some mates. I honestly can't remember.'

'Ok, let me help you remember. Does the name Anja Schmedding mean anything to you?' Peter said, looking Detlef directly in the eyes.

'Anja Schmedding, no, I don't think so. Why, should I have?'

'You were seen having a drink together in a restaurant in Soest on the night in question. Has that jogged your memory?' Detlef went quiet and Suzanne could have sworn his face took on a lighter shade of pale. 'Come on, easy question.'

'I would like to speak with my lawyer.' Detlef finally replied.

'Ok, and what is the name of your lawyer?'

'I don't have one, but I would like to speak with one.'

'Ok, we will contact one for you. Herr Krome, we are placing you under arrest. You are not obliged to say anything unless you wish to do so but what you do say may be given in evidence. Do you understand your rights?'

'Er, yes, I think so.'

'Interview terminated at 14:08.'

Detlef was escorted out of the room and placed in the hands of the duty Sergeant, whose job it was to sign in the prisoners, have them searched, photographed and fingerprinted and taken to one of the cells.

'Guilt written all over his face,' Suzanne said, 'did you see the way he changed colour to match the ceiling? Like a bloody chameleon.'

'Yeah, well, let's hope we don't start counting our chickens before they hatch.' he replied. 'Come on, let's get a brew before we call the legal eagle.'

As they headed up the stairs, Freddy was on the way down when they met halfway.

'Heard you have the suspect downstairs. Finished already?' Freddy asked.

'No, just that he clammed up, refused to answer any questions so we arrested him. Going to let him stew for a bit, let him wait before we call a lawyer, then we'll get to work.'

'Let me know when you start the questioning, I'd like to be there with you.'

Suzanne looked away but the movement was not lost on either of the detectives.

'Don't worry, love. You can still stay in the room if you want. Last thing I want to do is muscle in on your action. But if you could keep to "guarding" the door from the inside, then you may learn a trick or two.'

'Thank you, I'd appreciate the opportunity.' she replied, this time with a smile on her face.

'Right, see you later. Off outside to get a spot of fresh air, been stuck indoors all day' Freddy said, continuing down the stairs.

At the time of Detlef being led to one of the police cells, Rudolph was in the process of delivering a very important package. The package in question was a pretty girl in her late teens or early twenties and needed to get from the train station to her boyfriend's house pretty fast. She offered to pay him more fare if he put his foot down. When she had got in the car, he thought to himself that he wouldn't mind pulling her knickers down.

So, driving along the B1 heading towards the village called Horn, Rudolph ignored all speed limits hoping to get a nice glimpse of her legs when she got out of the car. Suddenly, he heard the sound of sirens and when he looked in his rear view mirror, he also saw the blue lights flashing on top of a police car. He automatically took his foot off the accelerator and shifted down a gear to slow the car down without using his breaks. This was an old trick so that the police would not see him suddenly breaking. When the police passed him by, he saw the "Follow" sign lit up in the back window and proceeded to slow the taxi down and pull up behind the police car that had stopped on the hard shoulder. The policeman in the passenger side got out and walked over to Rudolph's window.

'Good afternoon. Do you know why we have stopped you?' asked Trilling.

'Er, no. Did I not stop at the last stop sign?' Rudolph bluffed.

'No sir, we have stopped you for impersonating Niki Lauda. Do you know what speed you were driving back there?'

'Sorry constable, I wasn't paying attention. I'll be more careful from now on.'

'Glad to hear it. However, I'm going to need to see your ID and drivers license.' Trilling informed him, holding out his hand.

'Is that really necessary?' he asked. 'I mean, I've said I'm sorry.'

'Simple procedure, sir. Just need your details and we can all be on our way.'

'Can you please give the policeman want he wants,' his passenger complained, 'I'm in a rush and don't want to sit in here all afternoon.'

'Ok Fraulein, please let me deal with this.' Trilling said.

Rudolph lent across his passenger and his hand brushed the top of her bare leg as he was reaching to open the glove compartment where he kept his wallet and money. She gave out a shriek and told him to keep his pervert hands to himself. He straightened up and the exertion of bending down combined with the adrenaline of touching such a beautiful girl made him flush and sweat popped up on his brow and upper lip.

He reached inside, all fingers and thumbs and retrieved his driver's license and ID card and handed these to the constable.

Trilling looked first at the drivers license and then at the ID card. 'Sir, could you please confirm your name and date of birth.'

'Rudolph Mertens, 4th June 1943.'

'I am pleased to confirm that they are the details displayed on your driver's license. However, the details you have verbally provided do not match those written on the ID card. Sir, please step out of your vehicle and keep your hands where I can see them.' Trilling commanded loudly so that his colleague would hear and quickly came over to assist.

'What do you mean?' Rudolph enquired, 'my details are the same on both documents.'

'Then how do you explain yourself being in the possession of an ID card from a dead girl?' Trilling asked.

That was when the penny dropped and the ground opened up underneath Rudolph. He realized he had given over the wrong ID card. He knew he should have thrown it away or at least left it at home. It was his passengers fault. If she had only sat in the back and not worn a short skirt, then he would have been in control and none of this would have happened. Slowly, not out of choice but because he was not able to do it any faster even if he had wanted, he got out from behind the wheel and was forced to turn around. His hands were cuffed behind his back and Trilling radioed the station to update them on what had just happened. They were told to stay at the scene and another crew would come by to assist and another taxi would be sent to take the passenger to where she needed to be.

Some ten minutes later, Trilling and co were joined by another unit who took over possession of the taxi and passenger whilst the prisoner was squeezed and pushed into the back of Trilling's police car.

'You have got to be fucking joking me,' Freddy said joyfully when he was called down to the front desk, 'two suspects in the space of an afternoon. Hopefully we can have this wrapped up by teatime.'

'I wouldn't bet my pension on it,' the duty sergeant said.

'Oh thee of little faith, just wait until I have finished with both of them. Could you please get in touch with Erster Kriminalhauptkommisar Gerling for me and update him as to the situation we have downstairs in the cells.'

'Will do it right away, sir.'

'So, Trilling, looks like lady luck was on your side today. That's how many of the most wanted are often caught. Routine stop for one thing or another and Bob's your uncle, we nick them for something else outstanding. Good bit of work, glad you were observant.'

'Thanks sir, cannot see him being the murderer myself looking at the size of him, but how else would he have Anja's ID card?'

'That is the million dollar question and one I am planning on finding out. Do you want to sit in on the questioning with myself?' Freddy asked.

'Wouldn't mind if I did, sir. Thank you sir.'

'No worries, just keep your mouth shut and watch. Don't wander off too far, I'll get you when we start'

Freddy bounced back up the stairs two at a time, humming a tune he had heard earlier on the radio before he had been summoned downstairs.

'Hi Freddy, sounds like you have been kept busy and now may have some rewards to reap.' Sven punched his friend and colleague lightly on the shoulder. 'What do you reckon on our chances that one of them killed our girls?'

'That I cannot say, but Krome clammed up as soon as Anja's name was mentioned and the big fucker we questioned before has her ID card. How they both have gotten to be in contact with her time will only tell.'

'Yes, but don't forget, time is not on our side. Unless we have some real evidence, we can only hold them up till midnight tomorrow where we will have to let them go. Unless the prosecutor's office provides us with a forty eight hour extension.'

'So, we have about thirty three hours in which to question them. Shall we do bad cop, bad cop routine, or do you want one of us to be good?' Freddy asked.

'Let's see how we are getting on. Let's tag team between both interviews, keep up the pressure. You start with fat boy, I'll deal with Krome and we'll swap in one hour or so and keep doing this so they have no clue who they told what to.'

'Sounds like a plan. Just hope it works.'

'Alright, let's start interviewing bang on four.'

'Ok, please state your name and date of birth for the tape.' Sven commanded.

'I am Detlef Krome, born 29.05.1954.'

'And also present in the room are myself, Erster Kriminalhauptkommisar Gerling, Polizeiobermeister Trilling and Herr Buchwald, the lawyer appointed by the courts to assist the suspect.

'Now then, what can you tell me about Anja Schmedding? And before you start giving us the story that you didn't know her, just be informed that we have evidence linking you to her.'

Detlef looked over at his appointed lawyer and received a nod. 'Ok, yes, I do know her.'

'Did know her, past tense, she's been murdered.' Sven butt in.

'Well, I didn't kill her, we just went out for a drink is all.'

'Alright,' Sven interjected, 'let's start at the beginning. How long have you known her?'

‘I met her a few weeks ago. I took my mum in to hospital to get her ingrown toenail looked at as it was causing her jip and that is where we met. She was a trainee nurse and assisted the doctor with the procedure. I spoke to her after we had finished and asked her if she would like to go out for a drink as I wanted to say thank you for being kind and gentle to my mum.’

‘And how many times did you go out with her?’

‘Only two times. The first time she was a bit shy, probably because of our age difference, but the second time we went out, she wasn’t paying much attention and so we had a row and she left.’

‘Ok, where did you take her the first time?’ Sven asked.

‘Don’t remember the name, I met her outside the nursing accommodation where she lives and we just walked into the town centre and she steered me into a bar. Somewhere near the market square.’

‘And apart from appearing shy, what did you talk about?’

‘Mostly I asked her questions about her family life, she told me her dad was a dentist and that she wanted to qualify as a nurse and then maybe go to university to become a doctor herself. I told her I was a nurse and we talked shop most of the evening. You know, war stories of what we have experienced on the wards.’

‘How long were you out with her that first evening?

‘She said she had a big day the next day and couldn’t stay out too long, so I made sure she was back before midnight.’

‘I see,’ Sven said, ‘did she offer you to go back to her room?’

‘No.’

‘What about a goodnight kiss?’

‘Again, no.’

‘And how did you feel when she did not offer anything in return for you taking her out for the evening?’

‘We just went out for a drink. Nothing more and nothing less.’

‘Did you want the evening to end differently? Would you have gone back to her room if she had asked you to?’

‘Of course I would have, stands to reason. She was good looking with a nice body. Anybody would have jumped at the opportunity if she offered. Even you would have.’

‘Please refrain from making general assumptions and stick to answering my questions. Now, how did you plan to meet up the second time?’

‘As she was about to go inside, I asked her if she would like to go clubbing and she said she’d think about it. She said we should meet at the train station as she would be coming from visiting her family and we could then decide on what we would do. So we met and we went to the restaurant in town, you know, the old one.’

‘Im Wilden Mann, yes?’ Sven said.

‚Yes, that’s it. So we went in and ordered a couple of drinks. I was asking her about her day but she wasn’t really listening to me. She said that since we last met, she had met someone else and was planning to meet up with him that night. She said that she had to tell me to my face as it was not nice just not to show up. I then started asking who she was meeting but she wouldn’t say. We argued, she got up and left. That’s all.’

‘And you never saw her again?’

‘No.’

‘Thank you, interview suspended at 16:15.’

Sven got up and informed Detlef he needed to stay in the room as he would need to answer more questions after a quick break.

At the same time, Freddy was in full flow with Rudolph. Sitting next to himself was Peter with Suzanne standing at the door and another appointed lawyer was sitting next to Rudolph.

‘So, please tell me again how you came into having possession of the ID card’

‘As I’ve said before, I was cleaning out my taxi when I saw it on the floor behind one of the seats.’

‘Which seat? Behind the driver’s seat or the passenger seat?’
‘I can’t remember. Driver’s seat I think.’

‘And it was just lying there in the open?’

‘I had to bend down a bit to get it.’ Rudolph added. ‘I know I should have handed it in, that was my intention, honest. I put it in my wallet for safe keeping and then just forgot about it. It’s an easy mistake to make.’

'Ok, so just supposing I was to believe you. Can you remember her ever getting into your taxi?'

'Yes, I have already told your lot the last time I was here. Picked her up from Herzfeld and dropped her off at the train station in Soest.'

'Did you see her drop her ID when she got out?'

'No. I found it when I was cleaning my taxi and put it in my wallet. I was going to hand it in to the authorities but forgot all about it.'

'Interview suspended at 16:44' Freddy left the room.

'So, what have you got so far?' Sven asked Freddy.

'The creep is sticking to his story in that he found the ID card in the back of his taxi when he was cleaning it out and just forgot he picked it up and put it in her wallet.'

'Do you believe him?'

'It's hard to say. It is plausible that what he is saying is the truth. But something just doesn't feel right. I've asked for any records he might have to be pulled, so just waiting for any results to come up. How did you get on?' Freddy asked.

'Well,' said Sven, 'I think Krome may be hiding something. At the beginning he was being evasive, but then we learnt that they had had an argument when she told him that she was dating someone else. Either that is made up or we have someone else in the frame. Let's swap and you go in to Krome and nail him on the new boyfriend, I'll get fat boy to sweat some pounds off by tying him up with questions just to see what I can get out of him. Meet you within the hour when we can collaborate again.'

And after this brief interlude in the questioning, both detectives went and interviewed each other's witness.

After the introductions were made for the benefit of the tape, Freddy started the questioning from the beginning, checking on the notes that he had been given as to what was asked before and what answers had been given.

‘So you say that you had only met her twice socially and that the second time she had informed you she was seeing someone else. Have I understood that correctly?’ he asked.

‘Yes.’

‘And at no point after she left the restaurant did you ever see her again. Correct?’

After a slight hesitation, one almost too slight to notice, Detlef replied ‘Correct.’

Freddy ignored what he had noticed and put this little hesitancy in a box to be opened up and used later.

‘How did it feel to be dating such a beautiful young girl?’

‘What do you mean?’

‘Well, let’s face it, you’re no spring chicken yourself, you must have felt something when others saw you two together, no?’

‘Not really, we were just out for a drink.’

‘Yes, but you were having illusions that you would be a couple. Boyfriend and girlfriend stuff. Be invited to meet the parents, maybe get engaged before you got much older and marry her as soon as possible before you lost her to someone nearer her age.’

‘No, it wasn’t like that. I just fancied her is all.’

‘Of course you fancied her. Enough to throw a wobbly when she told you she was shagging someone else. That must have really hurt seeing that you did not have any opportunity in getting your own end away. What did you do? Follow her and decided that if you couldn’t have her then no one could? Did you follow her after she left the restaurant? Had she told you where she was going?’

‘No, it’s all wrong what you’re saying. Yes, it gave me a sense of pride to be seen with her next to me. No, I had had no thoughts of marriage or engagement. Yes, it had crossed my mind about what her parents would say if we were to go out with each other, but only because of the age difference. And no, she never told me where she was going when she left me sitting there looking like a prick.’

‘How did that make you feel? Did the other punters hear your conversation? Did you feel embarrassed? Or did you sit there and slowly let the rage build up inside you to such an extent you went out and slit her throat in cold blood?’ Freddy’s voice got louder with each question until he nearly shouted out the last one.

'I didn't kill her, it must have been the British soldier.' he stammered.

'What British soldier?'

'Her new boyfriend. She told me she was seeing a squaddie.'
'So why have you not mentioned this in the past? Why have you omitted to hold back this piece of information from us?'

Detlef sat quiet for several seconds, chin resting on his chest, eyes closed.

'Because I was embarrassed in that she would prefer to be with a foreigner rather than with me.' he answered finally.

'But surely you can see that the age difference would have been an issue sooner or later?' Freddy asked.

'Yes, but not until we had been out together a few more times. We had only been out once for a drink together, she did not give us a chance.'

'But according to your earlier answer, she went out with you the first time when you asked her because you wanted to say thank you for her being kind and caring towards your mother. Maybe you read something else into your "relationship", maybe she only wanted a social drink out of politeness.'

'Then why did she agree to another date?'

'You call it a date, maybe she didn't. Maybe she went back to her dormitory and told all the girls that she had been out with someone nearly as old as her father, that you were punching above your weight and that she was playing you along out of boredom? Who knows? I bloody well don't. And I'll tell you what else I don't know. I don't know a bloody thing about any British soldier up to this point. Now, let's continue from there shall we?'

'Ok, Herr Mertens, let me reiterate what you have said so far. You remember Frau Schmedding getting into our taxi and taking her to the train station. You did not see her drop her ID card but that you found this later when cleaning up sometime later. Is that correct?'

'Yes.'

'And everything you have told me is the truth, the whole truth and nothing but the truth?'

'Yes.'

'Well, going back through my notes, you informed my colleague that you found the ID card behind your seat, the driver's seat. But you have adamantly informed me that you found it lying underneath the passenger seat. Surely you would remember what seat you found it under? If you are not sure about where you found this item, maybe you are also not that sure if you ever saw her before? Maybe you had forgotten that she was indeed a paying passenger and that when you dropped her off at her destination, you cold bloodedly slit her throat and left her to bleed to death. Is that not what really happened?'

'No, no. How can you say such a thing? Anyone who knows me would vouch for me that I have never hurt anyone, that I am a gentle giant. Why would I kill an innocent young girl?'

'Seeing that I am the one asking the questions, you answer me'

'I have always been an honest citizen, never in any trouble. I keep to myself. Someone left it or dropped it in my taxi. That is all I know.'

'An honest citizen. Really? Then how comes you buried your mother in a shallow grave and did not inform the authorities?'

Rudolph was taken by surprise. He was being asked about an ID card found in his possession when all of a sudden his past was being raked up.

'Did you forget to tell the authorities that she had passed away? Or did you kill her yourself and buried the body? Was your mother your first victim? How many more have there been to date?'

'No, I did not kill my mother. Why would I? I loved her and she loved me. We only had each other and when she died I went into shock. I didn't know what I was doing and when I did start to understand, it was too late to back track. But I have paid my price, served my time in prison for that and I regret my actions every single day. Apart from that one mistake, I have been an exemplary citizen of the Federal Republic of Germany'

'So, apart from that one lapse of concentration, you have never had any violent urges? Never planned or dreamt of murdering someone?'

'No, never.'

'Interview suspended at 17:56.'

CHAPTER 19

11.09.1988

'Alright, who sang "Little Willy"? This is worth three points.''

'What year was it?'

'1972.' Taff replied.

'I was only three. Give us a tip.'

'Alright, er, it's what many parents call their babies.'

'Fucking hell, what's that for a tip? Sarah, Cindy, Michael, depends what sex it is.'

'No, I don't mean their actual names you thick sod, I mean in general.'

After a few seconds of contemplation Billy was still baffled. 'Nope, that tip is shit. Give me another one.'

'Ok, this is then now only worth two points. What does a paedophile use to entice his victims?'

'Pictures of puppy's. Got it, *Donny Osmond* with Puppy Love.'

'And where does "Little Willy come into it?' Taff asked.

'Maybe he's got a one inch wonder.'

'Nope, here's your final clue for one point, opposite of sour.'

'*Sweet.*'

'Correct. So, you now have seventeen points to my twenty two.'

'So, explain me your clues.' Billy said.

'Easy. Every parent calls their babies "sweet", and a kiddie fiddler uses "sweets" to get them in the car.'

'You've got a weird way of thinking. Ok, my turn. Ready?'

'I was born ready.'

'Ok, who sang "A Love Bizarre"?'

'Hum it for us.'

'Nope, that would give it away. Ok, first tip. It's what the Aussies call all their women.'

'Sheila.'

'Yes, but I need the full name of the artist.'

'Alright, let me think. *Ready for the World* sang "Oh Sheila". The only other one I know is *Sheila B Devotion.*'

'No. Last clue, she toured with *Prince* on his "Purple Rain" tour.

'Sheila E,' Taff instantaneously replied. 'Am I good or what?'

'Heads up, car's coming.'

Taff adjusted his camouflage smock and beret and went and stood by the main gate. If it was a soldier returning back to camp, then he would open up one side of the double gates to allow access after checking the identification. If it was a taxi, then he would open up the smaller gate that allowed foot passengers to enter. In the sangar, Billy stood with his rifle pointing towards the incoming vehicle, which he could follow with the headlights coming ever closer. The job that Billy had was to protect his colleague on "gate duty" and be ready for any sign of attack. The sangar itself was of brick construction and had three large slits starting at chest height so that he was not only protected, but was also able to see down the road in both directions and also see straight across the road where the fields were. Sandbags were set up on all three ledges to give comfort for when a soldier needed to take aim.

The car slowed and indicated to turn left into the camp, so Taff knew it would be someone returning from a night out dancing or coming back from the well known brothel in Dortmund. When the car came to a stop, Taff opened the main gate slightly and slipped through and approached the driver's window.

'Hi Jock, where have you been?' Taff asked the driver.

'Hi mate, been clubbing in Salzkotten in *The Zoo*. Not a bad night out.'

'Get off with anyone?'

'No, just went and had a good time. Grant here got lucky again, though.'

'Lucky he calls it. You've either got it or you ain't. It just happens to be that I've got it and you ain't.' replied the passenger. 'Not many guys can dance like me and that is what the ladies like. Not some bloke propping up the bar all night. They go out to dance and that is what I give them.'

'Come on Taff, let us in will you. I'm dying for a piss.'

'Yeah, alright.'

Taff opened the right hand gate and closed it as soon as the car had driven through. Jock parked the car outside the guardroom and jumped out to sign himself and Grant back in.

'Oi, Billy,' Grant shouted from the open car window, 'don't see you that often on guard duty. What's happened?'

'Nobody was willing to jump in for me. I offered up to fifty Deutsch Marks but no takers. Oh well, first guard duty for about half a year. Could be worse, I could be stuck out here with some dipstick or other. At least Taff is up for a bit of conversation to kill time.'

'Time isn't the only thing I've killed,' Taff replied, 'Killed him on general knowledge, killed him on geography and just killed him on music.'

'Well, see you boys tomorrow,' Jock said, getting back into his car, 'make sure Billy doesn't fall asleep in there.'

'Fuck you.' Billy answered back.

The approach, arrival and the departing of Jock and Grant had killed another five minutes of their guard duty. Anything that disturbed the boredom of standing outside was welcomed.

A typical weekend guard duty started on Saturday or Sunday morning at 09:00 and lasted twenty four hours. The guard duty involved twelve people in total. Eight were the soldiers on gate and Sanger duty, two JNCOs were in charge of the guard room itself and there was a duty sergeant and also a duty officer. The duty officer was seen at the beginning of the guard shift and normally went and spent the rest of the time in the officer's mess and the duty sergeant came down a few times during the day, the early evening and just before shift hand over in the morning. The Junior Non-Commissioned Officer was either a full Corporal or a Lance Corporal. These two shared and took it in turns to sit at the guardroom desk and made sure the "stag roster" was adhered to and that all comings and goings in and out of camp were correctly logged. The "stag roster" was for the two soldiers whose duty it was to stand outside for two hours at a time. What normally happened is that two would go out to start their stag, one going into the Sanger and the other standing near the gate and after one hour they would change between themselves. Then after their two hour stag, they would be replaced by another two, allowing them to go back inside, maybe have a brew or get their heads down to sleep. So, they would only stand outside for a total of six hours in a twenty four hour shift. Not too bad as long as it wasn't cold or raining. That was when the time dragged on.

'How much longer left?' Taff asked.

'Fifteen more minutes, then we've done all our stags. Then inside, quick wee and then beddy-byes.'

Billy went quiet as he waited to be relieved. It wasn't too bad having to do guard duty on the weekend, but his next one was scheduled for the thirtieth. This one he would definitely have to give up or pay someone to do it, whatever the cost. After all, he had been planning something special for this date.

'My client is asking how much longer you are going to hold him here. He has answered all your questions time after time and it is becoming repetitive.'

'We are able to hold him until midnight tonight if we so please. We can just have him sitting there if we want. But as you know, we are looking for a killer responsible for two horrific murders and as your client fits the bill, we will be keeping him here until midnight. If we receive more damning evidence, then we will apply for an extension for questioning. You know the ropes, so go along and brief your client to give us everything we need so that we can all go home, yourself included.' Sven smiled at the young lawyer, knowing full well that it was not only the prisoner who was feeling the long hours of questioning.

Now, at nearly 06:00 on a Sunday morning, all Sven wanted to do was find a bed somewhere and bury his head under a pillow. They still had eighteen hours in which to extract any other clues they could find, but with the last interview bringing nothing new to light, it seemed that they might have to release both suspects without further charge. But he wanted one last try at Krome.

Sven entered the interrogation room where Detlef sat with his head resting on his arms, his lawyer sitting with his head tilted back and mouth open, eyes closed. Suzanne had been sent home earlier but Peter was still present and had the appearance that he had only just started.

After the formal preliminary introductions were taken care of, the two detectives went back to work.

'So, let's go over this again.' Sven said.

'How many more times do I have to repeat myself?' Deltef asked.

'Until we are satisfied that we have all the facts.' Peter added.

'So, Anja told you she was dating a British soldier but did not tell you what his name is or where he is based. Correct? Then you tell us that she left you sitting there on your own and that when you finished your drink, you paid the waitress and left. Correct? At this time you were not drunk. Correct? When you left the restaurant, you decided on going on a bender as you wanted to drown your sorrows. Correct? You admittedly state you went from pub to pub looking for some quote "action" unquote and on finding none, you decided to go home. Correct? But on the way to the taxi rank, you state that you saw Anja coming out of *Old Germany* in the arms of a young soldier. Correct?' It was at this last question where Sven stopped and waited for an answer.

'Yes, I've told you. I was walking along the road and she came out with him on her arm. I don't think she saw me as I kept my head down. All I know is that the last time I saw her, she was healthy and breathing.'

'And would you be able to pick out the soldier in a line up or by looking through photographs?' Peter asked.

'They all look the fucking same to me, short hair and pale skin.'

'And you are positive that you have never seen this soldier before or after the date in question?'

'As I've stated for about the fortieth time, no.'

'Ok, Herr Krome, thank you for your cooperation. Interview ended at 06:25 on 11.09.1988.'

'Does that mean I am free to go?'

'No, it means you will be taken back to the cell where you might get a couple of hours sleep. We will be following up on the information you have provided and may need to speak with you later. Until then, I wish you happy dreams.'

Sven and Peter left the room, allowing the duty sergeant to take over and lead his prisoner back downstairs.

Both Sven and Peter walked up the stairs to the office they were all sharing and were pleased to see Freddy waiting.

'Find out anything new?' Sven asked.

'Nope, Mertens is sticking to his story of only finding it. Tried again to wobble him with his mother's death but he won't budge. I think we will have to release him. What about Krome?'

'So far all we have concentrated on is the death of Anja. Let's wake them up at 10:00 and start grilling them on what they were doing on Thursday evening when Nicole was killed. But I also want to look into this British soldier. We need to find out which barracks he is from, who he is and what his hunting grounds are.'

'That's going to be a bit more difficult,' Bernie Backhaus interjected as he walked into the office. 'We have several British camps around here. First we have San Sebastian, then we have Salamanca and then we have the camp in Werl. That is where the Scots are based. They come into Soest as it has a better night life here than in Werl. So, how are we going to interview and photograph all soldiers?'

'Well, firstly we'll have to contact the RMPs as we will need their assistance. Then if the Royal Military Police are able to help, finding the soldier will be like looking for a needle in a haystack.' Sven rubbed the stubble on his chin and shook his head. 'Seems like an impossible task, but let's get on with it and see what we can do. Bernie, can I leave the liaison with the RMPs with you?'

'Yes sure. I'll keep you updated as to what I can find out.'

'Right, wake me up at 09:45, I need a couple of hour's kip before I fall down. I'll be in cell number six. Already spoke to the duty sergeant to reserve it for me.' Sven said grinning as he walked out of the office and down the stairs.

At exactly 14:00, Rudolph was released from police custody and told to be available for further questioning if the police needed to ask him something further at a later date. At 14:20, Detlef was told the same and also released.

'Alright, I want everyone in my office by 16:00. I don't care if they are sleeping or having a wank in the toilets, 16:00.' Sven said.

After several phone calls and radio messages, the whole team were assembled in Sven's office, some sitting on chairs, others perched on one of the desks and several left standing.

'Ok, this is where we are currently at. Both Krome and Mertens have been released as we have nothing we can pin on them for either murder. Although Mertens had the ID card from Anja in his possession, his story about finding it appears to be true. He stated that on the night of the murder of Nicole, he was working and unless he is Superman, it would be hard to be in two places at once. We checked the taxi central and they confirmed he was on a pick up at the time of her murder.

'As for Krome, he may have killed Anja in a jealous rage but again, without any evidence, we will not be able to pin this on him. As for his alibi for the 8th, he was at home watching TV. This has been corroborated by his mother, so again we are at stage one.'

'I have some information regarding Catwoman,' Dennis interjected, 'I had her come in today to follow up on the shout she heard. This is what she has stated,' he said, reading from a sheet of paper in his hands, 'and I quote "I was asleep in my bed when all of a sudden I was woken by a man shouting loudly. He shouted something like "Mind what you are doing you stupid fucker. That nearly hit me on the head. If you can't hold it, fuck off and get me someone who can." I stayed in bed trying to listen if I could hear any more but after about five minutes the lights were turned on outside and I heard nothing more until you came ringing my bell." unquote.'

'So who was shouting?' Freddy asked.

'When speaking to the technicians, apparently one of the guys setting up the Arc lights could not hold on to one whilst it was being raised and it nearly hit his colleague on the head when it toppled over. It was this colleague who was heard to shout the profanities, not our murderer. So, as like you, no new clues I'm afraid.'

'Bugger it. Cheers Dennis. Anything else new come in that may help us with either murder?' Sven asked the room.

Everyone mumbled that no new leads were apparent and that they would start looking closely regarding the British military personnel in the outlying areas.

'Alright, there's nothing else we can do today. Let's all fuck off home to our nearest and dearest and be back here tomorrow morning for 08:00 sharp.'

CHAPTER 20

12.09.1988

On Monday morning, the Stattsanwaltschaft in Arnsberg informed the Institute für Rechtsmedizin that as all the evidence was documented and nothing more was needed, the body of Anja Schmedding was being released back to the family for burial. The murder squad were also informed as were the police in Soest.

The Schmedding family were now able to finally bury their beloved daughter and greave like any other family would at times like this. They had already contacted a funeral parlour and now just called to set a date, which was set for Friday, the 16th September 1988. This was to be a private affair, her body being laid to rest in the Herzfeld cemetery which was situated to the front of the primary school.

At 08:00, Sven opened up the meeting by informing everyone on the case that leads needed to be either followed up or new avenues opened.

'What we need to do is ask again any friend or colleague of Anja if they know of her being friends with any British soldier. We also need to have her photograph handed around to all the pubs and clubs to see if anyone remembers seeing her with a squaddie. Maybe we will get lucky, but we won't know if we don't try. Then I want all known associates of Nicole to be interviewed again and more door to door at both murder locations. And if that isn't enough straws to grasp, we then need to find if there is a link between both victims. Did they know each other? Did they share the same interests or friends? Questions anyone?'

'With the release of the nurse and the taxi driver, are we again back to square one?' Suzanne Baumgarten asked.

'Unfortunately, yes. All those hours of hard work you have all put into finding those two individuals may appear to be wasted, but rest assured, with correct police procedures, we will find the killer or killers.'

'What about the soldier? How we find out where he is based?' Trilling enquired.

'That will be for Polizeihauptkommissar Backhaus to contact the RMPs and see if we can get some help from them. The rest of us will just need to go over everything that we have so far and maybe find another route of identifying the killer. Is there anything else? If not, let's all jump to it and keep me informed of any updates or new leads.'

Everybody exited the room apart from Freddy, Dennis and Peter.

'Ok boys, looks like we might have a longer stay in Soest than what we originally planned. I'm driving back to Dortmund tonight to pack a bag and get some digs here in Soest. This driving back and forth is killing me. Anyone want to do the same?'

All three of them agreed and set a time when they would meet up with Sven so that they could all travel together.

'Ah, Erster KriminalHauptkommissar Gerling, I'm Erster PolizeiHauptkommissar Ulrich Schneider. I'm just back from holiday. Bernie has got me up to speed on the case. Is there anything you need to tell me or need from me?'

'Glad to meet you at last,' Sven said, 'no, we have everything under control and everything is going through Bernie whenever we need something. I must say, our intervention here has been widely accepted and all help as much as they can.'

'I'm glad to hear it. So, if you have nothing else, I'd better get back to my office and see if I can get through my in tray before it all topples onto the floor.' And with that, he turned and went along the corridor to the staff room. After about half a minute, they all heard him complaining loudly that since when did black coffee look and smell liked chicken soup.

'113 Company RMP, Captain Scott speaking.'

'Good morning,' Bernie said in his best English, 'Polizeihauptkommissar Backhaus from the German police in Soest. We have a situation where we might need your assistance.'

'Good morning to you. And how may I be of assistance?'

'Two ladies have been murdered here over the last two weeks and we have been led to believe that one of the victims was last seen alive in the presence of a British soldier. We would like to interview this soldier.'

'That shouldn't be an issue, just give me his name and I will see that he is picked up immediately and brought to your station under RMP supervision.'

'Ah, that is where we are stuck,' Bernie confessed, 'we do not have a name. The only description we have to go on is he has short hair and is pale in complexion.'

'That's not a problem, we'll get the whole of the British army on parade and check who has short hair and not tanned and see how many we have who fit that description.'

'How long would that take?'

'Ever heard of English humour? Of course it will not be possible. You'll have to provide us with a better description than that seeing we all have close cut hair. What we can do is narrow the field down. If you provide the dates, we can see who signed out of each barracks and if they returned after the murders. But, that will only help with the single soldiers. We would have no record of the married soldiers who do not live in the barracks. The majority of these live in Soest itself or in several smaller villages around the area.'

'Quite, I understand. But if by eliminating most soldiers, that would give us at least some help. Then we would only need to concentrate on those who were supposedly in the area on the nights in question.'

'Yes, that would work. Ok, what dates are you looking at?' Captain Scott asked.

'The first victim was murdered in the early hours of 31st August and the second was killed on the night of 8th September.'

'Ok, I'll contact all of the barracks around the area and I'll fax you the total of who went out from which camp on the nights in question. To keep the list shorter, I'll see if any name left camp on both of the evenings to narrow it down somewhat.'

'That would be a great help. Thank you so much Captain Scott for your assistance.'

'I'll be in touch.' And with that, the line went dead.

'And why would they keep you in overnight if you hadn't done anything?'

'I was helping them with their enquiries.' Detlef told his mum.

'Do you think I'm stupid?' she asked. 'They arrested you at work. Klaus told me. And when I called the station and asked to speak with you, I was told that it was not a good time and to see what happens over the weekend.'

'Look, I didn't do anything, they thought I was someone else and once I proved who I was, I was let out.'

'Rubbish. Do you think I was born yesterday? Of course they knew who you were. They arrested you at work. That just goes to prove that you are not telling me the truth. And then yesterday, I had the police knocking on my door asking where you had been on the night of the 8th, I told them you was here watching TV with me. But you weren't. You were out again God knows where. So, what have you been up to? So help me God I'll give you a good beating if you don't tell me what you have done. I don't care how big you are, you'll be sorry when I've finished with you.'

'Honest mum, I didn't do anything. I was out with a girl and she left me and went out with a Brit and then she was found murdered. Because they knew I was with her at the beginning, they were just asking questions about him.'

'And what were you doing on the 8th? Don't try to get out of answering that.'

'I just went to Lippstadt with a couple of mates for a few drinks. You don't really think I could murder anyone do you?'

'Who knows what goes on inside your head? Locked up with all those lunatics for eight or ten hours a day. Bound to drive you crazy and give you strange ideas.' she replied.

'Look, I need to get to work. It's embarrassing enough how I left the place on Saturday, now going back there and being late doesn't help. Look, we'll talk about it tonight over dinner. Why don't you cook some liver and bacon, you know it's your favourite. I'll buy us a nice bottle of wine to go with it. Ok?'

'If I find you've lied to me, just remember my words.'

Detlef kissed his mum on the forehead and was out of the door before she had a chance of continuing the conversation that had started the evening before.

Billy walked along the road that led from the cookhouse to the training wing. He opened the door and went inside, removing his beret as he entered.

'Hi, Gordon, is SSgt Bones about?'

'Yes, he's in his office. Want me to get him for you?' Signalman Gordon Bennett asked. His father was either drunk when naming the baby or he had a funny sense of humour.

'Can I go in? I need to ask him something.'

'Staff, Signalman Jennings is here to see you. Can he come in?' Gordon shouted.

'Yes, send him in.' came the reply.

'Cheers mate.' Billy said and walked around the counter and headed through a door that led down a small corridor.

'Ah, Jennings, and what do I owe the pleasure of your visit?' SSgt Bones asked. He was sitting behind his desk, surrounded by survival catalogues, climbing ropes and a canoe paddle.

'Good morning Staff, I was just wondering if there were any more survival courses going. I really enjoyed the last one and I learnt such a lot.'

'Glad to hear it. I don't have anything planned but I am sure I can ask for some volunteers and maybe we could go out over the weekend. Leave after duties on Friday and get back here for Sunday evening. Would you be up for sacrificing your weekend?'

'Yes, Staff. I could ask around who would like to go. How many can come?'

'If we keep it small, all fit in one vehicle, then it is easier to learn that way. Just find another three and I'll square it with the transport section. What would you like to learn?'

'Well, the way you killed that wild boar and cut it up. Maybe we could do some hunting and you could show us how to skin and gut other animals?'

'Ok, then I'll wait for you to get back to me with final numbers, no later than Wednesday before 17:00 hours.'

'Yes, Staff, thank you Staff.'

And with that, Billy walked out of the training wing and contemplated who he could ask to go with him.

'Listen Herr Mertens, you were not available for work on Saturday evening and you did not come to work at all yesterday. Now you are telling me that you will not be working today either. What is wrong with you? Are you ill or something? Or are you in the shit with the police? Did you think I would not find out? Of course I would. The bloody police called me on Saturday and informed me that your car would be in the police compound and would not be released until you were. They then came by my office and asked me all sorts of questions about you. Tell me honestly, what the fuck is going on?'

'Nothing, boss, honestly. I found an ID card in my taxi and forgot to hand it in. Just happens to be the one from the dead girl killed last month. So, after answering all their questions, they could see I was innocent and they let me go without any charge.'

'So why do you need today off work?'

'Well, my nerves are all shot to pot and I need to calm down. What with my heart and all. I'll be back tomorrow as if nothing had ever happened.'

'Ok, don't mess me around again, do you hear? If all the cabs were off the road, nobody would be earning any money. See you tomorrow and be prepared to do a longer shift to make up some lost time. Do you hear?'

'Yes, boss. Thanks.' Rudolph hung the phone up and slowly went back to his bed. He lay back down and started looking through the magazine he had collected the night before. Amazing what one could purchase if the need was there.

‘Hey, Detlef, what the fuck happened to you?’ Gary asked when Detlef was alone. ‘I missed all the fun. I was still out playing basketball when you were taken out. What did you do for them to come to your place of work? It must be something serious.’

‘A case of mistaken identity,’ Detlef answered, ‘all is sweet now, though.’

‘And I thought you’d be living in the room next to mine.’ Gary said, smiling.

‘And why would I need to be locked up here for?’

‘Just remember, if you did do anything bad and got caught, where would you prefer, here or a normal prison?’

‘Obviously in a place like this,’ Detlef replied, ‘but it isn’t as easy as that.’

‘Of course it is, just blame it on memory loss or blame your childhood. Say your mum used to beat you as a kid and you have a complex. That will have them thinking you’re a bit loony. I reckon half of this lot knew what they were doing when they committed their crime. They also knew how to play the system. Nice cushy number this. Bet I wouldn’t get any newspapers from England in prison. Plus I’d be the number one target for getting shagged up the arse, me being the only Brit.’

‘Yeah, well, I didn’t do anything and I don’t plan on being sent to either a prison or here.’

‘Whatever. Who’s escorting us to the group therapy today?’

‘I am,’ Detlef said, ‘just have to get the others together. Wonder what stories I’ll hear today.’

CHAPTER 21

14.09.1988

Betty Feldmaus had spent an extended weekend in London. She had travelled over from Düsseldorf to Gatwick airport on Saturday afternoon. She then collected her suitcase from the carrousel and headed towards the train station where she boarded a train that took her all the way to Victoria station via East Croydon and Clapham Junction. After an expensive taxi ride that took her past Buckingham Palace, Covent Garden and Fleet Street, she was dropped off outside the YMCA in the Barbican.

After registering and collecting her room key, she went upstairs, unpacked the clothes from her suitcase and took a quick shower. She then proceeded on blow drying her hair, painted her nails and then meticulously put her makeup on before dressing.

She walked out of the hostel wearing a blue and black skirt with matching jacket, a black roll neck sweater and a pair of black high heels. She carried a small bag that contained some makeup, a small hairbrush, a compact mirror, her purse, a packet of peppermints and some tissues. She walked down the road and around the corner and arrived at the Barbican Centre where she had a ticket to see the London Symphony Orchestra, something that she had wanted to hear for years.

After the concert finished, she walked around the lobby and picked up the many leaflets that were there for the taking, advertising boat trips along the river Thames, a tour of the Tower of London, many museums and other activities. She put these in her bag and headed out and sat in a pub near her hostel where she ordered a meat pie with chips and slowly drank a pint of Guinness. After she had finished, she walked back to her room, undressed, went to the bathroom and then got into bed and fell asleep pretty quick.

The next day, Betty rose early, washed and dressed in a different outfit and went to find somewhere to eat breakfast. Once completed, she took the map out of her pocket and followed the roads, sightseeing as she went. A walk up Regent Street and Oxford Street saw her buying items of clothing that were not yet fashionable in Germany. Two pairs of shoes and a new wardrobe later, she headed back to her room where she got rid of her bags and went back out again, this time heading towards the underground. She took the tube and got off two stops later at Liverpool Street.

On exiting the station, she saw what she was looking for and purchased a ticket for a tour of the old city. She walked to the meeting point and joined a group of fifteen tourists who had also purchased tickets for the same tour. Some were Japanese, two were Americans, a family of four were from France and three were from Germany.

'Hope this isn't too scary.' One of the German women said to the others.

'Shouldn't be, that family have kids, so it cannot be that bad.' said one of her friends.

After waiting five minutes, their guide arrived. He was in his early twenties and was dressed up in a pair of brown corduroy trousers, grey jacket, a black flat cap and a pair of scruffy black boots.

'Ok ladies and gentlemen, welcome along to the tour of the Old East End where you will be transported back in time to exactly 100 years ago, a time of crime and murder. Follow me and I will take you down the actual streets where Jack the Ripper slit open his victims, where blood ran along the streets and where policemen were scared to tread. Follow me at your own peril and keep your chin down to guard your neck, as Jack was never caught and it is said his ghost is still walking the streets looking for new victims.' And with this, the guide pounced towards the French family and gave out a wicked laugh, scaring the mother and daughter and making the father and son smile at their discomfort. 'Follow me and you will see. And please mind where you are walking and keep away from the shadows.'

The group followed the guide and within two minutes of starting out, they had entered a back alley that was dark and gloomy. They were taken down streets and alleyways and were shown where the Ripper killed his victims and which pubs his victims used to drink at.

The tour lasted a good two hours and after it had finished, Betty walked back towards her hostel thinking about the tour she had just had.

On Monday and Tuesday, Betty became a typical tourist and visited the many landmarks dotted around the city. Big Ben and the Houses of Parliament, she stood outside Buckingham Palace and watched the Changing of the Guard, she went to Trafalgar Square and Piccadilly, she visited the Natural History museum and she also went on a bus tour on an open Double Decker bus.

Now it was Wednesday and Betty needed to travel back to Germany, her plane leaving at 11:05 from Gatwick. She booked out of the hostel, took the train to the airport and sat around for two hours waiting for her flight to be called for boarding.

Now seated, she took out the pamphlets she had taken with her of the London trips and something caught her attention. Something was ringing in the back of her mind but she could not put a finger on just what it was. It was only when the plane jolted down on the runway in Düsseldorf that the idea came clear.

After she collected her baggage, she collected her car from the airport parking and drove as fast as she could back to Soest without even stopping at home. She walked straight into the police centre and asked to speak to Polizeihauptkommissar Ahrens on a matter of urgency. She showed the desk sergeant, Günther, her press credentials and was told to take a seat in the waiting area. She did not have to wait long as Bernie came down the stairs two at a time and walked to where she was sitting.

'Good afternoon, Polizeihauptkommissar Ahrens, how may I be of assistance?' he enquired.

'Hello, Betty Feldmaus, I was in the press conference on Friday. I have just come back from London and I have a strange idea that I know when the next murder will take place.'

'Excuse me? What do you mean?'

'Is there somewhere else we can go so that I can explain my theory in private?' she asked.

'Certainly, please follow me.' And Bernie led Betty through to an interview room on the ground floor.

After Betty had told Bernie about her idea, Bernie asked her to stay seated and that he would be back in a matter of minutes with the detective in charge of the murder squad.

'Hello, I am Erster Kriminalhauptkommissar Gerling,' said Sven when entering the room followed closely by Bernie.

'Betty Feldmaus, pleased to meet you.'

'So, Polizeihauptkommissar Ahrens informs me that you are either able to see into the future or that you have some weird idea of when the next murder will take place. Please, I'm all ears.'

'Well,' she said, 'I have just come back from London, a bit of shopping and the usual sightseeing stuff tourists do. On Sunday I went on a tour called "The Ripper Walk" where you are taken along the actual streets and sights of where Jack the Ripper killed his victims. It wasn't until I was on the way back and browsing through the tours pamphlet that something jumped out at me. Here, look.' She took the pamphlet out of her bag and laid this on the table so both policemen could see what she wanted them to see. 'Look at the dates. He killed his first victim, Mary Ann Nichols on 31.08.1888. She had her throat cut and suffered several stab wounds. His second victim, Annie Chapman, was murdered on 08.09.1888 and she also had her throat slit, and just like your last victim, she also was cut open and organs either displaced or taken. Now is this a coincidence or is your murderer copying Jack the Ripper's killings? Look, both his and your victims were killed on the same date exactly 100 years apart. They were also cut open exactly the same way. If that is true, then according to the pamphlet, he will kill again on 30.09.1988, but this time he will kill twice in one night.'

'Here, show me that.' Sven said, holding out his hand for the pamphlet. He read the complete thing from start to finish and then went back to the victim's death dates and injuries. 'On a scale of one to ten, how sure are you on this?'

'Honestly, I would say a twelve. It is too much to be a coincidence. Both the same MO, same dates 100 years apart. Do the math. It all adds up.'

'Polizeihauptkommissar Ahrens?'

'It sounds logical but still farfetched.'

'I couldn't agree more. But I do agree with Frau Feldmaus that this could actually be real. I just hope you are right as we can also do something to pre-empt the next murders. If our killer goes ahead with the Ripper's timetable, then he will not reckon on us knowing when he will strike again, which could play into our hands.'

'Yes, but how would you know where his next victims will be?' she asked.

'That we don't yet know. But look at your pamphlet and at the pictures of the locations. All are in small alleyways or back streets, all are badly lit and all are in the old part of London. Well, look at the two locations he has used so far. He has stuck to the old part of town where all the buildings are half timbered or in that 1700 or 1800 style. So all we need to do is reconnoitre the area, stake out certain locations and hopefully grab him on the way in before he can do any damage. I know that it is a long shot, but we are hopefully closer to catching our non faced killer than we were ten minutes ago.'

'Yes,' Ahrens added, 'if what you have said is true, you may have saved the next victims.'

Betty blushed and she sat up straight with a smile on her face.

'May I ask you a question?' Sven asked without waiting for a reply. 'For which newspaper do you work?'

'I don't, I'm a freelancer. I write my story and sell it to the highest bidder and also get royalties from other newspapers who print the story after it is released.'

'Then may I ask you to sit on this and not print it or tell any other living soul.' Sven stated.

'No, of course I won't. But when you do catch the killer, may I have first go at getting my print in first before the others get a whiff?'

'I am sure that you and Polizeihauptkommissar Ahrens can work closely together on this. You can get some inside information when and only when this murder spree has come to an end. Is that a deal?'

'Oh yes, I could not possibly ask for more.' she replied.

'So, now we have that completed, please, come to my office where we can share a pot of coffee and a packet of biscuits.'

*

'Ah, Sven,' Ulrich Schneider called as he walked along the corridor. 'Look what's just come in. A complete list of all of the British soldiers who left the barracks on both of the days as the murders took place. The RMPs have been able to whittle it down to fifty four from all three camps around the area. We have twenty one from Salamanca Barracks in Lohne Klei, nineteen from San Sebastian Barracks in Echtrop and fourteen from Vittoria Barracks in Werl.'

'Well, that is good news. From having around God knows how many hundreds or even thousands, at least this is a manageable number. If we can then ask the RMPs to take photographs of everyone on that list, then that would help us even more. Then all we need to do is show them to Anja's friends and colleagues, also to the staff in that disco she was seen coming out of and maybe we can get a match. It's a long shot but it is better than nothing.'

'I fully agree,' Schneider replied. I'll get Bernie on it when he gets back from his appointment. He shouldn't be too long.'

'Ok, I'm going to call my team back and brief them on what we have found out today. Can I have the conference room set up with a projector and screen and enough chairs for twenty people?'

'Of course you can. I'll get it made ready soonest.'

'Hi Staff,' Billy said as he walked towards the training wing. I've only got two names for Friday. Will we still be able to go?'

'Yes, the three of you plus me makes four. Good number. Who have you got coming?'

'Believe it or not, I was able to persuade L/Cpl White and Signalman Goodwin. Although they were not keen to go the first time, I think that this weekend could be fun.'

'That's good. Weather might be a bit on the damp side, rain is forecast, but heck, we have to deal with the elements if we want to learn how to survive.'

'What shall we bring with us, Staff?'

'This time you can bring a rucksack with spare clothes, your poncho to make a tent out of, don't forget some string and bungees, your mess tins and water bottle and your diggers. We'll concentrate on hunting and killing as you asked. Is that still what you want?'

‘Yes Staff. Where are we going?’

‘I know a great place in the Sauerland where we can hunt wild deer. Nice piece of countryside. I’ll teach you how to stalk and creep up on it real close and use your knife to kill it quietly.’

‘Brilliant. I can’t wait. Where shall we meet?’

‘Outside the Motor Transport section at 14:00 hours. I’ll square it with your OC so that you can knock off earlier. And tell the others to be at the MT on time or I’ll be gutting them instead of the deer.’

‘Ok, Staff. Thanks.’

‘So, as you have just heard, because of a lucky break and our fortune that a reporter went over the water for a short trip, she may have uncovered a plan so unbelievable that it is too good to be true.

‘So, we may be dealing with an individual who has studied Jack the Ripper closely. Is it too convenient that we are also searching for a British soldier who may know more about the Ripper than anyone else? I certainly was not aware of the dates or numbers he killed and certainly not how he murdered. But the evidence is there to be seen.

‘Would a German be able to get hold of this information? Why would anyone want to commemorate a centennial murder spree at all? This case is unique if it is all happening as we may think.

‘So, what have we learnt so far? Not much. Two victims slaughtered in such a horrific manner, no clues found at either murder site, no sightings of anyone coming or going where the bodies were slain, no witnesses coming forward with any information at all. The only two suspects that we have interviewed have alibis for the second murder, so that it itself should surely rule them out of killing the first victim if we are to believe the killer is one and the same.’ Sven paused and took a sip of water whilst he let his words sink in to all those present.

‘If I may just add,’ Freddy said before Sven had put down his glass. ‘If we can rule out the nurse and the taxi driver and we are able to find out the identity of the British soldier Anja was last seen with and we are able to find him in order to question him, we still have the hard task of proving he murdered anyone without evidence. If he is trained in interrogation techniques, he may not crumble like some others would.’

‘I agree, this is far from over even if we can find the boyfriend of Anja. If we were to interview him, would that be enough to make him stop if he thinks we are on to him? Would he not have a deadline he would like to keep to if he is able so that he could kill again?’ Sven asked the room.

‘Sir, if we were to identify the soldier, could we not put him under surveillance and track him when we think the next killing will be?’

‘Young Trilling, you have voiced a good question and one that I have already asked myself earlier,’ Sven answered, ‘and the nightmare to get something like that organized is difficult to say the least. Let’s not forget that he could be trained in counter surveillance techniques, he would know we were on to him before he even left the camp gates. And even then he would probably lead us one way, lose us somewhere far from where he plans to kill again and then head towards the sight without us being any the wiser until the next body gets spotted by the general public. No, we will need to think this through and plan our next steps carefully.’

‘So if the schedule is stuck to, the next killing will be on the 30th, which is in sixteen days. That gives us some time to prepare, but we still need to follow up with anything else we have open. Let’s hope the RMPs are able to photograph everyone on their list and also hope that the boyfriend is one of these soldiers. Just imagine if she was dating a married soldier. I was speaking earlier to Ahrens and he told me that most of the married soldiers live on the “patch”, which is a housing estate with its own shopping centre and doctor’s surgery for the army wives. So whilst we’re knocking on the camp gates, Mr. Married soldier tells his misses he is going out for a few drinks with the boys and is having an affair and gets away with murder, literally.’ Freddy shook his head and noticed he had spoken what others had been thinking.

‘And if it is not a British soldier, we’re really screwed.’ Sven commented. ‘So, now we know what we are up against. Get your ropes, crampons and carabineers together and let’s start climbing this mountain that we have in front of us. First one to reach the peak will get a reward. Now let’s get to it.’

CHAPTER 22

16.09.1988

Two army Land Rovers were dispatched to the barracks of Salamanca and San Sebastian. Salamanca is situated a few hundred meters off of the B1 between Bad Sassendorf and Schmerlecke and located next to a factory that disposes of dead farm animals. When the wind blows from the north, a foul odour can be smelt within the camp vicinity. To the east of the camp is a small airfield for the Army Air Corp which houses a few hangars for the helicopters, a few small private aircraft, a runway and a tower.

The camp itself was home to several Army units, these units being from the Royal Signals, Royal Electrical and Mechanical Engineers and two armoured workshops. This was known as “Bottom Camp”. San Sebastian was higher up in altitude and was known as “Top Camp” and was home to the Royal Signals.

Each Land Rover carried four RMPs, all armed with a 9mm Browning pistol and one also armed with a camera with a 28mm lens. Both vehicles were provided a list of soldiers and their units that needed to be photographed as being those that had booked out of camp on the nights of both murders. Each Regimental Sergeant Major, or RSM for short had been contacted by Captain Scott from 113 Company in Werl, asking for complete cooperation and that speed and secrecy was to be maintained at all times. Both vehicles were timed to enter each barracks at 08:00 and nobody was allowed out of camp until the RMPs had photographed all on the list. As the RMPs were stationed in Werl, it was somewhat easier for them to conduct the mission within their own camp.

Each RSM in turn informed each Officer Commanding (if one of the soldier’s was in his unit) that the soldiers were to present themselves on the parade square forthwith with no excuses.

When all of the soldiers had lined up in their respective camps, names were checked against their ID cards and each was photographed four times, once from the front, once from each side and once from the back. These were meticulously numbered and the soldiers were sent on their way when finished without even being told what it was all for or about. It was true what was said that soldiers are like mushrooms, them being kept in the dark and fed on shit.

Now completed, each vehicle travelled to San Sebastian where a small photography office was located and here the films were developed and each photo blown up to A4 in size. Once dry, each picture had the name, rank and unit of the soldier written on the back and they were then taken to Soest where Captain Scott was waiting outside the police station doors, drinking a cup of vegetable soup from the police vending machine. He had actually pressed the button for tea with milk and was shocked when he took his first sip. Not knowing how long this mission would last, he decided that it was better than nothing and wondered what liquid was available if one pressed the soup selection.

'Here you go sir,' said Staff SSgt Beatty, '216 first class photos of our fifty four models. All named and numbered on the backs, A4 in size as requested.'

'Thanks Staff,' Captain Scott replied, 'did anyone give any trouble?'

'No sir. All went as expected. One or two were turfed out of bed but all went smoothly.'

'Good. Well, you head back to camp and I'll let you know where we go from here if we are needed.'

Both soldiers saluted and SSgt Beatty climbed up into the waiting Land Rover and moved off. Captain Scott went back into the police station and was taken to an interview room through the glass doors.

'Good morning Captain Scott, we are so glad that the English military are helping us at this difficult time. I am Polizeihauptkommissar Backhaus and we spoke on the phone together. May I introduce you to the officer in charge of this investigation, Erster Kriminalhauptkommissar Gerling and our press officer, Polizeihauptkommissar Ahrens.'

'Good morning to you all,' Captain Scott replied, 'the British military are more than happy to provide any assistance that is necessary if any British soldier is involved with these terrible killings.'

'Thank you,' Sven said, shaking the hand of the army Captain, 'we will make copies of these photos and show them to the pub and club personnel here in Soest and also show them to the first victims friends, maybe we can then get a name of the British soldier she was dating. How far can you assist in this?'

'Well, as for doing the donkey work, that will have to be left to you guys. However, as soon as you have a name to one of the people in the pictures, then contact me directly 24/7 and I will move mountains to have the chap apprehended and brought down to your station for questioning. But just to warn you, we will need to have an army lawyer present before any questioning can commence. Do I have your word that you will wait for one to arrive before you proceed?'

'Of course, we are only too willing to oblige with your own rules and requirements,' Sven stated, 'let's face it, if it is a British soldier murdering German women, then the quicker he can be apprehended and charged the better. Don't need any red tape getting in the way.'

'Quite. So, here are my contact details and as I have said, as soon as you have someone in your cross hairs, call me immediately and I will have the soldier to you that same day.'

'Captain Scott, that is most kind,' Sven replied, 'we have other leads that we are following up on and may need to divulge to you one or two scenarios if and when we get there.'

'Sounds good to me. So gentlemen, stay in touch and reach out when you need to. Happy hunting.' And with that, Captain Scott stood, shook hands with all those present and left the interview room and was shown out of the building by Ahrens.

'Ok, let's get these copied and have the foot officers do door to door enquiries again, this time showing the pictures. I also want the photos shown to Anja's family, just in case they have seen a picture of her boyfriend.' Sven stated.

'I'll get the boys on it now and hope we get lucky.' Bernie said.

'What is in our favour is that if we are able to identify one of the soldiers here, then at least we can track and follow him for the night of the 30th. There we may need the help from the RMPs again.'

'Yes, that would be something we can have arranged. Maybe this will be the big breakthrough that we are looking for.'

'What the fuck was that all about this morning?' Tony White asked his roommate.

'To be honest, I have no fucking idea. All they said was we were needed on the parade square. When we got there, there were four Monkey's waiting to take our pictures. They didn't say what for and when we asked we were told absolute shit all.' Billy carried on packing his rucksack that he would need for the weekend.

'Maybe they are looking for the Army's new male pin-up.' Tony said laughingly.

'Nah, if it was something like that, why send the RMPs to take the photos?' Ian stated.

'True,' said Tony, 'so you two, what have you been doing that I don't know about? Am I sharing a room with a pervert or something? Been flashing your parts down at the local playground?'

'Don't be so fucking stupid. Talk like that sticks and you know it. No. I haven't been flashing to kids or their young mums. And no, you are not sharing the room with a pervert, well, not me anyway. I can't talk for the others. And no, I haven't been up to anything. Anyway, whatever it is can wait until after the weekend. Soon we are going to shoot shit out of some wild deer. I wonder what weapon we will be using.'

'If we can take what we want, I'll take the GPMG.' Tony said enthusiastically. The General Purpose Machine Gun is a belt fed weapon which is mounted on a bipod and fires 7.62 mm rounds up to a rate of 750 rpm with a sustained fire role of up to 1800 meters.

'I doubt if we'll able to take the Gimpy,' Ian said seriously, 'let's face it, the rounds will disintegrate the animal and there won't be anything left of it to eat.'

'Ok, what weapon would you like to use?'

'I'll sign out the Carl Gustaf 84mm bazooka. Not only will I hit the target, I'll also cook it at the same time.' Billy said laughing.

'Do we have a Charlie G here in the armoury?' Ian asked.

'Yes, along with a few 66's. Never fired one?'

'No, never had the chance. When did you fire one?' Ian asked Billy.

'When I was training for the Site Guard. You know, when I went to guard all the weapons and ammunition that time. Was taken out on the ranges and we went through firing most of the weapons, including lobbing a few grenades.'

'Cool. I wish I could do something as exciting as that.' Ian said.

'Well, you have to make your own excitement sometimes,' Billy replied, 'like this weekend. How many of the others will ever get the opportunity in expanding their skills like we will this weekend?'

'Seriously though, do you know what we will be using?' Tony asked.

'No, I think Staff Bones will bring along his hunting rifle or something. Just remember to sharpen your knives, may need it for slicing and skinning the deer.'

And with that, the three soldiers carried on packing their kit before their lunch break was over.

The funeral of Anja Schmedding took place at precisely 13:00, starting with the church service in the St. Ida Basilika in Herzfeld. Although scheduled as a private affair, the church was full of all the family members still alive and able to walk or be pushed in wheelchairs, friends of the family, friends and ex-school mates of Anja as well as her work colleagues. As is usual for small villages, those who had nothing better to do with their day also attended so they would have something to talk about the next time they met with their friends. Standing or sitting at the back of the congregation stood several reporters, photographers and plain clothed detectives. The reporters were there to catch and record the story of the first victim being buried, the detectives were scrutinizing all of those present in the off chance that the killer was present and had gone to watch his victim being put in the ground.

The service in the church lasted forty five minutes, many hymns being sung and several anecdotes were told of Anja by the priest and also those closest to her. They were then all led out of the church and walked solemnly along the road, past the junior school and all assembled at the freshly dug grave.

After another small ceremony, Anja was finally lowered into the ground and laid to rest under several birch trees that would provide shade in the summer months.

Cameras were heard clicking as the photographers took their pictures for the newspapers and reporters was seen writing in their notepads capturing the scene for the story they would unveil. There were not many eyes that stayed dry during the ceremony or the burial.

After the final prayers were said and the family and guests had all said their goodbyes to Anja and her family, they all headed back to their cars that were parked near the church and all headed to the funeral reception where sandwiches and refreshments were provided for those that had been invited. It was at this venue when a detective slowly approached Anja's parents and asked if they would be willing to look at several photos to see if they could recognize their daughter's boyfriend. After being told to have some decency and let the family greave, they agreed that they would be available for talking with the police at another time, just not today.

The detectives left and headed back to the station. The reporters and photographers were already back at their own work stations and were busy either hitting the keys or processing the negatives for printing.

It had been an uninteresting week for Detlef. After he had returned not just home but also to work, he had the impression that he was under scrutiny. He tried to keep apart from his colleagues at work but could not stay away from his daily duties. He had been called in to the head of the clinic and asked if he was indeed in any kind of trouble with the police. When he adamantly said no, then he was told that if it came about that he was lying in any way, the clinic would not tolerate any activities that could shed any bad light on the clinic or its patients.

He was again sitting at the back of the weekly group therapy session where Gary was telling all present a story of Jack the Ripper and what would have happened if he was ever caught back in the late 1880s.

'They would have sent him to trial and when found guilty, he would have been hung in Wandsworth prison.'

'But surely if he was mentally troubled, would he not have been sent to a mental institution for some kind of therapy?' asked Hubert, a patient who was addicted to arson. In his time, he had admitted to burning down three houses, five cars and an animal shelter.

'No, back then they didn't have anything like they do today.' Gary replied.

'But how comes nobody ever caught him?' Hubert asked,

'Because he didn't leave any clues behind. Some say that he was related to royalty, some say he was a doctor or surgeon. All we really know is that he planned his killings and made the police look like fools and scared the shit out of the women of London. To this day nobody knows the true identity of Jack the Ripper. He is well known in the UK, got away with a series of murders. It couldn't happen today. The police are more efficient and have more technology than back then.'

'And how do you know all about this?'

'Every kid in England grows up on the stories of famous murderers. We have of course Jack the Ripper. He was never caught. Then there is John Haigh. He killed six people and disposed of their bodies in baths or drums of acid in Crawley back in the mid 1940s. He was hanged when they found him guilty. Then you have the Moors Murderers, Ian Brady and Myra Hindley. Together they killed five kids and buried their bodies in the Saddleworth Moors. Both locked up for life with no chance of ever getting released. We also had John Christie, killed at least eight women including his wife back in the 40s and 50s. He buried some in the back garden and some he boarded up behind his kitchen wall. England is a haven for breeding murderers. It's a pretty fucked up place when you come to think of it.' Gary said.

'Yeah, well, every country has its own set of murderers, we just don't sensationalize them.' Detlef remarked.

'Well, that is because nobody was as good as Jack.' Gary said proudly. 'He came, he chose his victims, he killed, he disappeared. End of story. Nobody is that brash anymore. He's a fucking legend.'

'Alright, how would you murder someone and get away with it?' Detlef asked the group. This started them all off talking and contemplating who would do what and how and where etc. Each patient ripped shreds out of the others crime but many things all came back to the same point. The victims had to be random.

The three soldiers met SSgt Bones outside the MT section as ordered and placed their bags into the back of the Land Rover and all climbed in.

'Alright men, this is where the weekend begins. Here are the rules. You do what I say when I say. We are going out hunting so that I can show you the skills it takes to get close to your enemy and I will instruct you on different ways of killing. I will teach you evasive actions that you should take when you are compromised. I will show you how to kill silently and with stealth. Listen and learn and you will enjoy every minute of it.'

'Where are we going?' Tony asked.

'What weapons will we be using?' asked Ian.

'Patience is a virtue. Wait until we get there and all will be revealed.'

With that, SSgt Bones and his passengers drove to the camp gates and were let out without having to sign the exit book as it was still part of the working day.

After driving for around two hours, SSgt Bones drove the Land Rover onto a car park where they all got out.

'Ok, grab your kit and follow me. This is a hunting area and as I am a paying member, we are allowed to hunt only certain animals at this time of year. You are to do exactly what I say and when I say, no arguing. Got it? I am the only Brit in this club, so don't ruin it for me. So, follow me over to the trees and we'll start our basic preparation there.'

They all walked over to where the tree line started and stood waiting for instructions.

'Ok, as this area is being used this weekend to hunt deer, we cannot go walkabouts wherever we want to. We will all need to wear these orange vests so that other hunters can see where we are and we don't get shot at. Under no circumstances are you to remove them. Is that clear? We will try and stay away from the main hunting seats and we'll concentrate on finding something nearer to the west side of the forest, which means we will need to hike a few clicks before we reach our destination. I hope your water bottles are all full, but we will be crossing several streams along the way so you can replenish if you need.' SSgt Bones looked at each soldier and handed out the orange vests.

'Won't the deer see us if we are wearing this? And why are we then wearing our camouflage stuff if we are lit up like a helicopter landing pad?' Billy asked.

'Well, deer are colour blind so they will not recognise the orange colour we are wearing. This is purely for safety sake so that other hunters will see us and not mistake us for something else. I don't plan on getting my arse shot this weekend. Secondly, we are wearing our combat outfit as the pattern on the suit breaks up our shape so that we will not look like a human being if a deer happens to look at us.'

'Oh, right.'

'So, let's keep in single file and follow the track until we get deep inside, then we can start with some basic skills.'

They all followed in a single line and walked along an animal run through the trees. The forest was quiet and the tall trees were interspersed with small clearings where trees had either fallen or where fire breaks were, reducing the spread of wild fire if something should ignite during the summer months.

'So, remember what you have been taught before when walking through forests and undergrowth. Slow the pace down and slide your foot a few inches above the ground and then snuffle the toe of your boots through the soil where you want to place your foot, so that your toe takes the pressure first, then slowly put the rest of your boot on the floor. This will make sure that any twigs or leaves are brushed away by the front of your boot so that you don't tread on anything which might make any noise.' SSgt Bones demonstrated and watched and listened as all mimicked his actions. They continued doing this for the next twenty minutes until it became natural and they no longer needed to think what they were doing.

'Ok guys, well done. Last five minutes I couldn't hear any of you behind me. So, now we start moving into the undergrowth where we will make up a hide in which we will wait for something to come our way. Keep your eyes open for any natural hiding place, a fallen tree, a large boulder, a dip in the ground that can be covered by branches.' Now SSgt Bones let the other three pass him and he took up position at the back of the line, watching and listening as he had been trained many years before to do. 'Keep your eyes open and see if you can spot any animal droppings or hair or fur either left on the ground or caught on low branches and of course any animal footprints.'

Two minutes later, Tony White whispered back that he thought he had found some signs of animal activity. SSgt Bones walked past the soldiers who had stopped still and went towards Tony at the front.

'So, what have you spotted?' he asked.

'The bark on these trees has been stripped off, so I thought this could be an animal eating it or rubbing itself against the tree?' Tony said questioningly.

'Ok, let's move slowly off the track and keep quiet until I stop.' SSgt Bones quietly whispered. They all moved one behind the other and after two minutes all stood in a small huddle.

'Well done L/Cpl White,' SSgt Bones congratulated, 'that was spot on. Yes, eating bark is an important part of a deer's diet. During the summer, they will pull off the bark of a tree in long shreds and completely expose the wood. They also scrape their antlers against the trees that helps remove the velvet and they also leave droppings to mark their territory. So, if the droppings are dry and odourless, this shows that they are old, but if the droppings are moist and smelly, then they are fresh. And the easiest way to see if they are fresh is by observing if there are any flies buzzing around because we all know they like fresh shit to feed on. And remember, deer are most active at dawn and dusk. So, are you all ready to learn how to hunt your first deer?'

All three nodded enthusiasm simultaneously.

'So, as you may have noticed, I am not carrying any firearms and I will be teaching you how to hunt by setting traps. As we have just seen recent activity that deer have been in this area, we need to make sure that the surrounding area is left as intact as possible and that we only touch as less as possible, so wearing gloves is best. So, now that we know that they inhabit this area, let's make a hide nice and sharpish on top of that overhang of rocks so that we can look down on the trail. Let's gather some longish branches so that we can build a hide and also collect enough foliage to camouflage it.' And with that, all four soldiers got to work and within half an hour they had erected a place to stay whilst waiting for their prey.

'Right gents, let's get down to the trap. Trapping deer is not as easy as you might think as they are easily scared and will run at the first sign of something being out of place. What we need to do is prepare a spring snare which will trap them and hold them in place until we move in for the kill. We know which trail they take so that is the easy part. Let's go back there and start setting up.'

They all moved off, excitement showing on the young soldier's faces.

'So, we need a springy tree that is easily bent down over the trail. Come on, you two bend down that sapling over there and have the tip nearly touching the ground on this side of the trail.'

Both Ian and Tony went to work and as quietly as possible managed to hook the sapling near the top and were able to bend it towards where Billy and SSgt Bones stood waiting.

'Good boys, right, all we need to do now is tie the end of this cam-string firmly to the top and let the rest dangle to start with. Ok, is that tied off tight? Good. What we now need to do is attach this part of the cord to a peg, which in turn will be wedged under another branch or rock. Here, grab that large stick and tie the cord to it. Ok, now give it here and I'll gently place the stick under this tree stump like this. Now, whatever you do, don't go touching the sapling or the peg or branch. Is that clear?' All three nodded. 'Now all we need to do is make a noose over the trail so that when a deer steps through it, its head will get caught in noose, the stick will get dislodged from the branch and that will release the sapling to shoot up to stand as it should be. Understand the mechanics? Good. And what you also need to know is that the sapling is supple enough to keep bending as the animal will be fighting for its life. If we used something rigid, then the cord would snap easily enough, but as the sapling is pliable, then it allows the deer to fight against the sapling and not the cord, meaning the deer will wear itself out, in which time we move in to the kill. Got it?'

So, all of the soldiers got to work and completed the tasks set them and eventually stood back and admired their handiwork as SSgt Bones finished concealing the snare noose with some loose ferns and also covered up where the stick met the branch.

'Ok, let's move back to our hide and we will take it in pairs to watch and listen for when we catch our food. And no talking at all from now on. Hand signals only.' And with that they all headed back off the trail and gradually made their way back up the embankment to the overhang of rocks where they had erected their hide.

It wasn't until the next morning when Billy and Tony heard something moving below them. They had all taken it in turns to get some rest in pairs whilst the other two stayed watch. Now, just as it was starting to get light, they could hear an animal foraging on the trail. Not daring to move and each shielding their own breathing, they watched as a female red deer known as a hind walked slowly along the path, stopping every few paces and listened for any signs of predators. It stood still and both soldiers saw that the animal was just less than two meters in length from tip to tail and it weighed around 130 kg. Its reddish brown fur shimmered in the early light as it stood chewing grass roots, eyes and ears darting in all directions as a slight breeze moved the foliage. Slowly, the hind moved towards the snare trap that was across the path, well hidden if you did not know what you were looking for. Suddenly, the deer darted back but not before the sound of the sapling whooshing up to its full height and the sound of the stick hitting the trees nearby.

All four soldiers were now fully awake and were witness to the deer trying to pull its neck out of the snare and the sapling and cord holding it in place. Gradually, the female deer started to tire and SSgt Bones motioned for them all to follow him.

On reaching the stricken animal, SSgt Bones slowly approached it head on and kept as low as possible. The deer's eyes were wide and frightened and Staff Bones slowly extended his right arm towards the deer's neck and with the speed of a cobra he sliced through the carotid artery as if he was cutting through warm butter. Blood spurted in all directions as the animal thrashed around trying to escape one final time, but with the sudden loss of blood, this fight did not last long.

'So, as you see, we all went to bed hungry last night but now have the promise of some delicious venison steaks for breakfast.' SSgt Bones stated.

As soon as the deer had stopped kicking, he showed the soldiers the skill in preparing the kill. After making sure it was dead, he laid it out on its back and inserted the point of his curved knife where the sternum was and cut all the way to the crotch, making sure that he only cut deep enough to penetrate the hide and membrane and not the guts.

Then, starting from the crotch, he started to pull out the guts and also cut across the tissue that attached the innards to the spine. Then by cutting the last of the membranes, he yanked out the guts in one quick motion. Then he got to work in taking out the lungs and other internal organs, asking if anyone would like to eat the liver or heart for breakfast, these organs being tender. But soldiers being soldiers, they all wanted meat that looked like steak.

Once this was all completed, SSgt Bones then went to town on skinning the animal, making sure that his running commentary was also followed by the others having hands on experience, taking it in turns to help and assist.

Now fully prepared, SSgt Bones showed them how to cut up a deer in certain portions and informed them that as today was Saturday, they would need to keep enough meat for the next day also.

Billy was sent back to the hide to collect all of their kit and to bring it down to where the animal lay in portions and the soldiers stood looking down in awe and disgust as to what lay at their feet.

'Alright, let's get the packs back on and we'll take what we can eat with some spare and we'll set up camp some way off and start cooking breakfast.' All followed the instructions and all were handed various cuts to carry in their packs.

On reaching their new destination, they went back into survival mode and soon were shown how to make a fire safely and also how to cook meat over open flames so that it would not burn the outside and leave the inside raw. They then all sat around the fire and were soon eating their first meal since two days.

'How many times have you done this then Staff?' Ian asked between a mouth full of tenderloin.

'What? Kill a wild animal for survival purposes? Quite often, as during my army career, one had to live off the land.'

'How long have you served?' Tony asked.

'I'm now in my thirteenth year.' SSgt Bones replied.

'Seen any action?' Billy asked.

'Yes, and seen some more as well.'

'Have you ever killed anyone?' Billy insisted.

'A couple of times, yes.'

'Where? What unit were you in?'

'Well, I started off in the Signals and became a Physical Training Instructor. The next step was for me to go from being the units PTI to enlisting into the PT Corp itself. But as I was fit as fuck, I decided that why not go the whole hog and go for the elite unit. Did you know that you can join the Para's and Marines from day one in Basic Training, but to get into the Physical Training Corp or the Special Air Service, you can only do this through selection? Well, I went on a pre-selection course for the SAS and done rather well, so I got myself enrolled for the selection course itself.

'There were about 160 candidates all fighting for a place to get in. I was the only one from the Royal Signals. The majority were either from the Para's, the Marines or the Royal Engineers. Most of these were built like brick shit houses and at first I felt out of my depth. But then I realised that it is not size that counts but all round physical and mental ability.

'The first phase of training was in the Brecon Beacons and this is what is known as the endurance part. We had to show our fitness and navigational skills over three weeks where our hikes and yomps kept increasing in distance and so did the weight in our Bergen's. At the end we had to individually navigate through a set of checkpoints and cover a distance of 40 miles whilst carrying a Bergen that weighed 55 lbs in under 24 hours. The Directing Staff or DS would offer no word of encouragement or criticism. It was left to each of us to get through this part on our own. Those that cracked were Returned To Unit or RTU'd.

'Well, I managed to pass that phase and was then flown out to Belize for Jungle Training where we were taught the basics of surviving in harsh conditions. Quite a few cracked here as well. Most were all muscle and fit but had no mental discipline. We were in four men groups cut off from anybody else and quite a few just cracked under the strain of being secluded. Wasn't easy but I survived it.

'Then we were flown back to England where we started phase three. This is the Escape and Evasion and Tactical Questioning part. I thought this was the most fun. We were all dressed in old army trench coats with ill fitting boots with only string holding them together and we had to again get to certain map references without being captured. And as soon as you were either captured or were able to last the three days on the run, we were then taken in for the Tactical Questioning or interrogation as we call it. We had to stand for hours in the stress position, noise being blasted at us, not allowed to sleep, no food or water given us. Totally disorientated, we would then be taken in one at a time for questioning. Anything other than name, rank, number and date of birth and you were RTU'd before you even knew what you had said wrong. The only other answer permitted is "I'm sorry but I cannot answer that question".

'So, we started with about 160 candidates and only 15 of us got the beige beret with the winged dagger at the end. We had successfully passed the SAS basic training. Then it was onto the real stuff where we learned driving techniques, hand-to-hand combat, weapons training, hostage techniques, room and building clearance and so on.'

'Did you see much action?' Billy asked, just as a child would his Granddad who was talking about his time in the Second World War.

'Well, back in 1985 in Northern Ireland, three of us were in an OP, you know, an Observation Post which was located in a row of hedges that overlooked a site that was suspected of being an IRA arms cache. We had been living in this small hole for about ten days, shitting in tin foil and pissing in the mud when one night we saw three known IRA men coming back to the site carrying assault rifles, petrol bombs and anti-armour grenades. We opened fire and took them out. We then got the regular army to move in and they took away all the weapons.

'Then last year I was back over there again when British Intelligence received information that the IRA was planning an attack on a police station. A digger and a van had been stolen at around the same time so it was thought that these two vehicles would be used in the assault.

'Well, a few days later the digger was seen being moved from its hideout location on a farm and we were all told to get to our ambush positions outside the police station. We lay up out of site and we had several cut-off groups in case some of them were able to escape the main ambush.

'We were all armed with the Heckler and Koch G3 assault rifle rather than our usual M16s as the G3 has more stopping power, or as we say in the unit, more killing power.

'Well, the stolen van was seen driving slowly past the police station as if checking out the area first and a few minutes later it returned along with the digger. We all waited and watched as the digger crashed through the fence and three men jumped out of the cab wearing overalls and masks. One lit a fuse that was attached to an oil drum that was strapped down in the front bucket and they were soon joined by another five men dressed the same who got out of the van and they all started shooting at the police station. What they didn't know was that the police station was empty, everyone had been evacuated earlier. We opened fire and shot all eight down. The oil drum exploded and damaged the police station but we suffered no friendly injuries. That mission went down as one of the best planned missions of today. Set the IRA back a bit and they still think they have a mole in their ranks.'

'Fucking hell, what was it like? Were you scared or was it all adrenaline? Tony asked.

'It's what you train for. Yes, adrenaline is pumping but no, you have no time to be scared. You are an individual in a small team, all working together but with the expectation of carrying out the mission on your own.'

'Did you only see action in Northern Ireland?' Ian enquired.

'No, couple of other places but I'll keep those stories for another day.'

'And why did you leave the SAS?' Billy asked.

'I had my reasons. When I left the unit, I came back here and have been put in charge of the Training Wing where I can use my expertise in training the regiment in survival courses, escape and evasion, rock climbing, skiing and also hand-to-hand combat. So, that's all I'm telling you for now. Let's clear up here and we'll continue on with tracking techniques and I'll show you how to creep up on someone unsuspecting.'

And with that the four soldiers carried on until Sunday afternoon, where they then headed back to camp, wiser and more experienced than when they had left camp on Friday.

'Did you see the way he took out the deer and cut the fucking thing up in no time at all?' Billy whispered to Ian in the back of the Land Rover.

'Yeah, he's so casual but you can see a mean streak in him. Eyes are cold when he is doing something. Ever notice that?' Ian asked.

'Yes, so it's not just me that thought that. I wouldn't like to mess with him on a bad day. May not be the biggest bugger I've seen, but by fuck he's probably the most deadliest. Imagine what he could do if he lost it.' And with that, they fell into silence as they travelled back to camp.

CHAPTER 23

19.09.1988

'So how did we get on over the weekend?' Sven asked all present during the Monday morning meeting. 'Did you get the photos circulated to all the clubs and pubs of our British soldiers?'

'Yes, we showed them to all of the staff in the locales in Soest, Schmerlecke, Lippstadt, Hamm and Büren. So far nobody has confirmed ever seeing one of the soldiers with Anja or with Nicole on the evenings in question.' Ahrens stated. We have also shown the photos to friends and family of both the deceased and also turned up blank.'

'Shit, this doesn't get any easier does it? Freddy, have you anything new to add from your investigations?' Sven asked his best friend.

'Nope, diddly squat. We have no witnesses, no clues left behind and no suspects to speak of. Those we did have were let go due to no evidence or an alibi for one or the other of the murders. We have blanketed both areas with excessive door-to-door enquiries, nothing. Both the male nurse and the taxi driver have turned to be a dead end and all is resting on the killer as being one of the faces in amongst the photos. And if it is not one of them, we are back to the beginning again.'

'If I may ask, how far are we with the theory Frau Feldmaus has fed us?' Trilling asked. 'If we are still going to follow this theory, what can we do?'

'All we can do is to make sure that we cover the streets with enough police on the evening in question and either scare the fucker off or catch him either in the act or force him into making a mistake.' Sven answered.

'Well sir, looking on the board behind you and that leaves us only eleven days before he strikes again. I keep saying "he", could be a she. But it doesn't seem possible that we will be able to do much.'

'I totally agree with your train of thought. No, Soest is too big a town to be certain that we will catch whomever is responsible for the murders. But what we have on our side is that we may know when he may strike again, and yes, I am saying "he" because I do not believe that another woman would have it in her to rip out another woman's internal organs or remove her sexual parts.'

'So if the killer is mimicking Jack the Ripper, then he must either know his locations or will he just jump at any opportunity he can find? In the old town of Soest, how many streets and alleyways are there?' Trilling asked.

'There are far too many to mention. We will have to rely on a lot of luck and also carry on policing the way we have been taught. Maybe we will get lucky and catch the bastard before he has a chance to strike again.'

'I have been asked again for another press conference. What shall I tell them?' Ahrens asked.

'We can only tell them that we are still following up with our enquiries and that we are searching for new leads. I don't want it known that we suspect the killer is copying Jack the Ripper. That will send all the women in a panic and we have enough on our plate as it is. Can you hold them off for another couple more days? Maybe we can feed them something positive by then. So, we all know what we need to do, let's get doing it.' And with that, Sven ended the morning meeting and all shuffled out.

'Trilling, can you please stay behind? I need to ask you something.'

'Yes boss, what can I do?'

'I've been stuck down here in Soest for too long and I need to work out. I've been told that you belong to a local boxing club. Is there any chance that I might come along one evening and do some training with you?'

'Sure. If we knock off on time today, then we can go then. Training is only on Mondays and Thursdays. We share the gymnasium hall with other users, so it is not just a boxing club. That is why we are limited to training only twice per week there.'

'Sounds good enough for what I need. What time does it start?'

'18:00. Best to get there a bit earlier so we can get changed and be ready for the warm-up.'

'Ok, if nothing major occurs today, make sure to be here with your kit by 17:30. I'm already excited in hitting the bag again.'

The cremation of Nicole Kühn took place at one of the funeral homes in Soest. The press had not been informed of the ceremony as the family had kept this secret so that they could mourn in dignity and not have it turn into a circus. Seeing that Nicole was an only child, she had not had many direct family members. Sitting in the small chapel showed this. Only the closest friends had been invited and these only consisted of her work colleagues and one next door neighbour. The hair salon where she had worked was closed on a Monday anyhow, so all of the staff was able to attend without losing any pay.

Where the funeral of Anja was tear jerking, this ceremony was different. Anja was well loved by all, being so young and vibrant. Nicole was not and this showed. Yes, people came to the ceremony out of either respect or duty, but only family members were seen to be dabbing at their eyes with tissues.

But one person who was not invited had managed to sneak in and blend in at the back as if he was a statue and went most of the ceremony without being seen. Thomas Loch of the *Soester Anzeiger* had been vigilant and had been made aware that the body of Nicole had been released for collection from the fridge space she had been using since her post mortem. Thomas had waited outside the building and had followed the hearse with the Soest registration plates back to the funeral home.

Being a reporter, Thomas sometimes bent the rules ever so slightly to get ahead of the rest. He had called up the funeral parlour and stated that his mother had passed away and if they could find a slot for burial that week. The young girl on the end of the phone went through the appointment diary and basically informed Thomas of all the dates and times when they already had something booked and if he would be willing to be slipped between two cremations the following week. Thomas said he would get back to them to confirm and had hung up the phone. Now with dates and locations, all he had to do was follow the hearses that left and hope that he would be at the right ceremony of Nicole.

His luck had paid out and after his third cremation, he had found to be in the right one this time. He held a small camera and took several pictures without flash of the small, sorry looking congregation. Just before the final hymn was sung, Thomas exited the small chapel and stood outside under a tree, waiting to see if anyone broke down on the way back to the cars and the local pub for a free beer and sandwiches.

When all those present had passed and departed, Thomas went back to his paper and wrote up his story of Nicole's last few minutes before she was turned to ash. As no other reporter knew of this, Thomas had an exclusive and the paper's editor told him to juice it up a bit so that they could at least get it on to page five, if not nearer the front page. So, with some illustrious writing, Thomas produced a piece that was more imagination than fact but was still closer to the truth than mere fantasy.

The story was printed and set to be released the next morning.

They sat outside the *Eis-Cafe Venezia* which was only a few doors down from the hotel and restaurant *Im Wilden Mann* on the old town square. The day was warm for the time of year but the chairs outside all had blankets available for those who required them.

'So, tell me, off the record, what are you doing to be ready for the 30th?' she asked.

'Off the record, there's not much we can do. What do you imagine we can get in place on the off chance you are correct?'

'Erster Kriminalhauptkommissar Gerling, surely you can tell me more than that.' she replied.

'Call me Sven when we're out in the open please.'

'Ok, then you will have to call me Betty. Deal?'

'Deal.'

Both studied the ice cream menu card in silence for several seconds whilst deciding what they would like. All of the pictures looked so enticing. Just then, a good looking waitress walked towards their table wearing a tight white blouse, black leggings, flat shoes and a pouch armed with a purse, pad and pencil. She had shoulder length black hair, a tanned complexion and a winning smile which showed straight white teeth.

'Have you decided yet?' she asked.

'Yes, I'll take the Spaghetti ice please.'

'And you sir?'

'I'll go for the Nussbecher with chocolate sauce.'

'And would you like anything to drink?' she asked.

'Er, yes, I'll have a small Coke.' Betty said.

'Nothing for me thanks.' Sven replied and watched as the waitress turned and walked back to place their order.

'Put your tongue back in your mouth, you're drooling all down your shirt.' Betty stated with a smile in her eyes.

'I'm not,' he said, 'I was just watching to see if she got back to the cafe safely.'

'Rubbish. Would you say she was beautiful?' she asked.

'Being honest with you, if I had to give her marks out of two, I'd give her one.' he said grinning.

'Yes, I thought you'd like to give her one the way you were staring. Tell me, how would I score on your scale?'

'Well, seeing that we don't really know each other, I'd rather not say.'

'Come on, humour me.' she said.

'Alright, if ten is the highest and one the lowest mark, I'd score you an eleven.'

'Wow, I'm flattered,' she replied smiling, 'so would she score more or less than me?'

'Who, the waitress?'

'Yes.'

'Eleven and a half maybe.' he laughed.

'So what has she got that I haven't' she asked.

'Black hair.'

'Don't you like blondes?'

'Yes, but given the choice, dark hair would always win in a competition.'

'Well, looks like I've got some work to do to make you change your mind.'

'And what makes you think that I might need my mind changing?' he asked jokingly.

'Listen, you invited me out for an ice cream. I don't know your life story and I don't think we will be together long enough to fall in love, but you are a very attractive man and I think that together we could have some fun.'

'Well, now it's my turn to be flattered,' he said seriously, 'I just needed to get out of the station and get some fresh air and thought that we could sit down together and maybe I could pick your brains. Maybe you have another insight that I am not seeing.'

'So this isn't a date?'

'No.'

'Got you. You should have seen the look on your face. Absolute priceless.' With that, Betty started laughing.

'So then you'll have no qualms on me tapping off with the waitress then?'

'In your dreams. She's way too young for you and way out of your league.'

'Steady on, I was starting to warm to you for a moment.'

They sat in silence for a while and watched the shoppers passing by. Only busses and taxis were able to drive down this part of the town, so it was pretty quiet apart from the daily noise of kids screaming in their push chairs or of young mums shouting for them to be quiet. Eventually, the waitress walked back over to their table carrying a tray with their order. Betty watched Sven watching her approach.

'So, one Nussbecher ice, one spaghetti ice and a small glass of Coke. Enjoy.'

'Thank you. ' they both replied together.

'If I was your wife, I'd kick you right now.' Betty remarked as the waitress walked off.

'If you were my wife then I wouldn't be looking.' he said back. 'Let's face it, my wife cooks at home but it doesn't stop me from looking at a menu somewhere else does it?'

'But does it stop you from getting a take away?'

'Depends if I'm hungry.'

'Exactly. So try and keep your penis in your trousers long enough for me to enjoy my ice cream and we'll see if I can shed some other light onto my theory. Then we can see if you are still hungry later.'

'Come on, let's get serious. So, you had this thought whilst visiting London that our two murders here could be a copy cat for the Ripper murders exactly one hundred years ago.'

'Yes, it all made sense when I was walking through the alleys and later when I was checking out the pamphlet. The old part of Soest, the *Altstadt* is similar in that it is ridden with small alleyways and old houses to London as it was back then. Look around you at the architecture. You couldn't get older unless you visited Stonehenge or the Pyramids.'

'I can see that, but why would anyone want to copy the Ripper?'

'Who was Jack the Ripper?' she asked him.

'Well, what I have read up on him he was never caught, so nobody knows his true identity.'

'Exactly,' she replied, 'that is what makes our German Jack tick. He is playing with us and he wants to go down in the history books as having out foxed the German police exactly a century later, even though we have come on so far with crime scene technology.'

'But who would have all of the knowledge about Jack the Ripper to start with? And what about the medical knowledge that he would have to have in order to mutilate his victims the way he is going?'

'That I cannot answer,' she said, 'all I do know is that we have to do everything we can to stop him before he kills three more women, that is if he plans to stop.'

'Well, I have been talking about this case to a professor in psychology and also in profiling. He reckons that the murders will stop after five victims as that will be his goal, to go down in history as also never being named. So, we either catch the bastard before or during the next murder or we can sit back and sacrifice three more women being murdered with the hope that it will all stop after that. No, we have to know more. Do you have any suggestions?'

'Yes, I suggest you pay big tits for the ice creams and let's get out of here and back to my hotel and warm each other up under my blanket.'

'You know that that is the best offer I have had for a very long time, but firstly I have a lot of work to do, secondly I am married, thirdly I am going training tonight and fourthly you are too beautiful just to have a quick shag in a seedy hotel room.'

'Well firstly, you don't have much work to do as you are at a loss as to where to go next with the investigation, secondly I won't tell your wife if you don't, thirdly I can make you burn some calories by making you do all the work and fourthly, I am in a very pleasant hotel with an on-suite bathroom with a king size bed. But if you want to survive the rest of the day with the memory of the Ice Cream Queen, then be my guest. Just remember you have turned down a once in a lifetime offer of being entertained by yours truly. Never mind, I'm sure I can find someone else for my entertainment for tonight.' she stated adamantly.

'I have no doubts you will not be lonely if you went out hunting, but please let's keep this conversation we have had about the Ripper to ourselves and don't breathe a word to anyone, especially not the part where you have offered me some free afternoon sex.'

Sven motioned the waitress over and paid for both orders giving the waitress a nice tip and a wink. She smiled, said thank you and walked off.

'I saw that wink Erster Kriminalhauptkommissar Gerling.'

'That was harmless, just me recognizing the good service she provided. And I thought we agreed on you calling me Sven.'

'That was when we were getting to know each other, now we are back to being professional, need to get back to using the correct terms.'

'Ok, Frau Feldmaus, I hope you have a pleasant afternoon and find what you are looking for.' Sven grinned and escorted Betty back to the car park where she had parked her rental car. 'Keep in touch and hopefully I'll see you soon.'

'Get to work and catch the bastard. I'll reward you personally if you do.' she replied and drove off.

CHAPTER 24

20.09.1988

'Good morning Hauptkommissar Ahrens, Captain Scott here. I have some good news for you and I hope that you will be able to comply.'

'And a good morning to you too. What news do you have?'

'Well, I have spoken to my chain of command and I have been informed that we are able to collect every soldier on your list who happen to be present at this time in Germany and either bring them down to your station for interviews or, and this would suit us better, you and your detectives come to one of our barracks where it would be easier to interview them. What do you think?'

'Well, this is something that is out of my control. If you could give me two or three minutes, I will get the officer in charge of the murder enquiries, Erster Kriminalhauptkommissar Sven Gerling. Will you be willing to hold or shall we call you back?'

'No no, I'll hold.'

Ahrens placed the handset onto his desk blotter and rushed out of his office and down the corridor. The door to Sven's temporary office was open and he saw Sven chatting with Bernie Backhaus and Freddy Fischer.

'Sir, I've got Captain Scott on the line and he has a rather strange request. Would you be able to field it from my office?'

'Come on boys, let's see what he has for us.'

They all followed Ahrens back to his office and Sven took the offered phone. After the introductions, Captain Scott repeated what he had said earlier.

'Well, if we were to have fifty four soldiers come down to our station all at once, there would be no room to accommodate them all and I would not have enough officers on hand to assist. Your proposal for us to come to one of your barracks would suit us just fine. I can arrange for all of us to travel within the next half hour or so and wait for further instructions when we arrive.'

'I'll get everything set up from my end. All you need to do is to decide which barracks you would like to go to and I'll make sure that you have enough rooms to interview them all. I must add at this point that it would be better for us if you could limit the interviews to four at a time, as we will need to have a military lawyer present for each interview, and we don't have that many on hand.'

'I agree, four to interview at the same time would be good. Some interviews may be over within a few minutes whilst others may last longer. If we have a suspicion about one or the other, how can we make sure that he doesn't jump ship when we collect our findings?'

'That's easy. You give us the nod and we'll place them in a cell in the guardroom. Then you can always get them back for another go later.'

'That sounds ideal. Hauptkommissar Ahrens just whispered to me that Salamanca Barracks is nearest to us here, so would that be okay for you?'

'No worries. I'll have the duty officer made aware of your arrival and you'll be escorted to the place best suitable for the occasion. Let's say the first batch of soldiers will be ready for interviewing from 10:00 hours.'

'Perfect. Will you be present?' Sven asked.

'Yes.'

'Ok, see you in about two hours.'

Sven put the phone down and beamed at his colleagues who had followed one half of the conversation.

'I didn't know your English was that good.' Freddy said to his friend.

'You'll be surprised what I can pull out of my arse when the need arises.'

'So, what's happening then?' Freddy asked.

'I need you to get both Peter and Dennis here in my office pretty sharpish. I'll also like present young Trilling, Baumgarten and two other capable officers to assist with interviewing the British soldiers. We are travelling to Salamanca Barracks and they are expecting us there by ten. So, let's get moving. I want everybody downstairs and ready to go by 09:15.'

Three police cars travelled in convoy from the police station in Soest, along the B1 and turned right just after the Bad Sassendorf turn off. After several hundred meters, they were met by two white churches standing side by side on the right hand side of the road, directly opposite the camp gates. Another building stood further along, this one no longer in use. Once upon a time, it used to be an ice rink when the Canadian army were stationed here, but when they handed the camp over to the British army in the 70's, the Brits did not want to pay for the ice rink, thinking that the Canadians couldn't take it with them so they would just leave it for the Brits to use. The Brits thought wrong. On learning that the Brits had short arms and deep pockets, they systematically went to work with sledge hammers and crow bars and made the hall unusable unless someone was willing to spend a fortune in rectifying the place, which the Brits weren't.

Standing outside the camp gates stood the RSM, otherwise known as God, and beside him stood the Commanding Officer (CO) and Captain Scott of the RMPs.

'Welcome gentlemen,' the CO called when all three cars stopped by the open gates, 'we are only too willing to oblige and offer as much assistance as possible. Ghastly circumstances we find ourselves in. Let's see if we can get this over with so that we can all carry on with our normal lives. If you would follow the RSM, he will direct you where you need to go.' And with that, the CO excused himself and got onto his pushbike and pedaled off towards the officer's mess for some late breakfast.

'Sergeant Wilkins,' shouted the RSM in the direction of the guardroom, 'please escort out visitors to the car park outside the gymnasium and show them inside.'

'Yes sir.' came the reply from the open window. Seconds later, Sgt Wilkins strode out of the guardroom wearing a pair of green khaki trousers, a brown shirt under an olive jumper, boots bulled so you could see your reflection in the toe caps and a red sash over his right shoulder. He had a pace stick tucked under his left armpit.

'If you would follow the road around to the right and head straight up the road, you will be met by a member of my guard. He will direct you to where you can park. I'll follow on after you and I'll show you where you need to go.'

All three drivers followed the directions and were guided towards the gymnasium parking spaces by a soldier dressed in his camouflage uniform. They all got out and waited for Sgt Wilkins to stride towards them.

'Right gents and ma'am,' he said, acknowledging the only female present, Suzanne Baumgarten, 'if you'll all follow me, we have set up several tables and chairs inside the gymnasium and also put up partitions. The soldiers that will be waiting will all be at one end and cannot overhear what you talk about at the other end. Best we can do at such short notice.' And with that, Sgt Wilkins opened the door and walked inside. 'And we would appreciate it very much if you didn't wander around outside on your own. If you need to come outside for a smoke or a breath of fresh air, please speak to Cpl Tomkins here and he will arrange an escort for you. Hope you understand.'

'Of course' Sven said for all of them.

Sitting on benches in rows of four, forty six soldiers from the fifty four were present. They were informed that the other eight who were missing would be joining them later as they had either just finished duty, one was at the medical center and two were on an errand before the order went out to pick them all up.

Sven, Freddy, Peter and Dennis all chose a table behind a partition and each selected one of the other officers to assist them. Captain Scott introduced the four military lawyers and these split up and joined a group each. Captain Scott held a clip board with a list of names and photos. He called out four names and each one was allocated a seat behind one of the four desks.

'Over to you.' he said smiling.

Each soldier was asked his name and rank and this was checked against his ID card. Then the questioning began.

On the dates of 31.08 and 08.09 where did they go when they left camp? How did they travel to and from their destination? Did they meet with anyone? Could anyone confirm where they had been? Did the name Anja Schmedding or Nicole Kühn mean anything to them? Did they know of any friend or colleague who had mentioned dating one of these women? Were they aware that these two women had been murdered? Had they heard anyone mention anything about these murders?

The questioning went on for a long time. Some interviews were easily checked out and the name was crossed off of the list Captain Scott held. Others were marked and told to go and sit back down as they may be required to answer more questions later. The doors to the gymnasium were guarded by two RMPs at each door, one from each pair holding the leash of an Alsatian. At about 12:00, two soldiers appeared carrying trays of freshly prepared sandwiches and two urns of tea. They travelled back and forth to the Land Rover parked outside until two six foot trestle tables were full of food and paper plates and cups.

The detectives and police officers all grabbed a plate and a cup of tea when they had finished with the soldier they had been dealing with and noticed that the amount of soldiers still sitting had dwindled. Only three who had been interviewed so far had been asked to stay, the others had been allowed to leave.

When the police had all eaten, the remaining soldiers were told they could also have some refreshment as it was not clear how long they would be here. After a short break, the police started up again and Captain Scott rigorously called the soldiers forward and placed them at whatever table was now vacant.

‘Alright having some sarnies and a brew, but we’re gonna miss our meal in the cookhouse if we don’t get up next.’

‘Is that all you think about?’ Billy asked Ian.

‘No, I want to know what they are asking and why are we here. Don’t recognize half the people here.’

‘Well, that lot there is from the Black Watch. Look at their cap badges. The others must be from this camp. We’ll soon find out.’ Billy stated.

‘I fucking hate waiting.’ Ian replied.

‘Then what the fuck did you join the army for? All we seem to do is wait most of the time. Either that or we play “on the bus, off the bus”. We’re told to do one thing and when we do it we are told to do something else instead. Whatever it is, it gets me out of painting the 432.’ He was referring to the Armoured Personnel Carrier 432, otherwise known as the FV432 which was fitted with several radio sets for communication purposes when either on exercise or if it ever came to the real thing.

'Well, I'd rather paint than sit here.' Ian said with a sulk.

'Signalman Jennings and Cpl McEwan, your turn.' Captain Scott called out loud.

'Wish me luck.' Billy said to Ian as he got up and walked towards the other end of the gymnasium.

'Signalman Jennings, sir.' Billy said as he reached Captain Scott.

'Ok, take a seat there, Cpl McEwan, you're next door.'

Billy sat down and looked at the people sitting on the other side of the desk and at the officer sitting at the end.

'Good afternoon, I am a detective with the German civilian police, First Chief Inspector Gerling and this is my colleague, Constable Trilling. Also present is Major Hollingsworth from the British legal department. Can you confirm your rank and name please.'

'Signalman William Jennings.' Billy replied.

'We would like to ask you a few questions and we would like you to provide precise, honest answers. Ready?'

'Yes sir.'

'Good. What can you remember about the evening of 31st August of this year?'

'Er, what day was that?'

'It was a Wednesday. What did you do that evening?'

'I can't remember. Nothing special.'

'Ok, did you stay in camp or did you leave it at any point?'

'Sorry, but if I cannot remember that evening, then I would not know if I left camp.' Billy said matter of factly.

'Well, let me help you. The booking out ledger that is in your guardroom has you signing out at 20:36 on that evening, destination Soest and has you signing back in on Thursday morning, the 1st September at 04:12. Nearly eight hours away from camp on a Wednesday night and you cannot remember what you did?' Sven asked with a raised eyebrow.

'Well, if the book says I went out then I did, but you know how it is, we go out all of the time so one evening is like any other, regardless if it is a school night.'

‘A school night?’ Sven asked.

‘Yes, a week day, not a weekend.’ Billy informed.

‘I see. So you agree that you went out to Soest on that evening. How did you get there and back?’

‘By taxi I would say. Money was in the bank so would have been flush. Only at the end of the month do we either scrounge a lift or walk there. Saves money for beers’

‘So what locales would you visit on a Wednesday usually?’

‘Any. *Big Ben, Old Germany, Elli Pirelli.*’

‘And would you have gone alone or with some friends or colleagues?’

‘Depends. As I can’t remember anything about that evening, I cannot say.’

‘Would you have met any female whilst you were out partying?’

‘Sometimes I tap off with a local chick, not always.’

‘Ok, do you have a German girlfriend?’ Sven asked, steering his questions to where he wanted to go.

‘At the moment, no.’

‘And at the end of August? Were you seeing someone or were you in a relationship?’

‘A couple of one night stands. Nobody serious. May I ask what these questions are all about?’

Sven wrote something in his notebook and looked at Billy in the eyes.

‘What were you doing on the evening of 8th September? That would be a Thursday.’

‘Er, again I don’t know.’

‘Oh come on. That was only one and a half weeks ago. Do you suffer from amnesia?’

‘No sir, just as I have said before, most nights are the same as the others. Finish work, get showered, go to the cookhouse for some grub, go back and have a quick snooze then get ready and hit the town. Club here, club there. A few bevies, maybe get off with a girl, maybe not, back to camp for a few hours gonk and up the next day for work.’

‘What is a bevie and what is a gonk?’ Sven asked.

'A bevie is a drink, anything alcoholic, you know, a few beers or something. A gonk is another word for sleep.'

'If you could keep the slang down a bit so that our guests can understand what you are saying.' Major Hollingsworth added.

'Yes sir, sorry sir.'

'Ok,' Sven continued, 'the ledger states you also went to Soest on the said evening, signed out at 21:03 and returned early the next morning at 01:40. Would you still have had money for a taxi on the 8th? Where did you go? Did you meet anyone?'

'Sir, I cannot remember exactly where I was. Again, probably visited any of the clubs like before.'

'Do you know an Anja Schmedding?'

Billy thought for a few seconds and his temperature rose and he started to flush at the sides of his neck.

'Anja who?' he asked.

'Schmedding, Anja Schmedding. A trainee nurse in one of the hospitals in Soest.'

'No, I don't think so.' Billy replied, staring at the German detective.

'Take a look at this photo and tell me if you recognize her.' Sven pushed over an A4 size sheet of paper with a coloured picture of Anja printed on one side.

'No, but all the young girls look the same. Probably looks different when she goes out, you know, more makeup, different clothes. It looks like that picture was taken at a family party.'

'So you do not recognize her at all? Never seen her before?'

'I may have seen her in a club or somewhere but not personally. You know, she was probably on a dance floor or in a crowd and I saw her but nothing more if I did.'

'Does the name Nicole Kühn ring any bells?' Sven asked and again watched Billy closely.

'Nope, never heard of anyone with that name.' he replied adamantly.

'Again, please take a look at this photo and tell me if you have seen her before.'

'Again, no. Why are you showing me all these pictures?' Billy asked.

‘Because both of these women have been brutally murdered and we are looking for anyone who may have witnessed something that will help us catch the murderer.’ Sven stated.

‘If I knew them then I would say so, but I don’t. If the guard book says I was in Soest, then I was, but I didn’t go around killing anyone.’

‘Nobody has accused you of killing anyone. Major Hollingsworth, did you hear me mention that I thought Signalman Jennings had killed anyone?’

‘No, only that you are looking for witnesses who may have seen something.’ the Major replied.

‘All I know is that if I went out on both nights to Soest like normal, had a few scoops, sorry, drinks, probably had a dance or two, chatted up a couple of birds, you know, girls and then went back to camp. I didn’t see anyone stab any woman and I would have reported it if I did.’

‘Whoever mentioned they were stabbed?’ Sven asked quietly.

‘Er, you did.’ Billy stammered.

‘No I didn’t. I have only said they were murdered but not how they were killed. Interesting that you state they were stabbed. Why would you say something like that?’

‘Umm, it just goes to reason that someone would kill someone else with a knife. Not that many guns on the streets here.’

‘And what about strangulation? What about being beaten to death? What about being drowned? Many ways to kill someone, wouldn’t you say?’

‘Er, yes, but like I said, it was the first thing that came to mind.’

‘So you can honestly say you have never seen these women before on a personal level and you have no idea who would have killed them?’

‘No.’

‘Ok Signalman Jennings, you are free to go. Thank you for your cooperation. Please do not speak to anyone who we still need to interview about what we have spoken about.’

Billy stood up and came to attention in front of Major Hollingsworth. The Major nodded and Billy turned about and marched out of the small questioning area and walked towards the door. He took a glimpse into the next cubicle and saw that Ian was answering the same questions. Billy walked towards the exit and was let out by one of the RMPs who were not holding the police dogs.

'Polizeimeister Trilling, please mark his name in the book. I would like to investigate this one some more. He was doing so well and then let it slip at the end. What do you think Major Hollingsworth?'

'Exactly the same as you. Why did you not carry on with him?'

'Because I want him to believe he is free. It will be hard to pin anything on him with the lack of evidence we have so far. Let him go and we can keep an eye on him with the help of the RMPs. They can inform us when he leaves camp and where his destination is. And let's not forget, we have several names in the book that we are unsure of.'

'Ok, let me get some more tea before we get the next one in.' Major Hollingsworth said.

'Good idea, I think we'll join you.'

'So, what did you say?' Ian asked as they were being driven back to Top Camp in the back of the Bedford 4 tonner.

'I said I had never seen the women before and that I cannot remember what I did on those evenings apart from go downtown for a few sherbets and a knee trembler if I was lucky. What did you say?'

'Same thing but I left out the knee trembler stuff. Poor cows though.'

'Yep.'

'Hey, didn't you date someone called Anja? Did you not say she was a trainee nurse?' Ian asked in a very low voice so as not to be overheard.

'Anja is a common girls name over here. And how many trainee nurses do you reckon there are in Soest? No, I didn't recognize her.'

'If you say so. What time is it?'

Billy looked at his watch. '15:40. Get back in time to knock off. Not worth going down to work.'

'Yeah, I suppose you're right. What shall we do when we get back?'

'Well, I'm going back to the block for a dump and get my head down before tea. Saying that, sods law we'll get spammed for something as soon as the truck stops.'

'Yeah, but maybe we can wangle it by going to speak with SSgt Bones, say he wants to see us. At least we can skive over at the training wing.'

'Good idea. If we get given a task, we'll use that excuse, otherwise I'm going back for a shit and a kip.'

And just as if the angels looked down on the two soldiers, their prayers were answered and they were left alone allowing them to go back to their accommodation block, Billy to lose a few pounds on the toilet, Ian to fret about being caught skiving.

'Well, that is the last of them. Captain Scott, thank you so much for your assistance in getting all this organized in such a professional manner in such a short time. We managed to speak to all fifty four soldiers. If it had been left up to us, this would have taken us at least two days, maybe three to complete. We have five names on the list where we think we may need to either speak to them again or watch their movements closely on certain days. We would appreciate it if you could also help us when the time comes.'

'It would be my pleasure. I feel that building a good relationship between the British and German community can only help us all in the long run. After all, we are in your country.'

'So nice of you to say so. We'll be off now, if someone can show us the way out. I noticed it was a one way road we travelled down to get here.'

'Very observant of you. Yes, I'm also leaving. I'll jump in the lead car and the others can follow and I'll sign you out at the gates.'

'Ok, we'll be in touch.'

And with that, all seven policemen and the only policewoman walked outside and got into their respective cars after saying goodbye to the army lawyers.

‘Thank fuck that’s over. Heads killing me. Come on, let’s get out of here.’ Sven said and closed his eyes as the car drove once around the camps one way circuit.

During the next few days, the German police followed up with all they had found to date, which wasn’t much. The RMPs had been asked to keep an eye on five soldiers, two from San Sebastian Barracks, one from Salamanca Barracks and the other two from Vittoria Barracks in Werl. The RMPs had informed each guardroom to stall the soldier if they attempted to leave camp on an evening so that the RMPs could follow from a distance. This was all good if the soldier signed out. Sometimes one or another would stay crouched down on the back seat of a mates car or sometimes even be in the boot of the car when it actually left camp.

Sven asked daily for updates and spoke on a regular basis with Betty, who still informed him that they really should get into the sack together if only to release the tension and maybe have a brainstorming session under the sheets. So far Sven had been able to hold her off, but she was very persistent and so beautiful. He really needed to get back to Dortmund at the weekend and enjoy the company of his wife.

Billy went about his daily duties deep in thought and tried to stay away from his friends and colleagues as much as possible as he did not want to talk about his questioning ordeal again. Ian was proud that he had been questioned and told all those who wanted to hear and many more that didn’t.

Billy found solace with SSgt Bones and he visited the training wing nearly every day. They would talk about many survival topics and Billy tried to prise more information out of him regarding his SAS days but SSgt Bones kept the lid on anything that he did not want the boys to find out. Some of it was rather secret to say the least.

‘So, got over your ordeal with the police yet?’ SSgt Bones asked over a mug of tea and a chicken sandwich.

'Yeah, they were just fishing. Looking for any witnesses is all. Nobody has been accused of killing anyone themselves, so I think they are satisfied and all is forgotten.' Billy hoped they would. 'Staff, can I ask you a question?'

'Sure, fire away.'

'When you were in the SAS, did you ever take a lie detector test or something?'

'Yes, part of the training just to see how one would get on. It wasn't a fail and goodbye test, just to see what it was like.'

'And? Did you pass?'

'The first time, no. Everybody fails it the first time round. We were then taken into another room where we could see through the two-way mirror and we were allowed to watch an already serving member go through questioning so that we could learn. He passed with flying colours. Not a glitch on the paper. We thought he had just told the truth, but when we were shown his details and what he had actually answered, we werc all gob smacked.'

'And how did he beat the test?'

'That's what we asked after he had finished. He told us that every question posed had to be answered in the same way. No hesitation if you were going to give a truthful or wrongful answer. Sounded easy enough, but then he explained some more. He said that if you ever had the pleasure of being questioned, there would be two types of questions asked. Control questions and relevant questions. A control question would be something like "Have you ever committed a crime?" or "Did you ever steal money from your parents?" Then there are the relevant questions like "Have you ever used illegal drugs?" or "Have you ever spied for your country before?"

'So, how can you beat the test? When you are asked a control question, you should change your breathing pattern so that it is never the same rate. Make it faster or slower. Hold your breath as the question is being asked or breathe shallowly. This will then register on the graph as a high point, which would be seen as your "normal" scale. Then you will be asked relevant questions, so you would need to breathe normally for these as your heart rate may increase on its own, but should not register higher than your other answers on the graph.

'Another way to set your levels up on control questions is have something sharp in your boot or hand and stab yourself with it and this will increase your anxiety levels and when asked the relevant questions, do not use the object and your levels stay lower than your truths. Or bite your tongue. Also a good way is to do some mental arithmetic when a control question is asked. So, to put it simply, if you have a higher reaction to the control questions and a lower reaction to the relevant questions you will pass.'

'And were you able get to have the test done again?'

'Yes, several times. Each attempt got me closer to passing than the last. The breathing and using pain worked the best for me. Passed on my fifth attempt and never failed one since.'

'What about being interrogated without using a lie detector?'

'Well, that's easy as they cannot register if you are lying. They will just inflict some sort of physical or mental stress on you and hope that you crack. Keep you awake for days so you are mentally down, disorientation so you do not know what time of day it is. Or the good old fashioned beating. Only thing you can do is try and stay focused on a point in the room if you can and concentrate on it with all your heart. Look for a crack in a tile, a mark on a wall, a stain on the floor. And never deviate from what you have told them at the beginning. They will either believe you in the end or increase the torture and see if you crack then or they go too far and you die.'

'Ever happened to you?'

'I've told you, those questions are off limits. So, why do you want to know about polygraph tests?'

'No reason at all, just interested.'

'Alright, I think that is enough jackanory telling for today. Go on, you'd better bugger off back down the workshops otherwise I'll have your troop Sergeant on the blower.'

'Waste of time. I painted the 432 last month and because we are having some royalty visit, have to do it all again.'

'Is the paint in good order on the vehicle or is it all scratched and marked?'

'All good. Why?'

'Then why don't you get a bucket of Gunk and wipe it over the bodywork with a rag? Makes the paint shine like new and you'll have it finished within an hour.'

'What's Gunk?'

'You make a mixture out of petrol and diesel and wipe it on with a cloth.'

'And this will work?'

'If I tell you something, then believe me. Of course it will work. Don't they teach you these tricks in training anymore? So, fuck off and put the mugs in the sink on your way out.'

'Ok, cheers Staff. I might pop in tomorrow on my Naafi break. I'll bring you a Naafi Growly if you want.'

'Yeah, I'll have a Chicken and Mushroom. Whack it in the microwave first though.'

'Will do, see you tomorrow Staff.'

'See ya Jennings.'

Billy walked out and sauntered back towards his block. As everyone was down at the workshops, the accommodation block would be empty, so Billy stepped inside after checking he was not seen and went into his room, locking the door behind him.

CHAPTER 25

29.09.1988

'Ok, now listen in,' Sven commanded in the conference room, 'I would like to thank you all for coming in on this miserable Thursday morning and dropping all other work and tasks that you already have, but we need to get everyone up to speed so we all know where we are at this moment, what facts and fiction we have and what we need to get in place.

'Firstly, we still have no definite suspect we can pin either of the murders on. We are still hoping that something may turn up but I am not holding my breath.

'Secondly, we will need to go over the plans that we need to get in place for tonight if we are to believe in the Ripper copy cat killings.

'Thirdly, we will also have to maintain a huge police presence in the area and this has to be coordinated like a military operation. This is out of my remit, so I will also be relying on several of you to assist.

'So, before we begin and for the record, I would like to go through all of those present here this morning so that there is no confusion of who is responsible for what.' Sven looked at all the people present and smiled at them to ease the tension. 'We have present myself, Erster Kriminalhauptkommissar Gerling and I am in overall charge of the operation. Assisting me is Erster Polizeihauptkommissar Schneider who will be coordinating all of my calls from the station here. There will be four main groups all with their own teams. With me in group one will be Kriminalhauptkommissar Freddy Fischer and Polizeimeister Trilling, group two will be run by Kriminaloberkommissar Peter Schwarz with Hauptmeister Grote and Polizeiobermeister Baumgarten, then we have group three which will be run by Kriminaloberkommissar Dennis Schmidt with Obermeister Pister and Polizeimeister Grünewald and group four will be led by Hauptkommissar Bernie

Backhaus and assisted by Hauptmeister Zimmermann and Obermeister Horst. I would like to have Hauptkommissar Ahrens here at the station to help in all public relations issues that may arise and be the go between for us and the RMPs. We will need someone strong on the front desk, someone who has experience and is able to make decisions, so Günther, looks like you might be doing a long shift. Then we have both Doctors Stefanie Becker and Egbert Freckmann. I would like to have you stay here in Soest and be on standby for if and when this kicks off. And we also have the freelance reporter Bettina Feldmaus. I have invited her here to sit in with us as it was her idea about the dates of the Ripper killings, so maybe she is able to provide another way of thinking that could be outside of our normal point of view.'

'Thank you for inviting me. And please, everybody can call me Betty.' she informed the group.

All eyes turned from Sven towards where the quite voice had come from at the back and several glances stayed longer than was necessary. However, as she was sitting there radiating beauty, wearing a cling on black dress that boasted her ample breasts, tight waist and with her slender legs covered with black, sheer tights with high heels, she was not someone who you could overlook.

'Ok,' Sven continued, 'once you have all put your tongues back in your mouth, maybe we can continue.' Everybody turned back to face the front.

'We also have Captain Scott of the RMPs present with his interpreter, Herr Voss. Thank you very much gentlemen for coming and also assisting us in our time of need. So, according to the story, we have had two killings that have coincided with the first two Ripper killings exactly a century ago. If we are to believe that the pattern will continue, then the next killings took place on the 30th September 1888. So that means we need to be prepared for a double killing in the early hours of tomorrow morning.'

'Sorry sir, but I have been reading up on the Ripper reports that I have been able to get and I have a question.'

'Ok, young Trilling, don't be shy, you are among friends here.' Sven informed him.

'Well, the Ripper reports have the bodies of victim number three being found on 30.09.1888 at 01:00 hours and the second body being found some 45 minutes later at 01:45. These are all in the morning, or not long after midnight if you want to put it like that.'

'And your question is?'

'Does that mean that our killer will go for the same times?'

'Well, we can only presume that our pretend Ripper would want to keep it as authentic as possible. But without knowing the mindset of the killer, it is hard to make any definite decision.'

'If I may add something,' Betty said from the back and all heads turned to listen to the words ooze out between her luscious lips, 'I think we will need to take into consideration the date only, not the time. The original Ripper victims were found at those times but they went down in history as dates, not hours of the killings. Keeping that in mind, will our killer strike tonight after midnight or will he wait until tomorrow evening to make his move?'

'Good point,' Freddy interjected, 'if he just goes by date, we're gonna be sitting out there for around thirty hours. That is going to stretch us to the limits.'

'I agree,' Schneider said, 'but we will also have the forces from all of the surrounding stations. All leave has been postponed and all will be on standby and seconded under our command. We will be able to release people for a few hours of rest, which they will all take here back at the station. If any of the general public should get arrested today or tonight, then they will be held in another station keeping ours free for relaxation.'

'We will also have a large contingency of RMPs in plain clothes and several dog units on standby to assist and cordon off any areas that are required.' Captain Scott informed the gathering through his interpreter. 'Just on the off chance that it is a British soldier involved, but also to get this vicious bastard off of the streets so that we can make Soest safe again.'

'Thank you Captain Scott, glad we can rely on you.' Sven replied. 'So, as you can see behind me on the big map, the red pins represent the two murder sites of our first two victims. The blue line depicts the wall running around the Old Town and we have to believe that the next two murders will happen inside of this circle. If it happens outside, then we're screwed. There are so many streets and alleyways, we cannot have a policeman standing on each street corner and searching every individual who walks down the road.'

'We do that in Northern Ireland,' Captain Scott interjected, 'that way we can keep up to date with the whereabouts of all known IRA members.'

'Yes, but do we actually want to prevent the killer from killing again but have him still on the loose or do we want to catch him in the act so that we can take him off the streets?' Freddy asked.

'If you wait for him to attack, that is another life that has been taken unnecessarily.' Betty said.

'But on the other hand, one could look at it as being collateral damage. We run the risk of sacrificing one or two more victims in order to capture the killer for the majority.' Captain Scott said and this was translated for the group.

'That is a delicate matter but I agree with the Captain. We need to be out of site, dotted around the outskirts of the Old Town and able to move at a moment's notice. What we do not want is for our killer to spot us and go to ground and cause chaos and havoc at another time and place. If our killer knows the streets, then he will spot us if we are in plain sight, so with the knowledge of the local boys, I will leave that down to Erster Polizeihauptkommissar Schneider to come up with the locations for the groups.'

'I can have all the crime scene technicians with their equipment also on standby here in Soest if you wish.' Steffi Becker said. 'That way we are ready to get the immediate findings and hopefully we can also hopefully gather some evidence at the scenes whilst it is still fresh and not contaminated.'

'Right,' said Schneider, 'we will divide the Old Town up into four sections, each group responsible for its own section and only to leave their section with direct orders from either Erster Kriminalhauptkommissar Gerling or myself. These will be called the North East, North West, South East and South West.

'The North East will consist of the area from the upper point being Wallburgerstrasse running straight down to the Dom Platz as its southern point and then running to the east to the Nelmannwall.

'The North West will consist of the area from Schültingerstrasse as the northern tip, then heading straight down to the Sankt Patrokli Dom, then heading West to where Steingraben meets the Jakobi-Nötten-Wallstrasse.

'The South East will consist of the area startin as its tip the Ulrichtor going up to the Sankt Patrokli Dom and then heading East to where Bockum-Dollfs-Gasse joins the Osthofener-Thomä-Wallstrasse.

'The fourth and final group will cover the area staring as its southern point of Ulrichtor moving up to join in the middle at the Rathaus and moving west to where the Steingraben meets the Jakobi-Nötten-Wallstrasse. This will mean that all streets that are in your area come under the direct command of each groups leader who will need to provide step by step reports so that I can place the pins of who is where on the maps so that I can coordinate better from here. That way we can close down certain streets and pin the bastard in so that he cannot bolt out of the cordon. All agree?'

All heads nodded and watched as the map was updated with more markings being added by coloured marker pens notating the areas.

'I want you all to study these maps so that you can walk the streets in your sleep. Each group will have members of the Soest police in your team and will be able to show you the quickest way from A to B etc. The forces from other stations will be under my direct command and they will make the cordon outside the wall, blocking all streets and roads that lead out of the Old Town, but they will only move into place as soon as we here about the first murder being found. They will stop all traffic from leaving the area, busses, taxis, cars and also anyone on foot. They will have their names taken and will also be searched on the spot and taken to a location still to be decided and held until the all clear is sounded. OK, any questions?' Schneider asked the audience.

All stayed quiet and Sven stood back up again. 'Ok, we have a lot to do. Let's get our heads around this and if anyone should have any thought that might be of interest, do not keep it to yourself. Any suggestions at this point on can only help us further, so don't be shy in coming forward. I would prefer to have twenty stupid questions but have them covered than one unasked question which we later find out could have helped us if we were made aware of it. That is how good policing works so share your thoughts, no matter however stupid you may think them. So, please join your teams and the group leaders will take it from here. And good luck Peeps, it is going to be a long haul from now until the end of tomorrow night. Keep alert, take the rest when it is your turn and stay sharp. Does anyone have anything else to ask at this point?'

'Two things sir. One, when we are back here to rest, can we have the coffee machine spew out what we press as it is still a mystery what one gets. Secondly, what about food?'

'Good point, Trilling. Schneider?'

'I will get onto the vendors regarding the machine and I'll kick their ass to have this fixed. Thought this had already been done but I'll double check. As for the food, I'll have to look into that.'

'Excuse me sir,' Bernie Backhaus said whilst raising his hand, 'I could always ask a friend of mine who works as the head Chef in the Marienkrankenhaus kitchens. Sure she would provide food for the troops throughout the night and day when required.'

'Good idea, will she be able to get staff at this late hour to work overtime?' Sven asked.

'You will be surprised at her persuasiveness when it comes to her staffing roster. As long as the police will fit the bill, should not be any issues. I'll get on to her immediately and the local force can show the visiting forces where to go.'

'And I take it that my boys will also be allowed to share this hospitality?' Captain Scott added through Herr Voss.

'Of course, we are all classed as one team here so whenever we speak about the local or visiting forces, all are included.' Sven stated.

'And just on another note, we will also have the five "suspects" that you still want us to watch from the barracks followed if and when they leave the camp tonight or tomorrow night, all done discretely of course.'

'Fantastic. Let's just hope that with all our heads and manpower, something positive will come out of it. So, if there is nothing else, let's regroup with your team leaders and start putting the pieces of the puzzle together.'

And with that, all stood up and followed their group leaders to their relevant places of work space they had. Captain Scott left to get his troops briefed, Steffi got on the phone and called her office to move her team down in the afternoon and Betty flirted with anyone who gave her a chance.

‘41/01 to all, 41/01 to all, radio check, over’ Günther broadcast over the police radio to all of the patrol cars who had just dispersed to their areas.

‘41/17, in position.’ Sven replied immediately.

‘41/18, receiving and in position.’ Peter Schwarz said into the mic.

‘41/19, all quiet here.’ Dennis Schmidt added.

‘41/20, in position and all quiet.’ Bernie Backhaus reported.

The other patrol cars all reported back that they were all in position at the time and place where they had been informed to be.

‘This is where we now wait and see if the wanker decides to strike on the hour as Jack or just on the date.’ Freddy told his best friend.

‘And to think I’m going to have to spend all those hours stuck with you in the car.’ Sven replied.

‘Could be worse, you could be stuck in here with Smelly Schmidt. Remember the last stakeout we had and he had eaten that kebab for lunch? Had to have the windows open all night with the amount of farts he let out.’

‘How could I forget something like that?’ Sven remembered. ‘So Trilling, just so you know, if you need to release some sort of bodily function either in liquid or gas form, run it by me to see if it is safe to leave the car and relieve yourself outside. This patrol car will be our hotel for the foreseeable future. Got it?’

‘Yes sir.’

‘And any food that we eat, let’s keep it either all the same or nothing that will stink us out after an hour or two.’

‘And talking of food, not a bad bit of grub what Gaby laid on for us. Whoever said that hospital food tastes like shit. I especially liked the minced meat wrapped in cabbage. Just like my misses makes them.' Freddy said.

'Yep, and let's be thankful that she has been able to get special permission to keep one half of the canteen open for the police only. Makes you proud when everyone is willing to chip in and help. Even the RMPs. Normally not their issue as this is still a civilian case but to have them on board is ideal.' Sven reclined the front passenger seat that he was sitting in. Freddy removed his legs from behind Sven's seat and laid out on the back seat leaving Trilling sitting up in the driver's seat.

'So Trilling, keep your eyes and ears open, give us a nudge at 23:45. Then we will see if German Jack stays true to his word.' And with that, both Sven and Freddy closed their eyes and wrapped the blankets that had been provided to them over their bodies. 'And don't nod off yourself. You're on first lookout.'

'Yes sir, I mean no sir. I'll stay vigilant and wake you in two hours as ordered sir.'

'And one other thing, as we are all in this tin can together, try and stay relaxed and not so scared. We don't bite as I think you have found out these last few weeks. We both rate you and that is why you have been selected to be our slave for the evening.' Freddy added with a smile on his face that Trilling could not see.

'So Freddy shut the fuck up now and let me have a booboo. God knows when we will next have the chance of some shut eye.' Sven interjected from under his blanket.

And with that, silence took over and all stayed quiet and waited. Trilling cracked the front window open slightly so that the windows themselves would not steam up with three warm bodies in the car and not have to waste time cleaning them if they needed to move at a moment's notice.

'You fucked her yet?' Freddy asked after about ten minutes of silence.

'Have I fucked who?' Sven mumbled.

'Betty. I've noticed she's all over you.'

'I can't blame her. I'd want to fuck me if I was her.'

'Yeah, right. But have you?'

'Don't be so bloody soppy. Why would I do that?'

'Well, number one, she is so hot. I have looked for some fault in her, some imperfection and so far I have not found anything. Now if she asked me for a quick romp.'

'You'd get all tongue tied like you did with Steffi and go home to Heike feeling guilty. I've seen it all before. You just can't keep control. So shut up and sleep.'

After a few more minutes, Sven started breathing shallow and was slipping into sleep.

'So have you or haven't you?'Freddy asked his friend again.

'For fucks sake Freddy, why do you never let me sleep when I have the chance? It's like being in the car with a fucking child. Always needing some sort of attention. Do I have to spell it out? No, I have not slept, shagged, fucked or had a blow job from Betty. Are you happy now?'

'I'm only asking. Keep your hair on.'

Again the car lapsed into silence, Trilling not daring to make any noise or even move in his seat.

'So what about kissing or a quick fondle?' Freddy asked all innocently.

'Right, next assignment, you're on your fucking own. Do you want to smell my fingers to see if I've fingered her? Check my pockets for a pair of her knickers? Yes, she is probably the most perfect female form I have ever had the pleasure to speak to and be in her company. Yes, she offered it to me on a plate and I refused. Maybe I'm an idiot as Sabine would never find out. But maybe I love my wife so much that I do not need to cheat on her.' Sven knelt on his seat and reached over and punched Freddy a few times on his legs. 'Is there anything else you want to ask or are you going to keep me up all night? You know that I can wait for revenge and serve it when you do not expect it.'

'Keep the noise down Sven. I'm trying to get some sleep back here.' Freddy said with a wide grin on his face.

Sven turned back to the front and snuggled down again, this time unable to doze. 'Now look what you've done. I'm bloody wide awake now. Trilling, here's a tip for you. Never take your best friend on a stake out. You'll either land up killing each other or falling out. What time is it?'

‘Er, just coming up to half past ten.’ Trilling said looking at the car clock.

‘Sod it. I’m going for a piss. No chance of getting any rest when he’s in a playful mood.’ Sven opened up the car door, laid the blanket on the front seat and walked to the side where the bushes blocked off the railway lines and relieved himself.

‘Don’t forget to wash your hands.’ Freddy shouted from the back of the car.

‘I’ll just wipe my hands on your coat when I get back in.’ Sven replied with a grin on his face. He couldn’t stay angry with Freddy for long as they had been through too much together to let some childish prank come between them. He got back in the car and wrapped the blanket around himself again. ‘Seriously now, let’s keep it quiet. Either close your eyes or stay awake and let Trilling close his.’

And with that, the car went silent apart from the hushed radio traffic that came through sporadically.

‘Sir, 23:45 like you asked.’ Trilling said shaking Sven’s shoulder gently.

‘Ok, cheers boy. You ok?’ Sven asked back.

‘Yes sir. Nothing happened, saw nothing suspicious. Shall we stay here or shall we move closer to the center?’

‘No, we’ll stay here as we do not know when and where he will strike. From here we can get there within a few minutes and the others can also be directed. Freddy, you awake?’

‘Yeah, had a couple of minutes shut eye myself.’

‘Good. 41/17 to 41/01, sitrep, over.’

‘41/01, all is quiet. Nobody has reported anything out of the ordinary. Just waiting for someone to shout so that we can move in when needed.’ Günther informed all who were listening.

‘41/17, roger that. All units please stand by and stay vigilant. This is when he will make his first move. Keep out of sight. Out.’

The minutes ticked away slowly and when the time reached 01:00 hours, all of the police units and the RMPs were on high alert. The adrenaline was pumping through each body in expectation of something going down. Both of the pathologists were waiting in the waiting area of the police station with their technicians, all of the equipment already stowed in their vehicles. Cars past the unmarked police vehicles as normal, several people walked along the streets heading home from one of the pubs or bars they had been in.

At 06:00 on the dot, Sven picked up the mic. '41/17 to all units, 41/17 to all units. Stand down. I repeat stand down. Let's all meet up back at the station and have a quick debrief and then we can all go and get some breakfast and prepare for this evening. If it hasn't happened yet, he won't be doing it until later. Out.'

With that, Trilling started the car and headed the few hundred meters back to the police station and parked the car. Several minutes later the police station was alive with so many bodies from all of the local and supporting units from the area. The RMPs parked their Land Rovers along the road and one was left to let the dogs out for a walk, wee and water.

'Ok, I'll keep this quick. Thanks for this evening. Nobody reported anything so we have to assume that it will go down tonight. Get yourselves over to the hospital for some breakfast and get your heads down for some deserved rest. If you live local, get yourselves home. If not, use any space you can find. Normal police duties have been suspended for Soest, these are being taken over by Werl. So, you can grab a space in one of the cells or witness rooms. Blankets and pillows are in the staff room. Everybody, I want you all to report back here by 17:00 hours. Any questions? No? Then thank you for your efforts and bog off to breakfast. See you all later.'

Everyone walked out of the conference room and either climbed into their civilian cars to get home or walked over to the hospital where Gaby had stayed up just in case.

CHAPTER 26

30.09.1988

This day could not have come a moment sooner. Detlef had been making plans for this day for so long that he thought he would crack under the pressure of keeping his secret to himself. If only he could confide in a friend. But if he did, what would they think of him? Would he be judged just like the patients he cared for? Would a true friend be able to understand the strain that he was under and accept his stress outlet he had chosen? He would never find out as he could not risk the consequences. Just imagine if his mother found out what he had been doing these last few weeks. It would either send her to her grave or she would be blemished and shunned by all of the neighbours.

'Hey, Detlef. Are you ready?' his mother called up the stairs.

'As I have told you earlier, I will be down as soon as I am ready. What's the rush anyway?' he shouted back.

'I've told you, I'm off to the market with number 31 and I need you to hang the washing out in the cellar before you go to work.'

'And I told you I will do it when I come down. Why do you always keep on at me?'

'I don't keep on at you I just remind you is all because I know you'll forget if I don't tell you at least five times.'

'Well, I'm going to need another ten minutes or so, just having a shave.' he informed her.

'Well, I haven't had time to make you your sandwiches, so you'll have to scrounge around yourself and see what you can take to work. What would you like for your tea tonight?' she asked him.

'I'm going straight out after work so I won't be home. Cook yourself something nice. I don't know what time I'll be home so don't wait up. And tomorrow I'll cut the hedge if it doesn't rain.' This last part he added just to sweeten her up and to divert the conversation from where he knew she would lead it to.

'Where are you going to tonight?' she asked, not being led so easily away from the conversation.

'I'm just going downtown with a couple of work colleagues for a bite to eat and a few scoops. Maybe to a disco afterwards, depends how we feel.'

'Well, you be careful and don't go getting into any trouble. And don't mix your drinks. You know what you get like when you go over the top.'

'No mum, I won't. Sometimes you treat me like a child.'

'That's only because you act like a child, especially when you've had a drink or two.'

She went on and on and didn't stop her nagging until he had left the bathroom and went into his bedroom and closed the door behind him so he could get dressed. He heard her shout a few more comments up at him but these went ignored and he eventually heard his mother close the front door behind her.

Now that he was left alone, he came down the stairs and watched his mother through the living room window walk up the road with her friend and saw them heading towards the alley where they would catch the bus. He walked over to the telephone and dialled the station number where he worked.

'Station 15/2, Sandra speaking.'

'Hi Sandra, it's me, Detlef.'

'Hi Detlef, you don't sound too good. Is everything alright?'

'No, I'm going to stay home today. I've caught a head cold. All my sinuses are blocked and I'm getting a migraine. I'm off back to bed to see if I can sleep it off.'

'Ok, sorry to hear that. Are you scheduled to work this weekend?' she asked.

'No, I'm off. Just as well really.'

'Ok my darling, you get back to bed and let your mum take care of you. Is there anything you want? I can pop around during my lunch break if you want.'

'No, it's all ok. I'll be asleep and will probably not hear the doorbell and my mum has gone to the market. I just need some peace and quiet and I'll be right as rain later.'

'Alright, I'll let the others know. Hope you feel better soon.'

‘Thanks Sandra.’ He said and hung up the phone.

Now that was easy wasn’t it. Now he had got the day off and his mother was not in to spoil his plans. First he put the kettle on and put two slices of bread in the toaster and then scrimmaged around in the fridge looking for the cheese he liked and the packet of ham. He finished making his cup of tea and his cheese and ham toast and took his tray into the living room where he switched on the television and started watching some daytime TV, something he had not done for quite some time.

After about one hour, he put the dirty plate and cup into the dishwasher and put on his shoes and coat and went outside. He walked a couple of doors down and rang the doorbell, which was opened almost immediately.

‘Hey, Paul. I couldn’t ask you a big favour could I?’ Detlef asked his friend.

‘Yeah, sure.’

‘I don’t suppose I could borrow your car today could I? I have something really important to do any I need a set of wheels. I’ll put the petrol in it and also get you a six pack for your troubles.’ he said.

‘I need it myself.’ Paul replied.

‘Come on mate, I wouldn’t ask if I didn’t need to. You’d be a life saver and my hero for life if you say yes.’

‘Alright. Listen, no eating or drinking or smoking in it. I want it back with a full tank of petrol and any dirt, you clean it off. And the six pack will be a crate.’

‘You drive a hard bargain. Ok.’

Paul handed him the set of keys and the vehicle papers from his wallet. ‘Remember to treat my car like you would a woman. Be gentle with her.’

‘Like I always do.’ Detlef replied. ‘And thanks mate. I won’t forget this.’

‘Neither will I.’ Paul remarked.

Keys and papers in hand, Detlef walked back to his own house as Paul closed the front door. So, he had been able to get the day off and now he had a set of wheels. All he had to do now was to wait a bit and make sure that nobody saw him when he put the bag in the boot of the car.

Back in the house, Detlef went down into the cellar and emptied the washing machine like his mother had asked and hung the clothes up on the drying line. The time was now just past 11 o'clock and he still had a few hours to spare before he had to get ready and leave. Paul would be off to work in a few minutes and would not be around to see him leave, so that was a bonus. He didn't want to lie to him if he asked any questions.

Rudolph was still in bed when Detlef was in the cellar. Working nights this week was a bonus as he had been planning this evening for a while. What was worrying him was how he would be able to get away from driving for a couple of hours to carry out his long awaited plans. Well, he would have to think of something soon as the date was set in stone.

He tossed and turned as the light came through his curtains, disturbing his thoughts. He had so much to think of and with his physique he had to be extra careful that night. Wouldn't do him any good getting caught as he would not be able to run from anybody. All he could rely on was being covert. And the darkness, yes, the darkness was his friend.

Unable to sleep no more, Rudolph maneuvered himself out of bed and padded to the bathroom where he stood for several minutes urinating and staring at his complexion in the shaving mirror that was attached to the bathroom wall.

With his ablutions finished, he went into the kitchen area and made himself a fried breakfast and a large mug of tea with enough sugar that would last a family of four a whole week. He sat down and went through the plan again inside his head so as not to leave anything by chance, apart from getting away for a few hours during the night. That decision would have to be made on the fly.

Breakfast finished, he put the empty plates and frying pan into the sink and went back into the bathroom where he sat on the toilet and opened up the book of unsolved crimes he was currently reading. After about fifteen minutes and several pages later, he wiped himself, flushed the toilet and walked into the shower and lathered his rather large body with soap. Job done, he dried himself with a towel that had not seen the inside of a washing machine for at least three months and carefully shaved his cheeks and chin. After he was finished, he went back into his bedroom and turned on the TV and video recorder and played one of his tapes to get in the mood. At the same time he also continued to read his book, looking up when he knew something was about to happen, having watched this particular film about twenty times already.

At around 3 o'clock, he dressed himself in a black T-shirt, black baggy jeans and he carried a black jacket over his arm when he left his apartment and walked down the stairs and went outside.

Not long to go, he thought.

Billy had been aware that he had been followed twice this last week as he had left camp in the evening to go into town. He had spotted the first tail after about five minutes from being picked up outside the camp gates by a taxi because the headlights followed at a steady distance and only got closer the nearer he reached his destination. When he got out of the taxi, the car that had followed had also stopped but he was too far away to see the occupants.

The second time happened when he was walking into the guardroom itself. Normally the guard commander would have banter with whoever walked in just to lighten up his own duty but on this particular evening, the guard commander picked up the phone and dialed a number and informed the person on the other end that the soldier was leaving now and travelling to Soest. If the guard commander had waited and watched Billy leave the guardroom before placing the call, then maybe all would have been different. But Billy had stopped around the corner before leaving and was reading Part One Orders that were printed out and hanging in the guardroom entrance and caught the one sided conversation. So, now on his guard, Billy checked his surroundings and saw a car waiting up the road outside the GHQ compound. When Billy got into the taxi, he saw the other vehicle turn its lights on and drive down the slight hill towards the camp gates.

This time Billy instructed the driver to drive a different route and when halfway to Soest, Billy informed the driver to turn around and head back to camp with the excuse he had forgotten something. This is when he saw the car go past and stop further up the road before it too turned around. Now Billy was certain that it had something to do with the interview with the German civilian police and the times when he checked out of camp and back in again on those two dates.

Well, that wouldn't happen tonight because he had planned this evening and nothing would stop him from completing his mission. That morning, Billy had taken a change of clothes to work with him in a sports bag and had hidden this in his place of work. He then went about his normal day of cleaning the APC or making sure the vehicle batteries were in working order or that the storeroom was kept tidy. He went back up to the main camp for his morning Naafi break and back down to work with his colleagues. Back up for lunch and down again for the afternoon.

The time was now 16:00 and the troop was called together for the knock off parade. This was where they all stood in their ranks and had their names called off to make sure that everyone was present and correct. Names all taken, the troop sergeant reminded them all that anyone could turn up and watch the sergeant's mess play against the officer's mess at football on Saturday afternoon on the sports pitch. Then they were all knocked off for the weekend.

Nearly all headed out of the door and marched up to the camp, but Billy hung back with the excuse he had to lock up his store room. When nobody else was around, he went inside and closed the door and quickly changed into the other clothes he had in his sports bag. Finally dressed, he hid his uniform and boots behind a large storage box and closed and locked the door behind him. He walked quietly to the door leading outside and walked as swiftly as he could, but instead of turning left to walk up the hill to the camp, he turned right and walked along a track that led into the woods.

Walking along the track, he was careful to keep to the sides and away from the puddles or muddy bits. He had to walk a good two kilometers until he came to a road that would take him towards the nearest village, which was situated behind the German military camp, the *Graf Yorkk Kaserne*.

On reaching the German camp gates, he walked over to a waiting taxi and ignored the shouts of abuse aimed at him from three German conscripts coming through their camp gates as he stole their taxi ride.

'Quickly please, Stadtpark in Soest.' he instructed the taxi driver and stuck up two fingers to the soldiers across the road.

When he reached the Stadtpark, he paid the driver and left a small tip and got out and looked around. He still had some time to wait as it was not yet quite dark, but soon he would be able to slip away from where he had been dropped off and even if the taxi driver was ever questioned, he would not be able to inform the police where Billy's final destination was.

'Ok, welcome back. I hope you were all able to get some rest and recuperate somewhat earlier. We have still received no sightings of any dead bodies, so we now believe it will happen tonight. We'll keep the same teams and areas as before.' Sven informed all those present. 'Any questions or any points you would like to bring up?'

'Yes sir, just one. If we are to believe the killings will happen tonight, would it not be best to have several officers in plain clothes walk along some of the streets and alleyways and not rely on the general public informing us that they had found a dead body?' Suzanne Baumgarten asked.

'Good point.' Sven answered. 'Anybody see any flaws in that scheme?' he asked.

'As long as the people don't stick out like a copper and don't loiter too long in any one place and keep moving, don't see why it can't work.' Schneider said. 'All we need is hidden radios with earpieces and we can control the foot movement from here as well. What do you think?' he asked Sven.

'If it isn't too much of a big job coordinating, could work in our favour. Yes, I like it. So, we'll sort out the foot squad in a minute and we can also use some of the supporting forces for that task. Anything else?'

Everybody stayed quiet and just as he was about to speak, Betty stuck her hand up. 'I could also walk around and help out.' she said.

'If you could show me how to work the radio, I'd be willing to assist.'

'I am afraid that I cannot permit that as this is a police operation with the assistance of the RMPs and not for the civilian population. We cannot have you walking around and scaring the killer off.' Sven stated.

'Or of you becoming the next victim.' Freddy added.

'And that also.' Sven ended. 'Nothing else? Ok. All grab your gear and get to your start points soonest. Radio in once you are in position and please keep out of sight.'

The police all stood up and filed out of the conference room door and the noise of boots and trainers jogging or walking down the corridors and stairs was ear shattering.

'Sorry Betty, but you have to see it from my point of view. You would only be putting yourself in danger and you would be one extra worry for us all.'

'Yes, I understand Sven, just that the thought of me sitting here waiting when I could be doing something useful.'

'You can. How about assisting Ulrich Schneider with his plotting the patrols on foot? That way he will have two pairs of eyes instead of just one.'

'I suppose,' she said, 'but keep me updated and I want to come out as soon as possible as you promised me the exclusive for this story.'

'I haven't forgotten, don't worry. So, I'll see you later. Be a good girl and keep your legs together until this is over.' And before she could reply, Sven was out the door and headed downstairs.

At around 21:15, Rudolph radioed the Taxi central and informed them he had just received a passenger asking to be taken to Düsseldorf airport and that he would be away from Soest for a good 4 hours. What he didn't inform central was that he would start his meter and claim that on arrival at the airport, the passenger opened the door and with small bag in hand, ran into the building without paying. Of course Rudolph tried to chase the passenger but he was not as fit as he used to be etc. etc. This would now give him time to follow through with his long awaited plans.

He slowly drove away from where he had been waiting and headed towards the Jakobitor, one of the main routes into the town center and turned immediately right onto Ulrich-Jakobi-Wallstrasse. As this road was seldom driven, he believed that no-one would notice his car parked along this road. Plus it had the hidden bonus of it not being too far from his destination which he would have to complete on foot.

At 21:30, he had parked the car and sat for several minutes waiting to spot any movements and on seeing no-one, turned off the interior light so it would not switch on when he opened the car door and slowly got out. Once again he looked all around him. On seeing nobody, he closed and locked the car door and walked to where he needed to be.

When he arrived at his final destination, he again glanced around and when he was sure that he had not been noticed, he stepped back out of the light and waited for when it was time.

At 22:15, he saw a woman step out of the building he was watching and headed towards the small alleyway. Although big, he was quiet and moved out of the shadows without her noticing and followed.

Detlef had left his house a lot earlier in case his mother came home and also so that he would not be seen by any neighbours. He had left through his cellar door and carried with him a sports bag. At precisely 21:30, Detlef had reached Soest via the B1 and parked the car he had borrowed next to the Volkshochschule, the adult education center. Here he stayed in the car for several minutes, himself watching if anyone had observed his arrival and when he was satisfied that he went unnoticed, he quickly discarded his street clothes and put on the garments he had taken from his bag. Now dressed again, he adjusted his head gear and exited the car and hurried to get into the shadows before moving off down the streets to where he had planned the first action for tonight. He too blended into the darkness so that he would not be seen by anyone just passing by, they would have to be looking for him to be seen.

At 22:15, he saw someone appear and it was now or never. Holding his breath, he stepped out of the darkness and approached the figure from behind. All his planning had led up to this crucial moment.

Billy had stayed in the town park for quite some time. Waiting was no bother to him. He had a lot of patience and knew that to carry out the task he had set himself he couldn't rush things as any stupid mistake would or could get him found out.

He left the park and headed along the streets, head down so as not to be recognized. On reaching the street he needed to be at, one that he had meticulously reconnoitered before, he walked towards a doorway and stood in the darkness watching the door to the building directly opposite. He stood motionless as he had been taught and made no noise at all.

At 22:15, he saw someone exit the building he had been watching and they turned left. With his heart beating heavy in his chest and the adrenaline pumping through his body, he counted to five, glanced that nobody was watching and strode across the street, intent on his next actions. There was no turning back from here.

CHAPTER 27

Renate Bölte normally kept to herself and did not like socialising. She had been shy for as long as she could remember, never being able to look anyone directly in the eyes. But she had not been able to get out of this party, even though she did try. In the end, her work colleagues grabbed her by both hands and literally dragged her to the restaurant when it was time to leave the office.

She worked for a solicitors firm in the centre of town and one of her colleagues was celebrating their well earned promotion, so a meal with a few drinks was on the board. The company had put some cash towards the night out and everyone else put money into the kitty and would stay until it was time to top it up again.

The restaurant that had been booked was just off the main square and close to the Ratshaus or town hall. Being known for its fine international cuisine, the Ratskeller St. Georg was a fine choice for a good meal and a glass or two of fine wine. Not only was it a restaurant but it also housed a Kegelbahn, a German version of bowling but with smaller balls with a narrower alley. Several of Renate's colleagues were onto their fourth or fifth drink and she had not even finished her second, but she wanted to show them that she did belong to the group, even if it was by sitting on the outskirts.

At the age of thirty two, she had the appearance of a church mouse. She was small in every way possible from her height, stature and breasts. She had light blonde hair held together at the back of her head in a bun, she dressed in dark grey clothes and wore sensible shoes. She had never had a boyfriend and apart from her father, she had never been kissed by a man. She was a true definition of a young spinster. The only thing that she still needed to being complete was a cat or two at home, but as she was allergic, she had to do without.

She had ordered the schnitzel "Holsteiner Art" which is a pork steak fried in flour and breadcrumbs and served with smoked salmon, fried eggs, fried potatoes and a side salad. She had picked her way through this meal and gave up half way through as she was not used to eating such large portions. She turned down the offer of a dessert and watched the others devour their way through apple strudel with vanilla ice cream or a bowl of Stracciatella ice cream with Zabaionesauce and cream. She had ordered a glass of Barolo, a dry red wine from the Piemont region of northern Italy and this had gone to her head. She was too slow in rejecting a refill as she was still chewing on a piece of her schnitzel and did not want to appear rude and speak when she had food in her mouth.

Now, after the second glass was emptied, she decided that she had done her bit and it was time to be on her way home. Against all of the complaints about her being a party pooper and someone also said a bit too loudly that she was a bore, she left the locale at 22:15 and stopped just outside the doors to adjust her coat. Not living too far away, she decided that she would take the short cut as she wanted to get home quickly because she needed to pee and she did not like using toilets where the majority of the time someone would manage to pee on the seat.

She turned left, walked past the small crafts shop on the corner and turned left down the Ressourcengasse, a small alleyway that led down to the "large pond", which is rather small for its name.

The alleyway was poorly lit but as it was only sixty five meters in length, she would be down and out the other side in no time. All she then had to do was walk along the side of the pond, walk past the indoor swimming pool and walk down two more streets and arrive at her tiny apartment. The walk should have taken her about ten minutes from start to finish but not on this night.

As she turned down the alleyway, she had not seen the man standing in the doorway opposite the restaurant and was also not aware that the man had followed her.

The left side of the alleyway was made up of the side walls of the crafts shop which had no windows overlooking the alleyway and on the right side was the side walls of another building, again no windows on the ground floor but some above where several apartments were. Further along on the left side, the building stopped and a stone wall of around two meters in height ran the rest of the way to the end. With only one entry and one exit, this was a stupid place for a lone woman to walk when a killer was loose on the streets of Soest.

As she reached the middle of the alleyway, the ground ran slightly down hill and as she came level with the wall, she felt a hand snap around her forehead and something sharp slice across her throat, cutting through the silk scarf she had just adjusted.

The first cut with the knife shed no pain as it was so sudden, but she felt the second slash and pain engulfed her torso and bursts of light flashed through her head in shock. She was unable to scream as her windpipe had been cleanly severed from one side to the other and with the cutting of her carotid artery, her weak, miserable life splashed out of her within seconds. She was thrown to the ground and saw her attacker walk swiftly to the end of the alleyway and moved out of site. The attack lasted all of a few seconds and was over before it had begun.

Renate lay on the ground gasping for oxygen, her blood emptying onto the stones and running slowly down the hill, making puddles and pools in any unevenness of the cobbled stones and she lost consciousness some fifty seconds after the first cut was inflicted and died some two minutes later from hemorrhaging and shock.

If she had been able to see around the corner, she would have seen her attacker stop at the pond, walk down the four steps and wash his hands and knife in the water and then walk past the pond on Wippgasse towards the swimming pool.

That was good timing, he thought to himself. He had only been standing in the doorway for several minutes when the door to the restaurant opened and a single woman stepped out. He had already made sure that there had been no other people walking towards his position when he stopped in the darkened doorway and saw that the opportunity in claiming his third victim was a gift from God, handed to him on a plate. He followed the woman into the alleyway, checked that he had not been followed and walking swiftly on his rubber soles, quickly closed the gap. Without any hesitation, he grabbed the slight woman from behind and with his right hand snaking around the front, sliced deeply and forcefully with the blade of his sharp knife to make sure that he cut the right place like he had been trained to do. As soon as the knife was free from the flesh, he sliced again but this time he could not cut as deep as intended as his victim was already on the way down and he had to let go of her head so as not to get blood all over himself.

He knew immediately that he had cut her fatally and she would not be able to be saved even if the paramedics were standing next to her as she went down on the hard cobbles. He stepped passed her inert body and heard her fighting for breath and glimpsed the black liquid flowing around her upper body and head but not being able to spurt out due to her scarf being in the way. He glanced back up the alley and saw that no one was coming and so he continued down to the pond where he cleansed any blood that was on his hands and knife, which he then wiped with a handkerchief and placed back in its scabbard that was attached to his belt under his dark coat.

He then continued along the right side of the pond and noticed several people leaving the public swimming pool. Some people left in small groups, others in pairs and one or two alone. As he came to the end of Wippgasse, he looked left and right along the Wiesenstrasse and noticed a solitary figure walking towards the Damm. Was his luck in again? He quickly scanned the area and saw that nobody was heading his way, so he lengthened his stride and saw that the figure ahead was also a lone female. He glanced once more behind him and when he faced the front again, she had disappeared. It was only when he walked another ten meters or so that he noticed she had turned right into another dark alleyway, this one called the Kerngasse which led to the Domplatz.

The Kerngasse is a walkway that has several, small houses dotted along the left side and a wall that separates a driveway to a large apartment building. Twenty seven meters along this walkway, a streetlight normally shines but on this particular night, the bulb had blown and all was in darkness. Where the light is situated, the walkway curves around to the left and another two houses are located on the left side with a large house on the right. The path then splits into two. The right fork heads towards the Domplatz but the left fork leads to another house further down on the right, the path ending at a gate leading to one of the houses garden.

The woman was walking along wearing a long coat, a woolen hat, trainers and a pair of tracksuit bottoms and she carried a sports bag across her right shoulder. She was oblivious as to her surroundings, her follower or her fate as she hummed a song out loud.

As she rounded the first left curve, her killer was almost upon her and as his hand was reaching out to grab her, a sixth sense made her start to turn around. She saw a man with a glint of murder in his eyes and with another glint, this one coming from a bedroom light reflecting on a cold steel blade, a hand was clamped over her mouth and simultaneously reached forward with his right hand and sliced through her neck. That was about all she knew for after that, it was all down to her killer.

The first cut severed her larynx just below her vocal chords and carotid artery and the second cut was dealt to be sure that his latest victim would have no chance of survival. As he held her, he noticed the dark path that led to the left building, and so he dragged his latest victim along the ground and realised she was now just dead weight, not a living being. Blood had spattered along the ground and followed them as thcy waltzed their way towards the darkness, him to where no light shone and her to where no life existed.

Once out of sight of anyone looking down the walkway from the Domplatz, the killer swiftly tore and ripped the clothes off his victim so that he would be unheeded in his task. He laid her on her back and got down to the business he had to complete.

First, he placed the tip of his sharp knife on the breastbone and sliced her open from sternum to groin, slicing through skin and muscle, exposing all of her inner organs. Then he swiftly put his hands in and started cutting as if from memory or experience. Although it was dark, it was as if he could carry out this part with his eyes closed. He sliced away and removed her intestines and placed these carefully over her right shoulder, arranging them as if in an art club. With his hands inside her body, he made several cuts until he held her left kidney in his hand, which he removed and placed this in a plastic bag he had brought along. As her internal body temperature was many degrees warmer than the outside air, steam arose from the open wound and the stench of offal could be smelt. He cut some more inside her opened body, remembering what he had to do and then turned his attention to her face. It appeared as if she was sneering at him, edging him on to do something else. He stabbed and sliced across her face several times, cutting her eyelids and nose, cheeks and lips. The warmth of her body escaped and enveloped him so that he was sweating as he completed his attack.

All in all, it only took him about five minutes to complete the task he had set himself, or the task that had been set for him. After all, it was not he who had come up with this original idea of killing this way, he was just bringing to life the story that was one hundred years old. He too would go down in history and people would read and talk about him like they did old Jack.

Finally finished, he slowly got to his feet and listened to hear anyone approaching. Nothing heard, he walked swiftly back the way he had come and exited the Kerngasse, turned right on Damm and at the end crossed the road and walked down Kolkstrasse. He checked his clothing to see if it was possible to spot any blood stains on his clothes, but as the street lights were not that bright, his dark clothes hid any wetness that would be visible if scrutinized up close. He turned left on Thomästrasse and headed towards the Osthofener-Thomä-Wallstrasse which was the street that ran parallel with the town wall and the parks behind it.

Using the darkness wherever he could find it and stealth where he had to move across the lit streets, he was able to get from the second murder scene and onto the town wall by climbing up the embankment where many trees grew, giving him a foot-hold. From on top of the wall, he was able to look down onto the other side and allow him to plan his escape.

'41/01 to all units, 41/01 to all units. We have just received a report that a body has been found in the Ressourcengasse some two minutes ago. Apparently it is of a female with a slashed throat. 41/17, that is your area, please respond over.'

'Fuck it, the bastard has actually had the bottle to strike.' Freddy said from the back seat.

'41/17 to 41/01, copy that. We are moving in to the location. Are there any foot patrols nearby that can also attend over?' Sven said into the radio mic.

'41/01, roger, we have both 26 and 33 in the region. Do you want them both on scene, over?'

'41/17, send one to the scene and the other on standby, over.'

'41/01 roger that. 41/26, proceed to the location, 41/33 stand by for further instructions. Ambulance has been called and is on its way. All units, please secure the perimeter. Stop all foot and road traffic from entering or leaving the city center. Out.'

Before the radio message had ended, Trilling had the car turned on and was already heading towards the crime scene at a fast pace of knots. Oblivious to the late hour, he turned the sirens and lights on and tore down the streets and had stopped the car on Wippgasse within minutes of starting the journey.

All three jumped out and Sven instructed Trilling to seal off the alleyway where they were heading towards, only to let in the emergency services and the crime scene investigators when they arrived.

'41/17 to all units, I want the town flooded with foot patrols, stay in pairs and walk every street possible. Let's have the supporting crews pull forward and secure the outside of the town wall, get the RMPs in with their dogs and let's hunt the bastard to ground.'

'41/01, copy that.' Günther relayed the message and coordinated with Schneider and Betty who decided which team should go where and when.

Within minutes, the old town of Soest had turned from being a quiet, secluded area into a frenzy of running feet, sirens blaring and blue lights flashing, dogs barking and men swearing and police radios squawking in the night. As it was not too late, many people were still up watching either the late night news or one of the feature films being screened on a Friday night and all heard the cacophony outside. Lights were turned on, doors and windows opened and many thought that the town was being invaded. One old man went down into his cellar and loaded his Luger P08 pistol that he had kept as a souvenir after the Second World War and went outside to defend his property and wife from anyone who came to attack him. In the turmoil, the old man thought that one of the policemen who happened to be running down the street towards him was actually a Russian soldier from Stalingrad and so he decided to open fire, hitting his neighbour's car twice, the pavement once and the policeman three times in the chest. Now with an almost empty magazine, he went back inside to reload and keep out of the firing line.

The downed policeman's colleagues returned fire in the general direction they thought the ambush had come from and the shots were heard from the center of town. All this added confusion to the hunt as several radio messages went out simultaneously claiming that the killer had turned to using firearms in his bid to escape. 41/01 directed other units towards this gun battle and several units were pulled away from the key locations they were guarding and told to assist.

On reaching the house in question, they found that the injured policeman still lay on his back and was heard groaning in the middle of the road.

When the old man saw the enemy regrouping outside his house, he took several more loaded magazines and moved towards the front door, making sure that he turned off all the lights as he went. His wife was screaming at him but was ignored. If only her words could have registered in his brain that he had made a mistake and should hand himself in, then all would have worked out differently. But as his muddled thoughts took him back to 1942, he was only able to see the Red Army outside. He moved as swiftly as he could with his on setting rheumatism and scuttled towards the low garden wall with its wooden gate. Here he crouched down and let off single shots wherever he saw either movement or the shape of his enemy.

By now, the police were in full force and had been able to surround the house and block off all escape routes. One policeman, who was either brave or fed up with being shot at decided to get closer to the property by moving slowly through the bushes in the next garden, was able to locate the assailant and shot the old man several times in the upper legs and lower stomach. When no other shots were fired back in retaliation, the policeman shouted to his colleagues to cover him and slowly stepped over the low dividing fence and approached. This is where he saw that the man he had shot was someone of retirement age and was wearing a white string vest, a pair of pyjama trousers and a pair of carpet slippers. Not the attire that one would associate with a killer. This battle had taken some time, as getting all the units in position from one part of town to the other was not something that was practiced every day. As the smell of cordite hung in the air, it became apparent that not only were there several holes in the old soldier and the policeman in the street, there was also a huge hole left where the units should have been before they were redirected to deal with someone suffering from Alzheimer's disease. With the earlier euphoria of cornering German Jack as he had now been labeled, suddenly there was concern that maybe they had left the door open for him to escape.

'41/01 to all units, 41/01 to all units. Another report has come in and a second victim has been found. 41/17, again your area, this time in Kerngasse, I repeat Kerngasse. Copy, over.'

'41/17 received. Coordinate other units to the scene and send another unit to my current location. I'll go to Kerngasse. How is the lockdown? Over'

'41/01, closing the streets as planned went out the window when we moved as many units as we could to the gun battle that took place. I'll start moving them back to their positions and only keep the relevant units at the scenes, over.'

41/17, roger that. Let's hope that we have some luck and can close the doors before the horse bolts, otherwise we will need to wait until the next time. Out.'

'Did you get that Freddy?' Sven asked his partner. The shitbag has claimed his fourth murder tonight. Let's go and have a look. Leave this to the locals to guard and wait for Steffi and co.'

Both moved away from the inert body of Renate Bölte and walked the few meters to the end of the alleyway. Sven threw the hand radio towards Trilling and instructed him to drive him towards Kerngasse where the other victim had been found.

'Sir, it will be quicker if we went on foot, we only have to go between the buildings here, walk across the square and we are there.'

'Ok, lead on. Freddy, on me.'

With that, all three policemen jogged across the cobbles and had reached the entrance to the street where a policeman was seen crouching over, puking all over the floor and his own boots.

'Where's the body?' Freddy asked.

The constable pointed towards a house in the alleyway and continued heaving, making speech impossible.

'Ok, Trilling, stay here and wait for reinforcements. You coordinate who comes in and out.'

'Yes sir.'

Freddy had already walked towards where the fourth victim lay and Sven heard him gasp as he approached from behind, his view being blocked by Freddy's broad back.

'Ok,' Sven said, 'let the dog see the rabbit.'

'Dog see the rabbit? Looks like this rabbit was set upon by a whole pack of rabid dogs.'

Freddy moved to his left and Sven caught his first view of the body.

'Fucking hell, I'd say it was a pack of fucking werewolves, not dogs.' Sven added in disgust.

'We have to stop this cunt before he strikes again.' Freddy added.

Both stood up and took a step back. It was clear that the victim was dead. Nobody would have survived being drawn and quartered in this fashion.

'What's that?' Freddy asked, pointing to something lying next to the opened body.

'Fuck if I know, didn't do much anatomy at my school. We were into metalwork and woodwork.'

'We only got to dissect a frog in biology. Looked nothing like this.'

'I think we've fucked up tonight.' Sven confided in his friend. 'This has gone tits up. We have let him kill another two women and we also had the gunfight at the OK Corral. What could we have done differently?'

'Being honest, nothing. If the bastard has this planned, we are only playing catch-up the whole time. He will always be one step ahead and we will only catch him if we are either lucky in him making a mistake or we can get into position for the fifth murder.'

'Yeah, I suppose you're right. Come on, looks like the Techies have arrived. Nothing we can do here, let's back off out the way we came and leave this to the experts.'

*

Rudolph heard all the commotion of shots being fired and was also aware of cars starting and blue lights flashing from where he stood. He had a good vantage point up on the town wall and was able to see the area in which the police car lights moved towards.

Still taking no chances, he stayed to the shadows until he was sure that there was no longer any movement either on the wall or down on either side. He noticed that he had some dried blood on his right hand and he wiped this against the damp grass.

He eventually took courage and moved from his hidden location, satisfied that his plans had succeeded and had all gone as he had expected. He walked along one section of the wall until he came to some steep steps that led down to a street. He descended carefully and then walked towards where he had parked his taxi. With relief, he quietly unlocked the door and got in. He started the engine and drove to the end of the road, turning right towards Ulrichtor. He didn't get far as he was stopped by a policeman standing next to a barrier blocking the road. There was also a police car parked on the verge, engine idling and with another policeman sitting behind the wheel.

'Good evening, sir. Can I see some identification please? And where have you just come from?' he was asked.

Detlef was nervous. Because of his antics during the evening and the adrenaline pumping through his body, now that it was all over he was feeling weak and tired. He needed to sit down and take some deep breaths to stop the shaking of his muscles. He sat on the parapet of the town wall and looked across the night sky and saw the distant blue lights illuminating the other side of town.

His first encounter of the evening had finished so quickly, he had been dissatisfied with his performance and he had made sure to make an extra effort in his second encounter.

Now that it was all over, he wanted to get away from the area in case he was seen and this would compromise his return back home. He checked that his clothing was clean as could be when he noticed he had some blood on his hand. He took out a paper tissue, wetted this with his tongue and rubbed at the dried blood until it had vanished. He discarded the tissue under some bushes and headed towards where he had parked the car.

On nearing the vehicle, he again stopped in the shadows and seeing nobody, he quickly walked across the road, unlocked the door and got behind the wheel as fast as he could. Under darkness, he again undressed and got back into his street clothes, putting his other garments in the sports bag.

This done, he started the car and drove slowly away from the car park and headed out of the city wall towards home. He turned right towards the train station and was halted almost immediately by a barrier that was across the road blocking all passage.

'Good evening sir, may I see some form of identification please.'

Detlef's heart rate soared from a healthy 60 bpm to around 140 bpm within seconds.

Billy was sweating and breathing heavily after his escape. He had heard many sirens and saw a number of police foot patrols coming along where he had been, but with his skills, he went unseen.

His night had started good and he was able to move across the street from where he had been hiding without being spotted. After his first encounter, he had looked around and spotted another opportunity and headed their way. Now that he had finished with the second one, he wanted to leave but was aware that the night was turning into something that he had not anticipated.

He walked across the street and hid and saw several police cars and foot patrols moving around, but he went unnoticed as he slowly moved away from the scene. Extracting himself was harder than he had anticipated as he heard several police radios squawking whenever he turned a corner, making him to double back on a couple of occasions.

Now well away from the center, he walked along the road until he was near the town wall. Once at the top, he looked around and saw the lights across the town rotating with the colour blue and knew he was at last away from all eyes and ears. Not letting his guard down, he now had to get himself away from the area and back to camp and enter somehow so that he would not be seen entering. This would be harder, but after the training weekends he had done, he was sure he was capable.

He walked further along the wall and eventually climbed down some steep steps and he saw an underpass for pedestrians that went under the wall, taking them from the inside street to the parks on the other side. He walked along the park and saw a taxi that had been stopped by a police patrol, so he decided to cross the road now whilst they were busy and he walked up another road, not knowing he was now outside their cordon.

On reaching the next main street, he saw another taxi and was able to hail this down and asked to be taken back to Echtrop, the village close to the camp but was adamant he did not want to be dropped off at the camp gates. The driver asked for the fare up front in case the soldier ran off once the car stopped and Billy paid the agreed fare and sank down low in the back in silence, thinking of a way to get into camp without being seen or caught.

CHAPTER 28

01.10.1988

'41/01 to 41/17, come in 17, over.'

Sven took the radio set from Trilling and answered. '41/17 receiving.'

'41/01, we have stopped thirteen vehicles attempting to leave Soest so far. From these, eleven seem to have a good alibi that have so far checked out. The drivers and passengers are still contained but appear to be legit. However, two vehicles that were stopped have both provided stories that are not panning out. And the best bit is, both of these have already been in for questioning before. Over.'

'41/17, ok, make sure that we gather all the contact details of the eleven in case we need to interview them later. As for the other two, who are they? Over.'

'41/01, the taxi driver Rudolph Mertens and the male nurse, Detlef Krome. Both have provided a story that seems made up, over.'

'41/17, ok, get them two back to the station and have them locked up. I want their vehicles taken in as well and we'll have the Techies go over them with a fine toothcomb. I'll be here for a while but I want to be in on both interviews personally. Do not let anyone else start until I get back. Lock them up and let them stew first. And don't offer them any blankets. If I have to go without sleep, then so will they. Out.'

Sven handed the radio back to Trilling and walked over to where Freddy was standing, talking to a technician who was dressed in the usual paper suit, mask, hat and blue overshoes.

'Hey, Sven, on first inspection, it appears that some body parts have been taken from this victim.' Lucas Wilhelm informed him. 'All the cuts appear to be clean and not as if in a frenzy attack. Looks premeditated to me.'

'Cheers Lucas. Anything else unusual?'

'Not at first sight, Steffi is still examining. I've taken all the photos of the body and the complete area, in and around both entrances. I can see that she was attacked over in the corner and dragged along the cobbles to where she lays now. There are scuff marks from her shoes which suggests she was no longer in control of any leg movement and also I can see several footprints from the same pair of shoes heading towards her final resting place and going back down the alleyway. Obviously there was too much blood for the killer not to have stood in. Again, I've taken prints and these will at least tell us something about the size of our attacker.'

'At least that could be a breakthrough. We could do with one. Freddy, guess what? Both Krome and Mertens are back in for questioning. Both were trying to drive out of the centre and were stopped at the cordons. Maybe we have caught our killer and that the shoe marks will help us out. Good work, Lucas. Keep us posted. Hey, Steffi,' he called, 'anything yet?'

'I'll be finished in about fifteen minutes. I'll catch up with you then. Any news from Egbert at the other site?' she asked.

'He said it was a simple throat cutting. Exactly as like in the pamphlet Betty brought back from London. So far there are no apparent clues. Obviously we've got the door to door going on etc. Just need to get the identifications of the victims so we can start piecing together where they were, witnesses etc. But my gut tells me we won't find any witnesses who can point us in any direction. Both murders appear to be copycat killings, so all premeditated and that gives the killer the advantage in planning his attacks and also his escape. Let's just hope the footprints help us.'

'I'll meet you at the station once I've finished. Both bodies will be moved back to my lab in Dortmund and put in the fridge and Egbert and I will do the post mortems later today and send the reports via fax to you.'

'Ok, I'll see you back at the station before you head back to Dortmund. Thanks.'

Sven turned back to Freddy and moved his head, indicating Freddy to follow.

'Look, I've got a cracking headache. I'm gonna head back to the station and close my eyes for an hour or two. Can you wrap everything up here and get all the main heads in for a briefing for 8 o'clock? Then we can see where we're at and go from there. Look,

It's nearly 3 o'clock now. I'll start interviewing our two suspects once I've got rid of my headache and then meet you in the conference room.'

'Yeah, no probs. Need any tablets?'

'I'm sure I'll be able to find some. Just need a dark room to lay down in before the headache turns into a migraine. Nice hot sweet tea will also help. Be right as rain in no time. See you later.'

'Ok, mate, later.'

Sven asked Trilling to take him back to the station and then to come back and assist Freddy with whatever was needed. On the way back to the station, Sven kept going over the same thought. Had they let two women get killed for nothing or had they prevented the fifth victim from being killed by capturing the killer? Only time would tell.

'Sorry to wake you sir, but we've just had a phone call from someone who has identified the boyfriend of Anja Schmedding.'

'Fucking hell Günther, did I not tell you to let me sleep?'

'Yes sir, but I took this on as being more important than looking ones best for the camera.'

'You cheeky sod. What time is it?'

'Just gone five o'clock.'

'Ok, so, who called?'

Sven sat up on the concrete block that served as a bed and was thankful for the mattress and blanket that had made his short sleep more comfortable.

'Barmaid from *Old Germany*, just back from her holidays abroad and tonight was her first shift since coming back. She saw one of the photos we left behind and recognised the person immediately.'

'And? Any names?'

'Yes, she said it was a British soldier called Billy. No last name known.'

'Can't recall anyone on our list called Billy, can you?'

'No, but Billy is the shortened name for William. Billy Idol, Billy Joel and so on.'

'You could be right on that. Ok, can you get Captain Scott onto it and let's go through the list of anyone called William. And let's get the barmaid in for an interview and also show her all the photos of the soldiers for identification. Now, fuck off and wake me up with a nice cup of tea in one hour.'

'Yes sir. Would you like me to spit once or twice in the cup before I deliver it to his lordship?' Günther added as he walked out of the cell and closed the door, not quite hearing the blasphemy that was directed at his retreating figure.

'The time is 06:20 on Saturday the 1st of October, 1988. For the record, present in the room is myself, Erster Kriminalhauptkommissar Sven Gerling, also present are Kriminaloberkommissar Schwarz, Herr Detlef Krome and the duty on call lawyer Herr Schäffermeier. Now Herr Krome, we have been here once before not too long ago. Now what brings you back here so quickly?'

'You tell me. I was going home when you lot stopped me. I haven't done anything wrong.'

'Well, let's start at the beginning shall we? What was your purpose for visiting Soest this evening?' Sven asked.

'I'd rather not say.' Detlef replied, looking down at the table.

'And I'd rather not be in here at this stupid hour of the morning wasting my time with you.' Sven spoke loudly and banged the table with the palm of his hand, making Detlef jump in his seat. 'Now, I'll ask the question again. What was your purpose for visiting Soest this evening?'

'I just came for a few drinks. Weekend stuff, you know.'

'So, you openly admit to drinking and then getting behind the wheel of a motorised vehicle. We call that drink driving which carries a heavy penalty. Do you want to stick with that story? We will of course need you to take a mandatory blood test so that we can ascertain your blood/alcohol levels.'

'I didn't drink much.' Detlef added.

'Well, we'll see how much when we get the results back. Which establishments did you go to?'

'Er, I just went from one place to another, can't remember really.'

'Listen, stop feeding me this bullshit. You know that I will knock on every pub and bar door and ask if you were present. Help yourself and start telling the truth. Maybe your lawyer can talk some sense into you. The quicker you tell us what you were doing, the quicker we can move along. If you continue to play silly buggers, then I will have no other choice than to charge you with obstructing the course of justice and we'll hold you for a lot longer than you were here the last time. Do I make myself clear?'

Detlef moved his head towards his lawyer and nodded when the lawyer had finished whispering in his ear.

'I will cooperate with you, but I can honestly say that I have done nothing illegal. It is all quite acceptable nowadays.' Detlef informed the room and the tape.

'Well, we will see if it is acceptable when we find out what you have been up to, won't we?' Sven replied. 'So, starting from the beginning, I will ask my original question for the last time. What was your purpose for visiting Soest this evening? And if I don't get a clear answer, by God, I'll have you strung out to dry.'

'I, er, came to Soest for some entertainment.'

'What, did you go to the cinema? Bought tickets for the circus? What?'

'No, something private.'

'And would you care to enlighten us as to what sort of private entertainment you had? Did it involve the slicing of the throat of a young woman as she walked down a dark alleyway and then you decided you liked it so much you went for an encore where you took the time and gutted out another woman?'

'What? No, I haven't killed anyone. Are you again trying to pin a murder on me like the last time?'

'I'm not trying to pin any murder on anyone. What I am attempting to do is find out what you were doing in Soest and where you were all evening. If we can take you out of the equation, then we won't have to sit here all day guessing. So what were you doing?'

'I'd like to talk to my lawyer in private first.'

'Interview suspended at 06:35.' Sven turned off the tape recorder and said, 'You had better start cooperating. My patience is wearing pretty thin. Whatever you were doing, it cannot be as bad as killing two innocent women. Now speak to your lawyer and get some sense into your head for the sake of all of us. Understood?' And with that, Sven and Peter Schwarz left the room.

'So, for the benefit of the tape, could you please tell us where you had been in Soest prior to you being picked up?' Sven asked Rudolph in the interview room two doors down from Detlef.

'I dropped off a passenger at their address.'

'And which address was that?'

'Somewhere along Ulrich-Jakobi-Wallstrasse. He didn't give a house number, just told me to stop near a junction.'

'And what did your passenger look like?' Peter asked.

'Normal height, brown hair cut short, jeans and jacket, pretty normal.'

'Ok, so why has your central come back informing us that your last fare was registered to take someone to Düsseldorf airport? And how come they did not hear anything from you once you got there? And how come you can get from Soest to Düsseldorf and back within a couple of hours when it takes anyone else about four hours for the round trip? Would you care to elaborate?'

Rudolph went red in the face as he saw his story unravelling before his eyes. All of his well laid plans were about to come undone.

'Er, my passenger to Düsseldorf decided to go by train when I told him the estimated price of a taxi ride. I thought I informed central and picked up my last fare as he stopped me when he was walking along the road.'

'So why was this not logged in with central?' Sven asked.

'Ok, I thought I'd pocket some money. All drivers do it. Tips nowadays are pretty shit so we have to make some money other ways.'

'So, you are openly admitting to stealing money by not logging in your fares. Have I understood you correctly? If so, then I will have to charge you with theft and that will also lead to you losing your job and also your taxi license, which in turn will lose you your livelihood. So, are you sticking with your story or is there something else you are trying to hide? And believe me, this time I will apply for a search warrant and turn your place upside down unless you start telling me the truth. No more fabrications, no more hiding the truth. Understand?'

'May I have a few minutes with my lawyer in private, please?' Rudolph asked, head bowed forward and his voice very quiet.

'Interview suspended.' Again, Sven turned off the tape recorder and left the room with Peter following, allowing Rudolph to converse with his lawyer behind closed doors which was guarded by a constable standing outside.

'Alright troops, listen in. We currently have two men in custody downstairs conversing with their lawyers. We pulled them in before but let them go due to having alibis and no evidence. But these two were stopped when they both tried, independently, to leave Soest by car. I will let them stew for a bit and then we'll go in all guns blazing. It's time to stop playing Mister Nice Guy and get to the bottom of what they were doing last night.

'Then we have a positive identification on our British soldier. Captain Scott is on his way to the relevant barracks and will be bringing the soldier here for questioning along with a military lawyer and translator.

'Steffi, anything you need to add regarding the bodies?' Sven asked.

'There's nothing that I can be definite about without a post mortem back at the lab. Just that one died from a severe loss of blood due to having her neck sliced open by a very sharp instrument and the second died from excessive weight loss.'

'Weight loss?' Bernie asked.

'Yes, it happens when half of your insides become your outsides. Not much fun having your innards displayed for the Gods to look down at. But we will have a detailed report as soon as we have finished. My team found nothing at the scenes apart from several footprints at the last site. The ones closest to the body are the best and we can see that the killer walked down to the other end of the alley. Unfortunately the length of the alleyway made the blood collected on the soles of the shoes to wear off and we lost the traces half way down the alley. We sprayed a Luminol/hydrogen peroxide solution to see if we can find any blood traces as to the direction the killer may have gone after leaving the alleyway but we came up blank. When the solution comes in contact with certain substances, in this case blood, the iron in the blood will react with the Luminol solution and lets off a faint blue light known as chemiluminescence. What we do have is a nice print of the shoe the killer was wearing and will be able to provide you with shoe size and most probably the weight of the killer. Apart from that both crime scenes are as clean as a whistle.'

'Thanks Steffi. We'll get the two downstairs to strip off and you can test their clothes and shoes for blood stains. Dennis, have you searched their vehicles yet?'

'Not yet boss, got side tracked when we got back. I'll get it done when we finish up here.'

'Cheers. Steffi, can I have a couple of your techies to go over the cars with their magic tools?'

'Yes, sure. I'll let Björn and Lucas know to prioritize that.'

'Do we know the whereabouts of where the soldier was last night?' Freddy asked.

'No, not yet. We'll wait for the RMPs to bring in our suspect and see what we can find out. Anything else?'

'Yes,' Betty said raising her hand, 'can I report these latest murders before you have a press conference? You did promise.'

'Speak with Hauptkommissar Ahrens and work alongside him. But I think you do deserve first shout. Freddy, I want you with me in the interviews with the twats downstairs. Peter, Dennis, I want you two to concentrate on the vehicles and clothes of the suspects. The rest of you, the normal shit. Right, if that's it, all back to work and do what you get paid for.'

Conference over, they all headed out of the conference room.

'So, we left off with you wanting to speak in private with your lawyer. I hope he has made you see sense and you will now start telling us the truth and not feed us with the bullshit you have done so far.'

'What I'm about to confess to, will it be leaked to the public?' Detled asked.

'If you confess to the murders, of course it will. It will be splashed all over the tabloids and the international news desks. What do you expect? That we keep it quiet? Or are you confessing to something else?'

'Something else.' the lawyer said for his client.

'Well, I cannot promise, but if it has nothing to do with the bodies I have currently laid out in the refrigeration units in Dortmund, then we'll see. So, I'm all ears. Spill the beans.'

'Well, er, it's a bit embarrassing.'

'I don't give a monkeys tit if it makes you blush or not. I want to know what the fuck you were up to last night. I have to inform two sets of parents that their daughters will not be coming home tonight or ever again for that matter and you're embarrassed?'

'My client has confided in me and I can say on his behalf that he was nowhere near the murder scenes.'

'Well, seeing that we haven't said where the murders took place, how the hell does he know he was nowhere near?' Freddy interjected.

'Because I was doing something else.' Detlef said quietly.

'My patience is wearing pretty thin. Are you going to tell me so that I can discard you from my list of suspects and allow me to get on with catching the killer, or are you going to sit there and beat around the bush all day?'

'Alright, alright, I'll tell you. I'm a cross dresser.'

'You're a what?'

'A cross dresser.'

'And what the fuck is one of those when it's at home?' Sven asked.

'I like dressing up in women's clothing.'

'You like dressing up in women's clothing? What, the whole shebang? Boots, skirt, knickers?'

'Yes.'

'Why?'

'Because it gives me a kick.' Detlef answered.

'Kick? It gives you a kick? I'd give you a mighty kick up the arse if you were my son and came home dressed like a tart. And just when you think you've heard it all before. Ok, carry on. What did you do when you donned your glad rags?'

'I went into the park.'

'Don't tell us you went there for a ride on the swings.' Freddy added.

'No, to meet up with someone.'

'So you actually went into the park to meet someone dressed as a woman? What would you want to do that for?'

'You can guess what for.'

'No I cannot. I want you to tell me. It can't be as bad as someone seeing you dressed in frilly knickers with stockings, can it?'

'I go to the park to meet up with men for sex.'

'Do they know you have a wadger between your legs or does that come as a surprise later?'

'Of course they know. That's what turns them on.'

'Well, whatever rocks your socks I suppose. So, there you are dressed up as a woman and you get picked up by a bloke. What happens next?' Sven asked.

'Well, it all depends. Sometimes they just want a blowjob or a hand job, others want to have sex with me.'

'Are you telling me that you dress up as a woman and get your kicks off by getting banged up the arse by a shit stabber? Are there any witnesses to corroborate your story?'

'If you look in the boot of my car, you'll find my outfit under the spare wheel.' Detlef replied shyly.

Sven nodded at the constable by the door and it was understood what he needed to do. Several minutes went by and nobody wanted to break the silence. The constable arrived back and carried a sports bag into the room.

'Is this your bag?' Freddy asked.

'Yes.' Detlef replied.

'Ok, let's see what we have.' Sven opened the bag and put the contents onto the table. 'For the benefit of the tape, we have retrieved a sports bag from the boot of Herr Krome's car. On examination, the items inside the bag are as follows: A pair of high heel boots, black patent leather, size 44, a blonde wig, a black leather mini skirt, a cosmetic bag containing one red lipstick, a black mascara, a black eyeliner pencil and a blusher. Are these your item's?'

'Yes.'

'And where are the knickers?'

'I'm still wearing them.' Detlef swallowed with embarrassment.

'Would you be willing to undress here so that we can correctly identify your garments or do you wish to be taken back to your cell and strip down in front of another officer?'

Detlef stood up, unbuckled his belt and pulled down his trousers and lifted up his sweatshirt. A pair of red frilly knickers and matching bra looked out at everyone.

'So, tell me about your evening.' Sven said, lost slightly for words at the discovery that was unravelling in front of his eyes.

'Well, there is an advert in a contact magazine that I read and decided that I am able to live out my fantasy. I don't hurt anyone by doing it. So now and then I come to Soest and dress up and meet with men who like having sex with other men. I hide in the bushes or in darkened doorways and wait for people to walk past. Then I follow and when they look back, they register if they are interested or not. Then we find a quiet place to fulfil our urges.'

'And how many men did you have sex with last night?' Freddy asked.

'Just two. The first one didn't last long. He came within a couple of minutes. So I stayed and met another man, this time it lasted longer.'

'So what services did you provide this gentleman?'

'Everything. It started with a hand job, then I blew him and then I turned around and he fucked me. He was a bit rough and he pushed me a bit too hard against the wall. I cut my hand on the stones. Here.' Detlef held out his hand and all present saw the scrape marks on the palm of his hand. 'When he had finished, I heard sirens so I decided to go home. I saw the lights across the town so I know I was not near where the bodies had been found.'

'Ok, I want you to provide my colleague here with a detailed map of where you parked, where you walked, where you had sex. I also want you to provide any details you have of the men you allegedly met tonight. Understood?'

'Yes.' Detlef replied.

Sven excused himself for the benefit of the tape and left the room, flabbergasted at what he had seen and heard. It could not get any weirder than this, he thought. If only he knew.

'So, Herr Mertens, what have you decided to tell me?' Sven asked when he walked into the other interview room and started the tape recorder.

'Yes, I'm willing to confess to what I have been up to if you promise to not inform my taxi company of what I have said.'

'Now you listen to me you fat fuck. You have no bargaining chips to trade with me. I ain't gonna promise you shit until I hear the truth. Only then will I make the decision what I do with your confession. Got it?'

'Can he talk to me that way?' Rudolph asked his lawyer.

'I can talk to you anyway I want to. Now, do you want more verbal abuse or are you willing to play ball?'

'I'm sure my client is willing to provide you with his antics last night if you just curb the language.' the duty lawyer interjected.

'And I'm sure I'll remember to give him an apology if he stops fucking about and gets on with it. I have two girls looking at the inside of two body bags and getting colder as the time ticks by. They may have all the time in the world but I don't. And just so that you know, I am aware that you have a police record and I am not talking about the songs *Message In A Bottle* or *Walking On The Moon*. No, I am talking about when you were a naughty boy and decided to bury your mother in the middle of a forest. So I am beginning to think that you may have killed her and after such a long time, you haven't been able to resist and have started a killing spree to quench your thirst. Tell me if I am getting warm.'

'No, I never killed my poor mother. I woke up and she was dead. I was in shock and didn't know what I was doing when I buried her. Besides, I've been to prison for that and I wouldn't hurt anybody.'

'That is what you say but I am still sceptical. But it does shine a particular light on you. Now, are you going to answer my questions and enlighten me as to what you were doing?'

'Ok, ok. I arranged to meet up with a woman tonight. She's into BDSM and we arranged to meet.'

'Is that a name of a new rap group or initials for a sports club?'

'It stands for Bondage and Discipline, Sadism and Masochism. I like being tied up with ropes and having pain inflicted so that I can reach a sexual peak that is different from anything else.'

Sven stared at Rudolph in disbelief. 'So you came to Soest to get whipped and spanked by a woman so you can cum your duff. Have I got that right or have I misunderstood something?'

'If you want to put it like that, then yes. The world is changing and what you might call normal is not normal anymore.'

'Normal? I thought it weird when we had to suffer through the Glam Rock era with men wearing makeup and high heels. We're now just getting over that New Romance shit with men wearing frilly shirts and boots. Now you come along and tell me about getting tied up and spanked. No wonder you looked happy when we put the handcuffs on you. Surprised you don't go out of your way to get arrested more often. Anyway, where did all this take place?'

'Somewhere along the town wall where one of the towers used to be. I was told to wait at a certain place at a certain time as she was making a house visit and that she would deal with me when she was finished. We arranged to do it in the park or on the town wall when it was dark. I like it when others watch so I wanted to do it outside.'

'And do you have the contact details of your dominatrix so that we can corroborate your story?'

'Not on me, but yes, I would be able to provide it. If you look in my car, you'll find some rope and several whips and other instruments that she used on me. I'll even show you the whip marks on my back if you wish.' Rudolph confided with a smile, now starting to enjoy himself the more he saw disgust and disbelief cross the faces of all those present, duty lawyer included.

'I'll leave that to my colleagues. You just told me that you wouldn't hurt anybody but you also stated you are into sadism and masochism. Well, isn't that inflicting pain on somebody?'

'Yes, but I like the pain, I'm a receiver not a giver.'

'Are you telling me you also have titles for what you do? Ok, so we've established you're a lover and not a fighter. We will need to speak to your Mistress before we can make any further decisions. We'll get her details from you later after we have made other checks.

'Interview suspended at 11:26. Ok, constable, please escort Herr Mertens back to his cell and make him strip so that you can confirm his whip marks.'

Sven stood up and left the room and headed straight to the toilet where he stood looking at his reflection in the mirror, wondering if he was in a dream.

'Hey, Sven. How did the other interview go?' Freddy asked when they met up in the office.

'I've met some sick fucks in my time but it is hard to choose between them two who takes first place tonight. We've got Krome the Drag Queen against Mertens the Masochist. Krome likes to provide sexual services to perverts who like getting groped by a bloke wearing lace whilst Mertens likes getting whipped by a woman after being tied up.'

'He likes what?' Freddy enquired.

'Into something called BDSM. Bondage with Sadomasochism or something. He also likes to do it with a crowd watching too. I have a feeling that we should be able to find some witnesses who saw them both doing what they ascertain they were doing. Will just take someone brave enough to come forward and admit to being a weird pervert themselves.'

'Well, if we can rule the two out, we'll only have to concentrate on the soldier as a main suspect. At least we can divert our attention towards him and not have it wide open.'

'Yes,' Sven said, 'we only have to hope it is the soldier otherwise we are back to square one with no idea.'

'Proper Jack the Ripper style.' Freddy said and walked towards the vending machine.

CHAPTER 29

Billy was escorted into the police station by two burly RMPs and followed by Captain Scott, Major Hollingsworth and a civilian translator employed by the British army. They were shown into interview room 2 and asked to wait for a few minutes until the detectives were informed of their arrival. The detectives arrived some ten minutes later and made the introductions out of politeness and for the tape.

'Ok,' Sven started, 'I hope you will forgive any grammatical mistakes I might make and if there is something I cannot say in English, we can then revert to the interpreter. Is that ok with you?'

'Fine with me.' Billy said.

'Ok, can you confirm your name please?'

'My name is William Jennings.'

'That is what you said when we interviewed you before. Do you have a nickname that you may go by?'

'No.'

'Well, we have been led to believe you go by the name of Billy. Is this correct?'

'No.'

'Ok, so we are going to have to do this the hard way. I am sure that Captain Scott and his RMP colleagues will be able to drive to your barracks and ask every one of your friends what they call you. That will of course take time, in which case you will be locked up in a police cell. After we then establish that you have lied to us, we will find it very hard to believe anything else you say. So, I will ask you one more time and I want you to think hard before you answer. Do you go by the name of Bill or Billy?'

'May I ask why I am here?' Billy asked, deflecting the question.

'Listen Jennings, you had better start providing answers to the detective's questions or you will find yourself in more hot water than a NAAFI teabag.' Captain Scott interjected. 'Now stop being a prat and answer the questions.'

'Yes sir. Alright, some people call me Billy.'

'Now that wasn't hard was it? Ok, now let's go back to our first interview when I asked you if you knew an Anja Schmedding. You clearly stated no. Are you still sticking with that story or have you realized since that maybe you were mistaken and do actually recall seeing her before?' Sven asked, looking at his notes.

'No, I don't know anyone called Anja Schmedding.'

'Maybe she didn't tell you her last name. Here, look at this photograph and try to think.'

Billy looked again at the picture he had been shown previously and again tried to blag his way out of it.

'No, as I told you last time, I do not recognize her.'

'Well, that is where it gets rather difficult again as we have a witness who has identified you with being with her on the evening of the 31st August. Would you care to comment on that?' Sven asked, this time looking directly at Billy.

'Identified by whom?' Billy asked

'By a barmaid in *Old Germany* is who. Now it will only be a matter of time before we stand you up in an identity parade. That is when the shit really hits the fan.' Sven added.

'Ok, Jennings, like I said before, stop being an arse. These gentlemen have done their homework and if they hadn't, we wouldn't be sitting here. Now, I am ordering you to cooperate.' Captain Scott said sternly.

'Alright, yes, I recognize her. And yes, I went out with her a couple of times.'

'So why deny knowing her when we asked you?'

'Because you learn never admit to anything and when you said about her being killed, well, one goes into defensive mode.'

'So let's start again, shall we? How well did you know Anja Schmedding?' Sven asked patiently.

'We had met a couple of nights before and we got on alright, so we planned to meet up again. She told me she was seeing a German guy but it was nothing serious and she would rather be with me. So on that night, we met up in *Old Germany* and she told me she had just had an argument with him and she had left him in the restaurant and came out to dance. She just wanted to have fun.'

'And what happened when you left *Old Germany*?' Freddy asked.

'We went outside and I went with her to the nurse's home where she has a room. We stood outside in the car park and had a talk for about ten minutes and then I left.'

'Did you not go up to her room?' Sven asked.

'No, I did ask but she wanted to go slow.'

'Were you upset that she wouldn't let you up to her room?'

'Upset no. Maybe a bit disappointed. I mean, we were getting on well together and I thought she was up for it.'

'What does "up for it" mean?' asked Freddy.

'It means she is willing. You know, to have sex. But she wasn't.'

'When you were outside talking, did you agree to meet up with her again?' Sven asked.

'No definite date, no. She said we might see each other around and we could dance and such but no plans for a date. I think she was a bit of a cock teaser. You know, someone who leads someone on just for fun and not prepared to give anything out.'

'And then what? Did you leave first or did she?'

'We left at the same time. She went towards the door and I walked up the road to look for a taxi.'

'Did you see her enter the building?' Freddy asked.

'No, I didn't turn around. I thought if she was playing hard to get then that isn't what I want. So I just left.'

'So you did not see if she went into the building?' Freddy enquired.

'No.'

'Did you see anyone hanging around the entrance or the building?' Sven asked.

'Sorry, I didn't pay much attention.'

'So when you left, where did you find a taxi? And where did you go when you found one?'

'I walked towards the train station and picked one up from there. I went straight back to camp.' Billy said.

'Ok, let's move on to the night of the 8th September. Now that you are cooperating, what can you tell us about that night?'

'Honestly, nothing. I came into town like I normally do and after a few drinks went back to camp.'

‘And can you remember what bars you frequented on that evening?’

‘Like I said before, no. But it would have been one of the main three. Either the *Ben*, *Old G* or *Elli’s*.’

‘Have you ever had a drink in *Pesel*?’ Freddy asked.

‘*Pesel*? Never heard of it. Where is that?’ Billy answered.

‘In the middle of town.’

‘Well, I know all the haunts for the squaddies and that isn’t one of them.’

‘Alright, but can you remember anyone called Nicole Kühn? Here, take another look at her photo.’ Sven produced another A4 print and slid it across the table for Billy to look at.

‘No, never seen her before. Looks a bit too old to hang out in the bars I go to.’

‘So we can rule you out of being anywhere near the market square and the surrounding area for that night?’

‘Yes.’

‘Alright, where were you last night?’ Sven asked, watching closely for any reactions Billy might show.

‘Last night? In camp.’

‘And do you have any witnesses to that?’ Freddy asked.

‘You can get the guard book and check that I didn’t log out.’ Billy replied.

‘I have the book here.’ Captain Scott said, passing the book over to both detectives. Freddy took the book and looked at the pages and Sven asked the next question.

‘How easy is it to leave camp without having to bypass the guardroom?’

‘Well, seeing that we have a secure perimeter, I’d say it was pretty damn hard, wouldn’t you Captain Scott?’

‘Well, nothing is impenetrable, not if you had some mischief in mind.’ replied the Captain. ‘It has been known for soldiers to leave camp by travelling in the boot of a car if they have been restricted to barracks. And there is always the “over the fence” tactic wherever it is dark or secluded.’ he added.

‘Well, I stayed in last night and you can ask my roommates.’ Billy added.

'You can believe me when I say we will.' Sven replied.

'So, what happened last night?'

'For your information,' Sven said, 'another two women were murdered in the space of a short time.'

'Oh. Sorry to hear that.' Billy stated.

'I'm sure you are. And you were nowhere near Soest last night?'

'No, as I said, I stayed in last night.'

'And what did you do in camp all evening?'

'Nothing much. Stayed in my room and watched a bit of TV, went to the NAAFI venders for a meat pie, went to bed early. Nothing much.'

'Is there anything else you would like to add?' Freddy asked after he had read all the names of the soldiers who had booked out of camp and not seen Billy's name amongst them.

'No, not really. Look, I'm sorry for denying knowing Anja, but I had nothing to do with her being killed. She was a nice girl, but maybe she wound someone up the wrong way and they didn't want to take no for an answer, if you know what I mean.'

'Alright, interview ended. Captain Scott, I'd like to have a quiet word with you before you go if you don't mind.'

'Don't mention it. Ok Jennings, you wait outside and don't disappear.'

Billy stood up and exited the interview room and was shadowed by the two burly RMPs who had been waiting outside the room.

'Thanks for your help. Listen, you couldn't have a word with his roommates or something and see if his story is genuine could you?'

'Was already thinking of doing that before you asked. We want to get this straightened out just as much as you do.'

'Well, thank you again and when this is over, we would like to invite you both for a drink and a bite to eat.'

'Let's hope it is over soon.' Major Hollingsworth commented.

'Believe me when I say it will be soon, one way or the other.'

'What do you mean?' Captain Scott enquired.

'Oh, nothing really, just wishful thinking.'

*

Most of the national and regional papers printed the following story, taken from the Deutsche Presse Agentur, DPA for short:

"German Jack"

Jack the Ripper went on a killing spree in London in 1888, exactly 100 years ago. The killer was never identified and nobody was ever sentenced for the crimes that were committed. During this time, five women were brutally murdered in the East End of London, a place of poverty and prostitution.

On 31.08.1888, the first body was found, that of Mary Ann Nichols. Her throat had been severed and her body cut open from breast to pelvis. Several inner organs had been removed and placed around the body.

The second victim was found on 08.09.1888, this victim being Annie Chapman. Her throat was also cut and her uterus had been removed.

In the early morning of 03.09.1888, two murders took place. The first body found was a prostitute by the name of Elizabeth Stride and she died with only having her throat severed twice, dying of loss of blood and oxygen. The second body was found some 45 minutes later. This victim was identified as that being Catherine Eddowes. This time her killer took a step up in the way he killed his latest victim. Not only was Eddowes killed by the now familiar throat cutting, but she was also cut fully open and many internal organs removed and either placed around and on the body, or removed totally from the murder scene.

The fifth and last known victim of "Jack the Ripper" was found on the morning of 09.11.1888, this being Mary Jane Kelly, another prostitute. Again her throat had been severed and several organs removed from not just her body but also from the scene.

Well, what has this to do with a town called Soest in the western part of Germany? Well, quite simply this is what is happening as we speak. Yes, we have a copy-cat killer on our hands and he is not only killing his victims in exactly the same way as the notorious "Jack the Ripper" did, but these victims have been killed on the exact date 100 years later.

So far, we have witnessed four women killed and slaughtered in an exact replica as back then. "German Jack" is upon us, selecting his victims and killing them in the same manner as his name sake. Why? Only the killer knows. Who is the murderer? So far he remains anonymous. Do the police have any clues? No!

What we do know is that unless "German Jack" is found, then he will kill again on 09.11.1988. That we can be certain of. Until then stay vigilant and on 09.11.1988, all women should stay indoors for your own safety.

Bettina Feldmaus, Freelance Reporter.

CHAPTER 30

02.10.1988

The autopsy report had been sent from Dortmund and read by all those present in the briefing room. Sven looked around the room and only saw haggard eyes re-reading the papers or staring back at him like zombies. It had been a long night and there were still many things to do.

The local radio had already picked up the story and many people had already called the police station asking why the culprit hadn't been caught. The story of the veteran shooting the police was also a top story, and this also jammed the phone lines with complaints. Ulrich Schneider and his team on the switchboard did what they could to calm the general public down, but with the radio news and also the National TV channels getting involved, it was hard to keep the callers happy.

'Ok, where are we at?' Sven asked no-one in particular.

Freddy, with his eyes closed, was the first to speak.

'Just where we were when all this started. But now we have 4 dead bodies and still no clue as to who carried out any of the killings. We have checked up on the stories provided by both Mertens and Krome and their alibis look genuine. We have racked around and found some low-life's who have corroborated their stories, so it looks like they will be released later today.'

'Well, I would still like to keep them here and make doubly sure that they are just a couple of dirty bastards like they have admitted to. Will not hurt to keep them banged up a little bit longer.' Sven replied. 'Anyone else?' he asked.

'I do, sir' Suzanne Baumgarten said, raising her hand as she spoke. 'Who is informing the next of kin of the last two ladies?'

'That is being carried out as we speak. I have directed Hauptkommissar Backhaus with this task. Not the best job we have to do, but someone always picks the shitty end of the stick.'

'And what do we know about his latest victims?' she asked.

'Not much, the first found was a Renate Bölte and the second Julia Knaup. Miss Bölte was 32 years old, lived alone, had no friends to speak of and single. She has been identified by her ID she had on her and we have searched her apartment and have gotten the names and address of her parents. She was apparently out celebrating a colleague's promotion but left before the others. She left the restaurant not long after 10 p.m and was killed just around the corner very soon after.

'The second victim, a Miss Knaup was different. She was a young lady, 24 years old and liked keeping fit. She had just come out of the local swimming pool and was heading home when she was attacked and murdered. Again, her ID was on her person and she lived at home with her mother, parents are separated. I do not think that he is selecting his victims, he is just finding certain locations that fit the bill and waits for a lonely female to walk by. When he plans to attack again, it could be on any street in Soest that he has in mind. Does anyone have any ideas what we are missing or what we could do better?' he asked.

All was quiet, the only sound heard was one of the officers slurping their coffee.

'What about comparing what is written in the pamphlet that I brought back from England so we can prepare ourselves of his last victim?' Betty enquired.

'OK, what do we know?' Freddy asked.

'Well, for a start, his last victim was found in a house on her bed. The killer had stepped up his mutilation as it appears he had more time to carry out his planned deed without fear of being caught. The last woman Jack the Ripper killed had most of her internal organs removed and these were placed around her body in various positions. What makes this more ghastly than the rest is that not only were both her breasts removed, as were her nose, cheeks, eyebrows and ears but her face was slashed beyond recognition. As per all the other victims, her throat was severely severed and the cause of death was loss of blood, not forgetting the loss of all her internal organs.' Betty was reading from her notepad and trying to keep it simple so that all could understand the intensity of the killing. 'If German Jack decides to follow up this last killing, then it does not look good for us, as it could happen in any house.'

'Was there any common factor that linked any of the Ripper victims together?' asked Trilling.

'According to the pamphlet and the tour I took, no. The only thing familiar thing was that they were all prostitutes, but so were half of the women living in poverished London back in the late 1880s. According to the police reports as mentioned in the pamphlet, the women worked in different areas and would not have known each other. Remember, there was so much overcrowding that most people had to share a space on a floor covered in straw and pay nightly for the pleasure. Hardly anyone had their own room or house back then.' Betty stated.

'Well, it appears that his last victim had her own place.' Trilling replied.

'Yes,' Freddy put in 'but that doesn't matter with our guy. If he wishes to kill his next victim in a house, then we have our work cut out in finding the wanker.'

'What we need to do is inform the general public that live in Soest of the scheduled date for the last killing and instruct all women to stay indoors on said date. If there are any women living alone, maybe we could ask them to invite a relative or friend to stay with them for the night.' Suzanne said.

'Or we could have the mayor delegate several school gyms for bedding purposes, a kind of emergency refuse.' Peter Schwarz stated.

'That's not a bad idea, either of them,' replied Sven, 'who can you contact to get this rolling?' he asked Ulrich Schneider.

'Leave it to me and I'll make sure the mayor is aware of the seriousness for our request. I'll also speak with the Bundeswehr, the German army to get cots, pillows and blankets. I'll also contact the German Red Cross to provide food and drink for the evening in question.'

'Good, do we have any idea how many single women we are talking about?'

'No, but again I can get that information and by the end of the week. Will that do?' Schneider asked.

'Yes, we have four weeks or there about, so this is all logistics. If there is one thing us Germans are good at, that is organizing.'

'Sir?'

'Yes Suzanne?'

'I just had a thought. What about the Allerheiligen Kirmes?'

'What about it?' Sven asked.

'Well,' she replied, 'the fun fare is the biggest inner city fun fair in Europe and always starts on the first Wednesday in November after All Saints Day. This year it is scheduled to start on the 2nd and it will finish on Sunday, the 6th. I know that the fun fare will be finished, but it takes a few days to have all the rides and stands dismantled. What if this gets in the way of the next intended date?'

The Allerheiligen Kirmes went all the way back to the year 1338. Over the years the traditions changed as did the vastness and with modern technology, the original coconut shy, guess the weight of the bull or tug-of-war contests had given over to newer, up-to-date carousels. The original fare had been centralized in one place, but during the following centuries, not only had the population grown, so had the visitors from other towns and cities. Nowadays, the carousels were measured and placed all through the old town, in between houses and streets. The large chain swing was always in the same place each year, and it was so close to a particular building, anyone sitting on the outside of the ride would attempt to place their foot on the upper windowsill of the house. Or where the Viking boat would swing on a pendulum from side to side missing the building to its side by a mere 50 centimetres. The town is lit up with coloured lights, various smells of candy floss and popcorn, hotdogs and hamburgers, fried fish and mushrooms, the latest songs being played on the carousels, one tune outdoing the other. Crowds of people being pushed along with each other, all trying to see which rides to go on or deciding which food or drink to buy. Over the five days, Soest turns into a phenomenal attraction, millions of Deutsch Marks being spent for a good time. The town is simply transformed from a quiet, old town with cute houses to a cacophony of smells, lights and music.

'How long does the dismantling normally take?' Sven asked no one in particular.

'From experience, the streets are cleaned and the last of the trucks normally are gone by the following Wednesday, which will be the date of the next murder.' Suzanne stated.

'So that means that there shouldn't be a few thousand female guests walking the streets on the night. So, apart from the buggerance and interference of the fun fare next month, we are still where we are now. Fucking nowhere.' Freddy snorted.

'Do we have any news on the Tommy?' Zimmermann asked from the back.

'No new news,' Sven replied, 'the RMPs have kept the camp under scrutiny and Billy Jennings was not seen leaving or entering the barracks. I will ask them to lock him up on the date we have coming up, if only to deduct him from our enquiries once and for all. If he is under lock and key and in an army prison cell and no murder takes place, we could have found the murderer of the other four girls, letting us concentrate on his movements from under a microscope. If, however, the next victim is found and Jennings is locked up, then we can delete him from out list of suspects. I truly believe that we are only looking for one killer, so I want to concentrate all the manpower we have on going back over the witness statements and alibis between now and then and see if we have missed anything. So, if there is nothing else to add, all get back to work and do what we get paid to do.'

With that, the meeting was over and everyone filed out of the briefing room.

'Hey, Sven,' Freddy called to his mate, 'I'm famished. Come on, let's go over to the hospital and give Gaby Müller a visit and maybe she will rustle us up a nice breakfast. What do you think?'

'Yeah, not a bad idea. Come on Betty, let's introduce you to the best breakfast this side of the Rhein.'

'Breakfast, it's nearly midday.' she said.

'Well, we've been working hard, and I am sure we will get something filling to eat. And when we come back, I'll think about how long I will keep Mr Whippy and Mr Frilly Knickers in their cells. Will probably have to fumigate them when they leave.'

And with that, all three left the station and headed to the hospital on foot.

*

Both Detlef and Rudolph were released from the police cells on the morning of the 3rd, Sven making them sweat a bit and giving them enough time to think about their antics.

Over the following weeks, all documents and witness statements were looked at again and again, teams rotating so that a fresh pair of eyes would go over the same material in the hope that someone might see something that was not yet visible.

Life went back to normal for both Steffi and Egbert as they went about their daily life of carrying out autopsies and they were not needed in Soest for the time being but were on hand if needed.

Sven and Freddy were travelling back to Dortmund most nights to spend time with their respective wives and they were making sure not to go over a fourteen hour shift.

Betty was kept busy researching the last Rippers victim, hoping to find a clue as to where possible sights German Jack would choose for his next murder.

The funerals of both Renate and Julia had taken place, the first was a very quiet affair but the second was a celebration of her life.

The News broadcasts on the TV and radio dwindled slightly as there was no new news, but interest was rekindled when the date for the coming murder was flashed across the daily papers. Flyers were posted through every letterbox in the old town of Soest instructing any female living alone to either arrange for them to go away for the night or have a friend, relative or neighbor stay with them. For those who had nobody, the option to take them to alternative accommodation for the night was also in full swing. All they had to do was return the flyer with their name and address and transport would pick them up from their home along with an overnight bag and bring them back home the next day. Several requests for people to take their pets with them were declined due to health and logistical reasons.

Chapter 31

08.11.1988

With the fun fare over and done with for another year, Soest turned back to its normal self from the week of tourists and noise to being a normal town. Well, apart from the hundreds of TV crews and reporters who had flooded into the area, all hotel rooms and guest houses were fully booked. Several residents decided to move away for the duration and rented out their apartments or houses for those who were willing to pay an overpriced fee for the privilege. It was not unknown for a house owner to vacate their own bedroom and sleep on the couch in order to accommodate two or three reporters and cash in on the opportunity of making a quick killing.

At 09:00, the briefing room was filled to the brim. The only reporter allowed access was Betty, as she was now classed as being part of the team, if only on the outskirts.

All leave had been cancelled, units called in to assist from neighbouring towns and the German Bundeswehr had been put on standby.

Both Captain Scott and Major Hollingsworth of the RMP were invited to attend as was the translator. The mayor was given a seat near the front and both Steffi and Egbert were situated near the back of the room to answer any questions about the victims already found and what one might expect later tomorrow.

Bernie Backhaus was given the special task of providing enough refreshments for everybody and to make sure the vending machines worked properly and that the pictures of the beverages corresponded with the liquid coming out into the disposable cups. This was probably the hardest task he had to oversee in the last five years of his time on the force.

'OK ladies and gents, if you could all settle down so that we can get this meeting underway. We have a lot to get through and time is running away.' Ulrich Schneider stood at the front in his best uniform and stared at all the faces looking up at him on the podium. 'Sven, do you want to take it from here?' he asked.

'Sure.' Sven stood up from his seat and Schneider sat himself down. 'For all of you who do not know me, I am Erster Kriminalhauptkommissar Gerling and I am running this investigation along with my best friend and colleague, Kriminalhauptkommissar Fischer and with the assistance from Erster Polizeihauptkommissar Schneider from Soest. You have all seen and read the news these last months, so you should all be aware of what we have faced so far and why we are gathered here today. You were all given a folder on entering. I hope you have all taken the time to read it. If not, please make sure to do so before leaving the station. Nothing like being unprepared.

'So folks, tomorrow night is the night when German Jack plans to kill his final victim. He currently holds the high ground and has been planning this for months, if not years. That takes dedication. It is one thing to be a copycat killer but to do it on the same dates a century later, goes without belief.

'As it says in your folders, we know that German Jack is right handed, as confirmed by the pathologist's team of Dr. Stefanie Becker and Dr. Egbert Freckmann. We know this as to the way he has sliced the throats of his victims from left to right when standing behind them.

'What we don't know is who the bloody hell he is. Are we looking at a professional as in the way of a medical profession or a butcher? Or is the killer working only from reports that are available to the general public back in England. Let's face it, that is how we were informed of the Modus Operandi used by Jack the Ripper back in 1888 and the comparison of today's Jack. Is our killer old or young? Does he have military training or is he a hunter?

'You may think this is overkill and please excuse the pun, but we will set up a cordon using the Bundeswehr and police to make sure that every road leading into Soest and all paths, bridges, tunnels and walkways are patrolled. No male gets in without an ID showing that they live here. And each name and address will be recorded for our records. Yes, I know that this will cause some upset, but in all honesty, I don't give a damn. If it keeps another woman alive, then line up every male who wants to complain and I will take them down to visit the pathologists the next time they are elbows deep in a cold body. Understood?' Sven paused and sipped some of the coffee that was still in his cup, making him grimace as it had turned stone cold.

'So, we will also be putting a guard on the houses of both Rudolph Mertens and Detlef Krome, our two local perverts who, although having some sort of alibi, I want an eye kept on them until this is over. I have also spoken with Captain Scott of the British RMPs and he has confirmed that our other suspect, a Billy Jennings will also be placed under lock and key for the duration. At which point I would not only like to thank both him and Major Hollingsworth for their cooperation but also to all those who have been working in the background and providing all the necessary backup needed so far. Without any of you, we would not be able to carry out what we need to do for the next 48 hours or so.

'On the notice board outside this room, a list has been pinned up showing all teams and tasks that you will be put in. The section heads have already been briefed by me this morning, so listen out and they will inform you who is doing what with whom. Any questions, take these to your section head and they will make sure that this gets back to HQ here if they are unable to provide an answer.

'So, please all stay vigil, go about your designated duties with passion and gusto and let's see if we can catch this bastard before he kills again.'

Sven stood still and watched everybody leave the room before he turned to Freddy.

'Well, guess this is it.'

'You could say that. What do you think of our chances of catching him?' Freddy asked.

'Honestly, I think we are dealing with a sick individual who has had so much time to prepare for his sick fantasies, that he is always a few steps ahead of us and that he has already searched for his next killing ground. Will we catch him before he strikes again? I doubt it. Will we catch him after he kills? I doubt that as well. With all the technology we have to hand, we still have no clue or any identity. I think this could be spoken about for many years to come, especially if we are unable to identify him.'

'Somehow I have a feeling that we will get lucky this time. We have more manpower than ever before and let's not forget the advantage of shutting down who comes in and out from now until tomorrow night. Remember, anyone trying to get in will be recorded and we will then make checks as to their whereabouts for the other killing dates. I'm positive.' Freddy said confidently.

'If only you are right. Bet you a Mars bar that we don't catch him.'

'Alright,' Freddy said, holding out his hand to shake on the bet, 'you're on.'

'I don't give a monkey's fuck what he's doing. I want him escorted to the guardroom now.'

Provo Sergeant Ronny Hope shouted down the phone at the soldier who made the mistake of answering the phone on behalf of his troop Sergeant.

'But Sarge, he's on the loo and he normally takes some time to finish.' replied L/Cpl Tony White.

'I don't care if he's having a five knuckle shuffle, get that wanker up here now before I come down and jail the pair of you. Got it?'

'Yes Sarge, I'll let him know.'

'No, you will not let him know, you will escort him up to the guardroom as ordered. If that is beyond your capabilities, then I'll personally rip that stripe off your arm and shove it so far up your arse you could use it as dental floss.'

'Ok, I'll go and get him and I'll escort him up.'

The Provo Sergeant slammed the phone down on its cradle and looked at the two RMP officers standing before him.

'Sirs, he's on his way. Would you like to get some refreshments in the officer's mess? I could arrange someone to show you where to go.'

'No thank you Sgt Hope, we're willing to wait for Jennings here if you don't mind.'

‘Not at all. Would you like a brew whilst you’re waiting?’ Sgt Hope asked.

‘Yes please,’ said Major Hollingsworth, ‘milk and two sugars for me.’

‘Same for me too, please.’ Captain Scott said.

‘Smith,’ Sgt Hope shouted into the back room where the guards on rest were all situated. ‘three teas, NATO style. Quick as you can, there’s a good lad’

Several minutes later, all three teas were delivered and dished out. ‘Don’t suppose you’ve got a packet of biscuits knocking about?’ Captain Scott asked.

‘Sorry sir, no can do. Not done the NAAFI run yet.’

‘Worth a try, looks like we’ll have to drink this muck as is.’

After a further five minute wait, L/Cpl Tony White entered the guardroom, followed by another soldier.

‘Took your time, White. And where is Jennings?’ he asked.

‘Jennings? I thought you said Jenkins. I’ve not seen Jennings at all today. He wasn’t at breakfast so I thought maybe he’s gone to the medical center down bottom camp.’

‘Are you taking the piss and trying to make me look stupid in front of these fine officers?’ Sgt Hope ranted.

‘No Sarge, honest mistake. Was hard to hear as next door were banging doors and draws all the time.’

‘Right, you, get yourself inside, take your belt and beret off and lock yourself in one of my cells. I’ll deal with you later. And Jenkins, get the fuck out of my guardroom. You’re making the place look untidy. And go and get a haircut and report back to me once done. Now fuck off.’

Jenkins went through one door whilst Tony White went through the other where the cells were situated.

‘Ok, I want you to pull out all the stops and have Jennings located and placed under arrest. Not your fault, but we need him locked down.’ Captain Scott turned to his colleague and said, ‘I think the officer’s mess will have to do until we find the blighter. Sgt Hope, please keep us informed. You know where to find us.’ With that, both officers left the guardroom and drove their Land Rover up to the mess.

*

When Billy awoke that morning, he had long ago thought about skiving off of work, but was still wondering how to get off of the morning parade where the roll call was carried out. The only way he could think of was to go sick and visit the doctor in Salamanca barracks. But what to go sick with? If he went sick with something like a headache or backache, he would only be given two pain killers and told to get back to work. So, he needed something that would get him excused of all duties and be allowed to stay in his room.

He got out of bed and gathering up his toiletries, walked along the corridor to the washroom. During "rush hour", soldiers needed to queue up and wait for a sink to be vacated before the next one could use it, obviously the previous user would have to give it a quick rinse before leaving.

As he had woken earlier than normal, most of the sinks were not in use, so after mumbling good morning to the others already there, he chose a sink furthest away from the others. He refrained from joining in the morning banter that the other soldiers were having, and when asked why he was so quiet, he stated that he was not feeling well. Part one of his plan was complete, letting others know he was feeling sick. After he guided the razor around his face and whilst brushing his teeth, an idea popped into his head. He quickly finished off, scooped some water over his face and dried himself, gathered up his belongings and moved across the corridor to where the toilets were situated. He chose a cubicle furthest away from the door and locked his cubicle. After he had finished peeing, he flushed the toilet, put down the seat and sat down. He again opened up his toiletry bag and took out the toothpaste once more. He had only broken the seal a couple of days ago so the tube was nearly full. He took off the cap and placed the opening between his lips. His heart rate increased as did his breathing and he was sure that his temperature had also risen. Now or never, he thought to himself and gently squeezed the end of the toothpaste tube. After a small amount of paste was swallowed, he decided to speed up the process and squeezed harder. This time he nearly gagged on the strong taste of spearmint as it reached the back of his throat. Well, he had already started and he wasn't scared of a little discomfort, so he pushed some more. He squeezed and swallowed and squeezed and swallowed until the tube was empty. Not only did his breath smell strongly of mint, he started to feel slightly queasy. Part two of his plan was in place. After disposing of the empty tube in the rubbish bin, he left the toilet went back to his room.

'Hey, Billy, turn the light off, we're trying to sleep.'

'Sorry Paul, not feeling well today.' he replied.

'Well, feel sick with the light off, got another half hour before I need to get up.'

Billy turned the light back off and shuffled back to his pit. He sat on the edge of his bed and felt himself getting a bit warmer. He laid himself on top of his quilt and closed his eyes. Within 15 minutes sweat started to appear on his upper lip and brow.

'Oi, Billy, you ok?' his roommate, Ian Goodwin asked.

Billy opened his eyes to see that the others had already got up and were all getting dressed. The curtains had been pulled back and daylight was streaming through the window. Although the sun was shining, it looked cold outside.

'No, I think I have a fever,' he said, 'think I'll be going to see the quack this morning. Will you cover for me on roll call?'

'Yeah, course. You don't look that good either. Face is white as a sheet. Sure you're ok?'

'No idea. Probably a bug is going around. I'll be ok though. Fuck off to breakfast and I'll doze for a bit longer before the transport leaves.'

Both Ian and Paul left the room, turned off the light and went across the path to the cookhouse.

Billy slowly sat up and felt sick. He placed his hands on his knees, bent his head and started breathing deeply in and out, relieving the urge to throw up. He wiped his face on a towel and slowly got dressed. At 07:40 he was standing outside the guardroom waiting for the transport to take him to the other camp. At this time, the soldiers on guard had been staging on all night and the day guard had yet to arrive. Several other soldiers were also on the transport to see the doctor and nobody spoke.

On reaching the medical center, they all left the vehicle and queued up to provide their name, rank and number to the medical orderly, where they were then told to sit inside the waiting room.

Billy was fifth in line and it was not too long before his name was called. He got up and walked towards the doctor's office.

'Ah, good morning Jennings, you don't look to peaky today. Symptoms?' Captain Fitzgerald, the army doctor asked.

'Good morning sir, I think I have a fever and feel like I need to be sick.' Billy replied back, not looking the doctor in the eyes.

'When did this start?'

'This morning, sir.'

'Any bowel movement? Do you have any pain in your abdomen?'

'Just feel sick and hot.' Billy replied.

Captain Fitzgerald took a thermometer and put this in Billy's mouth, took his wrist between two fingers and a thumb and measured his pulse, the whole time looking Billy in the eyes.

After a couple of minutes, the doctor removed the thermometer and looked at the reading. Yep, Billy definitely had a temperature.

'Remove your shirt and lay down on the bench.'

The doctor then started to press and tap around Billy's belly and abdomen asking if he felt any pain or discomfort, which Billy replied no.

'Ok, looks like you may have a bug. I'll prescribe you some tablets that will fight the fever and something for you to take for your stomach. That should stop you feeling sick. If you need to vomit, don't hold it back. Whatever comes out cannot hurt. I'll also excuse you of all duties for 48 hours, so you should be right as rain for Friday's parade. If you still feel unfit, come back on Friday for another checkup. And lay off the booze.'

'I don't drink much sir,' Billy said, 'maybe a couple more on the weekends.'

'Well, your breath smells as if you have eaten a packet of mints before you came in here, so I am to think you are trying to disguise the smell of alcohol on your breath.'

'No, sir, honest sir. I didn't touch a drop last night.'

'Ok, Jennings, that will be all. Remember to take the pills, two tablets three times a day after meals.'

'Thank you sir.' Billy stood, adjusted his shirt and walked out of the examination room. He queued up at the dispensary and after collecting his sick note and medicine, he went back outside to wait for the transport which was scheduled to take all the sick soldiers back to top camp at 11:30.

'So, where the fuck is he?' Sgt Hope screamed down the phone to his friend and colleague.

'Steady on Ronny, you'll pop a blood vessel shouting like that. As I said, Goodwin informed me he had gone sick for today and that is the last I have heard. Call the quack to see if he was seen and if the transport has left to come back up.' Troop Sgt Cooper smiled at the thought of Ronny Hope getting red in the face. It was well known around the regiment that Sgt Hope's bark was deadlier than his bite and that the veins would stand out on his head and his face turn a dark crimson when bawling someone out.

'Right, if you see the little git before I do, make sure he has an escort up to the guardroom. He's really in the shit. I have no idea what he's done this time but the RMPs are here. Two officers, so it must be serious.'

'If he's visiting the doctor, you'll see the transport drop him off before I see him. Just grab him when he debuses. But keep me informed what is happening, will you?'

'Yeah, of course,' Sgt Hope replied.

After hanging up the phone, he called the medical center and was told the transport had just left the camp, and yes, Jennings was on board.

'Cpl Black, make sure to stop the medical run before it enters the camp and get Jennings off and into here sharpish, will you?' Sgt Hope said through the open window.

'Yes Sarge.' came the reply from outside.

Sgt Hope then called the officers mess and instructed the mess orderly to inform the RMP officers that their soldier was being delivered within the next fifteen minutes. On receiving this news, both officers finished what they were reading, thanked the staff for the tea and drove back to the guardroom, parking their Land Rover behind it. They entered the guardroom and after exchanging salutes with Sgt Hope, all three sat down to wait.

Billy sat at the back of the transport, a three quarter ton Land Rover and was squeezed in between seven other soldiers. Up front were the driver and in the passenger seat sat the highest ranking soldier who had also gone to see the doctor, this being a L/Cpl from the Pioneer Corp. Nobody spoke as it was hard to be heard above the throb of the tires driving along the tarmac. They turned right onto the new road leading to the camp and after a few kilometers, the camp came into sight. The driver passed the local pub, locally known as "The Shack" and slowed down as he neared the camp gates. The driver indicated and turned left to enter, where he was stopped by Cpl Black.

'Is there a Signalman Jennings on board?' Cpl Black asked, poking his head through the drivers open window.

Billy looked up and raised his hand.

'You're wanted in the guardroom, out you get.' Cpl Black ordered.

'But I've been written off sick, got a sick chit from the doctor saying I have to stay in bed.' Billy replied. All eyes from the other soldiers were on him.

'Well, I've been told to get you inside. You can take it up with Sgt Hope. So, get your arse inside. Come on.'

With that, Billy slowly and reluctantly climbed over the tailboard and making sure his beret was sitting correctly, he adjusted his trousers and jacket and walked into the guardroom.

'Cpl Black, get him out of here and have him march in like a soldier.' barked Sgt Hope.

Billy automatically turned around and went back outside, rolling his eyes as he walked back down the short path. Here he turned again and with the steps being shouted out by Cpl Black, he marched smartly back up the path and into the guardroom. After coming to attention, he was only then aware that there were more people in the front of the guardroom than normal. As he was facing forward, he could not make out the two figures standing off to the side.

'Ah, Jennings, nice of you to turn up.' Captain Scott said. 'Been to visit the doctor?'

'Yes sir.' Billy replied.

'Anything catching?'

'Don't know, sir. But I've been given some medicine and confined to my room. Bed rest. Here, here's the sick chit.'

Billy put his hand into his trouser pocket and withdrew a folded piece of paper and handed this over to the officer. Capt Scott looked at what was written and showed the document to Major Hollingsworth.

'Well, if you are confined to bed for the next two days, maybe you need some peace and quiet.' Captain Scott stated. 'Sgt Hope, do you have any spare cells so that we can keep an observational eye on him?' he asked.

'Yes sir. All are empty at the moment.'

'Ok, have him escorted back to his room so that he can get some essentials and have his food delivered here for him to eat.'

'Excuse me sir, but what am I supposed to have done?' Billy asked.

'Well, as you have been on the local police's radar, they think that something is going down over the next couple of days and we need to make sure that whatever happens, you are nowhere near Soest when it does. So, until I say so, you are to stay locked up here under the supervision of Sgt Hope or the evening guard duty. Understand?'

'But I'm sick.'

'Well, you can recover here in a private room and if you need help, you can always shout. I am sure Sgt Hope will only be too willing to assist. Right, Sgt?'

'Only too willing, sir.' he replied. 'Cpl Black, escort Jennings back to his hovel so that he can collect some possessions. Back here in 30 minutes.'

'Yes, Sarge. Ok Jennings. About turn. Quick march. Left, right, left, right, left, right, left.'

Billy marched out of the guardroom towards his accommodation block.

CHAPTER 32

09.11.1988

'Ok, I have heard back from Captain Scott that the soldier Jennings is under lock and key. What is the latest news we have on Mertens and Krome?' Sven asked Ulrich Schneider.

'As of this moment, Krome is being escorted home from his place of work and will be put under house arrest. We will have a car sitting outside his house all night just to be sure.'

'I would prefer if we had an officer in his house.'

'Unfortunately we do not have that jurisdiction. Both the back and front entrances will be kept under observation so he will not be able to get out.'

'And Mertens?' Sven asked.

'Well, we called his place of work and was told by his manager that he was in hospital, suspected heart attack. I have sent another vehicle to check and they have reported that Mertens is currently undergoing a triple bypass. I have ordered the constable to come back as I do not think that Mertens will have a miraculous recovery and be able to get out of bed so soon after today.' Schneider stated.

'No, fully agree. So that means all three of the earlier suspects are accounted for and pose no threat for tonight. If nothing happens, then we can look back at the previous murders and see who could fit the bill. If something does happen like we assume, then we have wasted so much time chasing the wrong guys and we still have no idea who the killer is. All we can do now is deploy all the forces we have to the agreed locations and wait it out. Time is now 10:25, let's lock Soest down and hope we get lucky. Remember, all males' names, addresses and ID numbers to be checked and recorded.'

'Yes,' said Schneider, 'all units have been instructed. I have Zimmermann driving around and checking that everybody, including the Bundeswehr and German Red Cross are in the right places. We just have to wait and bide our time. But I think that we have the killer under observation already. I still think it is one of the three.'

‘Feeling confident? Glad to hear. Let’s test and see if your faith and luck are on the ball today. You buy the beverages from the machine. I’ll have a hot chocolate. Wonder what I’ll get this time. Last time I selected this, I got to drink oxtail soup.’

Both policemen left the office and went to play lucky dip.

During the day, all streets, paths and walkways were cordoned off and anyone entering was stopped and their details taken. If they lived in the old town, they were allowed to proceed. If they didn’t, they were turned away.

The local radio kept broadcasting every half hour that all single, female citizens were to vacate their premises and proceed to the pickup point for the transportation to one of the many schools that would provide them shelter for the night. It also warned all women to stay indoors.

The TV and newspaper reporters had all been herded together and were parked, camped and kept under guard just outside the Wall. If any reporter was seen inside the Wall, they were escorted out. The whole road from the slaughter house right up to the corner of the Jacobistrasse was blocked off from normal traffic and this had been turned into a car park for the news crews, including many from abroad. The BBC and ITV had four vehicles between them and each team was trying to find a gap to get onto the Wall or onto the other side so that they could report live when things happened. However, the Bundeswehr kept them all in check and made sure nobody got near the Wall, as portable floodlights had been moved into place and switched on. As the sky turned darker, the floodlights lit up the reporter’s park like Wembly football ground.

Sven and Freddy drove around the old town, checking that everyone was staying vigilant and that all was going to plan.

‘When this is all over, it will be weird going back to work in Dortmund.’ Freddy said.

'Hmm, at least we won't have to get up too early every day to drive down here. It's really knackering me out, all this driving back and to.'

'I've promised Heike that I'll take her on holiday when we wrap up here.'

'Where will you go?'

'Thinking of visiting Ballermann. Ever been there?'

'I've been to Mallorca but never gone to Ballermann. Can't stand all the drinking and partying going on. Ok if you're a piss head, but not recommended for the normal folk.'

'Yeah, well, Heike wants a bit of excitement back in our lives. Been rejecting her a bit with all of this going on.' Freddy said. 'Need to make it up to her.'

They stopped the car at the end of Jacobistrasse and looked at the circus of reporters sitting or standing around like vultures waiting for something to die.

'Where's Betty?' Freddy asked. 'I've not seen her today.'

'Funny that, now I come to think of it, neither have I. Had so much on my plate, had no time to think about her.'

'Oh, I don't know. I think about her quite often. Only the other day I was giving Heike one and was imagining her being Becky. It was a real turn on. I nearly called out her name as well.'

'You're just a perv. But seriously, where can she be?' Sven asked.

Freddy used the police radio and contacted the police station and asked if her location was known. After drawing a blank, Günther, who was on radio duty, called all units to ask for assistance in locating her. One by one, each unit replied that her whereabouts was not known.

'Bugger, she said she wanted to pose as a single woman to flush out the killer. I think she has disobeyed our orders and gone freelancing again. I'll slap her tits when I catch up with her.' said Sven.

'Bet they're firm with small nipples.' Freddy replied.

'Knock it off, will you? She's off the grid and we don't know where she is. Let's hope she is not stupid and walking the streets on her own.'

‘Sure she will be spotted by the roving patrols.’ replied Freddy. ‘I know she’s blond, but I don’t think it’s her natural colour. She cannot be as stupid as one.’

‘Let’s hope you’re right. Ok, let’s drive around some more and keep your eyes peeled. Maybe we can spot her wandering around.’

Betty had her own plan for the day. She had kept out of the way of the police station, knowing that everything and everyone was being put into their respective places. And as the only reporter this side of the Wall, she decided to use her status and get some stories that her fellow reporters would not get first hand.

Her first story was of the evacuation of the single women. She walked to the pickup point and was allowed on the bus where she interviewed several women. After taking some photos of the school gymnasium and all the army cots placed out in straight lines, she got back on the bus and went back inside the Wall. She disembarked when the next passengers were getting on and she walked around the old town, camera in one hand and a map in the other. As it was still daylight, she was not afraid. The weather had turned cloudy and the temperature was down to around five degrees centigrade. Rain was forecast for during the night and she had a small foldable umbrella in her rucksack just in case but at the moment it was dry.

For lunch, Betty went into a café in the shopping walkway and ordered a cup of coffee and a cheese and ham baguette. She studied her notepad and looked at the street map that she had open on the table. She put her finger on her current location and traced a line to where the reporters were camped out and decided she would climb the Wall and take some photos of them. This would also make good reading, showing that she had special credentials over the others. She folded the map and put this in her pocket, zipped up her jacket and placed her woolen hat on her head and walked out.

After turning right and walking to the end of the shopping street, she crossed the market square, passed the street where the *Pesel* was located and walked further until she was at the end of Jacobistrasse. Here she walked along towards the Jacobitor and after fifty meters or so several arches appeared on her right. Three of the arches were the front of a wool shop on the right hand side and on the left two arches were the front for a hairdresser. The two shops were separated by an archway that led between the two and opened out into a courtyard. Betty was curious as to where this would lead and as it was still light, although it was diminishing because of the cloud cover, she decided to have a quick peep before continuing on as she had not seen this area before.

She walked through the archway and looked around. The courtyard was paved with cobbled stones and the buildings appeared to have been built haphazardly. Directly on the left was the back of the hairdressers and above this there were two large wooden balconies providing a small outside area for the houses above. Directly in front of her was another building, this being the side of a large house, boasting a large, metal lantern attached to the wall. The cobbled area ran further to the left and continued around the corner of this building. Directly to her right was another house with four floors. Wooden balconies were also fixed to the side of the building so that each apartment had its own walkout area for some freedom. Below the balconies and on the ground floor, two small steps led to the ground floor apartment. Because of the courtyard being surrounded on three sides by buildings and shaded by the balconies above, the light was even darker than on the main street.

She turned to the left and walked to the end where the courtyard moved around to the right and decided not to go any further, as this would lead her away from her destination. She turned around and headed back towards the archway to continue her journey when she noticed that the door to the bottom apartment was slightly ajar. She gingerly stepped towards it and called out 'Is everything OK?' She slowly put her hand on the door and pushed slowly. That is when her whole life fell apart.

At the time when Betty was pushing the door open, Sven and Freddy drove passed on the Jacobistrasse looking for her. If Betty had only carried on walking up the road and didn't make the short detour, she would have been seen by the two detectives and she would be sitting in the back of their car. If she had ignored the open door, all would have been different. However, as the saying goes, curiosity killed the cat.

CHAPTER 33

The evening before, he had gone to the hospital and walked to the visitor's toilet, where he entered a cubicle and locked himself in. Maybe it was not the spacious of places but it would suffice. It was warm, dry and he would not be disturbed. If someone knocked on the door, he would pretend he was a patient and bluff. He still had his sandwiches and flask of soup he had brought with him in his rucksack and he settled down for the night. He had slept in tighter places before and sleep would not be an issue.

The next morning, he woke when he heard talking outside the toilet. His bag was already packed and he waited until around 08:30 before moving out. He walked past the reception desk which was currently empty and walked out through the front door. Today was the day. He walked away from the hospital and headed towards the town center, constantly watching his peripheral vision that he was not being watched. Several times he doubled back on himself just to make sure he wasn't being followed, but there was no sight of any danger.

He continued moving along various streets, looking for a single woman to leave their house in order to walk towards the pickup point for the evacuation. From the spot he was standing in, he saw just that. The beginning always depended on luck, and today was his lucky day.

His fifth victim was called Katrin Werner, 48 years old, divorced with no children and lived alone. She opened her door and had in her hands a sports bag with a change of clothes, some night wear, toiletries and a nice book to while away the hours. As she turned to close and lock her front door, she was pushed heavily from behind and she fell through the doorway back into her apartment. As she fell to her knees, she was struck on the back of the head with such force that she lost consciousness immediately.

Her front door was then closed and locked from the inside and all the window shutters were lowered. Her attacker then turned on the light. He opened his bag and put on his balaclava. He had already donned his gloves earlier whilst keeping his hands in his pockets as he walked along.

He quickly looked into each room to see the basic layout of the apartment. When he was satisfied, he dragged her unconscious body to the bedroom, placed her on her own bed and went back for his rucksack. He took out his knife and went towards the bed, where he sliced open her coat so that the buttons fell off and he continued removing all of her other clothing, which he piled together and slid under the bed.

He could see that she worked out as there was not too much body fat and her stomach was flat and her legs were not afflicted too much with cellulites. He stood to the right side of the bed, placed his left hand on her forehead and sliced her throat from ear to ear, so deep that the knife nicked the spine. Blood instantly gushed out and he stepped away to stay out of the spray, only moving forward once it slowed to a trickle. Katrin Werner did not gain consciousness and was not aware that her neck tissues had been severed.

He put his hand into his pocket and took out his notebook. All of the pages were laminated and he flipped to the section named "Mary Kelly", who was the last Ripper victim. He read the bullet points these were confirmed by the pages of photos showing Mary Kelly in her last pose.

The bed sheets were by now saturated in blood where it also dripped and soaked into the brown bedroom carpet. He opened her legs wide apart at the knees so that he could see her pubic region, which was carefully trimmed, quite irregular for someone of her age.

He looked at his victim and admired her body with large breasts and firm thighs.

He cupped her right breast in his hand and with the other, sliced it cleanly off and placed this on the bed and done the same with the other breast. He then sliced the flesh off of her thighs, cutting deeper with each slice until both thigh bones were visible. He then sliced away the meat from her abdomen. He then slit her open from breastbone to pelvis. Here, he used two hands on the knife so that he would have the strength to get through the breastbone easily. Good job he had a proper knife.

On checking his notes, he then proceeded in taking out her insides, again placing these at the foot of the bed. Once he had completed this, he checked his notes again whilst taking a drink of water from one of the bottles he had brought with him. He was sweating under his clothing and balaclava but he could not discard any items of clothing just yet.

After a few minutes rest, he got back to work. This consisted in him slashing both her arms many times before hacking away at her face, making her features unrecognizable. He then moved her face, or what was left of it, away from him so that her left cheek was on the pillow. It was not that he did not want to see her but that is what Jack had done to Mary. He placed her left arm close to her body with forearm over the abdomen. The right arm placed slightly away from her body and rested on the mattress.

Now with notebook open again, he placed her uterus, kidneys and one breast under her head and placed the other breast by her right foot. Her liver was placed between her feet, the intestines by her right side and her spleen was placed on the left side of her body. The flesh that was sliced off of her thighs and abdomen were placed on the bedside table, the alarm clock being swiped to the floor.

When he had completed the last task he checked his watch. He had needed about two hours to finish his work and now he had to clean himself up. He walked to the bathroom, knife in hand and turned on the water. When the water was at a suitable temperature, he stepped under the shower, fully clothed and washed away the majority of the blood. He used soap and scrubbed himself from head to toe, or in his case, balaclava to boots. When he was sure that he was no longer covered in blood, he stepped out and walked back to the bedroom door, where he carefully undressed, placing his wet clothing into a black bin liner and changed into dry clothes. He put the knife back in its scabbard and placed his cleanly wiped notebook on top. He looked back at his last masterpiece, seeing that the bedroom walls were also covered in blood splatters and had dripped down to the skirting boards. He picked up his rucksack and adjusted the straps so that it fit snuggly. He left the bedroom door open and walked through the living/dining room, wiping surfaces he may have touched, such as the light switch and the door handle and lock. He stood by the front door, quietly unlocked it and opened it slightly, peering out through the gap.

Outside, the sky was still light but getting darker and the temperature had dropped during the day and was now around five degree centigrade. He was just about to open the door wide when he heard a woman's voice cry out 'Is everything OK?' He moved away from the opening and stood to the left side of the door, leaving it slightly ajar. The woman pushed the door open even more. That is when he struck.

He kicked the door open with his right foot and simultaneously propelled his body forward so that his left side was in the entrance. He pivoted his body and threw a punch with his right hand so fast and hard, it hit Betty full in the face, smashing her nose and breaking her two top teeth in the process. As her knees buckled, he grabbed her under the arms and dragged her into the apartment, where he closed the door once again.

Betty was out cold, blood flowing out of her nose and mouth and pooling under her head which was lying on the tiles near the closed door. She made no movement apart from the rising and falling of her chest when she breathed. He stood still for several minutes, waiting to hear if anyone saw or heard any commotion, but he was sure he was too quick and skilled to have made any noise. She had not been able to scream or make any noise herself as the attack was so sudden.

Now came the time for decisions. What to do with her. To kill her or leave her be? He did not know who she was but was sure that she had not seen his face. After all, his balaclava was in the black bin liner in his rucksack. Although curiosity killed the cat, Betty's guardian angel must have been working overtime as he decided that he could not risk spending too much time here when it was getting dark and he needed to make good his escape. Also, it would go against what Jack had done for his last killing.

Again, he opened the door slightly, looked out and when he heard nothing, he slipped out and closed the door behind him. He moved swiftly across the courtyard, down Höggengäßchen, along Elendsgasse and turned left on Rosenstrasse. He followed this to the end where he turned right onto Jakobi-Nötteln-Wallstrasse, which was the road running parallel to the inside of the Wall. Here he kept in shadows, stopping every few meters to make sure that he had not been seen and that there were no guards or patrols in front of him. When a vehicle or foot patrol swept by, he hid himself in hedges, behind parked cars and even in front gardens. Slowly but surely he made his way towards the Wall. This was a place he had scouted many times before when checking for escape routes. The sky was now dark and the floodlights that were shining brightly in the sky were to his left, some distance away. Once again checking that he was not seen or followed, he slithered up the bank and climbed and crawled until he was on the Wall. Locating the area he needed to be in, he moved to the edge of the parapet, looked down and saw blackness. He waited ten minutes and when he was satisfied that nobody had moved, lit a cigarette or coughed, he slowly lowered his legs over the edge, held onto the top and by pushing his feet against the wall, kicked and pushed himself away. He grabbed hold of the big, thick branches of the oak tree and wrapped his legs around it so that he was hanging like a sloth. Slowly he maneuvered himself towards the trunk and slowly climbed down the tree until his feet were back on the ground. After waiting a further fifteen minutes, he dashed across the open area until he came to the smaller, outside wall that was still present along this part. Just as he was about to climb up, several soldiers from the Bundeswehr came around the corner and walked along the path. They were spread out in a line, torches shining and lighting up the path and bushes in front of them. He was trained in escape and evasion and knew what to do to stay "invisible". He pressed himself into the ground making sure that his face and hands were not visible, as the whiteness of his skin would show out more in the torch light than his clothing. He stayed still and breathed shallowly, not making a noise. He was, however, ready to move if discovered. The soldiers were talking quietly amongst themselves and were not paying too much attention to the side he was on as their torches were aimed more towards the Wall.

After they had passed, he waited another five minutes before he climbed up the wall which was only three meters high. The wall was made of old slabs and it was easy to find hand and toe holds. Within seconds, he was on top and over the fence that was in front of him, placing him in someone's back garden. He crouched down and could see the road in front of the house and many cars driving along. He slipped around the side of the house unnoticed, opened the front garden gate and walked along the path. He was now outside the old town and outside the cordon.

CHAPTER 34

Betty regained consciousness after about an hour, the blood from her nose and mouth having congealed on her face and on the tiles she had been left lying on. She could not remember where she was or how she got to be in the position and state she was now in and her head throbbed. The room she was in was nearly pitch black, only the light from outside shining through the tiniest gap in the blinds.

She slowly sat up and after her head stopped spinning, she delicately stood up, holding on to the side of a wall. She moved along looking for a light switch, which she found before she reached a door. She turned the light on and quickly shut her eyes as the light blinded her and sent daggers into the back of her head. After several seconds, she slowly opened her eyes and looked around. She touched her face and ran her tongue over her teeth, knowing that all was not well. She saw a door open in front of her and went towards it. She turned the light on and entered the bathroom. The face that stared back at her from the mirror was one she did not recognize. Not only was her nose at an acute angle across her face, her hair was matted with blood as was the lower part of her jaw and ear. She opened her mouth and gave out a cry when she saw that her two top teeth were broken. Her eyes were puffy and were swelling up as was the colouring of her face with the onset of bruising starting to appear.

She turned on the tap and scooped up some water and gingerly started to wash her face. She tried not to touch her nose too much but was able to get most of the blood off. Her hair was rinsed under the flowing tap and she dried herself tentatively on a wet towel that was hanging on the bathroom hook.

Now that she had refreshed herself with the water, her head was clearing and she looked around some more. She walked slowly out of the bathroom, hand against the wall for balance when she passed an open door. She looked in and was not able to see anything as it was too dark. She was not able to smell due to her broken nose still being blocked by congealed blood but something told her to turn on the light in this room. She did and let out the loudest, shrillest scream she had ever heard come out of her throat. Betty fainted at the sight of Katrin Werner and for the second time that day, lay unconscious in a house of carnage.

Joachim Heidfeld was interrupted from watching the TV by a loud scream coming from the apartment below. He turned the volume down and called his wife, Sonya, who was in the kitchen preparing the evening meal. She came into the living room and he asked her if she had heard the scream also. As she had been using the electric tin opener to open up a can of peas to go along with the mince meat and potatoes she was preparing, she had heard nothing but encouraged her husband to go and take a look to see if Ms. Werner was alright.

Joachim went downstairs and knocked on the door. There was no answer and he could not see or hear anything from the apartment.

'I think she left for the shelter.' he called up to his wife.

'But you said you heard something. See if the door is open.'

'Nope, it's closed and all the blinds are down.'

'Hey, Joachim, did you hear the scream as well?' This came from the neighbor across the courtyard.

'Yes, but the door is closed and all the blinds are down.'

'Well, I think we should break the door down just in case. What do you reckon?'

'I don't know, Seb, what if the screaming was not from Katrin's apartment and we damage the door? What will she say when she comes home?'

'Listen, I'll fix the door and all the damages, come on, let's get it open.'

Being overweight and asthmatic, Joachim was not too keen on using force to gain entry, but seeing that he weighed at least double of Seb, it was left to him to move back slightly and rush the door with his shoulder. The Yale lock was no match for the colossal bulk of Joachim and readily surrendered. The door burst open just as Betty was coming round. With the sound of the door suddenly breaking open, Betty screamed again, as did Joachim as he was not ready to meet anyone inside. Seb stood frozen to the spot outside and wet his trousers.

Betty stood up and fell down almost immediately as her legs buckled from under her. Joachim had quickly recovered and walked into the room and bent over Betty, saying that everything was alright. Seb stood outside trembling.

'Are you hurt?' Joachim asked.

'Help me.'

'We're here to help, you're in safe hands now, isn't she Seb?'

Seb could not control his legs. Elvis would have been proud of the knee dance that was being displayed.

'Seb, get in here and help me.' Joachim said. 'Tell me, who are you?' he asked Betty.

'I was passing when I saw the open door. I got near and someone rushed out and punched me in the face. I found someone cut up in the bedroom.' she said.

'Ok, you stay here and I'll go and have a look. Seb, come over here and help.'

Joachim stood up and walked towards the bedroom. He smelt something wrong long before his eyes adjusted to the vision of the remains and mutilation of Katrin. Joachim instantly puked, not in a quiet way but a full on fountain that shot towards the bed.

'Seb, go and call the police.'

Seb stood stock still in the doorway, not able to enter the apartment.

'Seb, call the fucking police.'

At that moment, Sonya came down the stairs and was confronted by the sight of Seb, pale white, shaking and a puddle by his feet and a dark stain on the front of his trousers.

'Joachim?' she called.

'Sonya, don't come in,' he said, 'call the police. I think Katrin has been murdered.'

Sonya dashed back up the stairs to her apartment and called the police. She gave her name and address and asked for them to hurry. No, she had not personally seen the body but her husband was still there. And yes, she would tell him not to touch anything. She hung up the phone and went back down the stairs.

'Joachim, the police are coming. Don't touch anything.' she said.

She pushed past the immobilized Seb and was confronted with the blood that was left by Betty. As she stepped further into the room, she saw Betty sitting hunched over with her head between her knees.

'Are you alright dear?' Sonya asked.

Betty looked up and Sonya gasped in shock at the state of her face.

'Here, let me have a look. The police are coming. What happened?' she asked, looking towards Joachim.

'I was attacked and knocked out. When I gained consciousness, I turned the lights on and saw a dead body in the bedroom. Don't go in there.' Betty warned.

'It's ok, come with me my love, I'll get you cleaned up and give you something to drink. Joachim, you stay here and wait for the police. I'll call Beatrice to come and collect Seb.'

With that, Sonya took Betty by the arm and escorted her out the door and up the stairs. Seb was on another planet.

Sven and Freddy received a message over the radio that a possible victim had been found. Several units were sent to the address along with an ambulance and an emergency doctor. By now, all of the occupants of the surrounding apartments were gathered in the courtyard and a large crowd had gathered to see and record what could be the last Ripper killing.

'Right, get this lot moved out of the courtyard and get pictures of everyone here, along with names and addresses.' Sven told Trilling. 'Nobody enters the house without suiting up first. Freddy, contact Steffi and Egbert and get the forensics on standby. I want the street cordoned off and all cameras taken away from this lot.' He nodded towards the crowd. 'Baumgarten, I want you to start interviewing any witnesses. I'll suit up and take a preliminary look.'

He opened the car boot and took out the suit and over boots and swiftly put these on over his clothes and shoes. He walked to the entrance and Grünewald let him pass.

'How are you doing, son?' Sven asked.

'Ok, Sir. I haven't looked in.'

'Good, hold it together as you are now the face between the outside and this carnage house. Can you do that?'

'Yes sir.'

'Good lad.' Sven walked into the apartment, noticing the blood drying on the tiles near the front door. He had not yet seen Betty and was not even aware that she had been attacked. All he knew was that someone had been murdered.

Slowly, he walked towards the bedroom where the light still shone. He kept to the side of the floor nearer the walls and took large, exaggerated steps. He looked in and held his breath for about twenty seconds, which he slowly released through gritted teeth. He went no further and backed out the way he had come.

When he reached the front door, he nodded at Freddy, who spoke quietly into the hand radio and summoned the technicians.

Steffi, Egbert and the team of technicians all arrived to the address and methodically went about their business. Firstly, the photographer took pictures of the blood found inside the front door and slowly made his way towards the bathroom and bedroom. Steffi and Egbert stayed outside until the photographer was finished. Egbert went into the bedroom first whilst Steffi watched the other technicians get to work by collecting various blood samples from the tiles, bathroom and bedroom and also saw the carpets cut out where the major blood stains were. These were bagged and sealed and then they went to work in the bathroom, taking out the shower drain and the u-bend under the sink. Only then did Steffi take a deep breath and join Egbert in the bedroom.

'My God,' she gasped, 'what animal could do this to another living being?'

'Someone who is sick, but I have to admit, the body looks very similar to that in the Ripper photos. Our killer really has done his homework and tried to reciprocate it. All the internal body parts look to be placed in the correct position and the body left in the same pose as Mary Kelly.'

'Ok, I'll start cataloging the internal organs and you measure the body temperature, state of rigor mortis, time of death etc. It looks like we will need two bags for this one. Any identity?'

'No,' said Sven from the doorway, 'but we have six women unaccounted for at the temporary shelter. That means we will send a patrol to each of the registered addresses to double check and tick them off of the list. According to the guy who found her, the owner of this apartment is a Ms. Katrin Werner, but without proper identification, we cannot assume until we are sure.'

'Well,' said Steffi, 'I don't think that we can get a positive identification from the face of this lady. Completely cut up beyond recognition. Only her nearest and dearest will be able to help if she has any identifiable blemishes on her body that have not been hacked away. Or if a witness can place the owner as having been here when the killer called.'

'There is no sign of a break in, so it looks like she let her killer in. Maybe she knew him?' Freddy added.

'Or she was overwhelmed when she opened the door. Lots of blood on the tiles.' Sven added.

Everyone went quiet as Steffi and Egbert carried on with their tasks. Suddenly footsteps could be heard running down the stairs from the apartment above.

'Sir,' gasped Suzanne Baumgarten at the front door, 'you need to come upstairs immediately, please.'

'Sounds important.' he said to Freddy and went after Suzanne. He met her in the kitchen of Sonya and Joachim.

'Sir, we have found Betty.' Suzanne spurted.

Sven looked at the figure sitting hunched over the kitchen table whilst a medic checked out her facial injuries.

'Betty, what happened?'

Betty looked up and on seeing Sven, burst into tears.

'I don't know. I was walking around town photographing and interviewing the evacuees when I saw a door left open. When I approached, my assailant suddenly appeared from nowhere and punched me in the face. I woke up covered in blood and in a daze I went to the bathroom to see the damage.'

'Why didn't you run out as soon as you regained consciousness?' he asked.

'I don't know. As I said, I was in a daze and was not able to think clearly. Only after I had washed away the majority of the blood did I discover the body in the bedroom. It was horrible. I don't think I will ever get that image of her lying there out of my head for as long as I live.'

'Did you get a look at the killer?'

'No, he appeared from behind the wall and moved so fast.'

'Any guess on height, hair colour, weight? Can you remember what he was wearing?'

'No, as I said, it happened all so fast. He was normal height I think but I cannot remember anything else.'

'It's ok,' he said, 'you are alive, that's what counts. You need to get to the hospital to get your nose looked at. I'll send Suzanne with you so that you can provide her with a statement. I'll catch up with you later.'

Sven went back downstairs and informed Freddy of what had happened.

'Betty is one lucky lady,' Freddy added, 'she could have been victim number six.'

'Well, looking at the state of the bedroom, he would have needed some time to complete everything. It looks like he struck early so that he had time to complete his task as planned. I doubt that he would have killed Betty because everything had to be followed by the book. She was in the wrong place at the wrong time.' Steffi wiped her forehead with the back of her hand and looked at Egbert. 'I am missing her heart. Have you seen it?' she asked.

'No, sorry.'

'Sven, does it say in your reports of Mary Kelly if her heart was taken?'

Sven checked his notebook and confirmed that it was.

'Ok, let's get her bagged and back to the lab. At least this autopsy will be quick. Not much left for us to open up.' Egbert stated.

The other technicians helped roll, lift, scoop and bag up what remained of Katrin Werner and wheeled the closed transport boxes to their vehicles.

‘Any clue as to time of death?’ Sven asked.

‘Well, her body was still warm and there was no sign of rigor mortis setting in yet, so I would say she had been killed within the last few hours only, but I can give you an exact time when I’m back at the lab.’

‘Ok, thanks Egbert. Steffi, you too.’

Sven called to the officers outside, ‘you all know what to do. Witness statements, door-to-door enquiries, all the usual stuff we have to do and let’s tighten the perimeter if it hasn’t been done already. I want to catch this piece of shit before he disappears.’

He walked towards his home and emptied a small plastic bag of its contents in a large bunch of bushes. The heart would be found during the night by a cat and feasted on, leaving the rest to be devoured by other animals. Finally he got to the estate where he lived. Apart from being able to hear many emergency service sirens and could see the glow of the floodlights, all was as it should be.

He opened the main door to his block of flats and walked up the stairs to his apartment.

‘Hello love,’ his wife called from the bathroom, ‘how was your day?’ she enquired.

‘All fine, thanks. Nothing special. And yours?’

‘Stayed in this afternoon with the door bolted. Have you heard all the commotion over in the old town?’

‘Saw lots of police cars on my way home. Was there another killing?’ he asked.

‘Think so. Papers said it would be today and looks like they got it right for once. What sort of person could do that?’ she asked innocently.

‘No idea, love. World is full of weird people. At least you are safe.’ he said.

When his wife had finished in the bathroom, she came to the kitchen where he was putting in the washing powder and softener in the washing machine. She kissed him on the cheek and he patted her backside.

‘Had an accident at work, spilt some oil on me.’ he said.

‘Ok, I’ll fix us something to eat and you go and get changed.’

‘Just need to do something in the cellar.’ he stated, and picking up his rucksack, went back out the door and headed downstairs. When he was positive that none of his neighbours were down there with him, he took out his knife, notebook and boots and wiping them all down with a wet rag, placed the items in another black plastic bag and hid them under the bottom shelf where he kept his “junk”. The original plastic bag and the one that contained the heart were disposed of outside in one of the communal rubbish bins.

Epilogue

Several weeks passed without any new clues as to who the killer was. The last victim was finally identified by a small tattoo found on her left buttock, one that her sister was able to confirm as she had the same one on her right bum cheek. At the time it was a fun idea, both being drunk on holiday. Now it served to confirm her sister was dead.

The post mortem showed nothing that was not known or expected. The newspapers and news reports played for days after the last murder, bringing new speculations as to who could have been the killer. Some reported that it could possibly be the great-grandson of the original Jack the Ripper. Whatever was broadcast or published, the police found no clues at any of the murder sites nor had any idea of who the actual killer was. Fingerprints were absent and no hairs or skin was left behind or any other discriminating evidence. The police were able to discount Billy, Detlef and Rudolph from being involved as they were all accounted for when the fifth murder took place.

Steffi and Egbert were unable to provide any assistance as to who the killer could be. The only thing they were certain of was the type of knife used, but this would not help the police unless the killer was caught in possession of a knife with the dimensions of being around 15 centimeters long and about 2,5 centimeters wide. Business was back to normal, them cutting up bodies that had died under "irregular circumstances" or simple murder victims. Nothing was like the bodies that were left behind by German Jack.

Detlef was not able to go back to work as he was afraid of being spoken to behind his back, so he put in for a transfer to another clinic. His mother was sad to see him leave but promised he was always welcome home. He kept to himself until the beginning of 1989, when he started working in the psychiatric clinic in Dortmund and found himself a small apartment where nobody knew him. It wasn't long until he was wearing women's underwear again, what with Dortmund being a bigger city and more opportunity to meet others.

Rudolph was not so lucky. The heart bypass that he underwent kept him alive for several weeks and on being released from hospital and still being written off sick from work, he died of a massive heart attack in bed whilst watching a porno movie. His body was discovered four days later when a putrefying smell alerted his neighbours, and with the help of a locksmith and the emergency services, he was taken out of his apartment and to a morgue. He was buried in a pauper's grave several weeks later as nobody came forward to claim him.

After his name was cleared from any further investigations by both the civil police and RMPs, Billy learnt the lesson in following orders and started to become a sensible soldier. He kept up his friendship with SSgt Bones and was so inspired, decided he would like to join the SAS. SSgt Bones provided him with personal training to get him ready for the selection course.

Billy was sent to the SAS selection course and flew over to England where he was then transported to Hereford. Whilst on one of the vigorous exercises on the Brecon Beacons which included a 14 mile long march with full equipment over the 2,907 feet high Pen Y Fan (the highest peak in South Wales), Billy went down with hypothermia and died on the mountainside. His body was recovered and transported back to his family. Both his parents cried at his funeral but his sister was busy crying out in ecstasy on the back seat of a Toyota Corolla.

Sven stayed in charge of the operation after the final killing and kept his men busy until the New Year, where he was forced to admit that the investigation was not moving forward. Most of the other officers who had been working the case were slowly pulled away one by one and the team dwindled. He kept an office in Soest but was working more and more out of Dortmund when it was finally agreed for him to step down from the investigation as his skills were needed elsewhere on a fresh case.

Now that he was home more, he was obviously able to spend more time with his wife Johanna and their two children. He never let the job get him down and did not think of his investigation in being a failure because they never caught the killer. After all, they were always playing catch up to something that had been meticulously planned in advance.

As for Freddy, he took Heike, his wife on holiday to Mallorca as promised. Now back at work, he was in full swing with another investigation but was home every night, which suited them both.

On the day of the last killing, Betty was sent to hospital where she spent the next four days for observation and having her broken nose set back into place. The doctors had done a remarkable job on her nose but she swore that it was a bit crooked and was noticeable. Her teeth were also worked on by an endodontist and she received two crowns. Her smile was back and as beautiful as ever.

Many times she tried to write down what had happened to her on the day of her attack but was still not able to remember anything else apart from seeing the door open and a fist coming towards her. Although she had rights on writing up about the killings and German Jack, she somehow lost interest and stayed away from the subject altogether. She received several calls to publish something in a paper but she refused.

When she was physically repaired, she went back to her home and decided she needed to get away as she was still mentally fragile. After speaking with her landlord, she was able to get out of her contract and after contacting several estate agencies, she found an agreeable offer and moved up to Sankt Peter-Ording, a holiday and rehabilitation resort on the north coast of Germany just below the Danish border. Here she was able to go on long walks in the sea breeze, gather her thoughts and just be thankful that she was still alive and not dead herself.

She took a job as a travel agent and never took up reporting again.

Around about the time Billy died on the mountainside, SSgt Bones was clearing out his cellar and putting his belongings into an MFO box prior to being posted away from San Sebastian. His next unit was located in Münster, some seventy kilometers north of Soest.

Now in his new living quarters, he unpacked the boxes and put all of his uniforms in the wardrobe where they belonged. When his wife was busy with putting the cups and plates in the kitchen cupboards, he took a small box down to the cellar and carefully found a hiding place for it. He knew his wife would not look in his personal belongings but one had to plan for all eventualities. And it was always best to keep sharp objects out of the way.

Acknowledgements

Although the locations mentioned in this book are real, all the characters in this book are a fiction of my imagination apart from *Jack the Ripper*, who we still do not know his true identity.

Without the following people, it would not have been possible to get this book finished and I am grateful for their input and expertise:

Firstly to Kriminalhauptkommissar Frank Meiske for providing me an insight as to how the police would have worked back in the late 1980s.

Secondly to Dr. Zweihof of the Institut für Rechtsmedizin in Dortmund for allowing me to spend time with him and for him explaining about the procedures following a murder and what happens at the scene and on the slab thereafter.

Thirdly to Louis for his wonderful artwork in creating the book cover. It looks just like I imagined it. Thank you.

Not forgetting both Vanessa and Anastasia for your willingness and honesty in correcting all of my many mistakes and in believing in me. Without you two ladies, you would not be reading this part in print.

And last but not least, I would like to thank everyone who has read this book with the hope that you were entertained throughout, as that was my goal.

Printed in Great Britain
by Amazon

10461977R00169